HATING YOU,
LOVING YOU

CRYSTAL KASWELL

Copyright

This is a work of fiction. Similarities to real people, places, or events are entirely coincidental.

Also by Crystal Kaswell

Sinful Serenade

Sing Your Heart Out - Miles

Strum Your Heart Out - Drew

Rock Your Heart Out - Tom

Play Your Heart Out - Pete

Sinful Ever After – series sequel

Dangerous Noise

Dangerous Kiss - Ethan

Dangerous Crush – Kit

Dangerous Rock – Joel

Dangerous Fling – Mal

Dangerous Encore - series sequel

Inked Hearts

Tempting - Brendon

Playing - Walker

Pretend You're Mine - Ryan

Hating You, Loving You - Dean

Breaking the Rules - Hunter - coming fall 2018

Sign up for the Crystal Kaswell mailing list

About This Book

I hate him. I want him. I can't stop thinking about him.

Chloe

Nice to see you, sunshine, wearing black again?

Dean Maddox spent high school pushing *all* my buttons.

Seven years later, we're working together. So much has changed, but he's the same arrogant asshole with the same penchant for teasing me senselessly.

I still want to slap the cocky smirk from his face. And tear off his clothes. And kiss him like the ship is going down.

I hate him. I want him. I can't...

No, I will stop thinking about him.

Dean

Seven years ago, I took Chloe's virginity. It was supposed to cure my cravings for the pint-sized spitfire. But now that she's working *under* me...

The more she glares, the more I want her.
The more I tease, the more she eye-f*cks me.
The more I brag about my Prince Albert...
Let's just say it's obvious she's picturing me naked.
She owns my thoughts as much as I own hers.
I should stay away. She's my subordinate. She's off limits.
But there's no way in hell I can resist her.

For my husband, Dean's number one fan.

Chapter One

CHLOE

Why do people drink?

This stuff tastes awful.

I force myself to swallow another mouthful of orange juice and vodka.

My throat burns.

My head spins.

I reach for something to hold onto. Find the white banister. It's smooth, ornate, pure money.

This entire house is pure money. Pristine carpet. Glass tables. Three-thousand-dollar leather upholstery.

Six-dollar Trader Joe's vodka.

The cheap booze ruins the aesthetic. It clashes with the skylights, the sliding glass doors, the glowing aqua pool.

Not that anyone notices. My classmates are used to expensive furniture and two-million-dollar mansions.

But cheap vodka and an empty upstairs?

That thrills them.

I've heard enough rumors to know the drill. Rich kids. Nice house. Cheap booze. Parents out of town. *I heard Dean fucked Judy...*

Not that it's always Dean.

It's just those are the only rumors I pay attention to.

A giggle cuts through the big, white room. It bounces off the high ceilings. It bounces right into my ears.

There's Judy, all blond hair and long limbs, standing at the table, running her red nails over Dean's forearm.

His smile lights up his blue eyes. They're bright. Full of energy and life and lust for torturing me.

He raises a brow. Runs his strong hand through his shaggy dirty blond hair.

Shrugs his broad shoulders. Those are swimmer's shoulders. He has a swimmer's everything. I've seen him in a Speedo enough times to know—the guys practice a few lanes over.

He's more than a hot body too. He's handsome. Charming. Funny.

Evil.

My head knows better. My head despises the cocky playboy. For calling me sunshine. For taking nothing seriously. For throwing people away.

But my heart?

My body?

It's impossible to get over a guy you see shirtless five times a week. That's a scientific fact.

He laughs at Judy's joke. Shoots her that trademarked Dean million-dollar smile as he blows her a kiss.

She paws at his chest.

He shrugs *maybe, maybe not*.

He's indifferent. Effortless. Aloof.

He has so much female attention he could give or take a knockout in fuck me heels.

That doesn't give a nobody in combat boots much of a chance.

I force myself to look away.

Watch Alan—this is his place—pound his red solo cup. He finishes. Crushes the cup. Watches it fall onto the pristine white carpet.

Drops of brown liquor catch on the fibers.

He shrugs like he doesn't care, but the worry in his eyes betrays him. The jocks around him laugh. Pound their drinks. Whisper some secret.

There are a dozen people here. Half in that circle. The rest on the couch or in the airy, stainless steel kitchen.

Everyone here is casual. Comfortable. Used to parties. To money. To cheap booze in plastic cups.

I...

This is way out of my comfort zone.

My gaze shifts back to Dean.

His eyes lock with mine. He raises his glass. Smiles.

My combat boots tap together. My hands go to my tank top. I play with its edge. Try to figure out what the hell that means.

Dean and I have shared two classes a day, every day, for the last three years.

He spends most of his free time teasing me.

Calling me sunshine.

Mocking how seriously I take art, math, and science.

Mocking my all black clothes, my thermos of tea, my tendency to gush about cartoons.

He turns to Alan. Whispers something.

Alan laughs.

Dean nods *hell yeah*. "Everybody come here." His playful voice bounces around the room.

Everyone turns his way.

Looks at him.

Hangs on his words.

Dean commands attention, friendship, respect. All he

3

does is smile and a dozen girls fall over themselves trying to claim him.

A dozen guys want to be his friend.

The world is his oyster.

"Why should I listen to anything you say, Maddox?" Alan teases back.

Dean's shrug is effortless. *Why should I bother exerting a single ounce of energy on anything?* "If you don't want me to blow your mind, go ahead. Leave."

"Maddox, I don't want you blowing anything." Alan laughs.

I roll my eyes. How original.

Dean's eyes catch mine. He shakes his head *not great, huh?*

I fight my smile.

Every day this year, he turned our art class from my happy place to my *deal with Dean's constant teasing* place.

He doesn't get a smile now.

Even if my body is buzzing with nervous energy.

Even if my limbs are light and airy.

Even if my sex is aching.

I must be blushing, because he's smiling wider. Knowingly. Like he's sure I'm eating out of the palm of his hand.

He turns back to the group. "Truth or dare."

"I'm not fourteen," someone says.

"Sounds like you're chicken." Dean turns to me. "What do you think, Chloe? Are you chicken?"

"No." My heart thuds against my chest.

My head fills with ideas. Every dirty dare he could offer me.

His hands in my hair.

His groan in my ears.

His lips against mine.

God, those soft lips.

I want to slap them for all the stupid shit he says. For not giving a fuck about the classes his parents pay a fortune for. For calling me sunshine every three seconds.

But he's calling me Chloe.

He...

I...

My heart pounds so hard I'm sure it's going to break out of my chest.

It doesn't.

But a deep breath does nothing to help me calm down.

For three years I've been smitten. Ever since our first day in geometry, when he turned to me and asked to borrow my protractor. Then promised to make it worth my while with a wink and a smile.

Calm eludes me.

Sense eludes me.

Everything but a fangirl voice screaming *Dean Maddox* eludes me.

His lips curl into a smile. He holds out his arm. Motions *come here*.

My knees knock together.

Lightness spreads into my chest, neck, head. I'm dizzy. Like I'm going to faint.

Who knew swooning was a real thing? I thought Gia made it up.

My feet move of their own accord.

My combat boots sink into the plush carpet.

My hands slip from my pockets.

One finds his palm.

He wraps his fingers around my hand. Rubs the space between my thumb and forefinger with his thumb.

He looks down at me—he has to, he has a foot on me—like I'm the only thing he needs.

Like I'm *everything* he needs.

His voice is soft. Sweet. "Nice of you to join, sunshine."

The nickname breaks my trance.

Dean doesn't need me. He needs to push my buttons.

Gia insists he's teasing because he likes me, but what does Gia know about guys like Dean? She met her boyfriend at a comics shop. They read *Spider-Man* and play video games together.

Gia doesn't know Dean, but I do.

With him, you have to bite back.

I shoot him my best *fuck you* smile. "Nice to see you, dick face."

He chuckles. "You know I take that as a compliment."

I shrug *do you?* People mill closer. Take seats on the couch, at the table, on the ground.

"If you'd seen my dick, you'd know why." He steps forward to let someone pass. His hand brushes my arm. His chest brushes my shoulder. His crotch brushes my outer thigh.

My body responds with gusto.

Any sense of calm, of upper hand, of any hand, dissipates.

My body goes into overdrive. Every molecule screams the same thing: *more Dean please.*

A jock's voice pulls me from my thoughts. "Damn, Maddox. Stop bragging. We're playing a game here." He pats a spot on the packed couch. It's all designer jeans and BCBG dresses and pretty girls in hot guy's laps.

I take a step backward, but there's nowhere to go. My ass hits the glass table.

Dean turns to his friend. "Should I whip it out instead?"

A girl sitting on the couch claps with glee. "Hell yeah!"

The five girls sitting on the ground clap with her.

"There's a demand." Dean shrugs, effortless. He reaches for his jeans. Pretends to undo his button. "I can't let my fans down."

"Save it for the game," the friend says.

A dozen *awwws* and *no fairs* bounce around the room.

Dean turns to me. Winks. "Fair is fair." He offers his hand. "Sit with me, sunshine."

He leads me to the couch. Rests his ass on its arm.

I stand next to him. Shift my weight between my feet. Tap my toes together. Listen to the hollow sound the synthetic leather makes.

His hand brushes my hip.

My body responds immediately.

My pulse races. My nipples perk. My sex clenches.

I want him touching me. I think about it all the time. Too much.

He's everything I hate.

He's someone I hate.

But I still want him touching me.

I still stroke myself to orgasm thinking about him every fucking night.

"Why don't you start, Romeo," Dean's friend calls.

Ooohs and *ahhs* bounce around the room with *do its* and *Oh my Gods!*

The room wants Dean.

The entire world wants Dean.

He wants...

Who knows what the hell the manwhore wants.

He smiles, reveling in the attention. "With pleasure." He turns to me. "Chloe, truth or dare."

My head fills with ideas.

A dare to kiss him.

To flash him.

To touch him.

God, I want to touch him.

And to slap the smarmy smile from his face.

He did call me by my name.

Maybe there's some shred of decency behind his party boy façade.

Or maybe that's my hormones talking.

Either way.

I adopt his aloof posture. Watch clouds roll over the skylight. Watch the wavy lines of the pool bounce off the sliding glass door. Watch a dozen people turn their attention to me.

Deep breath. Slow exhale. "Truth."

His blue eyes sparkle as his smile spreads over his cheeks. "Are you a virgin?"

My cheeks flush.

My chest too.

Fuck Dean.

He must know I am.

Everyone at school knows.

I'm the weird loner who spends lunch drawing in her sketchbook.

Guys aren't interested.

Not that any guys appeal. The guy who tortures me is the only one I want.

Why am I here?

I step backward. Dig my heel into the soft carpet. My instincts scream *leave*, but I can't do that.

I'm not embarrassed of my inexperience.

I'm not letting him rattle me.

I'm not letting his friends think I'm some loser ashamed of her decisions.

"Yes." I shoot Dean my most serene smile. "I have standards. I'm sure that's hard for you to imagine."

He scratches his head. "Standards. Never heard of those."

His friends laugh.

Someone calls out, "It's when you need more than a pulse and two legs."

"Two legs? Look who's Mr. Picky." A jock laughs.

"I'd never discriminate against a woman with one leg. Or

no legs." Dean's eyes find mine. "I don't need a smile either. A million-dollar scowl is better."

I fight my scowl. I'm playing Dean's game. Indifference. Aloofness. Utter coolness. "Unfortunately for you, I do have standards."

Someone makes that *ooh, burn* sound.

The girls on the floor giggle. Whisper something. No doubt it's *who does she think she is? No way Dean wants her.* But I don't care about them.

They're seniors. They're graduating. In two weeks, they'll be out of my life forever.

Dean looks up at me with a wicked smile. "Your turn."

Oh. So it is. I scan the room.

Fuck the girls trading rumors.

Fuck the guys looking at me like they're deciding if I meet their standards.

Fuck this whole party.

My gut churns. Why did I let Gia talk me into this? Why did I think an invite from Dean could lead to anything but teasing and embarrassment?

I need to get out of here. Fast.

I look to Alan. He's a wannabe Dean. Not quite as cute or tall or blond. Not as funny or charming or attention grabbing. "Alan, truth or dare."

Everyone turns to him.

He leans back in his black chair. Revels in the attention. "Dare."

I have to fight fire with fire. "I dare you to streak around the neighborhood."

Alan jumps to his feet. Holds up his hand in salute. "I hope you ladies are in for a show." He sends winks in every direction. Even mine.

Then he marches over the carpet, the white tile foyer, the mat. All the way out the door.

It slams shut with a thud.

"Let's set up on the porch." Dean motions to the door. Leans in to whisper something to the girl next to him.

Even though she's sitting on some guy's lap, she giggles at Dean. "Sure."

She slides off her boy-toy's lap. "Follow me." Her red heels sink into the carpet, then they click against the tile.

She turns back. Motions *let's go*.

And everyone does.

One by one, people stand. File out of the room.

Someone, a guy about Dean's height, with a letterman jacket and dark hair, whispers something in Dean's ear.

Dean shakes his forehead. "Got something else to do."

The friend laughs.

Dean watches him leave.

It's just us in this giant house.

I move to the table. Fill my glass with more orange juice and vodka. Pray for it to erase that *you don't belong here* voice completely.

This is supposed to be the best time of my life. Parties. Boys. Fun.

I'm having fun, dammit.

Dean follows me to the table. "You don't want to watch?"

"Alan isn't my type."

"What is?"

"Smart guys." I take a long sip of my drink. "You know any?"

"Not one. But I can help with that drink." His hand brushes mine. Slowly, he peels my fingers from my cup. "Grenadine." He picks up a bottle of candy red liquid. Pours it into my glass. "Goes down smoother."

"Thanks." My stomach flutters as he hands the glass back.

This is intentional.

He's touching me on purpose.

He's helping me on purpose.

He's alone with me on purpose.

He fills his cup with Jack and Coke then lifts it to toast.

"To?" I ask.

"Good friendships."

"We're good friends?"

"Of course." His voice is earnest. Honest.

"I hate you."

"I know."

"That doesn't bother you?"

"Fuck no. It's what I like about you." He clinks his glass with mine. Takes a long sip. Lets out a low sigh of pleasure. "You keep me on my toes."

"You live on your toes."

"Should take up ballet." He makes a show of rising to his tiptoes. It's nowhere close to a ballet move. But it's Dean all the same.

Charming *and* irritating.

Gia says he reminds her of Han Solo.

But Gia isn't the one taking his constant insults. (And Gia needs to learn that *Star Wars* isn't the answer to all of life's questions).

"I do like you, sunshine." His eyes find mine. "Have for a while."

"So that virgin question?"

"I wanted to know something. So, I asked."

"What did you want to know?"

He moves closer. Until I can feel the heat of his body. Smell his cologne. "If I'd be your first."

What? My cheeks flame. There's no way he...

There's no...

I...

"Chloe?" His fingers brush the inside of my wrist.

"Huh?"

"I want to fuck you."

"But—"

"Let's go upstairs. I'll show you the night of your life."

My defenses crumble.

Dean wants me.

He's offering to fuck me.

He...

How is this possible?

My heart screams for him. My body aches for him. My head—it's still reasonable.

I throw up the only defense I know—sarcasm. "Of my entire life?"

"Yeah."

"Doesn't speak well for your future performances."

"You already thinking about round two?"

"No. I..." My cheeks flame. "I meant—"

"I know what you meant, sunshine. Round two will be just as good. But nothing is as special as your first time."

"Yours?"

He shrugs, effortless. "Wasn't lucky enough to have someone like me showing me the ropes."

"You're going to show me the ropes?"

He nods. "Yeah." His fingers trace circles over my skin. "If that's what you want."

"Judy offered to fuck you."

"And?"

"Why me over her?"

"I told you, sunshine. I like you. It's that simple."

"You're about to graduate."

"You will next year."

"But you're... you're leaving."

He shakes his head. "Not going anywhere."

"Where will you be?"

"Ryan is gonna get me a gig as an apprentice."

"Yeah?" I bite back my enthusiasm. Dean's older brother is a tattoo artist. It's the coolest thing ever.

"Yeah." He nods. "Just got this one." He pulls his shirt up his torso, showing off inches of taut abs.

He pulls it higher.

All the way to his side.

He turns to show off a tattoo on his ribs—the state of California, adorned with grey and red roses.

"How much did that hurt?" I ask.

"Like a bitch."

"Guys usually say it doesn't hurt."

"Liars."

"Can I?"

"Of course."

My fingers go to his skin. It's soft, but he's bone and muscle beneath it.

God, the feel of him against my fingertips...

My knees knock together.

"Didn't think you were the ink type," he says.

Words dissolve on my tongue. He's so close. And so undressed. And so hot.

My hand knows what it wants.

It traces his ink again and again.

I look up at him. He's so tall. I'm short, yeah, but he's on some other plane of height.

"Can you keep a secret?" I ask.

He pulls an imaginary zipper over his lips in a *my lips are sealed* gesture.

"I got one last month." I roll my jeans over my right hip to show off my new tattoo. A star. It's a little lopsided, but it's mine.

"Badass." He flashes me that million-dollar smile. "I have another one to show you." He offers his hand. "Upstairs."

There's weight in the word.

Upstairs isn't for conversation. It's for what I've been dreaming about for the last three years.

"Okay." I down half my drink. Pray for the liquid courage I hear so much about. "Upstairs."

I take his hand and follow him to the bedroom.

DEAN PRESSES HIS LIPS TO MINE.

He strips me out of my clothes.

He lays me on the bed and warms me up.

Pulls a condom from his jeans. Tears it open. Slides it on.

Then he's on top of me, easing into me, whispering dirty promises in my ear.

It hurts, but not as badly as Gia told me it would.

The pain fades to discomfort.

To pleasure.

To the thrill of knowing that Dean and I are one.

He takes care of me. Makes sure I come.

It feels like we go forever.

We finish. He helps me dress. Promises to stay in touch.

Never does.

He doesn't text, or call, or email, or IM.

The next week, he graduates.

And I spend seven years without hearing a peep from Dean Maddox.

Chapter Two

CHLOE

The bell rings as I push the door open.

Morning light floods the cozy shop. For a moment, the September heat competes with the air-conditioning. Then the door falls closed, and the air-conditioning wins.

It's freezing in here. December in Big Bear freezing.

It doesn't fit the cozy vibe. This place is awfully cute for a tattoo shop. Red and pink string lights, tattoo mock-ups in heart-shaped frames, black counter, white walls, shiny hardwood floor.

Two of the suites—there are three of them, oak half-walls on two sides, mirrored wall on one, lobby on the other—are empty.

The one in the middle...

That's his shaggy blond hair.

His broad shoulders.

His strong back.

His bright blue t-shirt.

I wrap my arms around my chest.

Suck a breath between my teeth.

Seven years, and Dean Maddox still fills my stomach with butterflies.

He still sends every bit of my sense packing.

No amount of reasoning—*he taunted you, fucked you, then threw you away*—helps.

I force myself to adopt a casual stance. Hand in pocket, hip tilted to one side, smile replacing my resting bitch face.

"Hey," I call to no one in particular.

Steps move closer. Not from Dean's suite. From the back.

Light surrounds Ryan in an angelic glow as he steps in the cozy main room.

He holds his hand over his eyes, blocking the glare.

Half-smiles as he nods hello.

Ryan's black-on-black Converse squeak against the hardwood floor. He extends his hand. "You're early."

I take it. Shake. "Always."

His chuckle is soft. "Not this early." He runs a hand through his wavy coffee brown hair. "Leighton won't be in for a while, but I can take you through her routine."

"Sure."

"Have to finish some shit in the office first. I'll be a minute." He motions to the black counter. "Feel free to set up."

He's a man of few words. It's one of the things I like best about him.

Ryan and I are the same kind of weird—too serious, closed off, always in black.

We spar with anyone but refuse hugs from strangers.

I was surprised when he offered me a job at Inked Hearts. Without an interview. All he knew about me was that I was as serious about aikido as he was. And as desperate to find a place to apprentice as anyone has ever been.

I lay my black backpack on the counter. Pull out my thermos. Find it empty. I drank my London Fog on the way here.

There's a Keurig in the lobby, right above one of the teal benches, but there's no sign of a kettle or a fridge.

Damn. I need that easy hit of comfort. Tea from a pod... no thank you.

Strong, steady footsteps pad the floor. "You miss me?"

Dean.

Anger and lust fill my veins.

That voice...

I can still hear him mocking me. *Sunshine, you never have any fun.*

I can still hear him groaning my name. *Fuck, Chloe. You're so wet.*

"You ever turn it off?" Ryan calls from the back room. He moves into the lobby. Shoots his brother a *really* look.

Dean makes that *who me?* gesture. He shrugs like he can't be bothered to think about anything he does.

Ryan ignores him. "Chloe, this is my brother. Dean. You guys went to school together."

This is a small space. We're close.

Dean is right there. Three feet away maybe. Close enough to kiss. To hug. To slap.

"I remember." My eyes refuse to obey my command. They focus on his narrow waist. His broad chest. His strong shoulders.

Those same bright blue eyes.

That same million-dollar smile.

He offers his hand. "Nice to see you again."

Ryan raises a brow. He shoots his brother a cutting look.

Dean shrugs, effortlessly aloof.

I dig my heel into the hardwood. I'm new and I'm nobody. He's a co-owner. And a blood relative.

Whatever problems I have with Dean Maddox, I'm going to have to get over them if I want this.

Ryan shoots me a look. *You okay?*

I nod.

He nods back. "If he gives you shit, let me know. I'll kick his ass." There's a hint of humor in Ryan's usually serious voice. He's teasing.

He must be.

Because Dean is wearing his amusement like it's his finest suit.

He waits for Ryan to leave then moves closer. "It's been a while."

God, I was such a stupid kid. I really believed that I meant something to him. "Yeah."

"Your hair looks good short."

"Thanks." I brush a dark strand behind my ear reflexively. At first, this style was a necessity, not a choice. But I grew to love it.

"You look even more like you can kill me."

"I can. I do aikido now."

"Ryan told me."

"Oh." I bite my lip. It doesn't mean anything, Ryan and Dean talking about me. He's the same carefree playboy. I may not be the same, but I'm still the artsy loner.

I'm nothing to him. Another notch on a bedpost covered with them.

"Ryan said you almost kicked his ass," Dean says.

"It's sparring. Not ass kicking."

"You beat him or not?"

Not. "I came close." Ish.

He offers his hand. "Show me something."

The thought of touching him sets me on fire.

The thought of hurting him satisfies somewhere deep.

This sort of anger isn't healthy. I've been through too much to care about a guy who failed to call seven years ago.

I need to get past this.

"Later." I take a step backward. My ass hits the counter. My heels too. "I don't want to break your hand."

"You're no fun."

"Was I ever?"

"Yeah. In your way, you were always fun, sunshine." His voice drops as he calls me by the old pet name.

It's the same charm as always.

He has no idea he hurt me.

Or he doesn't care.

Which is worse—stupidity or apathy?

"I should get to work." I move behind the counter. Take a seat at the stool. Pretend as if I know what I'm supposed to do with the computer.

"You want some help?" The light from the window surrounds him. Bounces off his hair, his neck, his chest.

He looks like an angel.

But that's all wrong.

Dean is a devil, plain and simple.

And he's not tempting me again.

I press my lips into a smile. "Ryan has it under control."

"Suit yourself." He takes a step backward, out of the bright light, into an even, diffuse one. "If you need anything, you know who to call." His voice gets soft. Seductive.

Is it an actual offer to fuck him?

Or more of his usual bullshit?

I guess it doesn't matter.

I'm not sleeping with him again.

I'm not letting him get to me.

I'm not taking any of his bullshit.

Chapter Three

DEAN

I roll my shoulders back. Focus on the neat line of black ink. This is almost done and it's fucking badass.

For a moment, my limbs fill with nervous energy. There's a thrill to marking someone's body. One that never gets old.

My eyes fix on the back piece.

This is it.

The end of a twelve hour, three session piece of art.

"You gonna miss me?" I ask.

"Not even a little." Randy squeezes the teal vinyl. He squirms, knocking his sandals together, turning his head to one side.

"You're brave." I turn the gun on. It hums. Vibrates against my gloved hand. "I could still fuck it up."

"Your ego won't let you."

"That's my favorite subject." I lower my stool. Lean closer. Until I'm out of direct sunlight. Why aren't the shades down? It's too fucking bright in here.

"I thought it was whoever you had last night."

I chuckle. Randy is, well, randy. He always fishes for details on my latest fuck.

Usually, I oblige.

Gladly.

Shooting the shit with customers is half the fun of the job.

I attract a certain type of client—guys who want to get crude or women who want to flirt. It works for me. Skin is skin. Doesn't matter if it's a middle-aged programmer like Randy or an eighteen-year-old model.

I kick ass, every time.

Truth be told, I went home last night. After leg day, I was dead tired. Crashed with takeout and TV.

But that isn't what he wants to hear.

I try to reach for an old story, one sure to please, but my brain is blocked.

Chloe is at the counter. Her almond eyes are fixed on me. Her short hair is sticking to her cheeks. Her black nails are tapping the counter.

Same as always. Impatient. Annoyed. Interested.

There's something about her that gets right under my skin.

Thinking about another woman is impossible.

My head is flush with thoughts of her. Those black jeans at her ankles. The shy smile when I wrapped my fingers around her cotton panties (black, of course). She was worried they weren't sexy. But they were.

There's something about plain cotton panties. The innocence. The sweetness. The Chloe no one sees.

My cock stirs.

I can still taste her cunt on my lips.

Still hear her groaning my name.

Feel her painted black nails against my back.

Three years of teasing and flirting and they ended exactly how they needed to.

Shit.

I can't think about this or I *am* gonna fuck up.

This tiger is too perfect for that.

"Must be a good one." Randy laughs. "Do I need to give you a minute alone?"

If I keep thinking about Chloe, he will.

I push it aside. Find a... not fiction, but an exaggeration. Sometimes a tall tale is what gets the job done. "You ever have a guy beg you to fuck his girlfriend?"

"No way."

"Way." It was a while ago, yeah, but it was also unforgettable. "It was his thing. He liked to watch."

"Yeah?"

"Don't tell me you're uptight, Randy."

His laugh is hearty. "No."

"I get the objection. I wouldn't let some asshole touch my girl—"

"Certainly not someone like you."

"Randy, stop being brave. You're on your stomach. I've got the gun. I could write *Dean Maddox owns my soul* on your ass."

"You wouldn't."

"You sure about that?"

"Yeah..." His voice trails off. "Pretty sure."

He's right. I wouldn't.

But I'm not gonna let him know that.

Focus returns as I bring the needle to his skin. This is where I belong. Don't get me wrong. I love a lot of things—weight lifting, surfing, TV, women—but nothing compares to doing ink.

Nothing.

I shift into the zone. "Last one. You ready?"

"And my details?"

"After." Everything fades away as the needle hits his skin. The breathy whine of a miserable lyricist—Leighton's pick— blurs into heavy guitar, conversation, the whir of the air- conditioning, the smell of rubbing alcohol and A&D ointment.

The afternoon light gets soft.

I only see the tiger's paw.

The line of black surrounding it.

Four fingers. Four claws.

There.

Done.

I turn the gun off.

Randy's sigh shakes his entire body.

"Did it hurt?" I ask.

"Nah."

Bullshit. He thrashed and blubbered with the best of them. It's a solid rule—the tougher the guy, the harder he cries.

He goes to push himself up.

"Stay," I say. "Gotta clean you up."

"Can't the cute chick at the counter do it?"

"Which one?"

"They're both hot."

True. Leighton is a certified babe. Back when she tended bar at Rock Bottom, I spent a lot of nights flirting with her. But once I got her a job here, and we actually became friends, my head threw up this road block.

I couldn't see her as a potential fuck.

Then she confessed her undying love for Ryan, and I drew a hard line in the sand. No way I step on my brother's turf. I have some standards.

Now, Chloe...

Fuck, the pint-sized firecracker still revs my engine. I'm

not sure what it is—the perky tits, the black panties, the *don't fuck with me* smile...

Shit. I'm getting distracted.

I drag my gaze from the counter. Look back to Randy. "You need to work on your game."

"Do I?"

"Girl's don't want to hear that anyone will do. You gotta make them feel special."

"Guess you'd know."

That I do.

Randy pushes himself onto his elbows. He looks up at me expectantly, like I'm holding the keys to the castle. "So. The guy begged you to fuck his girlfriend."

I grab the aftercare lotion. Squeeze it onto my gloved fingers. "She was smoking hot. I'd had a few. It seemed like a good idea."

"Yeah?"

I start at his shoulders and work my way down. "We go to their place. He's got this chair set up to watch. I figure I should pay it forward, help the guy live out his fantasies."

"That a policy of yours?"

I look back to the counter. Chloe is staring at me.

There's something in her dark eyes.

The usual mix of *I want you* and *I hate you*.

It stirs something inside me. Just like when we were kids.

She challenges me. To be a better version of myself. To be more of myself. To just be more.

Nobody expects more from me.

I'm a good time, a nice tattoo, a wicked story.

But Chloe...

She saw something in me. She still does. It's hard to explain. She hates me because I'm the court jester. But she sticks around because she believes I'm more than that.

"Dean?" Randy asks.

"Yeah." I shake my head. Push my thoughts away. Chloe is working here. Not for long—Ryan and I are gonna have a talk about this—but for now. That means I need to get my head in gear. "Of course."

"What was your fantasy?"

"You gotta seduce me a little more before you get that." I pour more lotion. Slather it down his back as I pick up my story. "We started. She was purring. She laid back on the bed and looked up at me like I was the only thing she wanted. Like she wanted something deep inside me. She had these dark eyes. They were usually on fire with frustration."

"You knew her?"

Fuck.

What the hell is wrong with me? Chloe isn't distracting me.

We fucked seven years ago.

Now, we're coworkers.

Soon, we're ex-coworkers.

End of story.

End of this story. I'm not about to replay the night I took Chloe's virginity. Not for Randy.

Maybe tonight, when I'm alone.

No, definitely tonight. Multiple times.

I shift back to bullshit mode. "Yeah. We got going. But as soon as I was inside of her, her boyfriend freaked. He pulled me off her. Threatened to kill me." I grab plastic wrap and get to work on Randy's backpiece. "I ran out of there in nothing but a condom."

"No way."

"Way. The girlfriend was kind enough to toss my jeans and shoes out the window. My phone landed on the concrete. Shattered."

He laughs. "How often does that happen?"

I shrug.

"Anything ever upset you?"

"Yeah." I make my voice dead serious. "Clients ignoring their aftercare routine."

"That's the one thing?"

"Worst thing in the world." I finish wrapping him up. Stand. "Keep it bandaged for a few hours. Wash with warm water and soap. Lots of A&D after. Don't cover it again. And no open water for three weeks."

"If I don't?"

"You'll disappoint me. What's worse?"

Randy laughs. Not cause I'm hilarious—I am, but that's irrelevant. It's the thrill of new ink. Guys think I'm their best friend. Women want to fuck me.

Not that I need help getting laid.

I'm tall, built, inked, charming. I have no trouble finding women to take home.

It's a good routine.

I make them laugh.

Make them come.

Get them screaming my name.

Then I say goodbye and I do it all over again the next day.

No muss, no fuss, no one gets hurt.

No women stick in my head and refuse to get out.

Randy bounces to the counter on cloud nine. He's still shirtless and he's without reservations about it.

I'm not afraid of pointing out a good-looking man. Randy's handsome, but there's more of him to love. When we started, he was embarrassed by his extra padding.

Not anymore.

I've seen it a million times. Someone comes in insecure about their stomach, back, thighs, arms, whatever.

They leave proud.

A little ink and someone's trouble spot becomes their favorite body part.

27

It feels good, helping people like that.

Not that I'd admit it to any of the guys here.

Certainly not to Leighton.

Or Chloe.

Leighton nudges her.

Chloe moves forward. Offers Randy a smile. "Can I see the whole thing?"

"Fuck yeah." He smiles. Spins to show off his back.

Chloe's gaze fixes on his ink. She studies it the way she studies art. Her eyes go wide as she traces the design in the air. "Amazing." Her eyes meet mine. They flare with something I can't place, then they're back on Randy. "Dean does great work."

"The best."

Leighton hands Chloe a receipt.

Chloe leans forward to offer it to Randy. Her tits spill over her tight tank top. The top of her bra peeks out.

All black.

Like the night we were together.

Like every fucking day of high school.

She catches me staring. Shoots me that trademarked Chloe *I want to kill you* look.

Randy hands over his credit card.

She forces a smile as she swipes it. Hands back the receipt. Motions to the tip line.

Leighton jumps in. "It really is amazing." She bats her eyelashes. Presses her arms into her tits for maximum cleavage. She has the flirting for tips thing down, pat.

Chloe...

She's more confused.

Even so, Randy leaves thirty percent.

I get his aftercare kit, walk him out, say goodbye with a high five.

Pull the goddamn shades down.

"Thank you," Leighton calls from the counter. She leans in to whisper something to Chloe.

Chloe whispers back.

Leighton's blue-green eyes fix on mine. She shoots me a *watch yourself* look then turns to Chloe. "Do you do yoga?"

Her eyes stay on mine. "No..."

"You should start. Tattooing kills your back. Ryan is like an old man." She twirls a purple strand around her pointer finger. It's her signature gesture. She thinks about Ryan, she plays with her hair.

"I heard that, baby," he calls from his suite.

She blows him a kiss.

He holds up his free hand to catch it.

She giggles.

They're so gaga it hurts. But I'm happy for them. Hell, I never thought I'd see my brother in love again.

It took forever for them to figure it out. They were idiots. Needed a lot of help. Help they fought.

But they're here.

Finally.

"Giving her flirting tips, Leigh?" I ask.

"What's with Dean and calling people by nicknames they don't like?" Chloe asks.

"He thinks it's cute." Leighton brushes her short hair behind her ear. "He thinks he's adorable."

"You suggesting otherwise?" I ask.

Leighton and Chloe share a *hell yes* look.

Leighton laughs. "I like you already. Too bad we won't work together much."

My eyes fix on Chloe. "Flirting for tips is Leighton's thing, but I don't see that working for you."

Chloe folds her arms over her chest.

"You're here to apprentice, aren't you?" I ask.

"Yeah." She bites her lip.

"Talk about the ink. Make them feel special. Important. Guys want attention from pretty girls. It's a fact of life."

Leighton nods. "It does work."

"What do you know about flirting with guys?" Chloe asks.

"Do what I gotta do." I wink.

She fights a smile.

Fuck, that smile. It lights up her dark eyes. It softens her brow. It convinces me there's some part of her that actually likes me.

What is it about Chloe?

She's the only girl who's ever pressed my buttons.

"I can take you out tonight. Teach you everything I know."

"I'm good." She unfurls her arms. Brings a hand to the counter. "But thanks."

"Suit yourself." I shrug.

Leighton moves out from behind the counter. She passes me with a shoulder bump. "Fuck with her, and I'll cut you."

I chuckle. I love when Leighton gives me shit. I love that she's already looking out for the new girl. That kind of solidarity is hard to find.

Even if it's gonna make it harder to talk Ryan of out un-hiring Chloe.

I should go back to my suite. Prep.

But I don't.

I move to the counter. "You like it here so far?"

Chloe gives me a long once-over. "I like most things about Inked Hearts."

"Ryan is the worst, isn't he?"

She just barely smiles. "Close."

"I missed this."

"This?"

"You."

She stares into my eyes, picking apart my intentions.

"Never thought I'd see you again. Figured you'd be in grad school by now."

"That was the plan."

"But?"

"Life happened."

It tends to do that. But Chloe was hardcore about school. Straight As, AP classes, all work and no play. "You in school now?"

"No. I graduated with a studio art degree a while ago. Then... I decided life was too short not to go after what I want."

"What do you want?"

"Hmm. I'm here apprenticing. Whatever could I want?"

"Leighton says she's here for the view."

"Uh-huh."

I pull my t-shirt up my stomach. Pat my abs. "This is what she means."

Chloe rolls her eyes. "I want to do tattoos."

It suits her—she's always been that all black, counterculture type. But it's still weird to think about. We used to compete for our art teacher's attention.

"Ryan swore he'd never take an apprentice." I lean in to whisper. "How'd you convince him?"

"He hasn't. He said I have to convince one of you to do it. Or all of you to share me." She presses her lips together. "Don't even."

"What? Suggest it would be dirty hot if all four of us shared you."

"Yeah, something like that."

"Fuck. That would be dirty hot. For you."

She shakes her head. "Not interested."

"You sure? You haven't seen Walker or Brendon since high school."

"Still sure."

"I'll introduce you tomorrow. See if that changes your mind."

She stares into my eyes, picking me apart. Finally, she nods. "That's it. You convinced me. Should we all go to the backroom now?"

"Yeah." I laugh. "You first."

"No. You first."

"Uh-uh. I have a strict policy. Ladies first."

"Is that right?"

I nod.

She catches herself smiling. Shakes it off.

The woman still despises me.

And I still love it.

I shift back to discussing work. "Ryan paying you?"

"You're a co-owner."

"And?"

"You don't keep track of that?"

I shake my head. I trust Ryan. Why take on extra work when he's got it covered?

"Yeah," she says. "Not much, but enough."

"You have a second job?"

She shakes her head. "I have a cheap place to stay."

"Nearby?"

"You're not invited."

"I wasn't asking."

"Not yet."

I can't help but smile.

Even after all this time, she knows me too fucking well.

Chapter Four

DEAN

"What's with the fuck me eyes?" Ryan asks.

I feign ignorance. Ryan can chew me out if he wants, but I'm not going to make it easy for him.

"She's a good kid."

"Are you her dad?"

"You scare her off, I make you hurt."

"You won't hurt me."

"Try me."

I mime pushing my sleeves up my arms. Make fists. "Let's go. I'll snap you like a twig."

"You want pain, say it again." His voice perks to that tone he used when we were kids. It's a challenge, not a threat.

It's tempting. I've always wanted to fight Ryan. Must be some primal thing, needing to prove I can take my older brother. I've always been bigger. Stronger.

Still am.

But he's a karate expert now.

This is an actual challenge now.

Even so, I motion *come at me.*

He shakes his head *you're ridiculous*.

"You're right." I drop my fists. "Can't stand to see you lose in front of your girl."

"Please. She'll get off on watching."

"I'm gonna tell her you said that."

"Fuck off." He chuckles. His gaze shifts to Leighton.

She's sitting behind the counter, half her attention on her laptop, the other half on us.

Her tongue slides over her lips. Her chest heaves. Anticipation fills her blue-green eyes.

She wants a show.

I'm game to let Ryan win.

But he's past my bullshit.

He leans in close enough to whisper. "You didn't tell me you knew her in high school."

"You didn't ask my permission to hire her."

"Guess we're fair."

"You fall in love with the hot bartender I hire and I get *guess we're fair*?"

"Yeah."

How the hell can I explain this to my brother? He's not gonna take any of my bullshit reasons. The truth isn't an option. But there must be something. "Chloe—"

"Fuck. Really, Dean?"

"Really, what?"

"You fucked her?"

Not a subject he needs to know about. "She's not a good fit."

"She's the female version of me."

I can't exactly deny that.

"If she doesn't belong here, I don't belong here."

"Been meaning to tell you—"

"If you have a real reason why you don't want her here, I'm all ears."

That's the thing. I do want her here. I want her glaring at my antics. I want her fighting her smile. Laughing despite herself.

I want her on the counter.

Her jeans at her ankles.

Her tits in my hands.

Her cunt pulsing around me.

"You there?" he asks.

"No. Thinking about your girlfriend naked."

He rolls his eyes. He's having none of my shit.

"She—"

"Hates you."

"She hates what I represent."

His blue eyes stay serious. He studies my expression like his life depends on it. "She hates *you*."

I shrug. Maybe she did, once. But it's been forever. It's all water under the bridge.

"After seven years?" I ask.

"Apparently." He runs a hand through his wavy hair. He inherited Dad's wild hair. I've got Mom's straight dirty blond locks. Though hers come from a bottle these days. "You gonna tell me why she hates you?"

"There are so many reasons. Could be any of them."

He laughs. "True." He turns back to Leighton. "You have any insight into why Chloe hates Dean, baby?"

"Does she need one reason?" Leighton offers.

Ryan chuckles.

"I can see why you love her," I say.

His cheeks flame red, but he shakes it off. "She's gonna shadow you tomorrow."

Uh-uh. Chloe isn't following me around. Not in tight black outfit she wears. Not with that short hair brushed behind her ears. Not if I have to keep it in my pants.

"Yeah," he says. "She is. You agreed. She's yours for the day."

"When did I agree?"

"You said I could hire anyone. I did."

"An apprentice?"

"You have an issue with her skills?"

"No." If she's half the artist she was in high school, she's better than any of us.

"Her attitude?"

That's a trap. "No."

"Her work ethic?"

"No."

"Then what's your issue?"

Fuck. He's right.

I can't take this from her. Even if it will make my life easier.

It's been an eternity.

This isn't high school

I'm not hung up on the girl who hates my guts.

I'm a grown adult.

I can work with Chloe without letting her get under my skin.

Better convince Ryan I don't actually care. "Will she really be mine?" I raise a brow.

"Don't."

"What if she's into it?"

"She's not. There's no fucking way Chloe wants anywhere near your dick."

I don't bother correcting him.

He takes a step backward. "Can I trust you with this?"

"Can you trust me with anything?"

He shakes his head *fuck if I know*. "I'll see you Wednesday."

"Until then." I nod my goodbye.

Watch him join Leighton at the counter.

He whispers something in her ear. She blushes.

He wraps his arm around her and whisks her to the door.

She waves on her way out.

It's just me and the machines.

I love the feel of Inked Hearts. The smell of rubbing alcohol. The red and pink string lights lining the walls. The framed art in the lobby.

It's a fucking thrill, knowing the place is mine.

But it doesn't fill me as deeply as it used to.

THE BARTENDER SHOOTS ME A SWEET SMILE. A *YOU FREE after my shift* smile.

But I know better than to shit where I eat.

She runs her fingers through her long black hair. "Usual?"

I nod. Move to the electronic jukebox. Trade a dollar for a grunge song. *Even Flow*. Pearl Jam is an obvious choice, but it's not like this thing has any b-sides.

Eddie Vedder's mumbling vocals pour from the speakers. I'm still not sure what he's saying. Only that his pain is spilling into his performance.

He's laying his heart bare, for anyone to see.

It's hard to imagine doing the same.

Earnest expression isn't my forte.

It suits this place and its utilitarian vibe. Concrete floor. Silver furniture. Plain white walls. Dim lighting.

Couples and friends crowd into the booths in the corner.

Singles line the bar. Stare at drinks or phones.

It's quiet tonight. Not empty—there are plenty of people here—but quiet. The grunge jam drowns out every hint of conversation.

That bartender sets a Jack and Coke on the bar. Squeezes

her arms against her chest, pushing her tits together. "Long day?"

"Same old, same old." I fish my card from my wallet and hand it over.

"Keep it open?"

"Yeah." The words are a reflex. It's part of my routine. A few drinks. A flirting partner. An offer to go back to her place.

I nod a *thanks*. Scan the bar.

There's a cute woman on the other side of some tech bro. She's staring at her phone. Tapping a text to her friend.

She takes a long sip. Sighs.

Looks around.

Her eyes catch mine.

Her red lips curl into a smile.

It's an invitation. Usually, that's all I need to get my blood flowing south.

But tonight...

Nothing is happening.

My body is apathetic.

She's hot—red hair, big tits, long legs. I can recognize it, objectively.

But that's it.

I approach her anyway.

Her long fingers curl around her pink cocktail. She looks up at me, her brown eyes wide with surprise. They get fuzzy as she stares.

I slide onto the stool next to hers. "I'm buying your next drink."

"You are?"

"Yeah."

"You're telling, not asking."

Yeah. It works like a charm. I lean in closer. Until I can smell her shampoo. Strawberries. Like Chloe's.

Dammit.

The feisty brunette isn't sticking in my brain.

It isn't happening.

I smile at the redhead. "Can I level with you?"

She laughs. "Sure."

"It's not for you."

"It's not."

"It's for me." I down half my Jack and Coke. "But I need you to play along. I'm not man enough to admit I want a pink cocktail for myself."

Her smile spreads over her lips. "It takes a lot of guts, admitting that."

"Thanks. I feel a weight lifted from my shoulders."

"I'm Allison." She extends her hand.

"Dean." I shake with a firm grip. Watch her pupils dilate as she gives me a long once-over.

She sizes me up.

Deciding if I'm worth fucking.

Deciding I am.

Her hand goes to her hair. She twirls a strand around her finger. Arches her back, thrusting her chest toward me. Practically screams *yes, I would like to come on your cock.* "It's a house special."

"Do tell."

"Earl Greyhound."

"Sounds like a lousy bus service."

Her laugh makes her tits shake. "It's Early Grey vodka and grapefruit juice."

"Creative." It sounds amazing, actually. Mixing bergamot with grapefruit is genius.

I hail the bartender. "Two more of these."

The bartender smiles. "On your tab, I assume?"

"Of course." I turn back to Allison. "Since you were kind enough to hear my confession."

"You hang at a bar long enough, you hear a lot of men's confessions."

"Why is that?"

"I guess they feel like they have to be tough. That whole macho boys don't cry thing. Until they start drinking and the walls come down."

"You sound annoyed."

"I'm not a therapist."

"Shit, there goes my plans for the night."

She brushes a lock behind her ear. "There's a couch in the back if you want to lie down."

"That's my backup plan."

Her cheeks flush.

Her pupils dilate.

She's thinking about dragging me to that couch.

About fucking me.

This is a done deal.

It should excite me, but it doesn't.

When I close my eyes, I see Chloe's pink lips. Her tight tank top. Her fierce glare.

That makes me warm everywhere.

The shitty pop music and the dim lighting and the cheap vodka—

Fuck, this is so done. I already know exactly how this night is gonna go. And I can't find any enthusiasm for it.

Two rounds of flavored vodka and grapefruit juice later, and Allison is pawing at my arm.

Hinting that her place is nearby.

She's hot. She's eager. She's sweet.

But I'm still apathetic.

MY APARTMENT IS QUIET. TOO QUIET. I TURN MY

Bluetooth speakers on. Pull out my phone to stream my favorite Sonic Youth album.

The powder blue couch is inviting—I'm fucking wiped—but it's nothing compared to the text on my cell.

Apparently, I'm your shadow tomorrow.

Chloe.

Something inside me stirs. It's not like with the girl at the bar. It's deeper. Achier.

She's an itch I'm desperate to scratch.

I tap a reply.

Dean: Who is this?

Chloe: Cute.

Dean: Is that Chloe with one e or two?

Chloe: Chloee isn't a name.

Dean: You sure?

Chloe: I think I'd know, Dick Face.

Dean: You remembered. Means the world to me.

Chloe: I figured.

Dean: You finally get why I consider that a compliment?

Chloe: I've seen better.

My chest warms.

Her hate fuels me. It feels good.

There must be something wrong with me, but I don't care.

I do a lot of shit to challenge myself—learn new styles, lift heavier weights, run farther distances—but none of it pushes me the way she does.

None of it makes me feel this alive.

Dean: Do tell.

Chloe: A lady doesn't kiss and tell.

Dean: What's that have to do with you?

Chloe: I don't want to bruise your ego.

Dean: It doesn't bruise that easily.

Chloe: I'm sure.

Dean: You just called your boss a dick face.

Chloe: You take it as a compliment.

Dean: True.

Chloe: Because you're operating under some delusion that it means your dick is beautiful.

Dean: If you're arguing otherwise...

Chloe: We're going in circles.

Dean: Are we supposed to be talking about something besides my dick?

Chloe: Yes.

Dean: Then how am I supposed to tell you about my Prince Albert.

Chloe: You do not have a pierced cock.

Dean: If that's some way of baiting me to send a pic, you should know it's working.

Chloe: Not interested.

Dean: Most of my ten p.m. texts head in this direction.

Chloe: Do you really think there's a snowball's chance in hell that I'm booty calling you?

Dean: You enjoyed it last time.

Chloe: You already warned me round two will be a disappointment.

Yeah, I did.

It wasn't that I didn't like Chloe—I did.

But I wasn't gonna let anybody into my heart.

And now...

Well that hasn't changed.

Dean: I've revised that.

Chloe: Have you?

Dean: Got a whole new way to blow your mind.

Chloe: Is this about the Prince Albert again?

Dean: I thought you didn't want to talk about my dick.

Chloe: Cute. Are you suggesting you blew my mind the first time?

Dean: Sunshine, I'm not suggesting shit. I know what it feels like when a woman comes on my cock.

The chat goes quiet.

When I close my eyes, I see her. In some tiny apartment, on a cheap black couch, staring at her cell, her cheeks flushed, her chest heaving.

Fuck, I want to be in that space with her.

I want her pressed against the wall.

Against the round kitchen table.

Under my white sheets.

Chloe: Does Ryan know?

Dean: Know what?

Chloe: My middle name. What do you think?

Dean: He signed your new hire paperwork. I assume he knows your name is Chloe Grace Lee.

Chloe: Cute.

Dean: Thanks.

Chloe: Are you going to answer me?

Dean: Where's the fun in that?

Chloe: I'll take that as a no.

Dean: Take it how you want.

Chloe: It was a long time ago. I barely remember.

Bullshit.

It was her first time.

She remembers every second.

I know I do.

The nervous look in her dark eyes.

That long, black hair in my hands.

The way my name rolled off her lips.

It was the only time in three fucking years that she said it without disdain.

And, fuck, there is something wrong with me.

Because I'm not sure which I like better.

The *ugh, Dean, you're the bane of my existence.*

Or the *fuck, Dean, you're the only thing I need.*

Chapter Five

CHLOE

There are a few facts of life in Los Angeles.

Seventy and sunny is a daily thing.

Strip malls are everywhere.

And traffic is a bitch.

The freeway is clogged. And nothing—not the blue skies, or the beige hills, or the grunge music flowing from my speakers—makes it bearable.

What is it about being stuck in a car that makes everything awful? I spend most nights sitting around, thinking, listening to music. But when I have to do it in my car, I start crawling out of my skin.

I find a spot. Jump out. Stretch on the sidewalk. I hate staying still. I did it for too long. I spent way too long thinking I'd never be able to move like this again.

Traffic is inevitable with the distance I'm driving, but I can temper it. Find a nearby gym. Leave early enough to zip along the freeway. Make up the time with bodyweight exercises and miles on the treadmill.

Strong body, strong mind.

Strong mind, strong body.

It's a cycle. And it works. At least, that's what I tell myself. My body and I aren't quite there yet. I haven't forgiven it for what happened. Or learned to trust it.

I stretch my legs on the five-block walk to the studio. This is a nice part of Venice Beach. Clean streets, fancy cars, palm trees lining the sidewalks.

They blow in the breeze, blue sky and ocean view behind them. Like a post card. *Hello, from Paradise. Your nemesis is waiting.*

He is.

He's sitting behind the counter, shaggy hair hanging in front of his blue eyes, attention on his sketchbook.

His expression is focused. Intense.

Some other Dean. One who takes shit seriously. Who finds pleasure in work and productivity and accomplishment.

Who doesn't live to taunt me.

He looks the same—white t-shirt hugging his shoulders, skinny jeans hugging his hips, gorgeous blue eyes on fire with something.

But everything else is different.

Maybe that's okay.

Maybe it's possible to forgive and forget. My life is bigger and broader than it was in high school. My concerns go way beyond a guy who didn't call.

A guy who didn't call...

I wish that was my biggest problem.

I roll my shoulders.

Lean my head to one side. Then the other.

I need this job. That means I need to play nice. It's possible. Really.

I go to pull the door open, but it's locked.

Dean looks up from his drawing. His focus fades as his eyes meet mine. His lips curl into a wicked smile.

The *I'm fucking with you* Dean.

I shift my weight from one foot to the other. Bite my lip. Play with my tank top.

He's not going to make my stomach flutter. He's not going to make me nervous. He's not going to make me feel anything. Period.

Dean moves to the door with steady footsteps. He stares into my eyes as he pulls it open. "After you."

I step inside. The bell rings as the door falls shut behind me. "Thanks."

"My pleasure." He turns. Places his body behind mine. It's a respectable, work appropriate distance—at least when your work involves touching people—but it's enough to make my stomach flutter.

My gaze shifts to the ceiling. Except for the string lights lining the room, it's plain, white. But they cast a soft pink glow over the top of the room. A pink halo.

"I should get started." I'm taking over half of Leighton's job. It's a lot of administrative work.

"After this." He motions to the office/back room.

I follow him past the counter, around the corner, into the cozy space.

It's a tiny room—smaller than my bedroom—lined with supplies on wire racks and a cheap Ikea desk. This room isn't like the rest of the shop. It's sparse. Empty. Soulless.

There's no love in this room.

Just function.

It's weird. The four guys who own the shop are artists—tattoos are art—and it shows in the main area. Hell, it shows in their clothes, their smiles, their skin.

But here?

It's basically a corporate cubical.

"You looking at something, sunshine?" Dean asks.

"No." My gaze shifts to the desk. Computer. Printer. Two office chairs.

He steps in front of the computer. The insanely old computer. "Come here."

I do.

He fumbles with the printer. "You have your portfolio?"

"Not on me."

He taps the strap of my backpack. His finger slips. Brushes my shoulder. "You have anything?"

My stomach flutters.

My nipples tighten.

My heart rises in my throat. My nipples haven't done that in a long time. They're usually...

But he...

I swallow hard. I'm not reacting to him. Really.

"Chloe?" he asks.

"I have my sketchbook."

"Show me a tattoo mock-up."

"Of course." I bite my lip, but it does nothing to clear my mind. Dean is touching me. But he's being serious.

It's weird.

Which Dean is this—the goofball or the artist?

No. I'm delusional. There's one Dean and he lives to make my life difficult.

Even so. He's my boss. My teacher.

I need his help.

I set my backpack on the desk. Dig through it for my sketchbook.

But what the hell do I show him? I scan page after page of figure drawings, doodles, mock-ups. None are right. None are good enough. Or me enough.

There.

I settle on the design I drew for Gia. A pinup style Han Solo. He's lying on the Millennium Falcon, his legs splayed open, his shirt cut to his belly button.

Dean chuckles as he looks it over. "Different."

"It's a riff—"

"On a classic pinup."

"Yeah."

"A parody. Han here looks hot as hell. But he also looks ridiculous with his back arched and his legs in the air. Making a pinup a male character underlines how ridiculous the whole concept is."

Yeah. That's actually exactly it.

His eyes find mine. "Yes?"

"Nothing."

"Your mouth is hanging open."

"It is not."

"You think I'm an idiot?"

"I didn't say that."

"You can." His fingers brush mine as they curl around my sketchbook. He raises a brow *you mind?* "It won't hurt my feelings."

"What would?"

"If I thought you meant it."

I motion *go ahead.*

He takes the book. Turns.

His ass brushes my thigh as he bends to lay the book on top of the scanner.

He smells good. Like soap and shampoo and Dean.

That's the same shampoo. It takes me right back to the dark bedroom. To fumbling hands and locked lips and low groans.

Get a grip, Chloe. You're working together. That's it.

The machine whirs on. Spits out a printout of my drawing. "You can close your mouth. I'm not gonna whip it out, no matter how much you beg for a taste."

I bite my tongue. Fight my desire to slap him. That's the Dean I know. God, he's so annoying. "In your dreams."

"No. My dreams of you are much dirtier than that."

"You haven't."

He shrugs *maybe I have, maybe I haven't*. He rolls up his sleeve, exposing his ink-free shoulder. "You ever do this?"

"*This?* Pretty sure you were there."

His laugh lights up his bright eyes. It lights up his entire expression. He becomes that charming, effervescent version of himself.

He's so...

Handsome.

And annoying.

How can one person be so endlessly frustrating?

He taps the printout. "It's a special adhesive paper."

"A temporary tattoo."

"Yeah."

I've seen these. They're examples. So people can trial run tattoos. Sometimes artists use them like tracing paper. Go freehand. The image is mirrored, because it's meant to be pulled off the paper and onto someone's skin.

"Cut it out." He picks up scissors and hands them to me.

I snip the edges from the paper.

"Paste it on me." He motions *come here*.

No. I can't move closer. I'm too close already. "Water?"

He motions to the cooler in the corner.

I move over. Fill a cup. The cotton swabs are on the wire rack behind me.

"Rubbing alcohol first," he says.

There. It's on the top shelf. I press to my tiptoes to grab it. Bring everything back to the desk. Leave it in a neat row.

A medicinal smell fills the room as I uncap the rubbing alcohol and wet a swab.

My left hand goes to his forearm. Holds him in place while the right cleans his shoulder.

There. I grab a paper towel from the corner. Pat dry.

"Take the temp tattoo and take off the plastic."

I do.

"Press it against my skin and hold it in place. Then wet it with the cotton ball."

"Sure." I press the temporary tattoo to his skin. Soak the cotton ball than dab it against the paper, inch by inch.

I can feel him, under the paper.

His warmth.

His hardness.

His pulse.

It's overwhelming.

Then he looks down at me and my body goes into overdrive. What's in those bright blue eyes of his? Is he assessing me? Figuring out how to teach me? How to torture me?

My head is uncertain.

My body is apathetic. It only cares that he's looking at me. That he's close. That he's here.

I force my gaze to the paper. "Is that long enough?"

"Thirty seconds."

That's an eternity. My eyes move around the room. Black desk. Black printer. Silver wire racks. Boxes of ink pads. Of K-cups. Of water bottles.

First aid kit.

Rubbing alcohol.

A&D.

Aftercare lotion.

Plastic gloves.

Plastic wrap.

Autoclave sterilizer.

His breath is even. Steady.

Mine is... not.

The air conditioner whirs.

My heart thuds.

There. That must be it. "You ready?"

"Yeah."

I drop the cotton ball in the paper cup.

Slowly, I peel the adhesive from his tanned, toned skin.

My breath leaves my body.

It's perfect.

It's amazing.

It's everything.

That's my work, my drawing, on his skin.

My work is on someone's body.

It's temporary, but still.

It's my work on someone's body.

On Dean's tall, sculpted body.

The back of his hand brushes the inside of my wrist. "You okay, sunshine?"

"Yeah." My fingers go to his skin reflexively.

"You gonna ask permission for that?"

"Sorry."

"I get it. I'm irresistible."

My cheeks flare. "No, I—"

"You can touch me all you want, sunshine. But you need to break that habit."

"Oh."

"You can't touch fresh ink. Not with bare hands. Not like that."

"Of course." I know the drill. I have a dozen tattoos. I... I'm better than letting my libido take over.

But, God, it's been so long since my body responded to anyone.

It hates me. This is more evidence. If it liked me, it would respond to someone else.

To anyone else.

"Come with me." He pushes past me. "Bring your stuff."

I grab my stuff and follow him into the lobby.

It's still empty. Just us. The store doesn't open for an hour. Walker is due in after lunch. Brendon too. Leighton showed me the schedule yesterday. (She also gushed about how hot they were. But not as hot as Ryan, of course).

Dean walks straight to his suite. All the way to the mirror.

He studies his reflection. He studies the ink. "What do you see?"

My work on someone's skin.

The rest of the world is a blur.

My thoughts are a blur.

My brain is screaming like a fourteen-year-old fangirl.

This is the coolest thing in the history of the world.

He makes eye contact through the mirror. "Chloe?"

"Yeah?"

"You want to do ink 'cause it's cool?"

"No."

"To piss off your family?"

"No."

"To prove you're a rebel?"

I fold my arms. "What the fuck?"

"If you love ink, you look at tattoos all the time."

"Of course."

"So, tell me what you think about my new ink." He pats his shoulder. "No holds barred."

Okay...

"I know it's tough concentrating. The bulging muscles are distracting. I tried to find a skinny model for this demo, but I was the only person available." His voice lifts back to that teasing tone. *I'm Dean Maddox and I take nothing seriously.*

"It suits you."

He stares at the reflection of the ink. "Yeah. But is it good?"

I tell the raging fangirl inside me to calm. Take a deep breath. Exhale slowly. Yes, it's amazing that my work is on someone's skin.

But is it the best it can be?

I study the reflection, but it's too far away. The details elude me.

I move into Dean's suite.

Past his chair. And the stool next to it. All the way to the mirror.

My fingers brush his upper arm.

The design looked perfect on paper, but there's something off about it on his shoulder. The top is too small. The bottom is too big. It curves around his arm at an awkward angle.

The lines aren't sharp enough.

The beige and brown blend into his tan skin.

"It needs work," I say.

"How?"

I drop his arm.

He turns. Stares into my eyes, hanging on every word as I explain what isn't perfect. When I'm finished, he shakes his head. "You're too hard on yourself."

"My sister says the same thing."

"Gia, right?"

"Yeah."

"She into you doing tattoos?"

"She thinks it's cool." I take a step backward. "I designed this for her."

"Oh."

"Oh?"

"And here I thought you had a thing for scoundrels."

"Cute."

"I try."

I bite back an insult. He tries to annoy me. To stay "hilarious." To press all of my buttons.

But why?

Dean's okay when he isn't being the most obnoxious person in the universe.

Where can I find more of that guy and less of this one?

"Redo it." He nods to my sketchbook. "Make it work better."

"You're the client."

"Yeah?"

"Shouldn't I be listening to your input?"

His smile spreads over his cheeks. "You'll do whatever I ask?"

"It's your tattoo."

"What if I want it to say Chloe Grace Lee has a fantastic ass?"

"That's a little obvious, don't you think? Might as well have it say 'water is wet.'"

His eyes brighten. "How about Chloe Grace Lee is madly in love with me?"

"If you want my name on your body that badly, just ask."

He smirks. "You're right. It's my ink. But some people have bad ideas. Want shit that won't work. It's your job to give them good ink. You have to steer them in the right direction."

"But—"

"You don't know shit yet, yeah. This is lesson one. You have ink."

I nod.

"Right here." His fingers curl around my wrist. He traces the word inked on it. *Hope.*

I cringe, anticipating his insult.

But he stays serious. "You pick this font?"

"Yeah."

"It's thin. Delicate. Perfect for a small part of your body. The tattoo is long. Not overly so—it's a short word. But long enough it stretches over your skin."

I nod.

"This was the right place for it." He pulls a marker from

his back pocket. "But here?" He scribbles the word *hope* in the middle of my forearm in cursive. "Doesn't look as good."

It doesn't.

"It's too small for that body part. It's swallowed up by all the skin. But this." He measures the tattoo on his shoulder with his fingers then brings it to my forearm. His fingertips tap my skin at my elbow crick and my inner wrist. "Fuck, you're tiny."

"Five one."

"This is too big for your arm. But mine." He holds out his arm. "It would work."

"Where else?"

"Curve of the hip. Lower back." His fingers brush my lower back. Press the cotton fabric of my tank top into my skin.

It's soft. Tender. Like the night he...

I swallow hard.

"I have an appointment at ten. I want you sitting by my side the whole time." He motions to the counter. "Set up. Do the work Ryan assigned you. If you finish early, fix this."

"Do you want it somewhere else or on your shoulder?"

"I need this on my shoulder. I'll die if I don't get it on my shoulder."

"Die, really?"

"Yeah."

"Aren't you supposed to motivate me to do my best work?"

"Yeah?" His eyes light up with epiphany. "Be careful, sunshine. If you bite, I bite back."

"You started it."

"Even so." He sits back in his chair. Spreads his legs in that *blow me* position.

I flip him off.

He chuckles.

I want to slap him.

And kiss him.

It's weird.

But it doesn't matter.

Dean is my boss. I'm keeping this professional. End of story.

Chapter Six

CHLOE

"Rick, Chloe. Chloe, Rick." Dean's voice is casual. Effortless. Like he's shooting the breeze at his favorite bar.

Rick, a tall guy with dark hair and a nervous smile, offers his hand.

I shake. "Nice to meet you."

"Yeah." His eyes trace a line down my body then fix on my chest.

My cheeks flame. It's been two years. I've spent them—no, I've spent my entire life living in tank tops.

I should be used to this.

But I'm not.

"Any way I can get her to do it instead of you?" Rick teases.

"It's her second day," Dean says.

"Even so." His gaze shifts to Dean.

Dean looks to me. "What do you think, sunshine?" He hands me the tattoo gun. "Want to do this freehand?"

Want to? Hell yes. I want to do ink now. But I'm not even close to ready for it. This isn't putting pen to paper. If I mess up, that's it. My mistake is on someone's body forever. "Not a good idea."

"Sorry." Dean shrugs. "I tried." He motions to his client. *Sit down.*

Rick follows orders.

"Get me the temp tattoo, Chloe." Dean leans in to whisper something in his client's ear. He shoots me a serene smile. "Please."

Is that sarcastic or earnest?

I don't know.

It doesn't matter.

This is a request from my boss. Not sass from my enemy.

I work with Dean.

I take orders from Dean.

Learning to do ink is worth dealing with a million obnoxious Deans.

There's a perfectly good temporary tattoo in the printer— Dean checked it a hundred times. Even so, I scan his drawing, hit print, wait for the machine to spit out the adhesive paper.

There. I snip it as small as I can and return to the main room.

The shop is still empty. There's no conversation, laughter, or grunting to drown them out.

I move close enough to eavesdrop.

"Come on. Be honest. You tapped that?" Rick asks.

Dean laughs. "Is she a PlayStation controller?"

"You know what I mean?"

"Is it the 90s? Is my hair rad?" He shakes his head, sending his long bangs flying in every direction. "Are my jeans fly?"

"Your hair is trapped in 2004. A little eyeliner and you'll be rocking the emo look," he says.

Dean chuckles. "You're brave, Rick. Braver than I am. But you know what they say—"

"Chicks dig guys with eyeliner?"

"Exactly." He laughs.

I'm not exactly opposed to the idea. Grey would suit Dean. Dark enough to line those baby blues but not dark enough to overpower them.

Shit.

This is...

It's just because I hit puberty when the emo look was popular.

It has nothing to do with that one time Dean dressed as some musician for Halloween. It has nothing to do with how badly I want to tug at his bangs and tear off his skinny jeans.

Besides, he's way too buff to look emo anyway.

This—

"Did you fuck her?" Rick asks.

"You gotta butter me up if you want juicy details like that."

"Girl like that. In those boots? Bet she's a tiny package of kink."

"Do you?"

"Yeah. Damn. How the fuck do you get all the hot chicks?" His cheeks flush as he catches me staring.

Dean laughs.

I blush. I get that I'm in a male environment. That tattoos are masculine and a lot of guys think they're in some *let's talk about babes and brews and sports* place.

But *tiny package of kink?* Really?

I suck a breath through my teeth. A lot of artists turned me down for an apprenticeship because *women just can't do tattoos*. I'm already at a disadvantage here.

It sucks, but I have to play nice if I want to level the playing field.

Dean's eyes catch mine. He motions *come here*. "Be honest, Chloe. You like this tattoo?"

It's a bicep piece, a classic sailor girl pinup. Vertical. Dark lines. Bright colors. Big, clear details. "It's good."

"Just good? Fuck, which of us should take offense to that?" Dean asks.

"It's great." It's bold, eye-catching, classic and original at once. "It suits you."

Rick looks to Dean and raises a brow.

"She told me the same thing about mine." He pushes his shirt up his sleeve to show off his Han Solo temporary tattoo.

"She was right about you." He looks to me. "I'm sure she's right about me."

"You know Chloe isn't just a masterful artist," Dean says.

"No?" Rick says.

"She does aikido," Dean says.

Confusion streaks Rick's expression.

"Martial arts." Dean jumps out of his chair. Sinks into his heels. Karate chops the air. "She kicked Ryan's ass."

My shoulders tense. I anticipate their stupid commentary. *Of course, the Asian girl does karate. Oh, you're only half Asian? Does that make you an egg or a Twinkie? What do you mean karate is Japanese not Korean?*

But the commentary doesn't come.

Dean threw a lot of bullshit at me over the years, but he never brought up my heritage.

Concern flares in his eyes. He notices my discomfort. Stares at me, asking me something.

I'm not sure what it is, but I trust him not to go there. I wave him on.

He turns back to Rick and launches into a story. "Ryan had no idea what he was in for."

I play my part. Shrug as if I had no problem defeating Ryan. Even though the truth is I've never bested Ryan.

Dean continues. "He was all pissy about his ex. You know the way he was before Leighton. And he was out for blood.

Saw Chloe. Saw that dark hair and thought of all the ways he wanted to hurt Penny. He went dirty. Did shady bar fight shit. But he was too slow. Chloe was bobbing and weaving. She wrapped her arm around his neck and threw him over her shoulder."

Rick hangs on every preposterous word.

Dean lights up like a pinball machine as he acts out our fight. He mimes my hold on an invisible Ryan. Throws the invisible Ryan over his shoulder.

Rick's eyes go wide. He looks to me with respect. "Badass."

"Thanks." I fight my blush.

"Dean, you think you could take her?" Rick asks.

"If I had a death wish, maybe." Dean shakes his head *no way*.

"But she's..." He looks to me. "You're so small."

"And agile. As soon as you see her, she's gone." He slaps his hands together. Lets one whiz past the other. "If you want to go, be my guest. But I'm gonna insist on charging first. In case you don't make it back."

Rick's jaw drops.

He's really buying this.

It's weird. He's looking at me with all this respect.

Ten minutes ago, I was nothing but a piece of meat.

Now I'm worthy of more than his boner.

Dean made me feel mixed-up, but he never made me feel like that. Not until I was staring at my cell, wondering what I'd done wrong, wondering why I wasn't worthy of his attention.

Dean winks at me. Turns back to Rick. "Stay still." He's quick about applying the temporary tattoo and peeling it off.

It's hard to explain how perfect it is. The lines fall over his muscles like they were made for them.

No. They were.

This is an art I don't understand. That I barely begin to understand. And Dean really is the perfect person to teach me.

He turns Rick to the mirror. "Still in love?"

Rick's eyes go wide. "Fuck yeah." He looks to me. "Would you clean it off?"

Dean nods. "Do the honors."

It's quick, a few swipes of rubbing alcohol, then a few of a paper towel.

Rick looks at me with goo-goo eyes. "You sure she can't do the ink?"

"Damn. This is why no one hires hot women." Dean shakes his head with mock indignation.

"Is it?" God, he's stupid.

"Yeah." Dean nods. "They steal all your attention."

"Wasn't gonna stare at your chest." Rick blushes. "I mean—"

"It's fine," Dean answers for me.

Who the fuck does he—

"Go wash up, Cloe." He taps the gun with his gloved hand. Nods to Rick's easy, breeze smile.

He's calmer than he was when he came in.

Because of Dean's stupidity.

Because he's too busy thinking about my boobs to consider the giant needle awaiting him.

I get his point. Really, I do.

But those are my boobs he's using as bait.

He could at least ask permission.

I wash and dry twice, return to the suite, pull on plastic gloves.

Dean already has the stencil taped to Rick's arm.

But Rick is lacking the cool of a moment ago. He's staring at the tattoo gun, his eyes wide, his jaw tight.

Dean motions to the stool next to him. It's teal, like every other chair in the room.

I sit. Watch Dean turn the gun on. Look to Rick.

"You ready?" he asks.

"Yeah." Rick fails to sell his sentiment.

"Let's play a game." Dean turns the gun on. "Truth or truth."

"What?" Rick asks.

"It's easy. You pick truth or truth. You in?" The gun buzzes against his hand. "Don't forget, I can still write *I have mommy issues* on your arm."

"I'm in." Rick lets out a nervous laugh.

"You first, Chloe." Dean turns back to Rick. Brings the gun to his skin. "On three."

Rick nods.

"One, two—" There's no three. The needle is already on Rick's skin.

Rick bites his tongue as he stares straight ahead. He's clamming up. Nervous.

This isn't a particularly painful spot, but a needle jamming your skin several times a second is always painful.

Especially if you hate needles.

"Chloe." Dean taps my toe with his. "Your turn."

"Oh." I have to distract the client. It's weird, but it makes sense in a Dean kind of way. "How'd you get into doing ink?"

"Damn, my ego." He looks to Rick. "Can you believe she isn't asking about my cock?"

He laughs.

"Who'd want to know something about my feelings?" Dean feigns confusion. "But fair enough, sunshine." He traces the outline over Rick's skin. "Ryan got his first tattoo at sixteen. Our parents freaked. Grounded him for a month. I thought it was the coolest thing ever. Talked him into taking me to the studio."

I can see that.

"The artist stared at me and said, 'what are you, twelve? Wait until you're eighteen, kid.' He wouldn't do it. Later, I found out, Ryan had arranged that. But I didn't forget it. As soon as I turned eighteen, I went back there. To the same guy. He remembered me. Did my first piece for free."

"What was it?" I ask.

He taps his side. "Our beautiful state."

The ink he showed me that night.

I fight my blush, but it doesn't work. My cheeks are on fire.

Rick looks between us. Arches a brow, angling for a story. He's eager for dirt. He's practically oblivious to the needle on his arm.

Dean is good at this.

"How'd you get from there to doing ink?" Rick asks.

"Ryan started apprenticing around then. Once he was a full-time artist, I guilt tripped him into getting me a gig at his studio."

"No wonder he's hesitant to teach anyone," I say.

Dean laughs. "Fucked that up for everyone. Sorry." He winks.

I don't know how to take it, so I focus on the work. The outline takes shape. A woman sitting on an anchor, her back arched, her lips parted, her chest in the air.

Classic.

He finishes the black. "Red."

I grab the pad, open it, place it on the tray.

Dean stops the gun. Switches needles. He's careful. Focused. Intent.

That other Dean. The one I don't understand.

Then he's back to the troublemaker. "My turn."

"Yeah," I say.

He turns on the gun. Draws the first line of red—the sailor girl's lips. "Chloe, what color panties are you wearing?"

Rick's cheeks flush. He barely notices the needle.

But that doesn't soothe my temper.

My eyes narrow. My fingers curl into fists.

"Black, I bet," Dean says.

Calm down, Chloe. He's helping the client. Look how calm he is. He's practically floating.

So what, if he's right about your panties?

That's an easy guess.

It doesn't mean he's thinking about your panties.

It doesn't mean he wants you out of them.

FOR FORTY-FIVE MINUTES, I SWALLOW MY ANGER. I PLAY along with Dean's game. Answer his question. Ask my own. Watch the tattoo take form.

Dean takes me through the after-care.

Has me check out Rick and walk him to the door.

Bright light floods the shop as I pull it open. It swings shut. Blocking the beautiful afternoon.

Keeping out the heat.

Breaking the dam holding back my frustration.

I march to the counter. Wrap my hands around Dean's wrists. Lean in close enough to glare. "What the fuck was that?"

"You're smarter than that question, sunshine."

"*What color panties are you wearing?*"

He smirks. "Are you pissed 'cause I was right?"

I fold my arms.

He reaches into his back pocket. Pulls a stack of twenties from his leather wallet. "I'll put a hundred bucks on it."

"On what?"

"You're wearing black panties."

"That's an easy guess."

"Is that a yes?"

"Fuck off."

He smiles as he slides his wallet into his jeans.

I reach for the first hint of upper hand I can find. "Ryan would kill you for asking that." It's the wrong thing to say. I know it as soon as the words are out of my mouth.

He shoots me a *really, that's your line* look. "You need Ryan to fight your battles for you?"

"No." I don't need Ryan. I don't need Dean. I don't need anyone. It's not like there's anyone I can trust. It's Dad and Gia. That's it. "I need you to mind your own business."

"You want the client freaking out?"

"No, but—"

"Figuring out how to keep someone calm is part of the job."

"I know what getting a tattoo is like. Most people don't—"

"Yeah, but Rick does. And our twelve o'clock does too."

"You must offend people with this frat boy routine?"

"Aww, you think I'm smart enough to be in college."

"No."

"Could have gone to UCLA."

"Because you were offered a swimming scholarship."

"Even so."

"That waives the regular application requirements."

He stares back into my eyes. "You don't like the way I handle *my* clients, you can leave."

"You're supposed to be helping me."

"You telling me you didn't learn anything?"

I bite my lip.

"You can handle your clients however you want. Do shit by the numbers. Talk about weather. Talk about celebrity gossip. Talk about the Dodgers. Fuck, be like Ryan and sit there in silence. Everybody finds what works for them."

"And perverted bro works for you?"

He presses his hand to his heart. "You know me too well, sunshine."

UGH. He's so...

He's right but he...

I...

I stare back at him. Try to find a calm, even response. Fail. "DON'T TALK ABOUT MY FUCKING UNDERWEAR."

"Sure thing, Chloe." He smiles serenely. "I wouldn't want to make you uncomfortable."

"Bullshit."

He holds up four fingers. "Scouts honor."

Total bullshit. He lives to annoy me. How did he live before I started working here? That's the real question.

It's just...

He's so...

UGH.

I take a deep breath. Cultivate all the calm I can manage. "Don't ask about my panties, or my sex life, or my taste in men."

"Of course."

"Good." I bite my lip. There's no way he's just agreeing. He must be up to something.

"You distract our client, I'll keep our conversation PG." He offers his hand. "Deal?"

There's some catch here. I know there is.

I shake his hand anyway.

This is just like high school. We're competing again. And, this time, I'm not losing to Dean Maddox.

Chapter Seven

CHLOE

Zack, our noon appointment, introduces himself with a nervous smile.

He's a bundle of anxiety.

We're doing a cover-up. As in, someone already fucked-up his first tattoo. As in, he has every reason to be cagey about ink penetrating his skin forever.

Dean watches me like I'm a monkey in the zoo.

Like I'm just oh so adorable and out of my element.

"It's going to look awesome." I cut out the temporary tattoo and apply it.

"Yeah." Zack's voice gets hollow as he stares at the tattoo gun. His eyes go wide. His jaw cricks. "How long is it gonna take?"

"About an hour." Dean stretches his arms over his head. "You good to sit?"

"Sure." Zack continues staring at the needle.

"Chloe is my apprentice," Dean says. "She's just gonna watch."

"Right." Zack nods.

"That's kind of her thing—" Dean catches himself getting dirty. Clears his throat. "You ever get a cover-up, Chloe?"

"Yeah." My hand goes to my hip reflexively. "My first tattoo was terrible. A lopsided star. I went to a really shady place. I was lucky I didn't get hepatitis."

Horror creeps over Zack's expression.

Shit. That isn't helping.

I back up. "We're really careful here. Sanitized needle. New pad of ink every time." I tap the ink on the shelf. "It's um..." I reach for a comforting response and find nothing. Dean makes this look so easy. But it's just... not. "We really are careful."

Zack stays horrified.

I bite my tongue.

Dean shakes his head. *Pathetic.*

No.

I won't prove him right.

"It's my favorite tattoo now. The cover-up." I roll my jeans over my hips to show off the ink. It's no longer a lopsided five-point star. It's a shooting star, trailing across my skin.

Zack's expression softens. "Nice." He turns to Dean. Throws him one of those guy looks *are you two a thing?*

"You haven't shown me the new version," Dean says.

This is artist to artist.

It's not him checking out my bod.

Not that I want him checking out my bod.

I...

Ugh.

I turn to Dean.

"Fuck. That is nice. Who did it?" he asks.

I relay the artist's name.

Dean nods knowingly. "Now put your clothes back on. We wouldn't want Zack distracted."

I fight a glare.

He smiles smugly.

Whatever. This isn't making it about sex. Nudity isn't always sexual. If anyone knows that, I do.

I shift my attention to Zack. "What do you think?" I motion to his temporary tattoo. "Is it perfect?"

"Yeah." He stares at his reflection. "It is."

Dean picks up the gun and turns it on. It buzzes against his hand. It hums that low, steady roar.

There's something relaxing about it. To me.

To Zack...

Every last ounce of calm fades from his expression. His face goes white. Really white.

I need to distract him. Now.

But...

How?

I've never been gregarious. Or chatty. I can hold my own in a conversation okay, but creating one from scratch?

Not as much.

I look for clues. He's in a plain blue t-shirt. Normal jeans and sneakers.

His other arm is covered in ink. A skull and crossbones. A dagger. A Nirvana logo.

Ah.

"Can I ask you for some advice, Zack?" I sit next to Dean. Stare into Zack's dark eyes like I find him endlessly fascinating.

"Yeah. Sure," he grunts.

"I want to get into grunge, but all I know are the five songs they play on KROQ." Total bullshit. But what's a white lie to bring someone comfort?

He chuckles. "Yeah, they play a lot of *Smells Like Teen Spirit*. Nirvana is my favorite, but I still get sick of it."

Dean turns the gun on.

"Seriously. It's that or *Like a Stone*," I say.

"Or *Even Flow.*" He laughs. "You'll never hear the best stuff on the radio. The singles have too many edges smoothed off."

"What would you recommend?"

He launches into a list of bands. Most, I know. A few are new. Zack is really into this stuff.

And he's really distracted.

He grimaces every time Dean changes needles or moves to a new line. But I manage to bring him back to music every time.

I keep him distracted for the entire cover-up.

When we're finished, he hugs me goodbye and leaves his card. Not in a *do my next tattoo* kind of way.

In a *call me so we can make beautiful music together* kind of way.

Dean shakes his head. "Not gonna stoop to sex?" He turns, tilts his hip into the air, rolls his jeans over his skin. "Low blow, sunshine."

My gaze refuses to budge from the tan skin on display. God, he has nice hips. I've never thought about a guy's hips before, but Dean's are so...

"My eyes are up here."

"I was showing him an example."

"You got any other examples? Here maybe." He points to my chest.

"Fuck off."

"Sure." He reaches for his zipper. "But only if you promise to watch."

"Is there some timer in your head that keeps you from being serious for too long?"

"I'm dead serious, sunshine."

I roll my eyes.

"Now you're hurting my feelings."

"I'm not."

His lips curl into a smile. "No. You're not." He rolls his jeans back up his hips. "We both know the truth."

"I don't want to watch you fuck yourself."

He smiles *yeah, you do*. "You had to resort to sex."

"I won't next time."

"Suit yourself. But there's no shame in taking an easy path."

"I..."

"It's hard enough doing this job. Why make it harder?"

The bell rings as a guy about Dean's height steps inside. He has dark wavy hair, dark eyes, and an easy smile.

He's dressed like Dean—jeans, t-shirt, sneakers.

Effortlessly casual.

Effortlessly hot.

He surveys the scene and shakes his head. "You must be Chloe."

"Yeah." I offer my hand.

"Walker." He moves forward. Shakes. Leans in to stage whisper. "If Dean's giving you too much shit, let me know. I'll kick his ass."

"Didn't work too well for you last time," Dean says.

"I let you win."

"If I thought that was true, I'd kick your ass for it."

Walker chuckles. He turns to me. "You can shadow me tomorrow, Chloe. I'm doing some cool shit." He moves into his suite. "Or you can stick with Dean. He's a good artist, if you can get past his personality."

"I'm not sure I can."

"I'm not sure I blame you."

Dean mimes being stabbed in the gut. He jumps over the counter—actually jumps—then stumbles forward. He lurches over. Grabs his chest. Stares at the imaginary blood on his hands.

"It's so... cold." He stumbles forward. Collapses on the ground.

He commits to his persona.

Even when it's stupid and annoying and rude.

And kind of funny.

Okay. Kind of really funny.

~

OUR THIRD TATTOO IS EASIER. THE CLIENT IS A WOMAN. A tall, curvy, gorgeous woman.

Getting a tattoo just above her ass.

Dean charms her. Teases her. Makes her feel special.

I try to focus on the ink—a blossoming lotus, adorned with spirals and swirls.

It's great work—rich colors, sharp lines, soft shading—but my thoughts refuse to settle.

Jealousy builds in my gut.

My stomach twists. My heart sinks. My shoulders tense.

Finally, we finish. She giggles as he cleans her up. Hugs both of us. Gushes thank yous.

She's so nice and sweet and genuine.

And I want to punch her in the face because his hands are on her body.

They should be on mine.

They should be under my clothes. Between my legs. Inside me.

Fuck.

It's like high school. Dean owns my thoughts.

When I spend my late lunch break on a picnic bench by the beach, eating my homemade almond butter and jelly sandwich, he owns my thoughts.

When I grab a cup of Earl Grey at the nearest cafe, he owns my thoughts.

When I return to Inked Hearts and finish up administrative work, he owns my thoughts.

The day crawls on forever.

Until he finally releases me. And I leave. And he stays in the forefront of my brain.

I drive to the dojo. Change in the car. Step into the gym with every intention of clearing my head.

No Dean.

No Inked Hearts.

No men staring at my chest.

Teasing me about my panties.

Reminding me of everything I can't have.

Thirty minutes until the next all level class. I warm up. Stretch. Let my mind wander past the padded floors and the bamboo screens lining the walls.

Back in high school, it took three days to realize Dean wasn't going to call. That his only interest was what was between my legs.

It killed me.

I was always cute enough, thin enough, petite enough. But I was the weird artsy girl who wore combat boots to prom. Without a date.

Back then, I had a hard time revealing myself to people. I guess that hasn't changed much.

I always pored myself into my art. And I always felt like Dean saw something in it.

Like he knew some part of me no one else did.

He knew exactly what buttons to press to get a reaction.

Before she died, Mom used to say that hate is the other side of love. They're both passions that consume you. That encourage you to throw away every bit of reason.

That keep you up at night.

But Dean...

I don't know.

Slowly, regulars file in. The woman who looks like a poetry teacher. The teenage geek who can handle himself against any jock. The newly divorced woman, finding herself after losing everything she thought she had.

The instructor joins us. Takes us through calisthenics. Strength. Technique.

Sparring exercises.

They steal my focus. Keep my thoughts from drifting to how much Dean annoys me. To how impossible it will be to survive another two years of working with him. Or living with Dad—I love him to pieces, but he drives me bonkers.

Staying at home is all I can afford.

Twenty-four and I'm restarting my life.

It's better than the alternative, but it's still frustrating.

After an hour of sparring, class ends.

It's late enough the drive home is quiet.

I park my sedan next to Dad's, flip on the kitchen light, head to the fridge to figure out dinner.

We've never been well-off—I only managed to attend our fancy high school with a scholarship—but we do okay. The little house in the valley is ours. It's decked with Ikea furniture (all black or white, but somehow it works) and adorned with family photos.

Dad works hard. I do what I can to make his life easier—grab groceries, cook dinner, clean up.

Tonight, there's no need. He's sitting on the couch with a box of delivery pizza and a beer.

He waves a hello. "How was it, Chloe?"

"Tough." I take a seat on the couch. Grab a slice of cheese, one that isn't touching any pepperonis, and take a big bite. "How was work?"

"Busy." He looks to the *Seinfeld* rerun on TV. "Have you seen this one?"

I've seen them all a million times—he watches sitcom

reruns nonstop—but I still shake my head. "I don't think so. I'll watch it with you."

His smile is bright. This, the two of us eating and watching TV together, brings him joy.

It feels good, seeing him happy.

But, honestly, I don't understand it. How can he be happy after losing so much?

How did he drag himself out of that misery?

How does anyone?

I finish the show and the pizza. Hug him good night. Shower. Climb into my pajamas.

I pore myself into my sketchbook, but it doesn't grab my thoughts.

They drift back to the beginning. The horror that streaked across my mind as I felt a lump.

Just like Mom.

It happened so fast. Exam. MRI. Needle biopsy. Scary words like malignant and gene mutation and preventative double mastectomy.

I knew the drill. I'd watched modern medicine fail my mother.

I was sure my fate was the same.

It was terrifying. I thought I had my life figured out—I was about to graduate UCLA. I was ready to start doing martial arts competitions. I was madly in love with my boyfriend.

But I misjudged him the way I misjudged Dean. To Alex, I was a fun way to fill time. We were never going to be serious. He left at the first sign of trouble.

My friends at college, the ones who drank with me, laughed with me, organized documentary screenings and bake sales with me...

They left too.

Gia and Dad are the only people who stuck around. And, yeah, maybe that wore on me.

Maybe it convinced me that people abandon you the second shit gets hard.

That men always fall back on their promises.

That no one wants the girl with a clock on her head.

But I...

Well, I guess I'm not over it.

I'm not filled with the survivor pride.

I'm not dancing over how lucky I am to be alive.

I'm alive, and I'm glad, but it sucks being alone.

Losing so much.

Mom was unlucky. The gene mutation that killed her wasn't easy to test then. She caught it late. She suffered.

But I knew early. Well, early enough for treatment. The doctors assured me I'd be fine so long as I lopped off my breasts then injected poison into my veins for a few months.

It was an easy choice.

I look the same. Better even. My boobs are bigger. Perkier. Nicer.

I wear clothes better.

I get more attention from guys.

But these fake tits don't feel like mine. They feel like they belong to someone else. To some woman who laughs at cancer. Who scampers around the beach in bikinis. Who drinks mimosas with brunch.

Not to me.

I'm the weird, artsy girl without a curve to her name.

I'm all skin and bone (and a little muscle).

I'm not a centerfold.

But these...

It was weird, coming out of recovery and suddenly turning heads.

I tried to revel in it. I tried to use it to my advantage. To date guys who used to be out of my league. To get free drinks and entrance to clubs (not that I liked them).

But it never felt right.

None of the guys felt right.

None set me on fire.

Or tempted me to tear my clothes off.

There's no reason why I can't feel desire. I still have my nipples. My hormones are normal. I'm not depressed. At least, not anymore.

But I can't find that deep need in my core.

That *if I don't have it now, I'll die.*

If I don't come now, I'll die.

But Dean...

He wakes up the part of me that's been dormant.

Because I had him before?

Because I want him now?

I don't know.

It doesn't matter.

Maybe I should listen to my body for once.

But my mind and heart are diametrically opposed to the cocky playboy.

Chapter Eight

DEAN

Friday night, I stop Ryan on his way out the door. "Chloe was a good call."

"No shit." He stares at me in that Ryan kind of way. Assessing my intentions. Picking me apart. "What the hell are you up to?"

"Me?" I feign offense. "What could I possibly be up to?"

"Something."

"You worked with her yesterday."

"Yeah."

"And?" I ask.

"She didn't mention wanting to kill you." His gaze shifts to Chloe. She's sitting behind the counter, working on a sketch. "Is that 'cause you're doing your job or cause she's not the type to narc?"

I shrug.

Ryan shakes his head. "You really think your bullshit fools me?"

"Sometimes."

"Sometimes, yeah. But not most times." He laughs. Steps

backward as he slings his bag over his shoulder. "You're staring at her."

"At her tits."

"No. At her." He smiles. "You like her or something?"

"I haven't liked a woman since high school."

"She went to our high school."

"Wasn't her."

"Don't believe you."

"It wasn't."

"Uh-huh." His smile widens. "Damn, Dean. Leighton is gonna flip—"

"I don't—"

"I don't believe you. But it doesn't matter. You *can't*. You're her boss. It's out of the question."

"Of course."

"Of course." He shakes his head. "Like you aren't picturing her naked."

"I can picture a woman naked then not fuck her." Or recall a past fuck. But Ryan doesn't need to know that.

"You put money on that?"

"You're picking up my bad habits."

He holds out his palm. Copies my *pay up* gesture. "A hundred bucks says you're gonna try to fuck her."

"Excuse you?"

"Yeah?"

"Try?"

He nods. "Not every woman finds you charming."

"She wants to fuck me."

"Hate fuck you maybe."

"That's still a fuck."

"Fair enough." He pulls out his wallet. Takes out a fistful of twenties. "What do you say? We settle this Dean style."

"You're freaking me out."

"You chicken?"

"No." Seriously, what the hell is Ryan doing acting like me? He's the stable, responsible one. "A hundred bucks says I keep it in my pants."

"Bet you've never said those words in that order."

"Sure, how much?"

He shakes his head, that same *you're ridiculous*. Turns to her. "Good night, Chloe."

"Good night," she calls back.

He waves goodbye then makes his way out the door.

Leaving the two of us alone.

Chloe stirs as I get closer.

For a split second, her dark eyes meet mine. They flare with something—some mix of frustration and anticipation.

It fades from her expression as she stares at her paper.

Her fingers curl into her pencil. She focuses intently on a curve. Outlines a flowering rose.

"Can I see?" I ask.

"You're asking?"

"I have manners."

"You sure about that?"

"No. Maybe you should test me."

"Okay." She looks up at me. Pushes her lips to one side. Taps her chin. "Should you ask your subordinates about their underwear?"

"Shit. I know I've heard this one before."

She fights a smile.

"Yeah. Right? Show them you're taking an interest in their personal life."

"No."

"Fuck. Really?"

"Really."

"But what if your subordinate is wearing tights jeans that are driving you out of your mind?"

Her tongue slides over her lips. "Are you saying she was asking for it?"

"No. I'm worried someone is gonna ask me about my underwear."

A laugh rises in her throat. She holds her hand over her mouth. Tries and fails to stifle it.

Her dark eyes light up.

Her expression softens.

She brushes a lock behind her ears. "You don't have a boss."

"Damn. There goes that." I lean closer. Raise a brow. "What if my subordinate asks?"

"I'm not sure this falls under manners."

"No?"

"More sexual harassment."

"That's bad, right?"

Her laugh is light. Soft. "Yeah, it's bad."

Fuck, her laugh still hits me everywhere. I want to do whatever it takes to make it happen again.

I should stay the fuck away.

Keep her at a distance.

Do whatever it takes to avoid her getting under my skin.

But I can't.

There's something intoxicating about being around Chloe.

I need more of it.

I need all of it.

And, right now, I don't give a fuck what that means.

I need to be around her. Period.

I move closer. Look to the paper. "You haven't shown me the mock-up."

"You want to tease me or you want to look at the mock-up?"

Both. I motion *give it to me*.

She hands the sketchbook over.

A rose unfurls over a Latin quote. Its thorns wrap around the words. Guarding them or destroying them?

Hard to say.

"You design this for anyone in particular?" I hand it back.

"That's all I get?" She presses her lips together. Shifts her weight from one foot to another. Nerves flare in her dark eyes. But still she stares up at me, unblinking.

"What do you want?"

"To know if it's good."

"Do you think it's good?"

She stares at the art. Traces its lines with her fingertip. "It's a good start."

"It's great."

Surprise streaks her expression. Her lips curl into a soft o. Her chest falls with her heavy exhale.

"You're a fantastic artist. Best at the shop."

"Really?"

"Yeah. But that's only a fraction of what you need."

"Oh." Her brow knits in frustration. She blinks and it softens. Fades into the fiery determination I expect from her.

There's no middle ground with Chloe. She's all fire and ice. She's passionate. Opinionated. Sure.

I wish I gave that much of a shit.

My eyes meet hers. "Where would you put that design?"

She studies the drawing. Thinks it over. Slowly, she holds out her arm. Draws a line from her wrist to the crook of her elbow. "Or a hip." She nods to my right hip. "You're ink free. Or you were, last time I saw that."

"It's been—"

"You pulled it out the other day. To prove how I had to stoop to sex."

So I did.

"Which was a dick move. And it wasn't even true. That was tattoo haver to tattoo haver."

"You're a hot chick. He's a straight guy."

"Nudity doesn't have to be sexual."

"Maybe for doctors. But the average guy—"

"You?"

"What do you think, sunshine?"

"Remember when we ended up in the same figure drawing class? The one at SMC?" She calls the local community college by its initials.

"Yeah." When I fell in love with ink, I got serious about drawing fast. Took every art class I could. My mom was delighted. She dragged us to museums every weekend. But that... That was fucked in all sorts of ways.

"Was that sexual?"

"When they were hot."

"If I thought you meant that, I'd slap you."

"You wouldn't."

"Yeah, I would." She stands. "If you can ask about my panties, I can slap you."

"Is that a deal?"

"No." She folds her arms. "I'm not violent."

"You do Aikido."

Her brow furrows. Her eyes flare. "Martial arts is about non-violence." She takes a deep breath. Exhales slowly. "You know that."

"Do I?"

"Yes. You do."

"Don't know a lot."

"You know more than you let on." Her eyes go to the paper. "Aren't you getting out of here?"

"You don't have keys yet."

"Oh. I'll pack up my stuff."

"No. I have something else for you."

"Can't it wait?"

I shake my head.

She slides her sketchbook into her backpack. Sets both on the counter.

She rocks back on her heels as she looks up at me. "Seriously, Dean. I can't handle any bullshit today. If it's—"

"It's not." I motion to the sink. "Wash up. Then meet me in my suite."

"Okay..." Her combat boots pound the hardwood as she stomps to the sink.

She scrubs her hands. Slides on gloves. Looks to me with that *what the hell are you up to* expression?

It fades into *I don't care. Whatever it is, I'm meeting this challenge.*

It fills some place that's usually empty.

I want to help her.

I want to teach her.

I want to show her things. I want to show her everything.

She takes a seat on the stool. Taps her heels together. "Yes?" Her voice is determined. Sure. *I can do this.*

She needs the confidence.

This is going to push her as far as she can take.

Further, maybe.

I lean back in the chair. Adopt an easy smile. "Do me."

"What?"

"You've never inked anyone before."

"Of course not."

My hand brushes hers as I lean down. I roll my jeans up my ankle. Turn my leg to show off the bare skin. "So do me."

Her eyes go wide. Not fear or frustration, but genuine shock.

She bites her lip. Stammers something that isn't a word.

I was as gung ho as anyone ever has been, but I was still terrified the first time I put a tattoo gun to skin.

To *my* skin.

I still have the shitty, uneven lyrics on my other ankle. They're ugly as fuck, but I wouldn't dream of doing a cover-up. It's a battle scar. No way am I hiding that.

And this, offering my skin to Chloe, that's another battle scar.

Fuck, never thought I'd be offering my body to a woman like *this*. To be honest, most of my fucks aren't exactly offering. I don't give anything of myself. I don't expect anything in return.

Expectations lead to disappointment.

To hurt.

To betrayal.

Who the fuck needs that?

Shit. I'm getting distracted. It's Chloe. She does something to me. She tears at the string holding my thoughts together.

A week ago, I was sure everything in my life was just right.

Now...

I stare into her dark eyes. "You want to be an artist?"

"Of course."

"You have to start somewhere."

Her gaze focuses on my ankle. My calf. My knee. My crotch. Her cheeks flush as she drags her gaze to my eyes. "But I don't—"

"Don't what?"

Her lips press together. "What if I mess it up?"

"Can you think of better revenge?"

"True." She fails to sell the confidence in her voice.

She slides off her stool. Leans into her heels to crouch on the ground.

Her gloved fingers brush my skin.

It's not like when she touched me before. It's clinical. She isn't looking at me like the guy she wants to fuck—she can deny it all she wants, but she does. That's clear as day.

She's looking at me the way she needs to. Like skin stretched over bone.

Like a canvas.

Then she isn't.

Her touch gets softer as she drags her fingertips up my leg. To the hem of my jeans. "Can you even do a tattoo with all this hair?" Her voice steadies. It's not quite confident, but it's closer.

"No." I chuckle. It's a good question. But, fuck, it makes it even more clear how little she knows. "That didn't come up?"

"I guess it did."

"What happened?"

"Walker shaved some guys arm." Her nose scrunches as she looks up at me. "Do I have to shave your ankle?"

"Yeah."

She sticks her tongue out *gross*.

"You do realize you have to touch people to give them ink?"

"Of course."

"Guys a lot less attractive than I am."

"Not possible. You're hideous."

"That so?"

"Yeah."

"You need to look at me again?"

Her laugh breaks up the tension in her jaw. "You're conventionally attractive, sure. But your personality ruins the whole thing."

"You'll have awful customers. It's part of the job."

"Thank so much, master tattoo artist. I had no idea I'd have annoying customers in a customer facing job."

"You're gonna pretend you know customer service?"

"I sold Doc Martens for years."

I can't help but laugh.

She flips me off.

"Just..."

"It suits me, yeah. I got an amazing discount."

"Didn't it bother you?"

"What?"

"Selling all that leather?"

"Sometimes. But we had a great vegan line. I got to talk people into that. And leather is a renewable resource, unlike plastic. So, it's not cut and dry." She bites her lip. Stares at the ground. "You really remembered that?"

"You wore a *Meat is Murder* shirt to class once a week."

She laughs. "I was sort of—"

"Confrontational?"

"Yeah."

"You give it up?"

"No." She drops to her knees. "I'm going to pretend you didn't say that."

"How long has that been?"

"Sixteen years. Not that I'm counting."

"But no *Meat is Murder* shirt all week."

"That's where you're wrong." She taps her tank top. "It's on here in all black. I could never give up my all black aesthetic. Even for my morals." Her lips curl into a soft smile. "I'm surprised you didn't notice it. With how hard you stare."

I can't help but smile. I don't stare, exactly, but I do look. I can't help myself. Chloe is my kryptonite. She always has been.

"You can't get out of this," I say.

"Seems like I'm getting there."

I shake my head. She's charming me, yeah, but she's not getting any closer to getting out of this.

Chloe is doing this ink tonight.

She drops the teasing to look up at me. "What do you want?"

"A shooting star."

"That's complicated."

It is. Way too complicated for her first tattoo. It's good she has some idea of her limits.

For being a week into her apprenticeship, she's doing fucking amazing.

Most people don't touch a gun for months. They don't start tattooing clients for a year or so. And then there's a year of doing shitty simple stuff for free before they're anywhere near good enough to charge.

I find something that will be easy for her to do. Well, easier. "Then a five point-star."

She drops to her knees. Her jaw drops. Her eyes go wide.

She isn't here to suck me off.

But the thought burns into my brain.

God, that smart mouth of hers...

What is it about the way she looks at me?

It's fucking irresistible.

She presses her lips together. "Did you draw it out?"

"You need me to draw a five-point star?"

"Some people are specific."

"No. Go ahead. Make a stencil."

"I will." Her voice wavers. "I'm going to do it."

"Good."

She rises to her feet. Presses her gloved hands together. "Are you really—"

"Yeah?"

Her knees bump mine as she moves closer. It's not a sexual thing. She's examining me the way Ryan does. Picking apart my intentions. Looking for meaning.

"I hate to disappoint, but there's no secret to my psyche." I tap my head. "This is empty."

She shakes her head.

"It's not."

"Beer and boobs."

Fuck, she really does warm my heart. "If only I had the wit for that kind of poetry."

"Uh-huh." She takes a step backward. Turns on her heels. Moves to the office with shaky steps.

She's terrified, but she's putting up a good front.

I do the odds in my head—two to three. She's working up all the confidence she can, but she isn't there yet.

She isn't going through with it.

Which means...

Tomorrow is gonna be a hell of a lot more fun.

A few minutes later, she returns with the stencil. "Should I tape it to your leg?"

"Should you?"

"No. I should clean you up first."

"You wore your gloves to do a bunch of shit."

"Okay, I'll change my gloves."

"Tape the stencil first. Let's see it."

"Okay."

"Gloves off."

"Fine." She peels the gloves off and tosses them on the tray. Picks up the medical tape.

Slowly, she drops to her knees. Bends.

Her fingers brush my leg as she presses the stencil to my skin.

She pulls tape over the top.

Then the bottom.

Her fingers curl into my skin. "Is that how you want it?"

Fuck yeah. "You have to shave it first."

"There's no hair in this spot. Look."

She's right. Clever.

I chuckle. "All right. Wash up again then grab the gun."

She tears the stencil off, ripping out a handful of leg hairs.

"Fuck. Careful with that thing."

"Sorry." She pushes herself to her feet and sets the stencil on the tray. "I have to clean you up first."

"Do it."

She raises a brow. Taps her toes into the ground. Confusion flares in her eyes. She has no idea what to make of me. "Is this a dare?"

"No. It's an order." I am her boss. I'm responsible for teaching her. A quarter responsible, but that's still a fucking lot.

"Shouldn't I get some experience."

"How else are you gonna get it?"

"Grapefruits."

"You've never?"

"Never."

Fuck, maybe this is a dare. I should have her do a hundred bananas before I let her anywhere near skin. But I've come this far. I'm not backing down now. "I'm your teacher. If I don't trust you to do me, how can I ask anyone to trust you?"

Her eyes fix on mine.

"Yeah?"

"You're being reasonable."

No. I'm being stubborn. And impulsive. But I guess, for me, that's reasonable. "I'm always reasonable."

"Uh-huh." She moves to the sink. Washes up. Returns with fresh gloves and an *I can do anything look* on her face.

"Pick up the gun."

She does.

"You know how to turn it on?"

"Yeah."

"Do it."

She yelps as it buzzes against her hand.

"New pad of ink behind you."

"You sanitized the needle?"

"Yeah."

She turns it off. Swallows hard. "I have to clean you up."

I motion to the rubbing alcohol on the tray.

"Right." She stares at the plain package. Slowly, she brings her gaze to me.

She searches my eyes for an excuse to get out of this. "You, um, you won't be able to go in open water for three weeks."

"And?"

"Won't that get in the way of your swimming?"

"Yeah." Damn, that's creative. "I'll live."

"When did you last hit the pool?"

"Last week."

"The beach?"

"It's been a while."

"It's still September. Still nice. I can't take you away from the beach."

"You can."

She shakes her head. "You should say goodbye to it."

My smile spreads over my cheeks. She's right where I want her. "All right. We'll wait until I say goodbye to the beach."

"Good."

"If you come with me."

She bites her lip.

"Two choices. You tattoo a star on my ankle. Or you show up at my apartment in a bikini first thing tomorrow."

"I don't wear a bikini."

"You want to go commando under your wet suit, I won't stop you."

"No, I—" She clears her throat.

"You want to skinny dip? My parents are in town, but I'm sure I can get them out of the house."

"I'm not getting naked at your parents' house."

"You're the one opposed to bikinis."

"You have heard of one-pieces?"

"Like the anime?"

"No." Her laugh breaks up the tension in her jaw. "But you... you watch anime?"

"Sometimes."

"That... seems wrong."

"Why? What about me says *I don't watch anime*?"

"Everything. You look like the quarterback who sleeps with the cheerleader."

I motion to the tattoo on my forearm.

"All right. The bad boy who steals the cheerleader from the quarterback."

"That might have happened."

"I remember. He was devastated. Then you dumped her and she was devastated when he wouldn't take her back."

"Nobody wants to be second choice."

"What anime do you watch?"

"Chloe, do the ink or put the gun down. Two choices."

"I'm not wearing a bikini."

"You are getting in the water."

"You aren't—"

"Yeah, I am. And if you want to work here, you're gonna listen to me."

"But you—"

"Call me a dick face all you want. Tell me you hate my guts. Insult my sexual prowess. I don't care. We both know the truth about the latter."

She bites her lip.

"Your choice, Chloe. The board or the gun. What's it gonna be?"

Chapter Nine

DEAN

At eight on the dot, Chloe knocks on my door.
It's easy to tell it's her. Her knocks are heavy. Like the door did her some wrong.

No. It's not the door. It's me.

I did her wrong.

Because I'm pushing her now? Because of high school? Because she straight up hates my guts?

I'm not sure.

But I do know one thing:

Nobody can talk Chloe into something she doesn't want to do.

If she's here, it's because some part of her wants to be here.

I pull the door open with a smile. "Hey."

"Hey." She taps her black sandals together. It's bizarre, Chloe in her *don't fuck with me* black outfit and sandals.

"You have other shoes."

"I do."

"I wasn't sure."

"You wore Vans every day this week. Why is that less interesting than my combat boots?"

"The high hit eighty every day."

"It's thirty below zero in the shop. What is your electricity bill to keep the air-conditioning that high?"

I chuckle. "A lot."

"Our customers are taking off their clothes. Aren't they cold?"

"You ever go to a tattoo shop without AC?"

"Yeah."

"You ever go back?"

She shakes her head.

"Bet it smelled like old combat boots."

"Yeah, but not mine. My boots smell like flowers."

"Fifty bucks says otherwise."

"Sure. We'll check Monday." She offers her hand to shake. *Deal?*

I love a bet. Even one where I have absolutely no chance of winning. I take her hand. "Deal."

She shakes. Pulls her hand to her side. Slides it into the pocket of her skinny jeans. They're black. As is her tank top. And the halter straps under it.

There's something on her forearm. Something that wasn't there yesterday.

Meat is Murder in all black.

Fuck, that's commitment to getting her way. "That isn't—"

"Sharpie." She holds it up. "Why? Does it suit me?"

"Yeah."

"I feel like that's an insult."

It isn't. She has principles. I have my own, but they don't ask me to sacrifice anything. They don't put me at odds with the majority of the people I meet. They're nothing like hers.

She looks up at me with a curious stare. Looking for a deeper meaning.

There isn't one.

That's what everyone thinks.

I'm the fucking court jester.

The easily placated idiot.

I know my role. Most of the time, I savor it. Keeping shit light is easier. Safer. Infinitely more comfortable.

I pull the door open. "You want a drink?"

"It's a little early for that."

"Caffeine."

Her gaze moves over the blue couch, the bookshelf over-flowing with DVDs and video games, the bare walls. "What do you have?"

"I keep coffee here for Ryan."

"For Ryan, huh?"

I can't help but laugh. "Ryan is one of the people who drinks it."

"Uh-huh."

"I have tea too."

Her eyes perk. Her tongue slides over her lips. She shakes it off. Shifts back to neutral. "You drink tea?"

"Something wrong with that?"

"No, it's just..."

"I can't watch anime. I can't drink tea. Anything else Chloe Lee insists I can't do?"

"Be serious for more than three minutes at a time."

She might be right about that.

She steps inside. Presses the door closed behind her. So, it's just the two of us in my six hundred square foot apartment.

Fuck, usually this place feels plenty big.

But knowing I *can't* touch her?

"What tea do you have?"

"Everything."

"Really?"

"Really."

"Golden Needle?"

"Yeah." No. But she's bluffing. I can bluff back. I'm not a Philistine. I know tea. Even if I'm lacking that particular rare tea.

"Gyokuro."

"Of course."

"Of course?"

I nod.

Incredulity spreads over her expression. "Of course, you have a rare tea that most people have never heard of?"

I nod.

"You're so full of shit."

I shrug. *Maybe I am, maybe I'm not.*

"Show me."

I pull the door open wider. "You don't need an excuse to come in."

"You already invited me inside." Her shoulder brushes my chest as she steps inside. Then it's her ass against my hip.

Her fingers curl into her jeans.

It's doing something to her, touching me.

Fuck, it's doing something to me.

I want to tear off those tight jeans and dive between her legs.

I want her groaning my name like I'm the center of her universe.

Like I'm the only thing she needs.

Her sandals pad the carpet. They squeak against the kitchen's beige tile.

She looks around the room curiously. "This is so... not you." Her shoulders rise to her ears as she stares up at the high cabinets.

She's way too short for this kitchen.

She looks adorable. Like a kid trying to sneak a cookie from the jar on top of the fridge.

"Tea's in the drawer on the right of the fridge."

She turns so her back is facing me. But I can still tell she's frowning. It's in her posture.

Then it's not.

She reaches for the drawer. Just taps the bottom.

She does it on her tiptoes. Still barely makes it.

"You need some help?" I offer.

"No, I've got it." She hoists herself onto the counter. Settles on her knees. Her tank top pulls up her lower back as she opens the cabinet. "I knew it."

"That I'd appreciate the view?"

She clears her throat. "You don't have Golden Needle."

"Do you even want Golden Needle?"

"No, but I—"

"You don't have to prove you're smarter than me. I concede that point."

"I just—"

"What *do* you want to drink?"

"Earl Grey."

Of course.

She grabs the tin of tea. Climbs down from the counter. Her lips curl into a frown as she takes in my expression. "You're a know it all."

"How's that?"

"Your smirk. It's not attractive."

"Thanks, Mom. I guess it is true you attract more flies with honey than vinegar."

She groans. "I just..." She grabs the electric kettle. Fills it with water and turns it on. "Did you invite me out to torture me?"

"Yeah." That's a part of it. A huge part.

"Why is it you love pushing my buttons?"

"'Cause it's fun."

"Is that your entire life, doing what's fun?"

Kinda, yeah. I try to keep it that way. Even when it starts to feel empty.

Those phases hit. But I always push past them. Get to the other side. To where the empty feeling is gone and it's just fun again.

I move into the kitchen. Grab cups from the cabinet behind her. Turn and hand them to her.

It's weird, having her here.

Not like with other women. There's always a purpose to that. An *I'm not gonna send you home hungry after last night*.

I'm in character.

But this?

This is domestic.

Like my parents sitting to their Sunday afternoon coffees.

And that—

Fuck that.

"Thanks." She sets them on the counter.

"Sure thing."

She turns back to the counter. Watches the water steam. Pours it into the mugs, one at a time. "You have honey?"

"Yeah. Stay there." I reach for the high cabinet, but I'm too far away. I move closer. Until my crotch brushes her ass. And her back brushes my chest.

Fuck, she's tiny. Her head is barely at my shoulders.

My arm brushes her side as I reach for the honey.

I set it on the counter. Step backward. But releasing her does nothing to send blood back to my brain. "Spoons are in the drawer in front of you."

"Thanks." Her ass brushes my crotch as she bends to pull it open. She grabs two spoons. "How do you like it?"

I drop into something comfortable. Teasing her. "Rough."

Her breath catches in her throat, but her sigh isn't one of desire. It's irritation. "Are you actively trying to get a rise out of me?"

"Maybe."

"You weren't..." She squeezes honey onto the spoon and stirs. "Why is it I can't tell when you're fucking with me?"

"Faith in me, I guess."

"No."

"I'm always fucking with you."

"That's the thing, Dean. You're not. You're an okay guy sometimes."

"I'll take your word for it."

She turns to me. Stares up into my eyes. She must find something, because she nods knowingly. "How *do* you take your tea?"

"Hot and sweet."

"Same way you take your women?" she deadpans.

"That's a good one. I'll have to add it to my repertoire."

"It's really not."

It's really not. But it's cute that she's trying. She's mocking me, yeah, but she's stooping to my level to do it.

"How sweet?" she asks.

"Enough to taste it." I place my body behind hers. Revel in the way her breath catches in her throat.

She wants me. She's not good at hiding it.

I want her.

It should be easy. Simple.

But it's not.

This, teaching her, is important. It matters. I'm not fucking it up.

"Tell me when." She squeezes honey onto a spoon. The amber liquid spirals over the silver.

"When."

She slides the spoon into the tea. Stirs. "Here." Her ass

brushes against me as she turns. There's no space between us. We're right there.

Inches from touching, kissing, fucking on that countertop.

She hands the mug to me.

I step backward. Release her.

But her expression isn't relief. It's like all the heat is leaving her body. Back to Icy Chloe.

The kitchen table is close. I take a seat. Motion *come here*.

She stays put. "Shouldn't we head out?"

"You make this tea just to toss it?"

She nods *fair enough*. Takes a long sip. Lets out a soft moan. "This is good."

"What did you expect?"

"I don't know." Her dark eyes find mine. "Your walls are bare."

Yeah, they are. They've been that way for a while. "And?"

"Why?" She moves into the main room. "You can't see any of the white in my bedroom. It's wall-to-wall art."

"Your art?"

"One wall. The rest is other artists. Magazine tear outs. Posters."

"Anyone hot?"

"No." She laughs. "Movie posters."

"*Fight Club?*"

Her brow scrunches with confusion. "Why *Fight Club?*"

"It just suits you."

"I thought maybe it was shirtless Brad Pitt."

"Can't object to that."

"Oh."

"Oh?"

"You're not going to start bragging about how you resemble Mr. Pitt?"

"In his dreams he's even close to as hot as I am."

"Uh-huh."

I nod. "Why? You see a resemblance?"

"A little." She takes a long sip of her tea. Lets out a soft sigh. With her next sip, she moves closer. She crosses the distance between us until she's standing in front of the table. "My posters are all old movies. Classics. The ones I used to watch with my mom."

Her mom is gone. I remember that much. "You miss her?"

"A lot." She takes a long sip of her tea. Lets out another soft moan. "What exactly is it we're doing today?"

"Surfing."

A laugh escapes her lips. "Of course. That's perfect."

"I'm not *that* laid back."

"Yeah, you are. You might as well write *nothing bothers me* on your forehead."

"You've got me pegged."

She imitates me. "Now, I'll return the favor, sunshine." She makes a show of winking. And throwing out a dorky thumbs-up gesture.

This time, her laugh spreads over her chest and torso. She pulls her hand over her stomach as she doubles over.

Fuck, it's adorable.

And hot.

But I play my part. "That hurts, Chloe."

"Yeah?"

"I'll never be clever enough for a comeback like that. Don't rub it in my face."

"Uh-huh." Her laugh gets louder. Heartier. "I hate to step on your dreams, but I know how to surf."

"So?"

"Aren't you trying to teach me something?" She takes her last sip. Sets her cup down.

Maybe. But it's not surfing. It's something deeper. There's a bright woman under the layers of black.

I want to bring her out.

Not 'cause there's anything wrong with Chloe's scowl or her clothes or her attitude.

Because I want to show her the beauty in the world.

'Cause I want to make her smile like this again and again.

Because she hates me.

Because she bites back.

Because she wears her misery on her sleeve.

This girl is under my skin.

It's fucking weird.

I take my last sip. "You ready?"

"Sure." She moves forward. "Are we walking or driving?"

"You up for a walk?"

She nods.

I grab my surfboard. Hand it to her. "Thanks. Carry this."

She wraps both arms around it. "Is that a challenge?"

I offer my best effortless shrug.

Fire fills her eyes as she lifts the board. It's way too big for her, but she holds it against her side like it's a tiny scrap.

She's strong. Or good at pretending.

I take it back. It's fun baiting Chloe, but I can't let her ride that board. It will swallow her whole. "It's too big for you. We'll rent one."

"What about you?"

"I'm coach today."

"The point of this is you saying goodbye to your hobby."

"Is it?"

Her smile is sly. It's there, in her eyes. *Of course not. We both know you're full of shit. I want to hate it. But I kind of like it.* "I can handle the board," she says.

"I thought you knew how to surf."

"I do."

"Then you should know that board is way too big for you.

You're barely five feet tall. Still can't believe you spar with Ryan."

"He's only got ten inches on me."

I raise a brow. "Fuck, Chloe. Don't let Leighton find that out."

She shakes her head *you're ridiculous*. Her nose scrunches as she looks up at me. "Really? Ten inches?"

I nod.

"How do you know?"

"Massive cocks run in the family."

"Even if that were true—"

"If? You gonna pretend like you haven't tested the equipment?"

"I didn't bring a ruler."

"You can take my word for it."

She shakes her head. "Everyone knows guys exaggerate about their height and their size."

God, she really is a tiny package of fire. I've never had a thing for short girls, but there's something about Chloe. I want to wrap my arms around her. To consume her.

"Which means you're only nine inches," she says.

"*Only* nine?"

"You're right. You're Dean. You exaggerate twice as much as normal. Only eight. Maybe even under seven."

"Eight gets an only?"

She nods.

"That's the size of your arm."

"No..." She holds out her arm, spreads her fingers wide. "This is at least a foot."

"Want to compare?"

"No."

"You can see my Prince Albert."

Her pupils dilate. It's a quick second, then it's gone. "Not interested."

I don't argue with her. It's not good for mission *don't fuck Chloe*. This probably isn't either. But I can't help myself. "Could you take me?"

"Really?"

"In karate?"

"Oh. Yeah. Sure."

"Show me something."

"I don't want to hurt you."

"I don't believe that."

She smirks. "Fine. Aikido is based around not hurting your attacker. But... shit happens."

"Of course.

"I'm not going easy on you."

"I'm counting on it." I move into the empty area in the middle of the room, between the couch and the TV. Motion *come here.*

"This is about self-defense. Not about proving something to you."

"Of course." We both know she's doing it because I baited her, but I keep that to myself.

She moves into the main room. Places herself three feet from me. Fire fills her eyes as she looks up at me. "On three, go. Attack me. I'll fend you off."

I nod.

She counts. "One, two, three."

I lunge at her.

She ducks out of the way. Darts behind me.

I turn. Reach for her.

She's too small. Too fast. Too short. She bounces off the couch. Gets behind me.

I reach back. Grab something. Get her tank top.

My arm finds its way around her throat.

Her gasp isn't fear.

It's a *yes, just like that, harder, please.*

It's a quick second.

It steals every bit of my attention.

I forget that we're sparring.

That I haven't figured out if I'm going to let her win or give it my all.

My thoughts go straight to Chloe under me.

She leans forward. Bends, Takes me with her.

Chloe flips me over her head.

I hit the carpet with a thud.

She dusts her hands off. Mimes a *no swea*t. "Told you."

I can't help but smile. Proud looks good on her.

It's the same as back in high school. I want to push her to be better. So she'll push me to be better.

I want the competition. The banter. The fire.

Nobody has ever pushed my buttons the way she does.

Usually, my buttons are too far out of reach. Nobody even tries to push them. Nobody thinks I give a shit. Nobody thinks I'm worth challenging.

Nobody but Chloe.

Chapter Ten

I stop at a red light. Look both ways. Cross and motion for her to follow.

She does.

A car whizzes by as we step onto the curb. It honks. The driver looks out the window with a *what are you, crazy?*

I wave back *hell yeah*. "You graduated six years ago."

"Accurate."

"When did you finish UCLA?"

"Two years ago."

"So..."

"So?" She raises a brow, trying and failing to look aloof. Her jaw cricks. Her eyes turn down. Her Fingers curl into fists.

"What have you been doing?"

"Life."

"Life?"

"Yeah." She stops at the next street. Looks both ways. Crosses.

I follow her onto the sandy sidewalk. This is it. Venice

Beach at its most beautiful. The sky is white. Soft. The puffy clouds diffuse the sunlight.

A hundred feet of dry sand. The crashing ocean. Surfers jumping onto a small wave.

Chloe steps onto the sand. She looks down at her feet with surprise. Shakes it off. Steps forward.

She keeps her back to me.

Whatever it is that knocked her off course, she doesn't want to talk about it.

I want to know.

I want to pry her open. Peel back her walls. Figure out why she's always frowning.

"I, um. I mostly just worked and went to school. There's nothing to talk about." She steps out of her sandals. Digs her toes into the sand.

She's drifting off someplace ugly.

It's something serious.

And serious...

Not my strong suit.

Even so. I want to know. I want to wipe the hurt from her expression. To hold her and promise it will be okay.

It's weird.

Really fucking weird.

I retreat to what I do best. "You fuck a lot too?"

"Huh?"

"You must have cleaned up at the Doc Marten store."

She turns to me. Throws her hand over her eyes to block out the sun. It's not enough. She squints. "Cleaned up?"

"You must have had punk guys leaving their phone numbers."

"No." Her laugh breaks up the tension in her jaw. "Punk guys are like other guys. They also want the blond cheer-leaders."

"I don't believe you."

"You should." She turns to the water. "Where are we setting up?"

"Let's get closer."

She nods and steps forward. With every step, she scrunches her toes, feeling the rough warmth of the sand. Her expression twists with this mix of surprise and delight.

It's enthralling.

"I had a boyfriend most of the time I worked there," she says.

"Did he have a Mohawk?"

She laughs. "No. He was clean cut. Liked good girls."

"You're a good girl."

She drops her backpack on the sand. Drops to her knees next to it. She keeps her back to me, her gaze on the ocean. "How do you figure?"

I move next to her. "How many guys have you fucked?"

She flips me off, but it's good humored. She's smiling.

"That many or that few?"

"Shut up."

"No shame in racking 'em up."

Her eyes light up as she turns to me. Back to fire. To challenging me. Pushing my buttons. "Wouldn't I be getting in on your turf?"

"Sunshine, there's no way you're anywhere near my turf."

"How many women?"

"I can't count that high."

She laughs. "You don't..." Her nose scrunches. "You don't really try to sleep with women for the sake of racking up conquests?"

"Fuck no. That kind of long-term goal setting is way beyond my abilities."

"Uh-huh."

I nod.

She shakes her head. "Then why so many women?"

"Why so few guys?"

"I had a boyfriend. He was—"

"Ouch."

"Not ouch. Just—"

"Your tone. It's bad." I take a cross-legged seat next to her.

She shakes her head as she leans back on her heels. "Maybe I'm bitter about the breakup."

"Maybe he's a terrible lay."

She half smiles. "What's it to you? Don't you... What are we?"

"You tell me."

"I hate you."

"You like me."

She shakes her head.

"Then why are you here?"

"You gave me a choice."

"If you hated me, you'd have done the shitty tattoo."

"Maybe." Her gaze goes to the ocean. "Where does that leave us?

"We're rivals."

"Rivals." She bites her lip. "I guess that's about right. Well, dick face—"

"You keep calling me that, I'm gonna get hard."

She rolls her eyes. "I'm sure you've never stuck around long enough to realize this, but when you're with someone for a while it can get stale."

"Ex wasn't creative?"

"This is really none of your business."

"Not holding a gun to your head." I want all of Chloe's secrets. But I don't want to take them. I want her to give them to me.

The breeze rolls over us. This is a perfect beach day. Warm sun. Gentle breeze. Salty air. Quiet scenery. In a few hours, this place will be a mob scene. But right now? It's perfect.

She turns to me. Brushes my bangs from my eyes. "Your client was right."

"About?"

"You have an emo haircut."

"You like it."

She shakes her head, but it does nothing to hide her smile.

"You're right. I've never stuck around with anyone."

"Why not?"

"Why'd you leave your ex?"

"Is this one of your games?"

"Sure, yeah."

She leans back on her elbows. Looks up at the sky. "Aren't we here to surf?"

"Say the word. I'll grab a rental board."

Her eyes get hazy. Dreamy. "How does the game work?"

"Truth for truth."

She nods. "Okay. Deal. But you first." She looks up at me. "Why don't you stick around?"

"It's easier."

She shakes her head. "I need a deeper dig than that."

I scratch my head. "Sunshine, you've made me forget my point completely."

"That's not an answer. Why is it easier? What is it you want or don't want?"

"I want to come."

"If it was just that, you'd fuck yourself. Nothing easier than that."

She's got me there.

"You... you went through the effort to seduce me."

"I liked you."

"But I'm sure... are you telling me you don't try to seduce women?"

Try is the wrong word, but I do make an effort. "I show women a good time."

"And it starts when you meet them. Not when you take their clothes off."

"Yeah."

"So what's easy about that? Let me tell you, as someone who's had both... casual hookups and relationships. A relationship is a lot easier if your goal is getting laid on the regular."

"Is that why you were with—"

"Alex. No. I loved him. Well, I thought I did. Now... I don't know." Her gaze shifts to the ocean. "I loved the guy I thought he was. But he wasn't that guy."

"How?"

"It's still your answer."

I don't actively think about why I do anything I do. Fucking a different woman every night is fun. It's a thrill. A challenge. A hobby even.

I leave because that's all I want.

One night. One time. No emotional attachments.

I don't hurt them.

They don't hurt me.

"I don't want anyone getting attached," I say.

"You or them?"

"Both."

"Ah." Her eyes light up with epiphany. "Dick face does have feelings."

"Don't tell anyone."

She pulls an imaginary zipper over her lips. Catches herself doing it. "Fuck, that's your gesture isn't it."

"Yeah, but—" I copy the gesture.

She laughs. Pushes herself up enough to play swat me. "Do you ever sleep with the same woman more than once?"

"Yeah. Sometimes. If I'm sure we're on the same page."

"Is that easier?"

"No."

"Why not?"

"Feelings always get involved."

"And you're afraid of intimacy?"

Something twists in my gut. Something I don't like. "You're gonna have to dumb that down for me, sunshine."

"Hmm."

"Hmm?"

"You got defensive. That must be it."

"You studying psychology?"

"Just Psych 101 in college. I'm sure you've never experienced this, but... when you spend a lot of time sitting out dances, watching everyone else, you get to be pretty good at reading people."

"It's your turn."

"It is." She stares at the sparkling blue ocean. The sun breaks through a cloud. Casts light over the azure water, the beige sand, the white and red lifeguard stand. "Alex was pretty good. Neither one of us was all that experienced when we started. We learned together. He made an effort. But we both got complacent. Fell into a routine. I guess you could say the passion died."

"How long did that take?"

"Six months or so."

Fuck, that's an eternity. "How long were you together?"

"Three years."

"Why'd he leave?"

She shakes her head. "It's my turn."

"Shoot."

"No." She shifts onto her knees. "I think it's time to hit the water."

"I won't forget it's your turn."

"I know."

Chapter Eleven

DEAN

I drop the rental surfboard next to Chloe. "You know how to do a pop-up?"

She pushes herself to her feet. "Yeah."

"Show me."

"Is this a challenge?"

No. It's safety. So she doesn't fall off the board and break her neck. But that isn't the way to push her. "Show me."

"You don't believe me?"

"Just show me."

"Fine." Irritation flares in her expression. It fades to that fire in her dark eyes.

She steps onto the board. Drops to her stomach. "This is barely smaller than your surfboard."

She's right, but, I can't say I'm disappointed. Being board-free leaves us with a lot of options for what we do after this. "You want to prove you can do it or you want to sass me?"

"Sass you."

"Then carry on."

"You can't make me surf."

"I know."

"Oh. Good." She looks to the teal board. Places her hands next to her chest. In one seamless motion, she jumps to a perfect surfing stance. "I know what I'm doing."

"When did you last surf?"

"Um..."

"That recently?"

She flips me off.

I blow her a kiss.

She laughs. Waves it away. Ducks to avoid it.

"Humor me," I say.

She tilts her head to one side. "My life is humoring you." The hurt in her voice is gone. It's all fire. She isn't thinking about her ex or whatever it is that knocked her off track. She's here with me.

It feels good, having her attention. Watching delight spread over her face. Maybe a huge part of Chloe hates me. But she loves the way she hates me. She loves teasing back. "Do five more."

"I'm doing them because they're a good idea."

"Uh-huh."

"Not because you said."

"What's scarier—me having a good idea or you doing what I say?"

"Good question." She drops to her stomach. "I'm getting used to the latter."

"Are you?"

"I worked with you twice this week."

"And?"

"It's a job." Her eyes light up as she laughs.

"You still have five."

"I'm good for them." Her hands go to the board. In one swift motion, she jumps to her feet.

Her form is good. Her sheer power is fantastic. She's

strong and she's tiny. Makes it easy for her to manipulate her bodyweight.

The aikido obsession shows.

I try to focus on her technique, but it's hard with the way her tank top hugs her tits. Fuck, she's hotter than she was in high school. Strong legs. Tight ass. Perfect tits.

They're bigger than they were.

How the fuck is that possible?

Chloe isn't the surgical enhancement type. Must be... fuck, I don't care what it is.

Only how much I want my hands on them.

"There." She jumps off the board, brushes her hands together in a *no sweat* gesture. "That's six."

Sounds about right.

Her chest heaves with her inhale. She's flushed and sweaty. From the exercise, but that's not where my head is going. "Any other lessons?"

"Show me your best paddle."

"I was on the swim team for four years."

"You swim recently?"

"At the gym, twice a week." Her feet sink into the sand as she steps off the board. "I'm getting in the water."

I point to the wetsuit I rented for her, the one sitting on the sand. "Yours if you want it."

She eyes it greedily. "Are you wearing one?"

It's a challenge. *I won't if you don't.*

It's a stupid challenge—why freeze when you don't have to-but then I've never been particularly wise about knowing when to back down.

"I can." I nod to my backpack.

"What are you wearing under that?" She motions to my jeans.

I laugh. "Eager beaver."

"Don't call me beaver."

"If I can call you sunshine."

"Can I stop you?"

"No."

"Sure. Call me sunshine. But only because I know getting my permission will ruin the whole thing for you."

"That's where you're wrong, sunshine."

She makes a show of rolling her eyes, but it does nothing to hide her smile. She may have hated the pet name once. Hell, she probably hated it Monday. But all day, she's smiled every time she heard it.

It's growing on her.

And I could be—

Uh-uh. Not going there.

"You know what? I don't care." She pulls her tank top over her head and drops it next to her bag. "I'm getting in the water." Her hands go to her hips. She unzips her jeans and pushes them to her ankles.

She's wearing a tight swimsuit. A lap swimsuit.

Like she wore every fucking day on swim team.

Fuck, that brings me back.

Sends my thoughts straight to the gutter. I spent a lot of nights in high school thinking about stripping her out of that thing.

And now she's standing on the sand, staring up at me with that fire in her eyes, daring me to strip and chase her.

It would be heaven if not for one ugly little fact:

I can't have her.

She picks up the board and hugs it to her side. "You're still dressed."

"You want a show, sunshine?"

She sticks her tongue out.

"You flatter me." I roll my hips as I bring my hands to the bottom of my t-shirt. Slowly, I peel it over my head. Toss it next to her pile of clothes.

She raises a brow *really?*

Hell yes. I do my best hip thrust. Make a show of unzipping my jeans and sliding them off my hips.

She laughs as I turn, bend over, shimmy the jeans down my legs.

"Oh God. You're..." Her breath catches. "You're not wearing that."

"But I am." I turn to her. Snap the waist of my Speedo. "Aren't you used to seeing me in this?"

"I've blocked it from my mind."

Bullshit. She's held onto it tightly. Thought of me the way I thought of her. But there's no sense in pushing her.

It's only going to make me want her more.

And I don't need the blue balls.

"Are you coming or what?" She turns toward the ocean. Watches tiny waves crest, foam, roll into the sand.

I follow her across the sand.

Even with the board, she's fast.

She squeals as her toes hit the water. "Fuck. That's cold."

"Not too late for a wet suit."

She shakes her head *no way* as she runs into the water. She shrieks as a wave hits her waist. "God. I... Fuck it." She sets the board on the water. Grabs the leash. Dives in headfirst.

When in Rome...

I do the same.

Fuck. That's freezing. But tolerable.

When I surface, she's already on the board, paddling into the surf.

She presses herself up to go over a cresting wave.

Fuck, is this a nice view. Every inch of her is on display. Her strong legs. Her tight ass. The folds of her cunt.

My cock stirs. I tell it to calm down, but that's a fruitless endeavor. My head is already filling with thoughts of bringing her home and stripping her out of that wet swimsuit.

"You coming?" She turns her head to look back to me.

At this rate, yeah. I dive under the water. Think of work and surfing technique and my brother erasing my existence from his mind if I do fuck Chloe.

None of that helps. But the cold water is enough to temper the heat building inside me.

Seeing her like this is not good for our professional relationship.

And even though I'd never, in a million years, admit it to her, teaching Chloe how to do ink matters to me.

I'm not gonna fuck it up.

She paddles past the break point. Pushes herself up and slings her legs over the surfboard.

"You look like a regular," I say.

"How many times do I have to say, 'I know how to surf' before you get it?"

"You keeping track?"

"No. I think I'll just round up to infinity."

"Good call."

She stares out at the white sky. There's a streak of blue to our right. Everywhere else, puffy, grey clouds cover the sun.

"How'd you get from college to Inked Hearts?"

"A lot of begging. I think Ryan would be happy to never hear my voice again."

I shake my head. "He likes you."

"I think so." Her gaze shifts to the water. "But it's hard to tell with him."

"He probably says the same about you."

"Probably."

"You have better credentials than any of us."

"But no experience." She looks up at the sky. "I'm grateful for the opportunity to work with Ryan, Walker, and Brendon. You, on the other hand—"

"You bow down at my greatness."

"Roll my eyes at your stupidity."

"To-may-to, to-mah-to."

Her eyes catch mine as she turns back. Watches a wave crest. "You were better than I was. In high school. You were the better artist."

"We were neck and neck."

"Mrs. White chose you every time."

"She didn't like you."

"She really didn't."

"What did you do to her?"

"Nothing." She spins on her board. Pulls her knees into her chest then folds her legs over each other. "I guess I'm just..."

"Prickly?"

She nods without offense. "Yeah."

"Isn't that what you're going for?"

"No... Maybe..." Her eyes find mine. "It doesn't matter. I have a good thing going now."

"Guys asking you to whip them?"

"Do I seem like a dominatrix?"

"Kinda."

"Are you into that?"

"I'll try anything once."

"You haven't?"

"Never."

Surprise spreads over her expression. "Bullshit." She pulls her arms over her chest. Rubs her triceps to stay warm. "As many women as you've been with. One of them must have tried."

"Never." The cold water nips at my toes. But everywhere else, I'm warm. This conversation is not a good idea. It's already doing shit to me.

"That shocks me."

I move closer. Until my hands are on her surfboard. And my head is six inches from her toes. "I live to shock you."

She looks down at me. "Anything else you haven't tried?

"A long list."

"Bullshit."

"Never taken it up the ass."

A laugh bursts from her lips. Her eyes light up. Her hand goes to her mouth. "Oh my God." She hugs her stomach. "That's the first place you go?"

"First thing that came to mind."

"Why would you even—"

"Lots of chicks are into it."

Her nose scrunches with distaste. "They are not."

I nod *are too*. All right. It might not be lots of women. But I have had the request before.

"What else?"

"Never been with a guy."

"What about a threesome?"

"With a guy and a girl? Yeah."

"You like it?"

"Depends. It's always been with couples. It's weird, being a guest star in their fantasy."

"Weird good or weird bad?"

"Both. It feels pretty bad ass. But it's impersonal. Like I'm a prop."

"You've never with a friend and a random girl?"

"Sunshine, I hate to burst your bubble, but I don't have those kinds of friends."

"Shit. I was kinda hoping you and Ryan." She winks. "Don't tell Leighton."

"I won't. You shouldn't either. She'll kill you."

"She seems tough."

"She is."

Her painted black fingernails tap the fiberglass. "What else have you never done?"

"I thought you were done with our game?" I push myself onto the board, turn, sit next to her.

"These waves are shitty."

They are. And I'd rather talk to her any day. Still. I brought her here for a reason. I need her feeling the thrill of catching a wave. I need that excitement in her eyes. That feeling that she can do anything.

Fuck, I thought this had something to do with being her teacher.

Maybe it does.

But that's not what's motivating me.

It's not wanting to teach her or wanting to fuck her or wanting to fuck with her.

It's wanting her.

Period.

I throw my head back, sending my wet hair with it. "Three waves. Then we talk."

"It's my turn."

"It is."

Her hand brushes my shoulder as she brings it to her hair. She moves closer. Until her shoulder is brushing mine.

Her brow furrows with confusion.

She doesn't get how we're this close.

I know better than to stay this close.

But I don't move. "I'm waiting."

"I, um, I have another idea."

"Yeah?"

"Ten fingers," she says. "First one out has to catch three waves."

"You're that interested in my sex life."

"You chicken?"

"Never." I offer my hand.

She shakes. "You first. I'll give you the advantage. Since you need it."

That's probably true. "Never have I ever taken it up the ass."

She makes a show of holding out all ten fingers. "Really?"

"Really."

"Do I seem like the type?"

"Yeah."

"What's that mean?"

"Well, you heard Rick. You're a tiny package of kink."

She flips me off. "Really?"

"No. But you seem game for anything."

"I feel like I should hit you."

"Just being honest."

She laughs. "It's ridiculous, but I believe that in your mind, that's a completely appropriate response." She runs her fingers through her wet hair. "Okay. My turn." She twirls a strand around her finger. "Never have I ever kissed a stranger."

"Fuck." I drop a finger. "You gonna continue this line of questioning?"

"Of course." Her smile spreads over her cheeks. "I play to win."

"You're cruel."

She copies my shrug. *Maybe I am. Maybe I'm not.*

It's adorable.

She taps my shoulder. "Your turn."

"Never have I ever taken an AP class."

"I thought this game was about sex."

"Didn't specify that."

She drops a finger. Shakes her head. *What bullshit.* "Never have I ever fucked a cheerleader."

"You like girls?"

"No."

"Not fair."

"There are male cheerleaders."

"Not at our school."

"Still. They exist." She nods to my pointer finger. "Drop it, dick face."

"You ever gonna realize I take that as a compliment?"

"You know, you're right."

"I am?"

"I can't call you a dick face anymore. Your dick is special enough to have jewelry. Your face on the other hand..."

"I need to get a nose ring?"

She laughs. "Eyebrow maybe."

"Lip?"

"Tongue."

"Never have I ever fucked someone with a tongue ring," I say.

"Bull."

"It's true."

"Whatever." She drops her finger. "How did you know—"

"Everybody knew about you and—what was his name?"

"Kurt."

"That was after you left."

"I kept up on gossip." Even though we're essentially alone out here—there are another half a dozen surfers, but they're spread out, focused on the waves—I lean in to whisper. "Is it true what they say?"

"What is it they say?"

"Tongue rings blow your mind?"

"Oh, when they're—" She motions to her crotch.

Fuck, it's adorable. "Yeah."

"No... not in his case. But I'm not ruling it out as a possibility."

"Scientific."

She does her best Dean impression. "*Should have stuck with me, sunshine. I would have blown your mind every night, three times a night.*"

"Sixty-nine times a night."

Her cheeks flush. "I've never."

"Really?"

"Drop it, Maddox."

Fuck, the way she says my last name... it's not burning hate or irritation or even raw desire. It's something softer. Something that hits me everywhere.

I drop my finger. "I'm sad for you."

"Uh-huh."

"You're missing out."

"Spare me the offer to enlighten me."

"You think I go down on any gorgeous woman who asks?"

"Yeah."

I can't exactly deny the allegations. "You think that little of yourself?"

"You can have low standards and still be with someone primo."

I can't help but smile. She makes an excellent point.

A wave rolls beneath us. Crests. Falls. Crashes into the sand and turns to white foam.

"That one was better," I say.

"It's your turn." She holds up her eight fingers. Nods to my mine. "You didn't drop your finger."

I do. "Never have I ever taken a self-defense class."

"I'm starting to think you entered this game under false pretenses." She drops a finger.

"I play to win."

"So do I." She turns to the horizon. Watches a set roll in. "Never have I ever suggested someone sit on a surfboard and talk instead of surfing."

"You suggested this."

"Did not."

"You started it."

"Absolutely not."

"All right. We both started it. Lose a finger."

She gnaws on her bottom lip, turning over my words. "Fine." She drops to seven fingers.

I'm down to six.

I pull my feet from the water. Copy her cross-legged position.

The air feels cold against my wet skin, so I move closer.

Closer.

Until I can feel the heat of her body.

Fuck, it feels good.

Too good.

I look down at her. "Never have I ever chickened out of giving a tattoo."

"I didn't chicken out."

"Bullshit."

"I was concerned about your mental health. You should be thanking me."

"Drop. The. Finger."

She does. She pulls her knees into her chest. Wraps her arms around them. "It's freezing, huh?"

"Not too late for the wetsuit."

"Nope. We have to finish this game so I can warm up properly."

No, she has to strip out of that swimsuit so I can warm her up properly.

My cock stirs.

I tell it to get lost.

That isn't happening.

No matter how badly I want it.

"Never have I ever tormented a subordinate," she says.

"Am I that awful?"

She nods, but it's with a smile.

There's a part of her that likes the way I tease her.
That wants more of it.
More of me.
More of us.
But now I'm getting ahead of myself.

Chapter Twelve

Truth be told, I haven't been surfing in ages.

Since way, way before my body betrayed me.

It's not like I was ever an expert. Gia and I went surfing a grand total of three times. We probably rode less than a dozen waves each.

I refuse to admit any of that to Dean.

He pretends like he doesn't notice. Cops some overbearing couch routine as he reminds me how to paddle, how to feel for the wave, how to jump.

It takes five tries, but I finally catch a wave.

Then another.

Another.

Another.

I surf until the beach is crowded with tourists and families. Until my lips are blue and my toes are numb and my body is screaming for food and water.

It feels good wanting something physical. Wanting everything physical.

I ride the wave into the beach. Return the board with Dean. Go back to our stuff.

"Freezing?" He pulls a towel from his bag and tosses it to me.

I wrap it around my shoulders. "Maybe."

He grabs another. Towel dries his hair haphazardly. It falls in messy waves as he wraps the towel around his shoulders.

He stays in his Speedo.

It's... I...

Why does he have to be so hot? It's wrong.

A deep breath keeps my expression neutral. "You're getting looks."

"Why's that?"

"Curious, yeah?"

He nods. "People are weird." He stretches his arms over his head. Lets out a yawn. "Don't know about you, but I could go for some Golden Needle."

My cheeks flush. It was a bitch move criticizing his tea selection. But Dean doesn't seem like a guy who drinks tea, much less cultivates an assortment of rare teas. And... well, that's no excuse. But Dean doesn't respond to earnest apologies. "You couldn't pick it out of a line up."

His smile lights up his bright eyes. "Is that a challenge?"

"Yeah." The words tumble out of my mouth without stopping in my brain. When it comes to Dean, I'm senseless. I'm compelled to push back. And to linger in his presence.

"I know just the place. But lunch first. I'm starving—"

My stomach grumbles at the thought of food.

"There's a nearby place with great cheese enchiladas."

Mmm.

"On me."

"I'm in."

~

THIS IS BLISS.

Cheese and tomato nirvana.

Some other plane of existence, where corn, red sauce, cheese, and guacamole meld into flavor perfection.

I let out a soft groan as I take my next bite. The enchilada melts in my mouth. Soft tortillas. Chewy cheese. Rich, wet sauce.

"Fuck, Chloe. You're giving me ideas."

I flip Dean off, but it's without enthusiasm. This lunch is too good. There's no room for anger or frustration or irritation in my brain.

I chew, swallow, suck water from my straw. Let out another soft sigh.

Dean chuckles. "You're gonna attract attention."

It's possible. We're at a trendy place on Abbot Kinney. The covered backyard patio is quiet but the half a dozen tables around us are full.

It's beautiful here. Cacti, flowers, red and white string lights shining against the green canopy.

Dean picks up the carafe. Refills my tiny water cup.

I finish it in three gulps.

Even sitting down, he's tall. I have to look up at him.

He's different than I remembered. But the same too. This guy, the one who insists on helping me, who fixes my tea, who cares about making sure my food is vegetarian—he asked the waiter if there was chicken broth in the Spanish rice twice— was he always there or is he new?

I don't know.

But I...

I really like him. This other Dean. And the original one too. As annoying as he is, that guy still pushes *all* my buttons —the hate ones and the love ones.

He takes a bite of his shrimp taco. Chews. Swallows. Licks guacamole from his lips. "You've been working at the shop a week now."

"Accurate."

"Who do you like working with best?"

"Uh." That's a loaded question if I've ever heard one. Even if Dean's the one asking it. "You really think there's a chance I'll say you?"

"How do you know that's what I'm getting at?"

"What else could it be?"

"All right. New question. You feel like you've learned a lot?"

I scoop another forkful of enchilada into my mouth. Chew. Swallow.

The last week is a blur of drawings, stencils, ink and skin, the buzz of the gun.

Dean's incessant teasing.

Ryan's quiet nods.

Walker's boyish laugh.

Brendon's... well, he's pretty much a more built, darker haired version of Ryan. Right down to the gushing about his girlfriend. And the girlfriend hanging out at the front desk a few times a week sending goo-goo eyes.

Not that the displays of affection send pangs of jealousy straight to my gut.

But you know, not all of us are lucky enough to be in love.

Or even believe in love.

They don't have to be so obvious about it.

"Chloe?" Dean scoops salsa verde onto his last taco. "You okay?"

"Wiped."

"Damn. Was gonna suggest a hike."

"Where?"

"Los Liones. Say, seven miles. Ten maybe."

"It's too late."

"In the morning."

"I'm good for it."

"You're that competitive?"

"You're not?"

His laugh is hearty. Knowing.

He leans back in his seat as he takes a bite from his taco. It drips over his hands. Onto his plate.

He finishes it with two more bites.

Licks salsa from his fingers.

His eyes meet mine as he sucks on his pointer finger. It's intentional, but it's not a come-on exactly. More a reminder of a possibility.

Dean still wants me.

But he's not offering anything.

At least, I don't think he's offering anything.

He's hard to read.

"I would, but I'm working tomorrow." He leans forward. Refills both our waters with the carafe.

"You have to work Sundays?"

"I have to work tonight. We all take weekend appointments."

"But I'm off?"

"'Cause weekends are busy and you're dead weight."

"Oh." I shrink back. He's being real with me, but the words still hurt. Right now, I'm in the way. I'm helpful, yes. I get coffee, I print mock-ups, I run errands. But when I'm sitting on the stool observing, I'm another person in the way. Like a friend or family member only without the benefit of distracting the client.

"You're a great apprentice, Chloe. Smart, dedicated, help-ful. But, tell me—do you feel like Ryan is trying to teach you?"

"Trying? Probably. But he's really quiet. He responds to most of my questions with one-word answers."

"Walker?"

"He's friendly but kinda distracted."

"Brendon?"

"He's intense."

Dean chuckles. "Yeah, he is. Hot though."

"Not my type."

He flips his drying hair. "You prefer blonds?"

Actually, yes. Light hair and light eyes any day of the week.

"Fuck. You do. You're easy to read."

"I am not."

"Yeah. You are. When you aren't pissed, you smile a lot."

"I do not."

"Maybe with other people you don't. But when you're with me—"

"I do not."

"I can start recording it."

I take another bite. Still tomato and cheese perfection. Still warm and rich. "That's creepy."

"You really don't notice it?"

No. But now that I think about it, he's right. I've smiled more today than I have any day the last month. I've smiled more this week than I have in the last year.

Yes, I've frowned and *ughed* and wanted to slap the stupid out of Dean a lot too.

But, overall, I feel good. Like I'm finally where I belong.

Like I'm with someone—

No. I'm not *with* Dean. We're hanging out. As friends or coworkers or mentor/student. I'm not sure, but I'm sure it's not sexual. Even if he keeps looking at me like he's thinking about me naked.

I don't blame him.

I'm doing the same.

God, the way that white t-shirt stretches over his shoulders. The cotton is damp. See-through. I can make out the ink over his right pec. Words, but what are they? And, God, the outlines of his muscles. He's just so...

Hot.

There's no other way to express it.

Dean Maddox is sex on a stick.

I look around the room. Find another hottie—a guy on a date with a short blond woman. He's tall, fit, with pretty blue eyes and dark hair.

Hot, even if he isn't my type.

But my body isn't responding.

Then I look to Dean. To his bright eyes and his wicked smile and his perfect pecs.

My heartbeat picks up.

My stomach flutters.

My sex clenches.

And my head... fuck, it fills with so many ideas.

He catches me staring. "I'm starting to think you invited me out just to picture me naked."

"You invited me out."

"To picture you naked. Fuck. Freudian slip."

"You know about Freud?"

"Yeah. He's my idol. With him, everything was about dick. Dick was basically the center of the psyche."

I can't help but laugh. That's dead on. "It sums you up."

"Can't go three seconds without thinking about what I'm gonna do with mine."

"Touch yourself?"

"Here? I'll get arrested. But if you want it that badly—" He stands. Makes a show of reaching for his button.

Actually undoes the button.

And the zipper.

He's still wearing that tight Speedo. But he's... He's not quite hard, but he's getting there. I can just make out the shape of his—

"More water?" The waiter drops off a carafe. Exchanges ours.

"Yeah. Thanks. I really worked up her thirst." Dean winks at me as he slides into his seat.

Tragically, he redoes the button of his jeans.

I force myself to stare into his eyes. This is so weird. Wanting him without all the hate rising in my gut.

Wanting him period.

The last time I wanted someone this much was...

That night in high school.

Don't get me wrong. I loved Alex. I loved having sex with him. But it was never tear your clothes off passion. It was comfortable. Easy. Safe.

"And me?" he asks.

"You?"

"How am I as a teacher?"

"Pushy."

He nods.

"Bossy."

"Of course."

"Annoying."

"And?"

I bite my lip. There's still a huge part of me that hates stroking his ego, but this is the truth. "You're a great teacher."

He beams. It's different than his usual bragging. There's no posturing to it. Just pride. "I must be good if you can admit that."

"You are. Ryan, Brendon, and Walker are friendly enough. But they just ask me to sit there and watch. You try to teach me things. Even if some of them are sexual harassment."

He chuckles. "I did stop."

"You did."

"But I can change that anytime." He takes a long sip of his water. "Balls in your court there."

"And it's staying there."

His laugh is loud. Hearty.

It warms me somewhere that's usually cold.

It makes every part of me feel good. It's the same as it used to be with Alex.

No, it's better.

I... I really like him.

"I have an offer for you," he says.

"I'm not wearing panties. I can't tell you what color they are."

"Your swimsuit is black. Like all your panties."

"They are not." They are too. But I'm not admitting that.

"Prove it."

"I will."

"You do realize you'll have to show me your underwear to do that?"

"Yes." I walked right into that. But... ugh, I just want to prove him wrong so badly. He stokes something in me. Desire. Need. Competitive fire. "What's the offer?"

"You can apprentice under me. Just me."

"In exchange for?"

"Your Saturday mornings."

"My Saturday mornings?"

"You do what I say."

"Extra lessons?"

"Yeah, but not about ink."

My brow furrows. What? "You want to teach me about..."

"There's more to tattoos than putting ink to people's skin. There's a philosophy."

"Which is?"

"Every artist has theirs. What's yours?"

"I don't know."

"I'll help you find it."

"How?"

"Living."

"Bullshit." I fold my arms. "What's your real motivation?"

"That ink line didn't land?"

"Not even a little."

He laughs. "It's simple. You don't have enough fun in your life."

"You don't know anything about my life."

"Yeah, I do. I've watched and listened all week. You get to work, you go to aikido, you go home. That's it."

"I draw."

"And what? Watch TV?"

"I love TV."

"I love TV too, but I love a lot of other shit. What do you love, besides drawing and ink and TV?"

"My family."

"And?"

"What business is it of yours?"

"That's the offer. I make it my business."

I bite my lip. There's something appealing about the excuse to spend more time with Dean. But that's dangerous. I like him too much to keep my hands off him. "What do you love?"

"Tea."

"I love tea."

"Surfing. Hiking. Hanging with my friends, shooting the shit. Hitting the gym with Walker. Teasing Ryan. Going out for drinks. Going to shows. I've done all that shit in the last two weeks. What about you?"

"I just went surfing."

He shoots me a *really* look.

"I like my life."

"It's just an offer, Chloe. I teach you everything I want to teach you—"

"You mean?"

"No. Ryan would kill me."

"Oh." Disappointment seeps into my voice. I hate how badly I want him. I hate how easily he wraps me around his finger. How good his read on me is.

But, mostly, I hate that I really can't hate him.

"Expires at midnight," he says.

"Won't you be balls deep in some babe at midnight?" I bite my lip, but it does nothing to chase away the jealousy brewing in my gut. I hate the idea of him with anyone else much less with some anonymous leggy blonde. Because, in my head, it's always a leggy blonde with curves for days and all the experience in the world and everything I don't have.

"I work first thing tomorrow."

"So, you'll be done by eleven?"

He gives me a long, slow once over. "You know me too well."

Chapter Thirteen

CHLOE

"Mmmm." I let out a soft moan.

This tea is perfection. Creamy milk, sweet honey, the astringent mix of bergamot, lavender, and black tea.

Is there anything better than a London Fog? Doubtful.

"I don't see it." Gia takes a long sip. Scrunches her nose in distaste. "It's so..."

"Robust."

"Weak." She stares at her mug curiously. "I'm trying, honestly, Chlo. But I just don't get tea." She takes another sip. "The honey is good." She reaches for a chocolate chip cookie.

After I got back from lunch with Dean, I needed to clear my head. I was too tired to go for a swim, so I started baking. Four hours later, the house is flush with sweet treats.

I grab an Earl Grey brownie and take a bite. Chocolate chips melt on my tongue. The Earl Grey flavor is subtle. Just enough to add depth to the semi-sweet chocolate.

Gia looks at the brownie curiously. "I don't know."

"I've made you espresso brownies a hundred times."

"But coffee and chocolate... that's everything that's right in the world."

"If you don't want it, don't eat it."

She tears a chunk from my plain white plate. After Mom died, Dad packed away all the fancy plates and cutlery.

At first, it was strange, like he was erasing her. But that wasn't it. He couldn't stomach the tiny memories of her. He couldn't handle scooping eggs onto his plate and seeing everything he'd lost.

All right. Maybe it was me as much as it was Dad.

But now the white plates and the dull silverware speak to her absence as much as the fancy plates do.

This is the plate for a life without Mom.

For a world where she doesn't exist.

Outside, the garage door whirs.

Gia slides out of her chair. Moves into the kitchen and starts scooping ground coffee into the machine. "You think he'll want some?"

"Probably." Coffee has always been Dad's drink. Tea was Mom's. I feel closer to her when I brew a cup. And, well, I guess after nearly fifteen years I'm desperate to hold onto her memory.

I savor the last sip of my London Fog then get to work on Gia's. It's lukewarm, but it's still good.

"There." Gia presses the button on the coffee maker. Reaches into the cabinet for two mugs. Lucky girl is five foot five. She never struggles to reach a high shelf.

She looks like Mom—round eyes, wavy hair, angled features.

She passes as white.

I don't. I take after Dad.

I'm proud of my heritage, but the *what are you* questions? I'd happily part with those forever.

Gia taps her fingers against the counter as she waits for the carafe to fill.

Dad's car pulls into the garage. The door opens and slams shut. Then he's in the hallway and the garage door is whirring closed.

"Do I smell coffee?" he asks.

Gia beams. "Hey Daddy!" Even at twenty-six, she's pure Daddy's girl.

He moves into the kitchen and hugs her hello.

"Go. Sit. I'll fix your coffee," she says.

His dark eyes pass over the counter. "Did you rob a bakery?"

"I'll bring them to work Monday." Or not. There's no food allowed at the shop. But I can wrap everything in plastic. Insist people eat it outside.

He takes a seat next to me. "You should have come to the movie."

"You know I don't like action." I tear off another chunk of brownie. Toss it in my mouth. Let it dissolve on my tongue.

He reaches for one, but Gia stops him.

"Careful, they're Earl Grey," she says.

He ignores her warning. Takes a bite. Shoots me a thumbs-up. "It was thinky. You'd like it."

"Thinky how?" I laugh. Dad loves movies. Great ones and terrible ones. "Did the spy have to outsmart the Russian super villains?"

"She's impossible, huh?" Gia teases.

"Oh?" I stare down my sister. "You want to see it—" I try and fail to recall the name of the weekend's latest spy thriller.

"Well..." She turns to the coffee maker. Pours two cups. "I would see it."

"I would see it too. But that doesn't mean I want to," I say.

Dad looks between us. Smiles wistfully, the way he does

149

when he's lost in a memory. "We can watch the first one after dinner."

Gia shoots me a *how do we get out of this* look.

He catches it. "Are you staying for dinner, sweetie?"

"Sure. Mark is at the office." She gets milk from the fridge. Pours it into both mugs. She and Dad take their coffee the same way—sweet and creamy.

"Are you hungry?" I ask Dad. "I can start cooking."

"Let's order pizza." Gia moves into the living room. Sets Dad's coffee in front of him. Slides into the seat across from me and sips hers.

I fight a frown. Cooking makes me feel good. It's how I show Dad and Gia I love them. "No. I'll cook."

Gia scrunches her nose. "I'm not in the mood for something vegetarian."

"Something like pizza?" I ask.

"It won't kill you." Dad takes a long sip of his coffee. "It's good for your cholesterol."

"You sound like Mark." She groans.

"Of course I do. Did you see the sandwich she posted on Instagram? The bread was made out of bacon," Dad says.

Gross.

"Oh my God. I'm dating my father. I'm going to marry my father." Gia's nose scrunches.

I do nothing to fight my laugh.

Then it hits me. "Mark is finally proposing?"

She takes a long sip of her coffee. "We're discussing it."

"Really?" They've been dating for ten years now. Since high school. I like Mark. He's a good guy. But he's also... well, they've been dating for ten years and he still hasn't proposed.

"You're too young," Dad says. "You should be like Chloe. Move back in to your room upstairs. Just for a few years. A decade or so."

She laughs *hell no*. "He wants to ask your permission."

Dad shakes his head.

"He's old-fashioned. It's sweet," she says.

"Take it into your own hands. Propose to him," I say.

"Would you really propose to a guy?" she asks.

"Sure. Why not?" I ask.

"With a ring for him or you?" She looks at me like I'm a science experiment.

"I haven't been on a date in two years—"

"What about today?" she asks.

"What about it?" I ask.

"You went out with someone." She continues staring. "You did. You're blushing."

Dammit. I *am* blushing.

"You did! Oh my God. You like someone." She claps her hands together. "Who?"

"I do not." I bite my tongue. Gia always believed I had a crush on Dean. I never admitted it. Even to myself. I certainly didn't tell her about our night together.

"Someone at the tattoo shop," she says.

"No."

"Yes."

Dad jumps in. "Does this guy treat you well?"

"Uh..."

"Bad answer." He shakes his head.

"It doesn't matter. He's basically my boss." If I accept his offer, he'll actually be my boss.

"Your mother was my boss," Dad says.

"That's different. No one will think a woman is sexually harassing her subordinate."

Dad's smile gets wicked.

Gross.

He looks to me. "Would I like him?"

"Maybe..."

Gia laughs. "Chloe is finally hitting her rebellious phase." She looks at my black tank top. The tattoo on my shoulder. The short haircut. "Well. With guys." She smiles knowingly. "Is he all inked up?"

For a tattoo artist, Dean is pretty light on the ink. But for a normal guy? "Of course."

"Oooh. Hot." She makes a show of fanning herself. "Is he hot?"

"He's attractive, yes."

"Let's see. I can't believe I haven't done this." She pulls out her phone. Taps the screen a few times.

I move around the table.

Shit.

She's looking at the shop's Instagram.

The first few pictures are finished tattoos. But then—

"Oh my God." Her hand goes to her mouth. Her eyes go wide. "That's Dean."

"Is it?" I play dumb.

"Why didn't you tell me?"

"It didn't come up," I lie.

"You still like him?"

"It's not a still. I didn't spend the last seven years thinking about him."

"I can't believe... Oh my God. You do."

"Who's Dean?" Dad jumps in.

"This guy from our high school," she says. "He was... "

I find a euphemism. "Casual with his body."

"Huh?" Dad's brow furrows with confusion.

"He was a slut," Gia says.

"So?" Dad asks.

"Oh my God, Dad. You're supposed to warn us about guys like that!" Gia says.

Dad shakes his head *kids these days*. He looks to me. "Go

ahead and make dinner, Chloe. If Gia doesn't want to eat it, she can order pizza for herself." He looks to her. "I thought you said you were on a diet?"

"It's my cheat day. I don't want to waste it on veggie stir fry."

Dad shakes his head. *Ridiculous.* He stands. Moves to the mail slot by the door—it's close. Our living room/den is a small space. The TV and couch on one end, the dining table in the middle, opposite the door, the kitchen on the other end.

He grabs something from the slot and brings it to me.

A letter from the hospital.

I don't have to open it. I know what it is. An appointment reminder.

Every year, for the next five years, I need a scan. To make sure I'm still cancer free. The odds are good. But not good enough for me to skip the scan.

I shove the letter into my back pocket.

Fighting my frown is useless. I know the reality of the situation. I *know* there's almost no chance I'm still sick.

But the thought still steals my oxygen.

It still makes the room dark and ugly.

I can't go through that again. And neither can Dad and Gia. It was like they disappeared with me. And watching them hurt... that was the worst part.

"I can take off work. Come with you," he offers.

I shake my head. "I'll be fine. Really." The words feel hollow. Empty. I'm already a nervous wreck and it's three weeks away. That day...

I'm not sure how I'm going to make it.

But if I am sick, if I am disappearing again...

I don't want them to know.

Not for a while at least.

I plant a kiss on my dad's forehead, I move into the

kitchen, and I start chopping vegetables. By the time I have them sizzling in the pan, I feel better. Calm. Centered. In control.

Like I can survive this.

Even if I can't.

Chapter Fourteen

CHLOE

I let my sister pick the movie. Focus all my attention on stirring sriracha into my bowl. Usually, I avoid the omnipresent condiment. It steals the flavor of the food. Makes everything taste like vaguely spicy ketchup.

But, right now, that's what I need.

I can't taste anything.

I can't concentrate on the weepy tearjerker.

I can't keep up with Dad and Gia's conversation—something about the director's latest movie.

For two hours, I sit with my family, with every ounce of my attention elsewhere. After the credits roll, Dad and Gia move to the kitchen for coffee. I decline. Head upstairs. Lock myself in my room.

Except for the moonlight streaming through the window, it's dark.

I leave the light off.

Pull the letter from my pocket. Tear it open.

I can just barely make out the words. It's a simple appointment reminder. Doctor's name. Time. Date.

The paper behind it goes into the test. An MRI. No jewelry. Expect an hour. Arrive early for paperwork.

Nothing about the possibility of life changing forever.

I fold the paper on my desk. Slide into my cheap Ikea rolling chair. My salary is good for an apprentice—most shops pay nothing or a tiny per diem—but it's still going to take me forever to upgrade my furniture. Moving into my own place is a pipe dream.

My eyes go to my alarm clock. The same one I used all through high school.

The time is there in red numbers.

Ten thirty.

An hour and a half until my deadline.

Dean wants to teach me. Exclusively.

I want to learn.

He may not be the best artist at the shop, but he's the only one really trying to mentor me.

He's my best chance to master ink.

And well...

I might not have a lot of time for that.

For anything.

Even if I'm okay...

I'm probably okay.

The odds are good. I repeat the words over and over, but they don't stick in my brain.

I say it again anyway.

I'm probably okay.

I probably have a long, healthy life ahead of me.

But I'm tired of wasting time.

This is what I want.

I'm taking it.

I pull out my cell and text Dean.

Chloe: I'm in.

My heart thuds against my chest. My face flushes. My toes

tingle. He can still change his mind. Back out. Find a way to get me fired.

I can still lose this.

And I can't lose this.

My phone buzzes with a new message.

Dean: Damn. Right down to the wire.

Chloe: Almost ninety minutes.

Dean: Even so.

Chloe: I had to weigh my options.

Dean: Smart.

Chloe: I try.

My palms get slick with sweat. My phone slips. Lands on my desk with a soft *thunk*. It drowns out the sounds of conversation downstairs. The *drip, drip, drip* of the coffee maker. The low murmur of the TV.

My stomach twists. Because of Dean or the test or the thought of losing everything again, I don't know.

I'm so tired of missing out on life.

On losing what I want.

It needs to change.

I need to change.

Chloe: What are we doing next Saturday?

Dean: Haven't worked that out yet.

Chloe: Will I need a swimsuit?

Dean: You might.

Chloe: Noted.

Dean: You own something besides that lap suit?

Chloe: Yeah.

Dean: Go on.

Chloe: I own bikinis. I just thought the lap suit would be more comfortable.

Dean: Was it?

Chloe: In some ways. Where are you?

Dean: Home.

Chloe: Alone?

Dean: Is this a booty call?

My fingers move of their own accord.

Chloe: What if it was?

Dean: I'd ask what color panties you're wearing.

Chloe: You can probably guess.

Dean: Black?

Chloe: Yeah. I only own black panties.

I wipe my hands on my jeans. Stand. Move to my underwear drawer. Pull it open.

It's a dozen pairs of the same thing—the black bikinis with cream trim. The ones I bought on sale at American Eagle.

And the lacy thongs I bought at Victoria's Secret.

I grab my phone. Snap a picture of the drawer.

I must be going out of my mind. I shouldn't send this to Dean. It's a *yes*. A *please continue your flirting.* A *please come over and fuck me senseless.*

But that is what I want.

He makes me feel good.

And, God, I need that. I need my body aching for his. I need him touching me.

There.

I hit send.

My blush spreads to my chest. Heat goes with it. Down my torso. Straight to my core.

Dean: Fuck, Chloe. You trying to make me hard?

Maybe I am. I don't know. I have no idea how to do this flirting thing. If I can even do this flirting thing.

I'm opening Pandora's box here.

But I have to do it.

Chloe: Are you?

Dean: Yeah.

My tongue slides over my lips. We can't do this. He's my boss. I need the job.

But I need this too.

Chloe: Can we talk like this?

Dean: Can we? Yeah. But we shouldn't.

Chloe: Oh.

Dean: It might shock you, but I don't always do what I should.

Chloe: You're my boss.

Dean: Yeah.

Chloe: Do you think about that? About ordering me around?

Dean: You sure you know what you're getting into, sunshine?

Chloe: Positive.

Dean: Yeah. I do.

Chloe: Me too.

Dean: You like me bossy?

Chloe: Sometimes. Other times... You annoy the fuck out of me.

Dean: I know.

Chloe: Doesn't that bother you?

Dean: No.

Chloe: Why not?

Dean: I like the fire.

I like it too. Dean makes me feel a lot—irritated, frustrated, needy, amused, curious, entertained. Some of it is bad.

But it's always something.

When I'm with him, I feel more than the dull, empty numb that set in with my diagnosis.

No one else does that to me.

Chloe: Do you think about me?

Dean: Yeah.

Chloe: I think about you.

Dean: I know.

Chloe: I should probably go before we get into trouble.

Dean: Probably.

Chloe: What about you?

Dean: What about me?

Chloe: What are you wearing?

Dean: Jeans. White t-shirt. Black boxers.

Chloe: Are you mocking me?

Dean: Like this? Never.

This is it. If there's a line, I'm officially crossing it.

But I don't care.

I have to do this.

Chloe: Prove it.

There's quiet for a long moment. The sounds of Dad and Gia's conversation flow into my room. Something about Mark. About whether or not Dad thinks she should marry him.

I flip open my laptop. Open my streaming app. Play my favorite grunge album.

It isn't sexy, exactly, but it feels right.

There.

My phone buzzes with a picture message.

It's a mirror selfie of Dean. From his chest to his knees.

He's wearing black boxers.

Only black boxers.

And he's hard.

The soft fabric is straining against him.

Fuck. My sex clenches. My nipples pang. He's the only person who can do this to me. Who makes me feel like a woman with desires.

And, God, my desire...

Dean: What are you wearing?

I flip the light on. Move to the floor length mirror across from my bed. Take a picture.

Send.

Dean: Fuck, Chloe.

Chloe: You asked.

Dean: Overestimated my self-control.

Chloe: I thought you were going to go out to pick up a woman.
Dean: I thought about it.
Chloe: And?
Dean: Thinking about you was more fun.
Chloe: You touched yourself?
Dean: Not yet. But after this I will.

I shouldn't do this.

But the reasonable, logical part of my brain is gone. Every thought is screaming *Dean*.

I roll my jeans over my hip. The one with the shooting star tattoo. The tattoo he traced that night that started everything.

Or maybe it finished everything.

I'm not sure.

I angle my cell just right. So the pic shows the tattoo, my skin, and my black panties.

There. I snap the photo. Hit send before I can chicken out.

Dean: You trying to kill me?
Chloe: Maybe.
Dean: You're succeeding.
Chloe: You're alone, right?
Dean: Yeah.
Chloe: So, if I ask you to take off those boxers?

My cheeks flush. I've never done this before. I've never asked a guy for a sexy picture. With my ex, I was too shy. And we weren't the type to talk about sex. To drag it out.

It was more rote. Get in, come, cuddle, get out.

It was good, but not like this.

Not something that set me on fire.

Dean: Are you asking?

My gaze shifts to the letter on my desk. Three weeks until I meet my fate.

Three weeks to seize life by the balls.

My fingers hover over the keyboard. I tap a yes. Go to hit send.

A knock on the door startles me.

My fingers slip. My phone hits the floor. "Yeah?"

"Gia wants to go out for ice cream," Dad calls from the other side of the door. "You want to come?"

Fuck, what a question.

I pick up my phone. Tap backspace until the text is gone.

I want to keep flirting with Dean.

I want to get his clothes off and his hand around his cock and his thoughts on me.

But my trance is broken.

Reality is sinking in.

Dean is my boss.

I need to be smart about this.

There's a line between fear and caution. I'm not sure which side I'm on. Only that I'm not pushing this forward.

"Sure. Give me five," I say to Dad.

"Not sure Gia has five minutes in her," he calls.

"Two minutes," I say.

He makes an uh-huh noise and moves down the stairs.

I tap a reply to Dean.

Chloe: I have to go. Family. I still live at home.

Dean: No shame in that.

Chloe: Yeah. But Dad knocking kind of ruins the mood.

It's bullshit. I'm still flushed and wanting.

I'm still desperate to get his clothes off.

Chloe: Next time.

Dean: Until then, sunshine.

Chapter Fifteen

CHLOE

Monday, I leave early enough to beat traffic. I spend my morning at a coffee shop on Abbot Kinney.

I drink endless Earl Grey.

I sketch mock-up after mock-up.

I push thoughts of Dean from my head.

We nearly talked each other into phone sex. And now we're supposed to work together like everything is normal. I have to sit next to him like I'm not thinking about pinning him to the wall and unzipping his jeans.

Like I didn't spend all of Sunday wishing I hadn't chickened out.

When nine thirty rolls around, I toss my tea and walk the dozen blocks to the shop.

Dean is sitting behind the counter working on a mock-up. His expression is intense. Focused. That other Dean.

I knock on the door.

He looks up at me with an easy smile. Motions *it's open*.

It is. And the AC is set to Arctic Chill. As usual.

"It's freezing in here." I slide my hands into my pockets. Shift my weight between my heels.

He nods, effortlessly casual. "You want my hoodie?"

"Sure." I bite my lip. Borrowing a sweater is a girlfriend thing. An *I like you* thing. But I guess that particular cat is out of the bag.

He knows I like him.

But does he *like* me? Does he want a fuck or a friend with benefits or a girlfriend?

My stomach twists as he disappears into the office. A moment later, his footsteps move into the main room. He slings his navy-blue hoodie around my shoulders.

It's warm and soft and it smells like him. Like his shampoo. Clean and masculine and beachy.

His fingers brush my neck as he pulls his hand to his side. "You need tea or something?"

"No. Sorry. Do I look—"

"In the clouds? Yeah. Shake it off, sunshine. Our client's here in ten."

"Ours?"

"You're my shadow now. This is a water color tattoo. New technique."

"A female client?"

He chuckles. "Yeah. She's bringing her boyfriend to hold her hand."

"Oh." It's common. Women usually bring moral support. Men tend to come alone.

His bright eyes find mine.

I stare up at him. "So, we're..."

"I was drunk and stupid. Don't worry about it."

"Oh. Right." I study his expression, but it doesn't give me a clue to his intentions.

～

THE SUITE IS TINY. ESPECIALLY WITH THE CLIENT'S boyfriend on the other stool.

I'm a foot from Dean. Less.

He's in the middle of the tattoo, but my body doesn't care. It begs me to touch him. To stop him. To do whatever it takes to get my clothes off and his hands on me.

I press my palms into my quads. Focus on the soft fabric of my black jeans. On the way my nails curl into the denim.

When I'm calm enough to concentrate, I bring my gaze to his right hand. I focus on the way his fingers curl around the tattoo gun. On the way his forearm flexes and relaxes as he works.

The tattoo takes an hour. I barely make it through the check out.

As soon as I can, I rush to the bathroom. But washing my hands in cold water isn't enough. Splashing my cheeks, fore-head, and neck isn't enough.

I'm burning up.

I'm not sure how I survive our second tattoo. The appointments are back-to-back. No time for lectures on tech-nique. Or teasing. Or staring at him like I'm desperate to get him naked.

This is a geometric design. It's cool, modern, trendy.

Dean is his usual funny, charming self. He turns the flirting off—he always does when a woman brings her boyfriend.

He doesn't ask about my panties or my night or when I last touched myself. He doesn't suggest a game of ten fingers or truth or truth or tell me yours, I'll tell you mine.

It's weird. But then it isn't. Not really. We had two appointments like this last week.

He's incredibly good at reading the mood in the suite. At tuning himself to what the client needs. And this girl needs quiet reassurance and distraction from her boyfriend.

Finally, we finish.

I gush over the work. Bring them to the counter so Emma can check them out—she's Leighton's more permanent replacement. Since Dean "can't have his apprentice running around doing errands."

Apparently, she's Brendon's younger sister. I can see the resemblance. They're both tall with intense brown eyes and dark hair.

"Nice." She smiles at the client as she hands over the receipt. "I want one just like that."

The client beams. Signs on the dotted line. "You should. I'm so in love." She turns to her boyfriend. Slides her arms around his neck. "Are you in love?"

"Yeah." He stares back into her eyes all goo-goo ga-ga.

She rises to her tiptoes to kiss him.

He wraps his arms around her. Kisses back. With tongue.

Emma shoots me an *ew gross* look.

I nod.

Dean chuckles. "Ink is an aphrodisiac."

"Since when?" Emma raises a brow. "That sounds like a load of bull."

He nods to the clients. *Shut the fuck up.* "How would you know, Em?"

"You don't have any?" I ask.

She nods. "When you grow up with a tattoo artist brother, the whole thing kinda loses its appeal." She looks to Dean. "I guess it's different when your brother is all old and weird. Like he's basically your dad."

"He does have a daddy vibe." My cheeks flush. Did I just say that? I'm not even sure what that means.

Emma's nose scrunches in distaste. "I did not hear that." She looks to the receipt. Points to the forty percent tip with a thumbs-up. "You guys are all done."

They keep making out.

Dean turns to Emma. "You got this?"

"Is it really part of my job description?" she asks.

"Get used to it. Happens with pretty much every couple. It's the ink. Or maybe it's me." He tugs his t-shirt up his stomach, showing off his taught abs. "I'm irresistible."

"God, I thought Dean was annoying in small doses. But large ones..." She wipes her forehead like she's wiping off the sweat of a heavy work out. "How do you deal?"

"I don't," I say.

"He's the worst, isn't he?" she teases.

"He's incorrigible," I say.

"Fuck, sunshine. You know you have to dumb it down for me." He motions for me to follow him.

I do.

He grabs my backpack from behind the counter and leads me to the back room. "You finish Han Solo?"

"Yeah. Why?"

He pushes his shirt up his sleeve. "Do me."

"Right here?" I pretend to undo my jeans. "Sure. You have a condom?"

His smile lights up his dark eyes. "I'm already corrupting you."

"Maybe I'm already corrupted."

He shakes his head.

I nod.

"Show me the goods."

"Oh. Right." We're not flirting. We're pretending like Saturday night never happened. Maybe. I can never tell where I stand with him. "You're holding my backpack."

He hands it over.

I set it on the desk. Dig out my sketchbook. Find the page with my latest Han. It's a little different. He's wearing only his vest and pants, no shirt, and he's kneeling on his blaster as it shoots a laser bullet.

It's all incredibly phallic.

"Nice." He taps his skin. "Make it happen."

He's in the way of the printer, but I don't ask him to move. My front brushes his as I pass him.

My nipples perk. My sex clenches. My veins buzz with nervous energy.

I'm shaking.

I steady my hands enough to set the mock-up on the printer. Scan. Print.

He keeps his body behind mine as I snip the edges from the design.

Stays close as I clean him up, peel the plastic from the paper, press it to his skin, wet it.

I'm right there. Inches from him. Touching him.

But it's not enough.

I want more than his shoulder.

I want him naked in front of me.

I want to be naked in front of him.

My blush spreads over my cheeks and chest. It's bizarre. I haven't wanted to be naked in front of someone since before my diagnosis.

My body has been my enemy.

Then a stranger.

But now, God, I want to kiss and make nice.

To get to know every inch and cranny.

Of me. Of him. Of us together—

"That's plenty of time," he says.

"Right." I peel the paper from his skin.

Perfect. The design transfers.

He looks down at me. "How is it?"

I study the tattoo like it isn't a silly joke. Like it's exactly what Dean wants. It does fit his cheeky attitude. And it fits his shoulder too. The lines fall over his skin just so. "It's good."

"Only good?"

"Really good."

He takes my hand and leads me back into the main room. Past Walker and Ryan—why are they in the lobby this early? All the way to his suite.

He studies the design in the mirror. "Fuck. That is good." He turns to me. "Good job."

The compliment does nothing to ease the flush in my cheeks. "Thanks." I stare up into his eyes. He's being genuine. It's weird. But I'm starting to get used to it. "But?"

"No buts."

"Do you want any changes? It is your tattoo."

"Yeah." He looks back to the mirror. Studies the reflection. "More details on the gun."

"I can't go too small. The ink spreads over time. In a few years it will be blurry."

He smiles knowingly.

"That was a trick question."

"Maybe." He shrugs. "Add a few. Big ones."

"Sure. I'll have it for you next week."

"Good." He looks around the room. Ryan and Walker are still in the lobby. But now Brendon is with them and the amorous couple is gone. "Let's do this."

"Do what?"

He's already in the lobby. "Hey." He claps his hands over his head. "Announcement. Chloe is gonna be my full-time apprentice."

Emma shoots me a curious look. Like she's trying to decide how I feel about that.

"That was your announcement?" Brendon asks. "Not sure anyone needed to get here early for that."

"All right. Don't care. I'm in heaven. Chloe working under me." Dean winks. "What more could I want?"

Walker rises from the bench with a chuckle. "In your

dreams."

"I'll make those nightmares." Ryan's threat is playful. He's even smiling. He looks to me. "You okay with this?"

I nod.

"You sure?" Walker asks. "Dean is—"

"Annoying?" I offer.

Emma laughs. "It's good she sees your true self."

"Em, baby. How could you say that? You and I, we're like this—" He presses his first two fingers together. "You get me."

"How horrifying." She shakes her head. "I do not." She looks to me. "Why Dean and not one of the other guys?"

"Well, the thing is, the other guys at the shop are smoking hot. But Dean... his personality ruins the whole thing," I deadpan.

"Fuck. Ow." Dean mimes being stabbed in the gut.

I shrug.

Walker laughs. "She is unfazed. I love it."

Ryan and Brendon share a knowing look.

Brendon shrugs *what are you gonna do?*

Ryan's brow furrows. He's working something out, but I'm not sure what it is.

"Is your ego okay?" Walker asks.

Dean makes a show of shaking his head. He leans forward. Wraps his arm around his stomach like his guts are falling out. "I don't know if I'm gonna make it this time." He stumbles forward. Then backward.

"You two fight a lot," Emma says. "I was only here one day and I saw it. You sure you want to deal with him?"

"I have to," I say. "His hideous nature makes it so much easier to concentrate."

"I can't... the shame." Dean reaches for an invisible weapon. Holds it in front of his stomach.

He drops to his knees and falls on the sword.

Then he falls flat on his face.

Rolls over. Lets out a death rattle.

His limbs go limp. Really limp. Like he's actually dead.

Walker shakes his head. "Was that it?"

Dean continues to play possum.

Walker looks to Ryan and Brendon. "I'm gonna get coffee. You want to come?"

Ryan nods.

Walker looks back to Dean. "Gym at five?"

Dean continues playing dead.

"I'll take that as a yes." Walker shakes his head *ridiculous*.

He and Ryan make their way out the door.

"He commits." Brendon steps over Dean on his way back to the suite. "I'll give him that much."

"He does," I say.

"Good luck." He moves into his suite. "Let me know if you need any help."

"Thanks." It's just me and Dean now.

Well, and Emma.

She studies me knowingly. Nods to Dean. Mouths *you like him*.

I bite my lip.

Her eyes go wide. She mouths *you do!*

Is it really that obvious?

She laughs. "He's dead. Let's check his pockets. You do it, Chloe. See if there's anything good."

"Sure." I play his game. Drop to my knees next to him. My fingers brush the waist of his jeans. Over his hip bone. Lower.

Fuck, my hands are close to where they need to be.

I drag my fingers a little lower. Brush the top of his pocket. Slide my fingers into it.

He's so warm and hard.

And—

Fuck.

His fingers curl around my wrist. "If you get any closer I'm gonna be hard."

"Oh." My cheeks flame. "Sorry."

"Don't be." He sits up. Looks to Emma. She's watching us with wide eyes. "You angling for a threesome, Em?"

"Ew," she says. "What's in the wallet for that kind of defensiveness?"

"If I wanted you to know, I wouldn't be defensive," he says.

"Or maybe you have a thing for Chloe getting you on the ground. Did you have a Xena Warrior Princess fantasy growing up?" she asks.

He looks to me. "What do you say? You go as Xena for Halloween. I'll go as Hercules."

"I'm good."

He shrugs. "I tried." He looks to Em. "How about you?"

She shakes her head.

"Got your eye on someone else?" he asks.

"Maybe." She clears her throat. Nods to Brendon, currently sketching in his suite, between clients.

"You need some help? I can make it happen. Take you to his hang out spot. Make him jealous." Dean releases my wrist. In one swift motion, he jumps to his feet.

He's not flirting with her. He's genuinely offering help.

It's weird. But sweet too.

"No. I'm good." She turns to the computer. "You have an hour until your next appointment."

"I know," he says.

I rise to my feet. "I should get lunch."

"No." He motions *come here*. "I have something for you to do."

"Oh."

"I need your hands on my banana."

Chapter Sixteen

DEAN

C hloe's shoulders drop from her ears as I pull a banana from my backpack. "This is fruit."

"What were you expecting?"

Her gaze goes right to my crotch. Her cheeks flush, but her eyes stay put.

After a long moment of staring, she shakes it off. "Whatever could I have been expecting? It's not as if you phrased that sentence to give me the wrong idea."

"Wrong idea? You sure you're thinking about me?"

"Pretty sure." Her dark eyes fill with fire. She folds her arms. Taps her combat boot against the ground.

"Come on." I motion for her to follow me. "No food in the main room. We have to do this in the office."

"Oh. Sure." She follows me into the office.

Brendon and Emma are the only people here. There's no need to close the door. If anything, it's a bad idea. It's an invitation. For her and for my body.

Being in this tiny space with her is hard enough with the door open.

I'm not doing anything that will ruin shit.

I'm not touching her. Period.

But caution isn't my strong suit.

I close the door. Motion to the chair. "Sit."

She does.

I place the banana on the table. Reach into the desk drawer. This is what she's been waiting for. This is everything she wants.

I set the tattoo gun in front of her.

Her eyes go wide. "You mean—"

"Yeah."

"Now?"

I nod.

She picks up the gun. Wraps her fingers around it with reverence. She's in some trance. One that doesn't involve me.

A gasp falls off her lips as she turns the thing on.

It buzzes against her hand.

She stares. Mesmerized.

Chloe is hard to impress. This is a rare look for her. But it's fucking intoxicating. I want more of it. I want all of it. I want to fill her with wonder and joy.

How the fuck do people deal with this? It's a head trip.

I focus on the shit I do understand. "Pick up the banana."

She does.

"Try the first one freehand."

She nods.

"What are you gonna do?"

"A star."

"Practicing for me?"

"Uh-huh." She nods, but the words aren't making it to her brain.

Her gaze fixes on the banana. She sets it on the table. Brings the gun to its flesh.

She gasps as the needle hits the peel.

"It's not quite like skin. But it's similar," I say.

She nods. Stares intently as she drags the needle up to a point, then down from it.

It takes her a minute to draw all five points.

She turns the gun off.

Sets it on the table.

Looks up at me with all the wonder in the world. "I really did that."

"How was it?"

"Awesome." She stares at the banana. Just stops herself from tracing the ink.

It's a good first attempt. The lines are messy, the symmetry is lacking, but the shape is there.

"Do five more," I say.

"On this banana?"

I nod.

Her eyes meet mine. "Are you going to stand there?"

"I dunno. Am I your teacher?"

"Oh. I just mean..." She nods to the chair on the other side of the desk. "You could sit."

"Sure." I grab the chair. Roll it next to her. Sit. But it's no good. She's too close. I can smell her floral shampoo. And the lavender scent of her soap. And beneath that, something all Chloe.

Her dark eyes fill with focus as she picks up the gun. She still gasps when she turns it on, but it's softer. Like she's getting used to it.

She draws another freehand star. It's better, but it's still not there.

I don't give her a chance to reflect. "Keep going."

She does.

It takes ten minutes, but she finally manages to do one star with straight lines.

The steady hum of the tattoo gun ceases as she sets it

down. The air-conditioning whirs, drowning out the sound of her soft, steady breath.

Her fingers curl around the banana. "How did I do?"

"It's a good start."

"But?"

"You tell me."

She looks to the first star. "It's almost as ugly as mine was."

"Yours was—"

"Horrible. But I did love it. At the time."

"Why?"

"Why was it horrible?"

"Why did you love it?"

"It was my first real rebellion. My parents were confused by the combat boots and the dark eyeliner, but they didn't really care. I got perfect grades. I did volunteer work. Made varsity swim team. I did everything I was supposed to do."

"I get that."

"When did you ever follow the rules?"

"Believe it or not, my parents adore me."

"Probably true. Everything falls into your lap."

That isn't true. But I don't bother correcting her. Chloe has some idea of me. I can't blame her for it. I'm the one who made sure she saw me a certain way.

"These are kinda lopsided."

"A stencil will fix a lot of that."

She nods.

"But so will holding the gun right."

"Oh."

"Like this." I pick up the gun with a soft grip. Model the proper technique.

She stares back at me like I'm crazy.

"Here." I motion for her to put her hand on the gun.

She does.

I place mine over hers. Press my palm into the back of her hand, modeling the pressure she needs.

Slowly, her grip softens. Her lips part with a sigh.

She leans backward, sinking into my touch.

Melting into me.

Fuck, it feels too good touching her like this.

I want more of it.

All of it.

Her eyelids press together. Her head tilts to one side. Her teeth sink into her lip.

Desire spreads over her expression.

I force myself to pull away. "Keep practicing. You'll get it."

She nods.

"Take this home." I motion to the gun. "Do a hundred by next Monday."

"A hundred stars?"

"Yeah. On bananas. Send me a pic of each one."

"Won't that be—"

"Boring as all hell? Yeah. If you're dying, you can switch to hearts or spades."

"Okay." She wraps her fingers around the gun then holds it flat against her palm. "This is really mine?"

"Yeah. You gotta swear something to me, sunshine."

Her voice is dead serious. "Of course."

"Fruit only."

She nods.

I stand. Offer her my hand. When she takes it, I pull her closer.

I pull her too close.

She's right there.

My hand goes to her hip. Rests there for a split second, until common sense gets the better of me.

Honestly, I'm not sure where this reserve of logic and will

power is coming from. I was *this* close to calling her and demanding she come for my listening pleasure Saturday night.

Fuck. I can't think about this shit when she's this close.

I take a step backward. "You can head home early today. Get started practicing this."

"Sure." Her ass brushes my crotch as she moves past me. She stops at the doorframe. Turns to me. "Thanks, Dean."

Her voice is soft. Sweet.

This is about work, but, fuck, it doesn't feel like that.

It feels like I'm the only thing she wants.

MY PHONE BUZZES WITH A NEW PICTURE MESSAGE FROM Chloe. A banana inked with a lopsided star. It's less lopsided than the one she sent five minutes ago. It's a hell of a lot better than the one she sent an hour and a half ago.

But it's still not there.

For the last two hours, she's been sending pictures like clockwork. Every five minutes. Without fail. The girl is a machine.

You'd think, at picture twenty-something, I'd realize I'm not getting a shot of her panties, but every time my phone buzzes, anticipation floods my body.

I tell my cock to calm down.

Chloe and I aren't happening.

No matter how badly I want her.

Walker finishes his last chest press. Sets the barbell in its stand. "You spotting me or flirting?"

"That a real question?"

He chuckles.

"You should see this. Kinky shit. Every fantasy she has about my—"

"Uh-huh." He stands. Motions to the bench. "You're up."

That I am. I slide my cell into my pocket. Load the barbell with an extra twenty pounds on each side.

Walker shakes his head. He knows me too well. Knows I'm going heavier to prove a point.

But I don't admit that. I drop to my back. Wrap my hands around the weight. Grunt through my first rep.

"Too heavy for you?" He looks down at me, half spotting, half taunting.

Fuck, I'm going to be sore tomorrow. But I can do this. Even if I have to cut it a rep short.

"You can load that thing with an extra hundred pounds. You aren't gonna fool me."

I grunt through my next set. Pause at the top. Fucking chest presses. "Why would I do something like that?"

"How long have I known you?"

"Easy to forget. Your life was empty before."

"How long have we been doing this?" He motions to the gym.

"Ditto." We've been working out together... forever, really. It's always been a competition to see who can lift heavier, run faster, go longer.

"You gonna tell me what the deal is with you and Chloe?"

"There's no deal."

"You do realize we went to the same high school."

"And?"

"You look at her the way you used to."

"Like I want to fuck her." I grunt through my next set. "Of course I want to fuck her. Look at her."

"You volunteered to help her."

"Time to give back."

"Bullshit."

All right, my motives aren't exactly pure. But I do want to help. Used to be I could do a lot of shit to help my friends. But now that they're all paired up, it's harder. They never went to me for assistance—most of them dread my assistance —but I always found a way.

Now, their problems are further away. They're off in their own orbits. Ones that only fit two.

"You want to get in her pants," he says.

"Think we covered this." There. That's four. Halfway through this set.

He looks down at me. "You're gonna drop that thing."

"Which is where you come in."

"Call it at six."

"I have eight in me."

"That's what she said."

"Fuck, I missed that." This weight is too heavy. And my head is too tuned to Chloe. The fire in her eyes. The earnest smile. The sigh of pleasure. I need more of it. All of it.

"You like her."

"She's my apprentice."

"You *like* her like her. High school like her."

I grunt through my fifth rep. Then the sixth. My arms shake. My chest burns. I don't have two more in me. But one?

I've got that.

"You gonna admit it?" he asks.

"You've been watching too many chick flicks."

"Iris hates chick flicks."

"Then all that fucking has scrambled your brain."

"You admit I get laid more than you do?"

"Who calls fucking their girlfriend getting laid?"

He chuckles *fair enough*. "You know what Leigh would say?"

All right, on three. One. Two. Three. There. I push the weight up.

His hands hover over the bar. He's ready to catch it if I drop the thing. Which is really fucking important. Two hundred plus pounds landing on your chest is bad news.

There's a lot of trust in working out together.

Hell, I trust Walker more than I trust anyone. He's been my closest friend forever. But I'm still not sharing this with him.

Nobody needs to know how I feel about Chloe.

I don't even understand how I feel about Chloe.

There. I lower the weight. Leave it in its stand.

"Fuck. It's bad if you can't think up something snappy," he says.

"Leigh would kill you for calling her that."

"Yeah, probably."

"She'd obviously say *Dean, you're so hot. Why'd I end up with your broody older brother when I could have nabbed you instead?*"

"Yeah, I see her doubting that relationship."

"Gotta figure the moping gets old eventually."

"Not like she pined for his brooding ass for two years or anything."

"You know women. Want to fix the broken guy."

"That why none of them stick with you?"

"I'm just too functional," I say.

He laughs *no fucking way*. "Are you jealous she's with Ryan?"

Once upon a time, maybe. I wanted Leighton, but it wasn't her I wanted. It was that she played hot and cold. It was the challenge.

Yeah, I'm an asshole. But it gets old having women eating out of the palm of my hand.

"I thought she was into you for a while," Walker says.

"Nah. Ryan is her everything."

"They're disgusting."

"And you and Iris?"

"That's different. We're poetry."

"Poetry, huh?"

He nods.

"So, *baby, I want you to come on my face—*"

"If you're trying to suggest that isn't poetry, I'm not hearing it."

"Should we ask Kay?"

He laughs. "You're deflecting like a fucking mirror."

"Mirrors reflect."

"Whatever. You know what I mean."

Yeah, I do.

"What is it Leighton says?"

I shrug like I don't know. Leighton likes to pull out the Shakespearean quotes. And there's one that fits this situation.

The lady doth protest too much.

I have a million excuses for my feelings about Chloe.

Keep deflecting attention.

Avoiding the subject.

Even with myself.

My phone buzzes in my shorts. Five minutes. Right on time. Another banana. But this time it's a heart. And it's a mirror selfie. Chloe holding the thing in her bedroom.

Her twin bed behind her.

Plain white sheets. Grey bedspread. Not what I expected. Not what I imagined.

But now...

Fuck.

Walker's gaze shifts to my cell. "Fuck. She likes you too."

"She hates me."

"She wants to fuck you."

"Look at me."

"Ryan will kill you."

"I can take him."

"He'll fire her."

That's a bigger concern. I do like Chloe. I'm not taking this from her.

"But fuck Ryan. We co-own the shop. I vote for her to stay. We can sway Brendon."

"Brendon doesn't give a fuck about us."

"Yeah. But he likes her." Walker runs a hand through his wavy hair. "You're really worried."

"No."

"Yeah." His eyes meet mine. "Shit. You're really into her."

"No idea what you're talking about."

"I can help."

"Horrifying."

"I will."

I shake my head. "You wouldn't know where to start."

"You admit it?"

"That I want to fuck her? Yeah. But that's it."

He smiles *that's not it*.

I shrug.

It's as close to an admission as I'll get.

But he knows it.

It's as good as saying *yeah, I'm fucking crazy about her*.

Chapter Seventeen

DEAN

All night, my phone buzzes with picture messages from Chloe. They slow, but they don't stop until she wishes me good night.

The next day—now that she's on my schedule, we're both off—it's the same thing.

When she isn't tattooing, she sends an explanation in image form. Tea and breakfast. The lap pool at the gym. A grilled cheese sandwich and tomato soup. A takeout iced tea. A sitcom rerun on TV. A pot of pasta. A selfie in her pajamas.

They're tiny things—shorts and a tank top that barely cover her.

The image sticks in my head all day at work. When she sits next to me, wraps her fingers around my forearm, peers over my shoulder to study a mock-up.

When she leans close to watch my technique.

When I send her to the office to do another dozen bananas.

When I watch the way her hips sway as she walks away.

All fucking week, my head is flush with thoughts of Chloe. Every time she's close, my body begs me to break. To touch her. To kiss her. To throw her against the wall and order her to scream my name.

Somehow, I don't.

I push it aside. Tease her about her lopsided hearts. About how seriously she's taking everything. About how much she needs to relax.

Then I go home and I think about exactly how I want to help her *relax*.

For the indefinite future, Chloe's Saturdays belong to me. I finalize plans for this one. Insist on picking her up.

Five minutes to eleven, I park on a sunny street in the Valley. Chloe's place—her dad's place, I guess—is nice. The taupe two bedroom is classic Southern California suburbs. Wide green lawn. White trim. Rose bushes lining the walkway.

I make my way to the coffee brown door.

The second I knock, Chloe pulls the door open.

She looks up at me with frantic eyes. "Let's go."

She takes my hand as she dashes outside. Yelps as her bare feet hit the hot concrete.

She's halfway to the car when a hearty voice stops her.

"You won't get away that easy, baby girl," an older man calls. He pulls the door open wider. Steps onto the patio. He's on the short side with black hair and dark eyes. He looks just like Chloe. "I'm Brian." He offers his hand.

"Nice to meet you." I shake.

He looks to Chloe. "I see what Gia was talking about."

Chloe turns bright red. She drops my hand. Hugs her combat boots to her chest. "She wasn't..." She clears her throat. "Dad. We have to go." She turns to me. "We're in a rush. Right?" Her eyes plead *go along with it*.

If I was a merciful guy, I would. But I'm not. "No. We have all the time in the world."

She groans like a teenager.

Which I get. I feel like a teenager around my parents.

"Well, you might have all day. But I have a hundred oranges to tattoo." She takes another step down the walkway. "So..."

"I didn't show you oranges."

"I saw it on YouTube. It's the same, isn't it?"

"Grapefruits are better."

"Oh." She looks back to her dad with a wave. "We do have to go."

He smiles, good humored. "All this rushing just because you don't want me to say Gia thought Dean was cute."

"Oh my God, Dad!" Chloe turns. Surveys the scene. Refuses to accept defeat. She taps her combat boots together. "I'm sure you're teaching me something important today. So, we should get to it."

She's so full of shit.

But then so am I. I tried to think up some way to explain this as a lesson, but it's not. I want to hang out with her. Period.

"Thank you," I respond to her dad's compliment.

Chloe takes my hand. She looks up at me *please, for the love of God go along with this*.

I shrug, playing coy.

She just barely stifles a groan. "I'll be home late, Dad. Okay?" She waves goodbye.

He nods *sure thing*.

"What happened to your work?" I ask.

Her cheeks flush. Her brow knits with frustration. "Love you, Dad." She ignores my taunting and drags me to the car.

I open the door for her.

She slides inside then slams it hard.

She's pulling socks from her combat boots when I get into the driver's seat.

She slides a sock on. Slips her foot into the boot. Laces it tightly.

"You do own sandals," I say.

"I like these." She slides the other sock on. Foot in boot. Laces. Done. "Perfect."

"Aren't you hot?"

"Nice of you to finally notice."

"That's bad. Even by my standards."

Her eyes go to the ignition. "Are we ever leaving or are we sitting here?"

"Kinda fun watching you stare at your dad like he's evil for standing on the porch."

She hides behind her hands. "How were you so polite to him?"

I slide my key into the ignition and turn it. "Told you. Parents love me."

She peeks out from behind her hands to look at the house. Her dad is still standing on the porch with a knowing smile. "Can we go?"

"Yeah. Sure." I put the car into drive. Wave goodbye to Mr. Lee.

He waves back.

Chloe drops her hands as I pull onto the street. "I love my dad. But..."

"I already knew you thought I was cute."

She ignores my joke. "I'm twenty-four and my dad is screening my dates."

"Is this a date?"

"Oh. No." She bites her lip. "But he thinks it is."

I turn onto the main road. "And you?"

She looks around curiously, like she's trying to figure out where we're going. "We can't, right? So, what's it matter?"

"Yeah." I stop at a red light.

She taps her black fingernails against the dash. "Where are we going?"

"You challenged me the other day."

Her brow scrunches with confusion. "I did?" She sinks into the fabric. Plays with her seat belt. "I figured you'd have a nicer car."

"What's the point?"

"Image? Status? Coolness?"

"I don't need a car to be cool."

"Of course."

"But?" The light turns green. I hit the gas. Focus on the road.

"I'm surprised you know that."

"Teasing me isn't gonna get you any clues."

"Not even one?"

I shake my head.

"I challenge you all the time. You should give me something."

"Sorry. It's against my policy."

"You're the worst."

"That's the sweetest thing you've ever said to me."

"I mean it. You're intolerable."

"Stop." I feign modesty. "You're going to make me blush."

"Do you blush?"

"Yeah." I turn right at the next intersection. There. This street will take us most of the way. "I don't think you need any hints on making that happen."

"Oh." Her cheeks flame red. She gives me a long, slow once over. Her dark eyes fill with desire. Then caution. She considers her options. Settles back into her seat.

I give her a minute to take the bait, but she doesn't.

Better change the subject before my thoughts are too far gone to come back. "How long have you lived at home?"

"Always. It's kinda—"

"It's sweet."

"Really?" Her nose scrunches. "The last time I tried dating, guys seemed to think it was pathetic."

"They were just worried about where you'd fuck."

Her laugh is soft. "God. You're probably right. I never thought about it like that."

"We're all the same."

"You really are."

"Where did you fuck?"

"Alex had his own place."

"After that?"

"Where do you have sex?"

"I usually go to a woman's place."

"Why?"

I stop at a red light. "Easier to leave than to ask someone to leave."

"That's really—"

"Cold?"

"Smart. For you."

"Must have read it in a magazine or something."

"Probably." Her teeth sink into her lip. Her eyes flare with jealousy.

She pries her gaze from me to look out the window. Studies the shop fronts of the strip mall.

This street is rows and rows of strip malls.

"What if they want to go to your place?" she asks.

"Then I do that."

"No roommates in the way?"

"Haven't had a roommate in a long time."

"You don't like it?"

I nod.

"I'm not sure if I would either."

"It doesn't crimp your style as much as living with your dad, but it doesn't help."

"Right." She bites her lip. "Are you still sleeping around?"

"Still?"

"Never mind. It's none of my business." Her voice wavers. "And I don't even care." She fails to sell her apathy. Her lip corners turn down. Her nails sink into her black jeans.

"I'll tell if you do." The light turns green. I take off. Zoom straight to thirty miles an hour.

"No. That's okay."

"Has it really been that long?"

"Well..." She clears her throat. "Longer than you could imagine."

"My imagination is limited. That isn't hard."

"True." The tension in her jaw eases as she laughs. "It's been a while."

"Who was the last guy?"

"Alex."

"Fuck, that is a while."

"Two years." The words are matter of fact.

But they feel like a bomb. Two years. That's an eternity. "How is that possible?"

"It goes faster than you'd think."

"No way. It's been three weeks and I'm dying."

"But that was when I started—"

"Yeah."

"So you haven't?"

"No."

"Why not?"

"I keep thinking about you."

"You... you're waiting for me?"

"No. Just don't want to be with anyone else."

She leans into her seat. Lets out a soft sigh. "But we... has anything changed?"

"No." I'm still her boss. She's still my subordinate. And teaching her is still the most important thing in my life. Nothing can fuck this up.

"So, we..."

"Still shouldn't."

"Right. Of course."

The devil on my shoulder whispers in my ear. *Doesn't mean we can't.*

But I keep that to myself.

Chapter Eighteen

DEAN

Chloe's eyes go wide as she steps into the tea room. She studies the floral wallpaper, the clean white tablecloths, the ornate wooden chairs.

This is a swanky joint. It's old-fashioned, all doilies and lace. Everyone in their Sunday best with the manners to match.

"Are you sure you're in the right place?" She looks up at me. "You probably can't drop f-bombs here."

"It's gonna be tough. Really." I lead her to the host stand. "Reservation for eleven thirty for Maddox."

"Right this way." The host beams. He leads us through the crowded room, to a round table near the window. The guy even pulls out Chloe's seat for her.

She nods *thank you* as she takes it. Unfolds her napkin and drapes it over her lap.

I'm not sure who looks more out of place—me in my surfer boy shorts and sandals or her in her artsy rebel combat boots and tight jeans.

We're not this place's usual crowd.

"Oh." Her eyes light up with epiphany. "The Golden Needle."

I nod.

"You're still thinking about that?"

"Man has to defend his honor."

"And you're doing that how?"

I point to the host. He's walking toward us with two tasting trays. Tiny white cups line white platters.

He sets one in front of Chloe and the other in front of me. "The key is right here." He motions to the paper in his hands then places it face-down. "I have you down for two vegetarian afternoon teas."

I nod. "That work?"

Chloe nods.

"Earl Grey?" I ask.

Under the table, she kicks me. "Yes, please." Her voice is sweet. Serene. Like she isn't bothered by how well I know her.

"And for you, sir?" he asks.

"Russian Caravan." I nod a *thank you*.

He heads back to the kitchen.

Chloe sinks into her chair. Her gaze settles on the tea. "How do we know who wins?"

"Whoever gets it right wins."

"Seems fair." Her eyes go to the paper. "How do I know you didn't cheat?"

"Winning isn't fun if you have to cheat."

Somehow, she believes me. "We both decide. Write it on a piece of paper face down. Reveal at the same time."

"Deal." I pick up my first cup. Take a long sip. Astringent. Grassy. Not Golden Needle, but good.

Her eyelids press together as she sips. Her lips part with a sigh.

Her brow relaxes.

Her chest heaves.

Her satisfaction does something to me. Warms me some-place that's normally cold.

I forget about our game.

Watch her drink instead.

She savors each cup. Studies flavors carefully. It's different than the way she stares at art. Less analytical. More emotional.

She picks up the third cup again. Takes another sip. "I think I have it."

Fuck, I don't. I rush through my teas. All four of them are good, but none stand out as Golden Needle. The second is too smoky. The third is nutty enough, but the fourth has a clearer flavor. I pick that one. Use the sharpie in my pocket (you never know when you need to draw a tattoo mock-up) to scribble it on a napkin.

She pulls a pen from her purse and writes her answer. "Ready?"

"On three."

We count down together. "One, two, three."

Flip. Hers reads three. Mine reads four.

I turn over the key.

It's one.

She laughs. "You were wrong. I think that means I win."

"I think it might."

Her chest spills forward as she leans in. "You do realize I was just"—she drops her voice to a whisper—"fucking with you?"

I hold my hand over my mouth to stage whisper. "You do realize I wasn't born yesterday?"

Her lips curl into a smile. "Doesn't explain your immaturity."

"True."

She picks up the first cup. Takes a long sip. "How did you get into tea?"

"My mom."

"Are you close?"

"No. But we were."

"What happened?"

I press my palms into my jeans. This is not a conversation I'm having. Not with her. Not with anyone.

The server spares me from finding a deflection. He drops off our lunch. Or maybe I should call it a feast.

Matching three-tiered plates are flush with finger sandwiches, cookies, scones, butter, jam, and lemon curd. The same shit my mom always ordered, only sans meat.

Another server drops off our tea.

Chloe stirs honey into her Earl Grey. "Was it that bad?"

"You could say that." I pour from my pot. Take a long sip. It's dark, rich, smoky. Perfect as is.

"Does she know how you feel?"

"Yeah."

"Does Ryan?"

I shake my head.

"Hmm." The gears in her mind turn. She pores over the possibilities. Tries to put it together.

But she won't. This is the kinda thing nobody thinks about their parents.

She brings her mug to her lips. Takes a long sip. Lets out a soft sigh. "How did your mom get you into tea?"

"She used to take us here. On Sundays. She'd dress us up in tiny little suits and meet her friends for afternoon tea."

She smiles at the mental image. "Were you already a troublemaker?"

"I was born a troublemaker."

"That's supposed to sound badass."

"Doesn't it?"

She shakes her head.

"You're killing me, Chloe."

"I'm sure." She plucks a cucumber sandwich from her plate. Takes a tiny bite. "This is weird."

"What about it?"

"You're being nice."

"I am not."

"You are so."

"Definitely not."

"Definitely so."

"I'm going to keep saying it."

She finishes her sandwich. "I'm sure you could go in circles for hours."

I nod. I could. But I don't want to waste my time with her. I want to know more about her. To peel her open and pry her apart.

I can't have her body.

But we can be friends.

I'm capable of getting to know her without getting her clothes off. "How'd you get into tea?"

"My mom. She loved her morning ritual. She made a strong black tea every day. Waited until it was steeped just right then added a little milk, a little honey. I'd always try to get her to add more, but she'd say, 'you need balance, Chloe.'"

"She sounds like a monk."

"She was like that." She takes a long sip of her Earl Grey. Lets out a soft sigh. "It's funny. All my stories about Mom make her seem so wise and worldly. She was, but I didn't see her like that when she was here. And then... at the end..." Hurt fills her eyes.

I want to wipe it away. "How did it happen?"

"She got sick when I was eight." Her lips press together. "Breast cancer. An aggressive one. She was already stage three. She did everything. Mastectomy. Chemo. Radiation.

But it wasn't enough." Her eyes turn down. Her finger glides over her cup. "It didn't seem fair, for her to go through all that only to die all the same."

"It never is."

"No, it's not." Her gaze shifts to the three-tier plate. She picks up a madeleine and dunks it in her tea. "Sorry. I'm killing the mood."

I shake my head.

"This is serious. And you're not."

"I'm a lot of things."

She brings the cookie to her lips. Takes a bite. Chews. Swallows. Crumbs fall onto her plate as she breaks off another piece. "I guess it's only been two minutes."

I arch a brow.

"That you've been serious."

I can't help but laugh. "I'm developing a tolerance. Might make it to four."

"I doubt it." She smiles, but there's a sadness to it. Those heavy memories are still weighing on her. "Your parents ever get sick?"

"Yeah. My dad. When I was a kid."

"What happened?"

"He lost a ball."

She drops the cookie. "What?"

"Testicular cancer."

"Oh." Her shoulders relax. A laugh rises up in her throat. "You... you really are ridiculous."

"You think this is ridiculous? Should have seen me at twelve. I was fucking terrified it would happen to me too."

"Really?"

I nod. At the time, it was the scariest thing in the world.

"Is he okay?"

"Yeah. It's treatable, as far as cancer goes. He caught it early."

"Did he have to do chemo?"

"No. Just radiation treatment for a few weeks. He took it in stride. Acted like it never fazed him. But now... I don't know. He must have been scared."

She nods. "It's scary when someone you love is sick. Not knowing what's gonna happen. Trying to be strong for them when you're falling apart inside."

"With your mom?"

"Yeah." Her voice trails off. Her gaze shifts to the cookie on her plate. "When she looked at me, and she saw the concern in my eyes... she had to swallow all her fear to placate me. She had to hide her feelings."

"You were a kid."

"But if I wasn't?"

"Doesn't matter. You were."

"But it must have been hard for her. Feeling like she had to convince me I was okay. Like she was the one who took the weight of everyone else's grief."

She's not talking about her mom anymore.

She's talking about someone else.

But who the hell is it?

Chapter Nineteen

CHLOE

Dean never quite gets back to his carefree self. We finish our massive lunches, sip another round of tea, drive back to my place with Stone Temple Pilots filling the car.

Hug goodbye.

I push my thoughts aside. Pour myself into tattoo mock-ups. Into swimming laps. Into inking bananas.

Sunday is work. I'm officially on Dean's schedule.

I sit next to him as he tapes a stencil to a pretty girl's ribs. I watch him flirt just enough to set her at ease. But it's not the same as it was. He holds back. Keeps the conversation tame. Glances at me every few sentences to check my reaction.

I barely manage to hide my jealousy.

I barely manage to keep my hands to myself.

I barely manage to swallow all the confessions that rise into my throat.

It was me. I was the one who had to convince everyone I was okay with dying. That their preemptive grief wasn't tearing me apart.

And it might be me again.

Even though our schedule is packed, the day passes slowly. My thoughts keep turning to kissing him. Touching him. Telling him.

We finish, I head to aikido, stretch, spar, drive home, make dinner for Dad, watch sitcom reruns on the couch, hide in my room with my sketchbook.

The entire time, I think of Dean. I consider calling him. Texting him. Demanding a shoulder to cry on, or a silly joke to make me smile, or a dirty demand to make me hot.

He wants me. He does. He's holding off for me. Because he knows this will explode in my face.

I can text him another picture of my panties. Demand he reciprocate. Ask him if he's hard. If he wants to fuck himself.

If I can watch.

I can do a lot of things.

But I don't.

I text him a request to take next Thursday off. For personal reasons.

And he texts back a perfectly professional *sure.*

And I fall asleep with my thoughts split between him and the terrifying reality check awaiting me.

Then I wake up, and I do it again.

OUR SATURDAY MORNING DATE (IS IT A DATE? DO I WANT it to be a date?) is Dean's challenge to me: a long hike starting at Los Liones Drive.

At five to eight, he pulls onto the street. He shoots me a wink as he drives past me and parks three cars up.

I push off the hood. Hit my key fob to lock my sedan. Stretch my arms over my head. It's early, but the sky is already a brilliant blue.

Dean steps out of his car. Slides his hands into the pockets of his loose running shorts. "Nice to see you, sunshine."

I tug my backpack straps. Between his shorts and my backpack, this feels too much like high school. "Miserable to see you. As usual."

He brushes his bangs from his eyes. "That's what I like to hear."

"Should I have thrown in a dick face?"

He presses his hand to his heart. "Fuck. I'm not sure I'm ready for that."

"Uh-huh."

Dean offers his hand. "You ready to go?"

"Yeah."

"Can you do me?" He pulls his t-shirt over his head then stuffs it into his bag.

My heart thuds as he brandishes a bottle of sunscreen. This is standard friend stuff. But with Dean... it's just not.

Deep breath. Slow exhale. We're coworkers hiking together. Rubbing sunscreen over his bare chest is no big deal. It's absolutely, positively not a big deal. Not even remotely.

My fingers brush his as I take the bottle.

He looks down at me as I squeeze lotion into my palm.

I bring my hand to his chest.

Soft skin. Hard muscles. Lines of ink.

Fuck, he feels good against my fingertips.

I swallow hard, but it does nothing to calm the butterflies in my stomach. I'm rubbing sunscreen into Dean's chest. And he's so... tall and broad and hot and...

He's still looking down at me with those bright blue eyes.

I force myself to focus on my work. It's like a tattoo. Skin is skin. That's what Dean says.

So what if this skin belongs to the guy I want more than I want anything?

My body ignores my logic.

Desire races through my limbs. It builds in my fingertips, my nipples, my sex.

My toes curl into my sneakers.

My fingers curl into Dean's skin.

I force my palm to flatten, but that's no good. Now I'm touching more of his broad chest.

"You okay?" He brushes a stray hair behind my ear.

"Why wouldn't I be?"

"You're red."

"I am not." I rub sunscreen into his taut stomach.

"Yeah, you are."

There. That's all his front. "Turn around."

He spins on his heels.

There. I can blush in peace. He's doing it on purpose. He's winding me up even though there's no way we can act on our desire.

He's evil.

The thought runs through my brain as I rub sunscreen into his muscular back and shoulders. But, bit by bit, my body takes over. My fingertips linger on his skin. I move closer. Inhale the scent of him.

Linen, sunscreen, and something all Dean.

He steps forward, breaking our touch. "Need me to do you?" He turns so we're face-to-face.

I shake my head. "Already done." For a second, I curse my habit of applying sunscreen every morning. But this is a good thing. If Dean starts running his fingers over my skin, I'm a goner.

He offers his hand. "I've got extra water in my trunk."

"I'm good." I press my palms into my sides. Move toward the trail. "Come on. Stop stalling. Let's do this."

He nods and follows me onto the trail.

It's all dirt and dry brush. The plants are short, waist high at most. Shade is rare.

He places his body behind mine, blocking the glare of the sun.

"Thanks." I dig my heels into the dirt, but my heels don't have enough grip. I need to keep my footsteps light.

"Need the tan anyway."

"Is that right?"

"Don't tell me it's a bad look."

"No, it suits you. Like a Hollister model."

"Hollister? Fuck, sunshine, how could you say that?"

I round the first bend in the trail. Duck under a short tree for a brief respite from the sun.

He's right behind me. Then next to me. He shoots me a smile. "At least give me Abercrombie and Fitch. Those are some hot models."

"I wouldn't know."

"Yeah." He nods to my black leggings and black tank top. "Where do you buy that gear?"

I move forward. "You really think I'd be caught dead in a preppy store?"

"No." He keeps his steps in time with mine. So he's next to me. "Just wanted to see your reaction."

"And?"

"Gold."

"I'm glad I can entertain."

He follows in silence for a few moments. The canyon fills with the gentle breeze, the sound of our footsteps, the feel of my heart thudding against my chest.

By the time we're at the top of the next hill, I'm panting and flushed. But it's not from the hike. It's him being right there. Shirtless.

He stops. Throws his hands over his eyes to block the sun

then takes in the view—the canyons flush with grey-green trees, the multi-million-dollar mansions, the rolling ocean. It goes for miles. Forever. From Malibu, all the way to Long Beach Harbor and beyond.

He turns back to me, those blue eyes on fire.

My knees knock together.

My body begs me to touch him.

I reach for the first distraction I can find. "How was your last appointment?"

"Should have seen the look Ryan gave me after he saw the tattoo." He imitates his brother's disapproving frown. Then his voice. "Why would anybody want this trendy shit?"

"It was water color?"

"How'd you know?" He laughs.

"You've never told me what your opinion is."

"Not my body. Not my place."

I nod. Hug the brush to give two friends room to pass.

Dean follows suit. He places his body right behind mine.

His crotch brushes my ass.

The back of his hand brushes my hip.

His breath is cool against the back of my neck.

They pass. Finally.

I play with the waistband of my leggings. "Would you get one?"

He shakes his head. "Not that secure with my masculinity."

"If you were."

"Hard to envision a universe where that's true."

I laugh, even though I don't believe it. "You're incredibly secure about that."

"About my cock? Yeah. Of course. You want to see so you can remember why?" he teases.

"No. About how manly you are. You're not afraid to hug Ryan and tell him you love him."

He smirks. "Ryan hates that."

"Yeah. And you'd probably say that's why you do it, but it's not. You care about your friends and family."

"Who said otherwise?"

"You."

He arches a brow.

I step over a mass of rocks. "You act like you don't give a fuck. But you do."

"Maybe." He turns to the view. Lets out a heavy exhale as he takes it in. "You act like you hate everything."

"I do."

"Nah. You barely hate anything."

I shake my head.

He nods. "You mostly talk about shit you love."

"That's because I mostly talk tattoos."

"You're obsessed."

"That's why I'm here." I round another corner. Ah, sweet, sweet shade. I hug the hillside.

"Why are you here?" He moves forward. So he's in front of me, then he turns and walks backward.

"Here? You have some sort of plan to make me see the beauty in the world."

"And?"

"It's gorgeous here, yeah. But it's not filling me with zest for life."

"I'm wearing too many clothes."

"That must be it."

His eyes meet mine. "Why are you at Inked Hearts?"

"I told you. I decided to start going after what I wanted."

"Tell me the real story."

I want to.

I want to let Dean in.

But the last time I did that, he left me high and dry.

Can I trust him now?

"You know the real story." I move forward. "I finished college, had a family problem, figured it out, begged anyone who would listen for an apprenticeship. The end."

"You're skipping over 'family problem.'"

"It's not an interesting story."

"You're not a good liar."

My shoulders tense. "Why should I tell you anything?"

"Because you want to."

That's the thing. I do. My heart is begging me to share with him. My body is on fire just from his proximity. But my head... "Last time I ignored my common sense, I went seven years without hearing from you."

He stops in a patch of shade. Leans against the hillside.

"Forgive me if I'm apprehensive about trusting you again."

"You're still thinking about that?"

"I wasn't. Until I saw you again."

His eyes find mine. "You were better off."

"I was better off crying into my pillow all of June?"

Something fills his eyes. Some realization. "I meant that much to you?"

"Yeah." I bite my lip. Here am I, awkward and vulnerable again. And here he is, aloof and in control, again. "I thought about you for three years straight. You and I... we always understood each other. Maybe we hated each other—"

"I never hated you."

"I hated you. A lot. But I always liked you."

"I love the way you hate me."

"You're disturbed."

"Yeah."

"So." I dig my toes into the dirt path. "When we went upstairs... I knew you weren't the boyfriend type. But I thought it meant something. That I meant something to you."

"You did."

"Then why didn't you ever call?" I bite my lip. This isn't how this conversation is supposed to go. I'm supposed to slap him and scream *fuck you for ditching me, you asshole* not stare into his eyes begging for an explanation.

I waited for him for seven years.

I'm still waiting.

I'm still under his thumb.

He's still holding all the cards.

"Honestly?" He stares back at me.

"No. I want a lie."

"I gotta watch myself. You could push me off a cliff."

"You must be—"

"You gonna guess my weight again?"

"You're all muscle. Don't pretend like it offends you."

His lips curl into that million-dollar smile. It's a second, then frustration streaks his expression. "It was for you."

"Fuck you." I push off the hillside. Move forward. He can shill out all the bullshit he wants. I'm not hearing it.

"Sunshine, wait."

I don't.

I climb the damn hill as fast as I can.

He follows.

He's taller. Faster.

I break into a jog.

A full-on trail run.

Dart around the curve.

Down a steep hill.

Up the next.

My heart races. My breath becomes a struggle. My focus shifts to the trail and the placement of my feet.

Fuck his stupid excuses.

Fuck him for calling me sunshine.

For inviting me out to show me the beauty in the world.

We can't be anything.

Not if he's still refusing to be honest.

With the next hill, he catches up.

His fingers curl around my upper arm. "You were going someplace. To a good college and a guy with a real job. A guy who could buy you a car and a vacation and a house with a white picket fence."

"What about me says white picket fence?"

"Besides the combat boots and the eyeliner, everything."

"Fuck you."

"I thought we were both better off."

"Both of us includes you." I turn to face him. To try to find some explanation in his expression.

Hurt streaks his blue eyes. "I told you. I don't do relationships."

"So that whole 'I didn't want to hurt you more' thing was bullshit?"

"No. I..." He runs his fingers through his hair. "I was crazy about you. I thought fucking you would cure me of that. But it didn't."

"You're really bad at apologizing."

"Chlo—"

"You were crazy about me. You kept thinking about me. Why didn't you ever pick up the phone?"

"I didn't want to get hurt."

"So?" I pull my arm to my side.

"You're right. I was an asshole."

The earnest apology catches me off guard.

"I'm sorry. It was one of the worst things I ever did, hurting you. It still eats at me."

"Oh."

"If I could take it back, I would."

"How?"

He raises a brow.

"Would you not seduce me? Or would you call? Would you stick around?"

"I'd call."

"And then?"

"I don't know, sunshine. This kind of thing isn't my forte."

"You really—"

"Yeah." He moves closer. "We can leave now if you want."

"No... Let's just... let's talk about something else."

"Anything in mind?"

Did you really think about me that much?

Are you still thinking about me?

Do you want me as badly as I want you?

I swallow hard. "Let's just talk about work."

He nods, accepting my answer.

But it lingers in the air.

He wishes he called.

He wishes things were different.

He wishes we had a chance.

Chapter Twenty

CHLOE

We make it through the rest of the seven-mile hike without another mention of the night we spent together.

But my thoughts never turn to the Malibu canyons or the Pacific Ocean or the million-dollar houses on the cliffs.

They stay on Dean.

He's sorry he hurt me.

He still regrets it.

Still thinks about me.

But is that enough?

He's still my boss.

This is still a terrible idea.

And my heart...

It's still committed to his.

Chapter Twenty-One

CHLOE

"**D**o your best with my banana." Dean slaps the piece of fruit on the desk.

It's Wednesday. The night before the test. Four days since he apologized. Since I fell asleep thinking about all the ways he could make it up to me.

Okay, that's bullshit.

I've fallen asleep thinking about him every night for a month straight.

I pick up my gun. Stare at the yellow flesh. I'm at work and I'm paying attention, dammit. "A star?"

"Whatever inspires you."

"Sure." My fingers curl around the metal. At this point, the weight and feel of the gun are familiar. It belongs in my hands. It makes sense there.

Dean goes into a trance when he's working.

Maybe I can do the same.

I turn the gun on. Focus on bringing it to the fruit's flesh.

There. I draw a curved line. Round it. Finish the other half.

The room quiets as the tattoo gun's hum ceases.

It's October now. Even in Venice Beach, even five blocks from the beach, the weather is cooler. Which means the air-conditioning is at brisk rather than ice box.

At the moment, it's silent.

Our breath is the only sound in the room.

My inhale is sharp. My exhale is heavy.

Dean moves closer. Until he's right behind me. Inches away.

Then pressed against me.

His hard chest against my back. His crotch against my ass. His arms around my shoulders.

My heartbeat picks up.

My stomach flutters.

My body buzzes with desire.

His touch feels so good.

Right now, I need good. This might be my last chance to kiss and make up with my body.

But can I trust him?

Can I muster up the guts to turn around and kiss him?

His fingers trail down my arm. My wrist. The back of my hand. He picks up the banana and studies it. "Good."

"Yeah?"

"This is it."

"It how?"

"You're graduating." He sets the fruit on the desk. Steps backward enough to release me. "Do a more complicated design this time."

"You have a banana?"

"Not one you can ink."

"In your dreams."

"Pretty sure needles on my dick falls into nightmare."

"Then how did you get the piercing—"

"Raw willpower."

"Bullshit." I need to tease him. I need to feel like today is a normal day and not the one before I meet my fate. "It was narcissism, plain and simple."

"Damn, sunshine. Slow down. I don't know those SAT words."

I turn and stare up at him. "It was all your ego."

"It is massive." His smile lights up his bright eyes.

"But that wasn't enough. You needed jewelry."

"And this." He takes my right hand between his. Traces the lines of each ring with his thumb.

"What about it?"

"Why is it you're adorning your right hand?"

I wiggle my left hand. I'm wearing rings on every finger there too.

"So, you use both?"

I can't help but laugh. "That's where you're going with that?"

"Unless you've got nipple piercings I don't know about."

So much for keeping my mind off my boobs. I bite my lip. Fail to force a smile. This is silly. I can't kiss Dean *and* keep my thoughts off my chest. If I kiss him, I'm tearing off his clothes. And he's tearing off mine. And his hands are going right to my chest.

And, fuck, I want that.

I want that so badly.

"You okay, sunshine?" His voice pulls me back to the room.

"Yeah. Just tired."

"You forget your London Fog?"

"Haha." I flip him off with my left hand.

He releases my right. "Do the design. Then you can head out."

"That's all for today?"

His gaze shifts to the clock. "You've been here for ten hours."

"But I..."

"I know I'm irresistible, but I'm taking my tired ass home."

"Don't you have a gym date with Walker?"

He arches a brow. "Didn't realize you had my schedule memorized."

"I notice things."

"Notice tattoo designs."

"I do."

"Pick one." He nods to the banana. "For the other side."

"Oh."

"A Latin quote."

I stick my tongue out.

"Who doesn't love *carpe diem*?"

My nose scrunches.

"You don't want to seize the day?"

I do. That's why it's awful. Because it's cheesy and pointless and cliché and completely true.

"Not sure how you say seize the dick. I can call Kaylee. Ask her."

"Don't berate the poor girl on my account."

"Guess you're stuck with *carpe diem*."

I barely manage to muster up a laugh.

His brow furrows. He stares at me like I'm crazy. "You sure you're okay?"

"Yeah."

"You've been spacey all day."

"I'm distracted."

"By?"

"Your body. Did your jeans get tighter?"

He laughs, disarmed. "They're new." He moves into the main room.

I follow him. "They look good."

"Yeah."

"Why is it you try to dress like an emo musician?"

"'Cause you like it."

"I do not."

"How about this. I borrow Emma's eyeliner. Put some on. Come back into the room. Check if your panties are drenched."

Desire flames below my belly. Yes. Let's skip all those pretenses and get right to taking our clothes off.

I swallow hard. My body screams for his touch. My head screams *bad idea*. My heart... it's a confused mess.

He looks down at me, his eyes heavy with desire.

This is an invitation.

I can take it.

I should take it.

But I still can't muster up the courage to say yes.

Or maybe I'm being sensible. Protecting my job. And my heart. And my ego.

I don't know anymore.

I try to find the right response. Something flirty. Something that says *yes, I want you*.

But it's too late.

The door is opening.

Someone is stepping inside.

A tall guy with gorgeous blue eyes.

Like Dean's, only deeper. Stiller.

He's familiar. And serious. It's all over his strong posture, his furrowed brow, his half-hearted attempt at a smile.

There's something weighing on this guy.

Something big.

Maybe he's also finding out his fate tomorrow.

Maybe he's as fucked as I am.

Dean turns to the guy. "About time you showed up." He greets the guy with a high-five.

The broody guy nods a hello to Dean. Then to me.

That's familiar too.

But different somehow.

Dean introduces us. "Chloe, you know Hunter."

Oh. Hunter. He went to our high school. Hung out with Dean. Slept with all the pretty cheerleaders. And the band geeks. And the nerds.

He had a reputation for sneaking Jim Beam into parties and spiking the punch at Prom.

And, well, for being... casual with his body.

He was never as easy, breezy as Dean, but he wasn't all quiet and tortured either.

This is... different.

He looks older. Not wrinkled or worn. More battle-scared.

Like he's wiser.

Like his last seven years were as brutal as mine.

And, hey, maybe they were.

Tattooed manwhores go through shit too.

There's something about the hurt in his eyes.

Or maybe that's more his broad shoulders and strong arms.

If things were different, if I was a normal girl with a normal body, if my only concern was getting over my boss...

I wish this was as simple as finding a hot rebound fuck.

Why can't it be that simple?

Dean moves to the desk. Crouches to rifle through a drawer. "Hunter is filling in for Brendon while he's away."

"Oh." Figures my hypothetical rebound also works at Inked Hearts. Not that it matters. Nothing is going to help me get over Dean. Not even the hottest guy in the world.

Dean stands. Places a thin stack of papers on the desk. "You gonna shrug off that chip on your shoulder?"

Hunter meets him there. Half-smiles. "You gonna be serious for five minutes?"

Dean shudders. "Never."

"There's your answer." Hunter's voice is playful, but there's an honesty to it too. He knows he's miserable.

But he's not like Ryan. Well, pre-Leighton Ryan.

He doesn't seem okay with it.

They go through the paperwork quietly. Then Dean backs off to let Hunter read.

The broody tattoo artist—he must be an artist if he's filling in for Brendon—signs on the dotted line.

Dean's eyes flit to me. "You can head home, sunshine."

"But..." I want to stay here. I want to eavesdrop on their conversation. To know what Dean is saying about me. If he's saying anything about me.

Guys talk.

Not the way girls do.

Dean's not about to pour his heart out.

But maybe he'll spill some detail I need.

I can't leave yet.

I can't be home.

I can't face tomorrow.

Dean's blue eyes fix on mine.

"You gonna be okay until then, sunshine?"

Not a chance in hell. But I smile a yes anyway.

Aikido fails to wipe tomorrow from my mind.

It's late enough traffic is clear. But I can't be home yet. I can't sit across from Dad as he asks if I'm ready for tomorrow. I can't listen to that edge in his voice. The one he's trying to hide. The one that screams *I'll fall apart if you aren't okay*.

I pull out my cell. Tap a text message to Gia. But then it's the same with her. If she knows I'm scared, she'll be scared. Then I'll be pissed at her for being scared. For putting her inability to deal with my mortality on me.

This is a routine test. It's probably okay.

She can tell me that.

But if it's not...?

I leave my backpack in my car, slide my cell into my pocket, and find my way to the bar down the street from Inked Hearts.

It's a dozen blocks from the aikido studio, but the walk feels good. Crisp, clear air, big silver moon, salty ocean breeze.

The pounding house music of the bar. It's packed for a weeknight.

"Vodka and orange juice, please." I slide onto a black stool. Take in the utilitarian decorations. It's like someone crossed a dive bar with an industrial music club. It's weird.

The bartender, a busty woman with long hair, nods. "Well or call?"

"Well." Tonight is a cheap vodka kind of night.

She scoops ice into a glass. Adds a heaping serving of vodka and plenty of orange juice and hands it over. "Close it out or keep it open?"

I hand her a twenty. "Make it two."

Her expression gets knowing. It's not quite understanding, but it's not judgmental either.

It's weird.

I ignore her. Take a long sip of my cocktail. It's not good booze. It burns my throat. Warms my chest. Sends my thoughts swimming.

I finish the thing in three long gulps.

Pound the glass on the bar.

It lands with a thud. It feels good. Purposeful.

Someone nods hello. A guy sitting on the other end of the

bar. He's tall. Dark hair. Dark eyes. Business casual outfit. The kind of guy who likes tattooed bad girls.

He probably thinks I'm some kinky alt model.

I nod back anyway. Gia would tell me I'm jumping to conclusions. Maybe the guy likes my eyes. Or my smile. Or my haircut.

Maybe it has nothing to do with my combat boots and tattoos. Maybe he's as desperate for a distraction as I am.

He slides into the seat next to mine. "Can I buy you a drink?"

Right on cue, the bartender drops off my second orange juice and vodka.

I look up at the guy. He's cute. If things were different, if I was a normal girl with a body that responded to cute guys, I'd flirt back. Kiss him. Invite myself to his place.

The glass is cold against my fingers. Then against my lips. I take a long sip. Let the vodka warm me everywhere. "Sure." My face and chest flush. From the drink, not the attraction. But isn't this close enough?

He's here. He wants me. He's not my boss. He doesn't drive me out of my mind. He doesn't grab my heart and refuse to let go.

There's no risk in sleeping with him.

I can get in, come, get out. Dean style. No feelings. No strings. No attachment.

"Give me one second." I set my drink on the bar. Slide out of my stool. Slip between tables full of friends and lovers to make my way to the electronic jukebox.

A dollar per song. It's a crime. But right now, I'm willing to pay to set the mood.

I trade a five for a set. Pick my songs carefully.

Alive by Pearl Jam pours from the speakers as I make my way back to the bar.

But I'm not even thinking about the angsty themes of the song.

I'm imagining Dean chuckling as he tells me that Pearl Jam is a euphemism for semen. Back in eleventh grade, he reveled in my embarrassment at that fun fact.

But now...

It's kind of hilarious.

The guy smiles at me. I'm sure he has a name, but I can't say I care. I guess I'll call him Anti-Dean. With Anti-Dean, my head is screaming *yes* but my body is apathetic.

This might be our last chance to kiss and make up and the damn thing still refuses to obey my wishes.

It's willing to kill me.

I guess attraction to a guy who isn't off limits is too much to ask.

My fingers curl around my drink. I bring it to my lips. Finish it in two gulps.

The guy looks at me curiously. Like I'm an amusement or an easy lay? I don't know.

It doesn't matter.

He fails to interest me.

"I haven't seen you in here," he says.

"Don't usually go to bars." I hail the bartender, but he's already on it.

He smiles at her. "Another round."

This time, the look she shoots me is judgmental. Like there's something wrong with going to a bar to drink your thoughts into oblivion. Where does she think her business comes from?

"What brings you in today?" he asks.

"Looking for a distraction." I press my lips into my best smile. Will my body to get in gear.

The bartender drops off our drinks.

My body remains apathetic.

Anti-Dean presses his palm into my lower back. Leans in to whisper. "Let's talk somewhere more private."

"Sure."

I rest my head on his shoulder.

Close my eyes.

Block out the world.

But that only sends my thoughts straight to Dean.

To his cocky smile and his bright eyes and his soft touch.

I don't want to be here.

I want to be there.

Anti-Dean's hand brushes my hip as he slides into the booth. I take the spot opposite his. Finish my drink as he introduces himself properly and tells me about his job.

I give myself one more round to let reason overwhelm my senses.

To let my body find a way to find Anti-Dean appealing.

I don't.

It doesn't.

The jukebox belts out a peppy pop song. Two college girls squeal as they lock hands and dance. They're wearing matching designer dresses. One is hot pink. The other is red.

They're the kind of women Dean usually takes home.

Only he doesn't.

He hasn't.

He wants me.

Maybe it's the booze talking, but this is seeming like a better and better idea.

I say goodbye to Anti-Dean. Leave a five for the bartender. Slide my second-hand leather jacket over my shoulders.

His address is still in my cell. It's ten blocks away. Far enough for the cool air to temper the heat racing through me. Too close for logic to find a way into my brain.

There.

I walk the concrete path.

Knock.

"One minute." His voice booms from behind the door.

I shift my weight between my heels. I can't wait. I can't give myself any time to think up excuses.

This is my chance.

One night before everything goes to shit.

One night to soak up every ounce of bliss.

Carpe fucking diem.

Footsteps move closer.

The handle turns.

And there's Dean, standing in front of the door in nothing but a towel, completely nonplussed by me crashing his place.

"Wasn't expecting you, sunshine." He motions for me to come in.

I shut the door behind me.

He stares back at me.

All tall and broad and lickable.

I tell my brain to fuck off.

I wrap my arms around his waist.

I rise to my tiptoes.

And I kiss him like the ship is going down.

Chapter Twenty-Two

For a split second, he kisses back.

For a split second, everything in the universe is where it belongs.

Then his hands are on my shoulders.

He's pushing me backward.

Against the door.

It's not *take your clothes off, spread your legs, and wrap your arms around me.*

He's pushing me away.

My eyes blink open. Focus on his.

They're not heavy with desire or excitement or need.

He's pissed.

"Never mind." I go to turn the knob, but his fingers curl around my fist. He grabs me hard.

He stares down at me.

I stare up at him.

What the fuck?

He's been flirting with me for a month straight. He's been teasing me, touching me, straight up telling me he wants me.

And now he's glaring at me because I had the balls to do something about our mutual attraction.

Fuck Dean.

My teeth clench. "Let me go."

"No."

"It wasn't a request."

"Yeah, it was." His eyes bore into mine. "What the hell are you doing?"

"Isn't that obvious?"

"You're drunk, Chloe. You're going to regret this tomorrow."

No. I'm going to celebrate this tomorrow.

Fuck him for telling me what I want.

He has no fucking clue what I want.

This is exactly what I want.

My fingers brush the edge of the towel wrapped around his hips. "You think that little of yourself?"

His eyelids flutter closed.

A groan falls off his lips.

He wants this too.

His fingers wrap around my wrist. "Let's say you tear this towel off, drop to your knees, and suck me off."

My sex clenches. Let's not say anything. Let's do that. Let's do everything.

"What happens tomorrow?"

The awful test happens tomorrow. "The sun rises."

His brow furrows. "You think you can fuck me and everything can stay the same?"

"You managed okay."

"I didn't. And if you don't believe that, then you should go right now."

I bite my lip.

"I'm sorry I hurt you. I am. But that was seven years ago. I was a stupid kid. I know better now. I know there's no way

I can fuck you and leave again."

"I don't want you to leave."

"This will change everything."

"So?" I push off the door. Move closer. Everything changes tomorrow whether I fuck him or not. He doesn't get it, but then, how could he? He doesn't know. "What if everything is supposed to change?"

He releases my wrist. "What if it's not?" His foot sinks into the carpet as he takes a step backward. "I wasn't the kind of guy you needed seven years ago. And I'm not now."

"You don't know what I need."

"Then tell me."

"I did." I stare up at him. "I need you to fuck me."

He moves into the main room. "I'm gonna get dressed."

"Don't."

"The towel isn't gonna help your case," he says.

"What will? What do you want to hear, Dean? That I like you. That I can't stop thinking about you. That you were the best I ever had. I do. You were. That's why I'm here."

"Which part of it?"

"All of it." I take two steps toward him. I'm begging him to fuck me. It's pathetic. But I don't care. I need to think about something else. I need to turn off my brain. To take this last chance to seize the fucking day. Night. Whatever.

His brow furrows. "You felt like this yesterday?"

"Yeah."

"But it took God knows how much vodka to get you here, telling me, today."

"I'm not here because I'm drunk."

"Then why?"

"I want you. It's that simple."

"Bullshit."

I reach for some way to explain it without telling him. Find nothing. "I've been fucking myself to you for the last three weeks straight." My hands go to the bottom of my tank top. "Why does it have to be complicated?"

"Stay there." He moves around the corner. His footsteps pad the hallway as he moves into the bedroom.

The towel hits the floor.

A drawer opens. He changes into something. Moves into the main room in jeans, no shirt, black boxers poking out from the waist band.

"If you're trying to tell me you don't want to fuck me, it isn't working." I brush past him as I move into the main room. Take a seat on the powder blue couch. My eyes find his. They beg for kindness, affection, mercy.

He offers none. "You gonna tell me why you're really here?"

I swallow hard.

"That's what I thought."

"Are you going to tell me why you were so afraid of getting hurt seven years ago? Why you still can't do relationships?"

"All right." He looks down at me. "Truth for truth."

"Only if you go first." I pull my feet onto the cushion. Sit cross legged.

He nods *fair*. "It's not easy to explain."

"You can try."

"All right." His footsteps sink into the carpet as he moves into the kitchen. "But I'm too sober for this conversation."

"I want you sober."

He reaches for a high shelf. Wraps his hand around a bottle of whiskey. "Right back at you, sunshine." He fills a glass and slams half in one gulp.

"Fine, but I—"

"You can have water." He grabs another glass. Fills it with water. Brings it, and the bottle, to the coffee table.

His fingers brush mine as he hands the glass over.

He sits on the couch next to me. His knee against mine. His shoulder touching mine.

I take a greedy sip. Wet my parched throat. Devour the drink in three sips. I'm still thirsty, but I don't want more water. I want him.

His knee rubs mine as he turns to face me. "Who starts?"

"You."

"All right." He drops the glass on the coffee table. He pours a shot's worth of whiskey. "Fuck. I'm too old for this." He wraps his fingers around the glass, brings it to his lips, slams it.

My gaze stays fixed on those soft lips.

His tongue slides over them.

His cheeks and chest flush. "Guess it's pretty simple." He turns to face me. "I don't trust women. Not when it comes to love."

"Why not?"

"It started a long time ago. At one of my parents' parties. I left the kid's room—I was tired of Ryan's music and I was really fucking tired of hearing him talk about Penny. That was before they started dating. When he was sure she wanted nothing to do with him. Our parents are family friends. But I guess that's irrelevant to my point." He runs his hand through his wet hair. "Fuck. Why'd you give me those shots?"

My lips curl into a half smile. "Take some personal responsibility."

"I'd rather blame you."

"What happened at the party?"

He presses his palms into his quads. "Mom's door was open. She was in there. With another guy. A family friend. They were kissing. Groping. I didn't see his dick or anything, but I saw enough."

"Oh."

"She realized I caught her. Freaked. Explained that we

needed to keep this a secret. 'Cause telling Dad would only hurt him. I was fourteen. I got what was happening. Started keeping tabs on her. Even then, I knew it was fucked-up spying on my mom, but I didn't care. I had to know what the fuck it was."

"And?"

"She was in love with him. Wanted to leave my dad for him. But he got cold feet. Made up with his wife. For a while, she was miserable. Then things got better. Seemed like she and Dad were happy."

"Does Ryan know?"

"Maybe. I don't know. We never talked about it."

"You held onto all that?"

"Yeah."

Damn. That's a big secret to carry. Especially at fourteen. Especially as a younger sibling. "That was after he got sick?"

He nods. "I guess the stress pushed them apart."

That happens. But, still. There's no excuse. "Did you hate her for that?"

"Yeah."

"I would too." My hand goes to his thigh.

He looks down at it like he's not sure what he wants to do with it.

Then his eyes are on mine. "What are you doing, Chloe?"

"Why do you keep asking that?"

"You don't want this."

"Yes, I do. I want you."

"As?"

"As everything."

"I don't want to hurt you again."

"What does that mean?"

He sinks into his seat. "You haven't answered my question. Why is it you're here tonight?"

"What happened with your parents?"

"They made up. Lived happily ever after, I guess."

"You never told your dad?"

He shakes his head. "She was right. It would have hurt him. He still loves her more than anything. Why take that away?"

"It's a lie."

"Is it a lie if you believe it?"

"That's kind of deep."

He chuckles. "I guess it is."

"So... ever since that, intimacy issues?"

"You're making light of my trauma?"

"No... well, I'm not trying to. I'm sorry if it feels like that."

"I know."

"You... uh... I'd never do that."

"I know."

"If you know—"

"I *know*, but I don't feel it. I can't."

"I don't trust guys either. Not after the way Alex left things. But I... God, I don't know how it happened, but I do trust you. I don't think you'd abandon me again." I drag my fingers up his thigh.

His eyelids press together.

His lips part with a sigh.

He wants me.

But he holds strong. "Your turn."

"We could not talk." I press my palm against his stomach. Soft skin. Hard muscles. He's still warm and wet from the shower.

His hands go to my hips.

He pulls me into his lap so I'm straddling him.

We're nearly eye to eye like this. I'm just barely looking down at him.

And we're so close.

"Dean..." My fingers curl into his hair. "Please." My eyelids press together. "Please."

"Your turn."

He wants to hear this.

I...

I want to tell him.

But, God, I can't deal with anyone else's grief or fear or concern.

I can't pretend I'm okay.

Not right now.

"You have to promise you won't freak out," I say.

"Can't make that promise, sunshine. Not until I know."

"Then promise you'll try."

He cups my cheek with his palm as he stares up at me. "Promise."

My shoulders relax. I trust him. It's terrifying, but I trust him. "I have a test tomorrow."

His brow scrunches. "What kind of test?"

I take a deep breath and exhale slowly. "A medical test. It might be bad news."

"Bad how?"

"Just bad."

Confusion streaks his expression.

He's going to make me say it.

Or maybe he doesn't see it.

For the last two years, my life has been breast cancer. But that isn't how it is for him. For anyone else. It's not on their radar.

I nod to my chest. "You didn't notice?"

"Notice what?" He follows my gaze.

I shift out of my jacket. Toss it on the ground behind me. Tug my tank top lower. Lower. Until my bra is peeking out.

But he's not getting it.

I go to pull it off but Dean stops me.

"I don't have the self-control to stop if you start."

"I don't want you to stop."

"I want to hear this."

I swallow hard. I want him to hear it.

But...

God.

"Look." I take his hand. Bring it to my chest.

He cups my breast with his palm.

"They're fake."

His brow furrows.

"It's obvious if I take my bra off."

He stares at me like I'm crazy. "You're not the type."

I know.

Epiphany fills his expression.

He understands.

I say it anyways. "I had a double mastectomy."

"You had breast cancer?"

I nod.

"When?"

"Two years ago. That was when it started. It's been a year since I finished treatment. I guess... I guess this is my anniversary."

"That story about your mom?"

"That was true. Just... also true about me."

"Are you okay?"

"Probably. But there's a chance." I swallow hard. "It happens. Even with the preventative treatment."

"Fuck." Something fills his eyes but it's not fear, or pity, or need.

It's sympathy.

"Do me a favor, sunshine. Fill the glass and hand me the bottle."

It takes a bit of maneuvering to do it without climbing out of his lap, but I manage.

He wraps his hands around the bottle.

I hold up the glass. "What are we toasting to?"

"Don't know. Just know we need another round after that."

Chapter Twenty-Three

DEAN

My throat burns. It's wrong drinking good whiskey this fast.

It's a bad idea, drinking at all.

This conversation is too serious for it.

The trust in Chloe's eyes is too intense for it.

My cock's whine is too loud for it.

Fuck, she's a lot braver than I am. Facing that. Telling me. Letting her guard down.

I don't deserve it, but, fuck, I want it so badly.

I want to become the kind of guy who deserves her.

Chloe licks the last drop of whiskey from her glass. Its soft, slick surface glides over my shoulder as she wraps her arms around my neck.

Her crotch rubs against mine as she moves closer.

Her dark eyes fill with nerves. "You aren't saying anything."

"Girl's never told me she had cancer before."

Her laugh breaks up the tension in her brow. "You get around. That's surprising."

"Is it usually considered an aphrodisiac?"

Her long bangs fall in front of her dark eyes as she shakes her head. "Alex left after I told him."

"Asshole."

"Yeah." Her fingers dig into my hair. "He wasn't committed. He would have left sooner or later."

Maybe. But that's not the story she's selling. Hurt seeps into her voice, her jaw, her eyes.

She isn't over her ex leaving.

Not that I blame her—fuck that asshole.

I want to punch his stupid face. To make him hurt as much as she did.

But that isn't gonna do shit to fix this.

She's still going to have the weight of that abandonment on her shoulders.

And I...

My eyes close as her fingertips brush my neck. Inch by inch, she presses her body against mine. First, her pelvis, then her stomach, her chest.

Her cheek brushes mine.

Her hands dig into my hair.

I've wanted a lot of women in my lap, but this is different. I want more than her body.

I want her heart.

I want her soul.

I want her everything.

And here she is, offering it.

It should be perfect. Easy.

Everything inside me is begging me to reach out and take her.

Everything but the one shred of decency buried deep.

I can't grab her unless I'm sure I won't let go.

I can't fail her like everyone else has.

Somehow, I knew that seven years ago.

But now? Now that she's laying herself bare for me...

"Dean." She drags her fingertips over my jawline. "Please say something."

"I'm sorry."

Her eyes turn down. "Oh."

"No." I drop the bottle on the couch. Reach up and rest my palm on her cheek.

Her eyelids press together. She turns her head to one side, leaning into my touch. Soaking up the affection in it.

"I'm sorry you went through that, sunshine."

She just barely nods.

"I want to fuck you. I'm going out of my mind over how badly I want to fuck you."

"It's not a boner killer?"

I can't help but laugh. "Is that the normal reaction?"

"I've only ever told Alex." Her tongue slides over her lips. "Does it change the way you think of me?"

"Yeah."

"Oh." Her chest slumps with her exhale.

"Not like that, sunshine. I want you just as badly. More."

"More?" Her eyelids blink open. Her dark eyes fix on mine. "Why?"

"'Cause you're letting me in."

"Is that what you want?"

"Yeah."

"You don't sound happy about it."

'Cause I'm terrified. "This is uncharted territory for me."

"Me too." She runs her fingertips over my jawline. "I need you to kiss me now."

Fuck, I need to kiss her now.

My free hand goes to the space between her shoulder blades. I pull her closer. Until every inch of her is pressed against every inch of me.

I kiss her softly.

Then harder.

Her need pours into me.

My need pours into her.

It's overwhelming.

How the hell do you let yourself need someone?

Trust them to be there?

Trust yourself to be there for them?

For the last decade, I've kept women at a distance. I've convinced the entire world I don't give a shit about anything.

Hell, I convince myself most of the time.

But Chloe...

My fingers dig into her soft skin.

My tongue dances with hers.

Her groan vibrates down my throat.

I need more of that groan.

I need her coming on my face.

She pulls back with a heavy sigh. "You're good at that."

My cheeks flush. It's weird feeling shy. I've fucked more women than I can remember. But this? Kissing someone I care about—

Not sure I've ever done that.

Not with anyone else.

"Oh." Her lips curl into a half smile. "That isn't how I thought I'd get you blushing."

"Me either."

"You're scared?"

"Not exactly."

"Then what?" Her voice is soft. Sweet. Understanding.

After all the shit I give her, she still sees the good in me. She still wants to dig past the guy I convince everyone else I am.

I have no idea what the hell I've done to deserve her.

My thumb rubs her temple. It's impulse. It must be right, because it's making her lips part with a soft sigh. "I could never be casual with you."

"But before—"

"Was before. I was a stupid kid. Now... I'm still an idiot half the time, but I've got a bit of sense."

"What does that mean?"

I want to be the guy she can lean on. Fuck, I want it so badly I can taste it.

But can I trust myself?

That, I don't know.

My hands go to her shoulders. I don't push her away or pull her closer. I keep her exactly where she is. "I want to fuck you, Chloe. I want to bury myself in you. But not tonight. Not because you're drunk and scared."

"It's not because of that."

"But you are."

"A little."

"I want to erase every ugly thought in your head. I do. But not like this. If you still want this tomorrow, come over after your test. I'll fuck your brains out."

My stomach flip-flops.

My hands shake.

My toes go numb.

I've done a lot of crazy shit in my life, but this is the first time I've been this fucking terrified.

"You... you want to be with me?" she asks.

"It's never been a question of whether or not I wanted to be with you."

"Really?"

"Yeah."

She leans in. Presses her lips to mine. It starts soft. Then it's harder.

The warm affection fades into a hungry heat.

Her tongue slips into my mouth.

Her fingers dig into my skin.

My body roars awake. My heart thuds. My lungs strain. My cock stirs.

"Oh." She pulls back with a heavy sigh. Her cheeks flush. Her tongue slides over her lips. "It's been a long time since I've made anyone hard."

I shake my head. "You have no idea how many times I've fucked myself thinking of you."

"How many times?"

"Too many to count."

Her fingers dig into my neck. "You're a tease. Do you realize that?"

"Yeah."

"It's cruel."

"That's me."

"Dean I... I understand what you're saying. Why you want to wait. But I can't. Everything might be wrong tomorrow."

"Even so."

"No." Her hair falls in front of her eyes as she shakes her head. When she blinks, a tear catches on her lashes. "What if I'm sick again?"

I have no fucking idea how to answer that, so I pull her closer.

Hold her tighter.

"When it first happened, I was in shock. Then I got angry. At the universe. At my parents. At everyone who didn't have to deal with cancer at twenty-two. But, mostly, I was angry with my body. It betrayed me. I know It sounds ridiculous."

"It doesn't."

"Really?"

I nod. I can't imagine how I'd feel if I were in her shoes. There's no way I'd handle it with half the grace.

"My body and I... we aren't friends. Friendly, sometimes. But not friends. I can feel it in everything I do. I'm not as good at aikido, I'm a slower swimmer, I don't notice when I'm hungry. I drink too much tea and get too little sleep. And I... well, up until a few weeks ago I'd given up on trusting my body enough to want someone."

"You didn't want anyone?"

"No. I did. But only in an intellectual way. And that meant I stayed in my head. I kept thinking of the way Alex looked at me like I was broken and unlovable. Of how strange my—" She looks down at her chest. "It's weird. Having fake boobs."

"Nobody's ever—"

"Never."

Fuck, that's an invitation if I've ever heard one.

But I meant what I told her earlier. I don't have the self-control to stop if I start.

Fuck. I barely have the self-control to keep my hands to myself at the moment.

I can't let her know that.

I'm sober and I'm not facing a life changing test tomorrow.

I've been the responsible one before—fuck knows I've dragged Leighton's and Walker's drunk asses home a million times—but it's never felt like this much of a responsibility.

"It means the world to me that you're telling me this, sunshine." I run my fingers through her hair. "But I still can't fuck you."

"You *can*." She sinks into my lap. "You're still hard."

"Well aware of that."

Her smile is sad, but it still lights up her eyes. "Is there a line?"

"A line?"

"You've kissed me twice now. So that's in."

"Are we negotiating?"

"If that isn't too pathetic."

"You're scared. It's brave, admitting that. Facing it."

Her laugh is happier, but just barely. "I'm not facing it. That's why I'm begging you."

"When's your test?"

"Eleven."

"Someone coming with you?"

"No. It's routine. Not a big deal." Her words are rote, like she's reading off a piece of paper. "I should be fine. Odds are good. Better than good. Ninety-five percent chance. More even."

"You're allowed to be scared about unlikely things."

"Maybe. It feels like... I didn't ask Dad or Gia to come because I knew how that would go. I knew they'd keep reciting the party line. *It's going to be fine. You'll be fine. Odds of developing breast cancer after a double mastectomy are almost nothing.* And then... I don't know."

"You want to tell them to fuck off."

"Kinda, yeah." She laughs. "But I know they're trying to help."

"They want to help."

She nods.

"Maybe you need to let them know how."

"Maybe." She stares back into my eyes. "You're smarter than you let on."

"Wiser maybe. But not smarter."

"Both."

"I..." I bite my tongue. Hesitation isn't me. But this... fuck, this might be the most I've ever asked of anyone. Or the most I've ever offered of myself. "I want to come with you tomorrow."

Surprise streaks her expression. "You do?"

"Yeah."

"You'll mostly sit in the waiting room."

"I don't care."

"I..."

"You can tell me to fuck off if you want."

"No... I... you have to promise you won't mention the odds."

My lips curl into a smile.

"What?"

"I knew you had a thing for scoundrels."

Her brow knits with confusion.

"That's Han Solo's famous line."

"Oh. Yeah. But his is about how he doesn't want to hear bad odds."

"Still."

"I guess I do have a thing for scoundrels." She runs her fingers through my hair. "Since I'm here begging you to fuck me."

"Sweet talk isn't going to get you anywhere."

Her laugh is hearty. Full. "How about taking off my clothes?"

"That will probably work." I bring my hands to her waist. Pull her a little closer. "If I'm being honest."

"I knew that." She looks down at me. "If I'm being honest."

This time, I laugh. "You think you know me so well."

"Sometimes. Other times... I'm not as sure. But I want to."

"I want you to."

"Where does that leave us?"

"You didn't respond to my offer."

"Oh." She presses her lips together. "The hospital is by my place. In the valley."

"I figured."

"Can, um... can we have sex after?"

"You'll have to drag me away."

She smiles like a kid on Christmas morning. "Yeah?"

"Fuck yeah." Fuck me. The thought of unwrapping Chloe isn't doing shit to get blood back to my brain.

"I... I don't know how to say this, Dean, but it killed me when Alex left. Not because I loved him. I did. But what hurt more was how wrong I was about him. I thought he loved me too. I thought he was the kind of guy who really wanted to be with me through sickness and through health. I can't go through that again."

I nod.

"So, yes, I want you to come tomorrow. But only if you're sure you're going to stick around if the prognosis is bad. Only if you're sure you can handle it."

"I get that."

"So... I mean, you don't have to answer now. You can think about it. Sleep on it. But if you want to come, I need to know. And I get it if you aren't in. If you're not ready to take that on. It's... it's not what I'd expect from you."

Me either.

"Watching my mom die was the worst thing I ever felt. Worse than worrying I might die. Worse than the looks Gia and Dad gave me every three seconds. Worse than forgetting how to want someone."

It's a fair question.

I'm not sure it's one I can answer. Not honestly. Not without really *knowing* what it means to love someone who might be dying.

Even if the odds are good.

Even if the odds are negligible.

Can I honestly promise her that?

I have to be sure.

"Come here." I wrap my arms around her and I kiss her hard and deep.

I let every feeling in my body rise to the surface.

Every place I ignore. Every thing I hide. Every ugly corner.

She holds onto me like I'm a life raft.

It's what she's asking.

This is a huge responsibility.

I have to treat it like one.

"Well?" Her fingers dig into my chest. Her eyes go saucer wide. They bore into mine. Beg for every bit of affection in the world. "Did that help you figure it out?"

Chapter Twenty-Four

DEAN

Every molecule of my body screams the same thing.

Somehow, I know this deep in my bones.

I press my palm into Chloe's lower back to pull her closer. "I'm sure."

"But what if I'm sick?"

"I'm still sure."

She stares back at me, assessing my words, looking for cracks.

After what she's been through, I don't blame her.

Hell, after the way I've treated her, I don't blame her.

I don't have a way to convince her.

Talk is cheap.

Sticking around every day is what counts.

But I can't do shit about that at the moment.

"What if I'm dying?" she asks. "What if we only get a year to be together then you have to watch me disappear?"

"Sounds like *A Walk to Remember*."

Her laugh erases the tension in her expression. "The Nicholas Sparks book?"

"Book? Please. I've only seen the excellent film. Starring certified hottie Mandy Moore."

"Is she a certified hottie?"

"Yeah. But she's no Chloe."

Her lips curl into a smile. "What if we're a Nicholas Sparks movie?"

"Guy in the movie seemed happy."

"So, you're basing your life decisions on a sappy romance writer?"

"I'm not gonna pretend I understand what it means to fall in love with someone with an expiration date. But I can't imagine a universe where I don't want to protect you."

"Is that what you've been doing?"

I nod.

"I guess you have. In your way."

"Exactly."

"It's not your strong suit."

"I know."

She leans in to brush her lips to mine. "How can you be so sure?"

"Nobody has ever made me feel the way you do."

"Ever?"

I nod. "You look at me like I'm worth your time. Like you see this guy who can be better. When I see that in your eyes, I want it. I want to be better. I want to earn your respect. Your trust. Your love."

"Dean..." She drags her fingertips down my neck. "You can't tell me I make you want to be a better person and keep to this no sex thing."

"I can't?"

She nods. "It's cruel."

"I thought we agreed I'm cruel."

"But you want to be a better person."

"A better guy would fuck you when you're drunk and vulnerable?"

"Semantics." She squeezes me with her thighs as she leans closer. Her lips brush mine. It's soft. Sweet. *I need you* not *I need your cock inside me.*

She tastes good. Like whiskey and like Chloe.

But that doesn't add credence to her claim of sobriety.

I pull back with a heavy sigh. "You play dirty."

"Sometimes you have to. To get what you want. You're the one who taught me that."

"Too smart for my own good."

"You are." She smiles as she shifts her hips away from mine. "You never told me where the line is."

If she kisses me one more time, I'm going to throw away the fucking line. "My self-control isn't getting better the more you sit in my lap."

"Mine either." She slides off me with a heavy sigh. "I just want to state, for the record, that this is entrapment."

"Is it?"

"Yeah." She takes a seat next to me and rests her head on my shoulder. "You insisted we toast then said I was too drunk."

"Fuck. I'm evil. It's not like you were angling for more booze."

"Not at all."

"I talked you into that."

"Yeah." She drags her fingertips over my leg like she's doodling on a piece of paper. "I was stone-cold sober before that too."

"Uh-huh."

"Glad we agree." Her laugh bounces around the room. It fills me with this deep, pure warmth. One I don't recognize. One I want more of. "So, um... I'm pretty sure I'm going to start taking off my clothes if we sit here talking."

"Are you?"

"Yeah. And I... I do get your point. You're wrong that I'll regret this. That I'm only asking because I'm vulnerable. And, quite frankly, I can't comprehend the reality that Dean Maddox is suggesting we wait to have sex."

"Me either."

"But then... I do see it. The guy you really are." Her dark eyes fill with affection as she looks up at me. "He's merciful enough to distract me."

"Is he?"

"Not like that." Her cheeks flush. "But somehow. And he needs to. Or I'm going to take my clothes off. And we all know how that will end."

Fuck, I can't believe I'm turning her down.

It goes against twenty-five years of instincts.

But it's the right call.

"How do you suggest I distract you?" I ask.

"I pitched one idea." She laughs. "I think that means it's your turn."

∾

AFTER TAKEOUT THAI, I PUT ON ONE OF CHLOE'S OLD favorites. *Bringing Up Baby*. There's a poster in her room—I caught a glimpse in one of her banana selfies.

She settles into the couch with a ceramic plate in her lap and her eyes on the screen. Somehow, she manages to eat without taking her eyes off the TV or spilling a drop.

She's practiced at this.

Not that I can talk. When I'm not out, picking up women, or drinking with my friends, I'm here.

There's something intimate about sharing a meal.

It's domestic.

Like we're playing house.

We finish dinner halfway through the movie.

I take our shit to the kitchen. Clean up.

She stays transfixed on the screen until I move back onto the couch.

All her attention turns to me. "You never put a shirt on."

"It's hot."

She laughs. "It's really not."

I shrug, coy.

"You get off on this cruelty, don't you?"

Not usually. Usually, I'm not into teasing. But with Chloe? Fuck. That's a whole different ball game.

"Why did I say get off?"

"You like torturing yourself."

"I must if I'm here." She looks up at me with hunger in her eyes.

But she doesn't push it.

Her hands go to my waist.

Her fingers dig into my skin as she pulls my body toward hers.

I suck on her bottom lip.

Fuck, her groans are music. Poetry. Everything.

Pulling back is torture.

She sighs as she settles into her seat.

Rests her head on my shoulder like she isn't dying to tear my clothes off.

I hold her close like I'm not dying to tear hers off.

We make it through the rest of the movie. Then the first half of the next—she picks *His Girl Friday*. Falls asleep an hour in.

She melts into me.

Usually, my skin crawls when a girl falls asleep on top of me. It's an intimacy I don't want.

It's still fucking terrifying.

But it feels good. Right.

I run my fingers through her hair. Watch her chest rise and fall with her exhale. Watch her lips part with a sigh.

Chloe stirs as I wrap my arms around her and carry her to the bedroom.

Her hand slides around the back of my neck.

Her head rests on my chest.

She murmurs something into my skin. I have no idea what it is. Only that I want more of that soft, needy tone.

I lay her on the blue sheets.

Her eyes blink open. Fix on mine.

She smiles a wide, nervous smile. The same one she gave me all those years ago.

I sit next to her. Pull the comforter to her chest.

"Good night." I press my lips to her forehead.

She lets out a soft sigh. "Good night."

It's agony tearing myself away, but I manage it.

I move into the main room. Pour a glass of water. Channel surf.

Nothing is as interesting as the thought of Chloe in my bed. But this spy thriller TV show is entertaining enough.

As the first episode ends, footsteps move across the hallway. The bathroom door opens. The water runs.

I start the next episode. The title splashes over the screen in big black letters.

The water turns off.

Her footsteps move closer.

"Dean?" Her fingers skim the wall as she moves into the main room. "Will you sleep with me?"

My cock stirs.

"Not sex." She tugs at her tank top, trying and failing to cover her black panties. The same ones from her picture—from every masturbatory fantasy I've had since—cotton bikinis with cream lace trim. "I know you want to wait. I just... I want you to hold me. I can't sleep. I keep thinking about it."

I can't say no to that. "Give me five minutes to brush my teeth."

"Okay." She turns and moves into the kitchen, hips swaying as she walks.

Fuck, she has a nice ass.

I try to pry my eyes away, but they won't go. My body is already roaring. It's already begging to get between her legs.

She fills a glass with water and brings it to her lips.

I move into the bathroom. Try to get my thoughts from the gutter as I brush my teeth and wash up.

Fail.

I stay put as I listen to her move into the bedroom.

She leaves the door wide open.

Yellow light floods the dark room. It casts highlights off her nose, the edge of her shoulder, those strong legs.

For someone barely five feet tall, she has long legs.

I want them wrapped around my waist.

Pressed against my cheeks.

Fighting my hands.

Fuck. For the first time in my entire life, I wish I'd done more to cultivate restraint.

How the hell does this work?

I step into the room and out of my jeans.

Chloe gives me a long, slow once over. Desire spreads over her expression as she pats the spot next to her.

I pull the door closed and climb under the covers.

She nestles into me. Rests her back against my chest, her ass against my crotch, her head in the space between my chin and shoulder.

I wrap my arm around her.

Intertwine my fingers with hers.

She's so close.

I can feel her heartbeat.

Her inhale.

Her exhale.

She squeezes my fingers. "I'm probably going to keep you up all night."

She's right about that.

"I keep thinking about the test. Worrying it's going to be like last time. Everyone told me it would be fine. That it was just a precaution. That I was too young." She melts into my chest.

"That must have been terrifying."

"It was. But it was more dread than fear. I knew what was waiting for me. I watched my mom fight. That's what everyone called it. The entire time, up until the end, she was fighting. But she was losing. The chemo took everything from her. I didn't want to go through that."

"Did you?"

Her nod is soft. "I did a short treatment. But it was enough... Do you know how it works?"

"Not exactly."

"It's poison. And it feels like it. It's killing you, only it's killing the cancer cells faster. It was awful. I wasn't sure if I wanted to live or die."

"Fuck." I run my fingers through her hair. "I'm sorry."

"I try not to think about it. I don't know if I could do it again."

The odds are nearly nothing that she's sick.

But it's not what she needs to hear. "Then don't."

"But I'd be accepting it."

"If you're sick, you're sick whether you accept it or not. It's your life. It's your body. It's your decision."

"Maybe. I don't know if I could do that to Dad and Gia. Or you even."

"Don't worry about me."

"I'm not. I'm just thinking."

"About."

"There are so many things I gave up on after my diagnosis. But I can have a lot of them. I just don't."

"What do you want?"

"Well..." She lets out a soft laugh. "I'm not trying to get in your pants. I swear."

"You're gonna hurt my feelings, sunshine."

Her laugh spreads over her chest and stomach. She shakes against me. Squeezes my hand. "You overuse that line."

"'Cause you keep bruising my ego."

She turns so we're face-to-face. "I want to feel at home in my body." Her fingers curl around my wrist. "Like it's capable of making me feel good." Her eyes bore into mine. "I used to. God." Her cheeks flush. "I used to love when guys would play with my chest. But now... what if I don't like it anymore? What if I can't feel anything?"

"You've never tried."

"Only on my own. But it's not the same. It's not enough."

Fuck, I want to give her that.

I want to give her everything.

My fingers skim her cheek.

Her eyelids press together.

Her lips part with a sigh. "Dean..."

My hands move of their own accord.

I trace a line over her chin. Down her neck. Along her collarbones.

Her voice is soft. Needy. "Don't tease me. Please."

She arches her back, pressing her chest against mine.

I bring one hand to the small of her back. Hold her close as I kiss her.

Her leg hooks around my thigh.

Her fingers curl into my wrist.

She breaks our kiss with a heavy sigh. "Please." Her chest

heaves with her inhale. "I have to know if I can still feel good."

Fuck, I'm being a fool.

This is what she needs.

I peel her tank top up her stomach. Over her chest. Her head.

I toss it on the bed behind me.

She looks up at me with nervous eyes. "No one has ever..." Her cheeks flush. "Do they... Are they..."

"Fucking amazing." I bring my lips to hers. Kiss her hard and deep.

She rocks her hips against mine.

Groans as her pelvis brushes my hard-on.

Fuck, that feels good.

My hand goes to the waist of her panties. I drag my fingertips up her stomach.

Her breath hitches as I bring my hand to her chest. "Dean?"

"Yeah?" My voice is heavy with need. Fuck, I can't remember the last time I wanted someone this badly.

No.

I've never wanted someone this badly.

Her hips rock against mine. "I... please."

I press my lips to hers as I drag my thumb over her nipple.

She groans against my lips.

Her palm goes flat against my stomach.

Her fingers dig into my skin as I rub her with my thumb.

I do it again and again.

I do it until she breaks our kiss with a sigh.

"Fuck." She looks up at me, her eyes wide with a mix of relief and desire. "That—"

I draw circles around her nipple with my thumb.

"Fuck." Her eyelids press together. "Don't stop."

Like hell.

I watch pleasure spread over her expression as I rub her harder.

Harder.

There.

"Dean." Her nails dig into my skin. "God."

Fuck, she's beautiful wracked with pleasure.

I toy with her nipple with my thumb. Harder. Softer. Slower. Faster. Circles. Zigzags. Up. Down. Left. Right.

I play with her every way I can, then I move to my index finger and I do it again.

Chloe tilts her head toward the bed. She bites her lip. Squirms under my touch.

She's wound up.

Ready.

But, well, I can't exactly live up to that *no teasing* request.

I kiss her hard as I toy with her.

Her tongue slides into my mouth. She kisses back, aggressive and hungry.

Her need pours into me.

Her groans vibrate down my chest.

Her fingers tug at my boxers.

Right now, she isn't thinking about her test. Or her future. Or tomorrow.

Right now, I'm the only thing in her universe.

And, fuck, the thrill of that—

I drag my lips over her chin.

She writhes under me as I kiss my way down her neck.

Over her chest.

I take her nipple into my mouth and suck softly.

I tease her every way I can.

Soft flicks of my tongue. Hard ones. Long ones. Circles.

I suck softly.

Then harder.

Then hard enough her groans echo around the room.

Her hand finds my shoulder. She claws at my skin like it's the only way she can express exactly how pent up she is.

"Dean." Her hips rock against my stomach. "Fuck me. Please."

I drag my lips over her chest. Take her other nipple into my mouth. Tease it just as mercilessly.

Her shoulders relax as a sigh falls off her lips.

Relief spreads over her expression.

But it's short lived. A few more flicks of my tongue, and she's clawing at me again.

Her expression is pure *make me come, now*.

My cock whines. It wants inside her. It wants every sweet, soft inch of her.

Soon.

Very fucking soon.

I bring my hands to her hips as I suck on her nipple.

There. I push her panties off her right hip. The left.

She arches her back. Shimmies out of her panties. Kicks them off the bed.

Chloe is naked under me.

And, fuck, it really is everything.

I toy with her until my name is a curse on her lips. Until her moan is more whine than pleasure.

Then I drag my lips down her stomach.

My fingers curl into her thighs. I pry them apart. Pin her to the bed.

"Fuck." Her hand finds my hair. "Dean. Please."

Fuck yes. I plant between her legs.

Nip at her inner thigh until she's panting.

Move to her other leg and do it again.

She tugs at my hair. Rocks her hips. Begs for more with her groans.

I hold her in place as I lick her up and down. I do it softly. Slowly. So I can savor the taste of her.

Fuck, the way she writhes against me—

It's magic.

I drag my fingertips up her stomach. Over her breast. Around her nipple.

I toy with her tender bud as I lick her up and down.

Again and again.

Until her nails are digging into my skin hard enough to draw blood.

Enough teasing.

I need her coming on my face.

I plant a soft, slow lick on her clit.

Her toes curl.

I try faster. Harder. Up. Down. Right. Left. Every fucking combination until I get it.

There.

A gasp falls off her lips.

One hand tugs at my hair. The other claws at my shoulder. "Dean..."

"Louder."

She groans my name again. She groans my name like it's her favorite thing in the whole fucking universe.

I lick her just how she needs me.

Toy with her just how she needs me.

Her brow knits. Her eyelids press together. Her hand knots in my hair.

She's there. At the edge.

A few more flicks of my tongue, and she tumbles over it. She pulses against my lips, groaning my name as she comes.

I hold her in place. Suck on the soft skin of her inner thigh for just long enough for her to catch her breath.

Then I bring my mouth back to her.

No teasing this time.

I wind her up.

Pleasure spills over her expression.

She comes fast and hard, bucking against my lips, clawing at my skin, groaning my name again and again.

I plant a soft kiss on her thigh. Her stomach. Her chest.

Her lips.

She looks up at me with heavy lids. "That... You..."

I wrap my arms around her.

"Fuck." She melts into my touch. "You're..." Her voice gets soft. Sincere. "Fuck."

I pull her closer.

Slowly, she falls asleep in my arms.

Chapter Twenty-Five

CHLOE

Morning light falls over the blue sheets and the navy comforter. I roll away from the window, press my eyelids together, soak in the feeling of the sun on my back.

Slowly, I stretch my arms over my head. Shake my legs. Wiggle my toes. There's this bliss in my bones, this satisfaction I haven't felt in a long, long time.

Last night...

God.

Memories threaten to derail the day's plans. They promise to keep me in a happy world filled with pleasure and connection and love. They promise to lock out ugly realities.

I want to stay there.

I want to buy a fucking house there.

But I only have...

Shit, how much time do I have?

I throw the comforter off. Slip out of bed. There. My backpack is sitting on top of my jeans. Phone in the front pocket.

The screen displays a sassy text from Dad (I swear, he's more older sister than Gia sometimes).

Dad: Staying with a friend, huh? Wonder if his name rhymes with bean.

He could at least pretend he's bothered by the thought of me hooking up with an inked sex god.

I find my spare pair of panties (I keep it around for period mishaps, but this is a much more fun use) and slide them on. Then my jeans. Bra. Tank top. Socks. Boots.

My clothes are scattered around the room. Collecting them is like living last night in reverse.

It's a head trip.

It's too much for nine o'clock. I have two hours until that test. I have two hours to feel like a normal person. To be a girl gushing over great sex. Over the thrill of falling in... well, I think a part of me has loved Dean since high school. But now... I don't know.

There are too many feelings whirling around my brain.

I move into the bathroom. Brush my teeth, wash my face, run a comb through my hair. This is where short hair excels. No fuss.

My reflection stares back at me with messy raccoon eyes and dark circles, but there's no denying the satisfaction in her expression.

A little makeup remover and a fresh coat of eyeliner and mascara fix the raccoon situation. The makeup looks good, but it feels unnecessary. I don't need a shield right now. I don't need my defenses up.

I can trust Dean.

The thought bounces around my head as I move into the main room.

Dean's standing at the stove in nothing but his black boxers. "You eat eggs?"

Fuck, he wears those boxers. The waistband is slung low

around his hips. The fabric clings to his tight ass and his strong legs. His entire back is on display.

My eyes trace the tattoo running over his shoulder. An abstract, geometric design with a modern flair. Classic. Bold. Pure Dean.

"Do I what?" My gaze goes back to his ass. Perfect doesn't begin to describe it. He's on a whole other level of hotness.

He lets out a hearty chuckle as he flips whatever is in the pan. "Do you eat eggs?"

"Yeah." I move into the kitchen. Until I'm two feet from him. "Most vegetarians do."

"Still gonna ask."

"Thanks." My stomach grumbles as the smell of said eggs wafts into my nostrils. "Tea?"

He motions to two mugs sitting on the dining table. A container of honey and a spoon sit between them. "Earl Grey."

"I drink other things."

"No shame in knowing what you like." He flips the eggs. Turns to me. Gives me a long, slow once over. "Was hoping you'd come out here naked."

"I thought about it."

"Damn, where did I go wrong?"

"It was when you insisted you wouldn't fuck me until after the test."

He shakes his head with mock regret. "It's the little things, isn't it?"

"Yeah." I can't help but laugh. He's just so... Dean.

"Sit down. I'll bring you breakfast."

I do. I watch him cook as I stir honey into my tea. He's focused. Intent. Careful. That other Dean, the one that cares about things.

No. That is Dean. He's both guys—the one who has to crack a joke and the one who perfects his tattoo mock-ups.

He turns the stove off, scoops eggs onto ceramic plates, and brings them to the table.

He slides into the seat next to mine and hands over a fork.

"Thanks." I groan through my first bite. "These are amazing." Fresh, soft eggs with tender tomatoes, sharp green onions, and tangy cheddar.

"Sure thing." He wraps his hands around his mug and takes a long sip. "How's your head?"

"Okay. I drank a lot of water last night." My eyes go to the clock. Nine ten now. That still leaves a lot of time to feel normal. I don't want to leave that yet. "How about you?"

"That was nothing for me."

"You are—"

"If you're gonna guess my weight again—"

"I was going to say experienced."

He chuckles. "True."

"With drinking."

"Still true." He scoops eggs with his fork. "Fuck. I usually chow down on bacon when I have a hangover."

"That sounds like you."

"Do you ever get tempted to eat meat?"

"When I first started, yeah. But after a while, meat seemed gross to me. After fifteen years, the smell of it makes my stomach turn."

"Fuck. That's dedication. I don't think I've believed in anything for fifteen years."

"What about lust for pussy?"

He laughs so hard he drops his fork. His hand goes to his stomach. He holds onto it like he's about to bust a stitch. "Lust for pussy?"

"What would you call it?"

"Lust for pussy is perfect." He wipes a tear of joy from his eye. "Fuck, Chloe. You... you're perfect."

"It's the boots." I show off said boots. "You can admit it."

"You can admit sandals are more comfortable."

They are comfortable. But—"They aren't me."

"You gonna wear combat boots to your wedding?"

"I don't know. Are you proposing?"

His eyes light up as his smile spreads over his cheeks. "You shouldn't dare me like that, sunshine. I'll do it just because."

I have no doubt Dean would marry someone on a whim. But not just to win a game of chicken. Because there's this lonely part of him hiding behind the cocky front.

He craves connection as much as I do.

"Who says that isn't exactly what I want?" I tease back.

"It's only four hours to Vegas."

"Don't I know it."

His laugh bounces around the room. "Don't you know it?"

I nod.

"You're hitting Vegas on the regular?"

"Is that really so implausible?" I take a long sip of my tea. Let out a soft moan. God, that's good. Bergamot really is a wonderful thing.

"I can't think of much that's less plausible than you at the Vegas clubs, getting wasted, bringing home some boy toy."

"That's because I'm all about roulette."

"Put it all on black?"

I wave my hand over my tank top and black jeans. "Of course."

He leans back in his chair with a knowing smile. "No fucking way."

"I have been to Vegas."

"And?"

"Well..."

"You hated it?"

"Only almost everything about it." I laugh. "Just that."

"It's not your kind of place."

"Yours?"

He shrugs. "It's was a thrill when I turned twenty-one. But the whole bar, club, hookup thing got old fast."

"You should have been putting it all on red."

"Maybe that was my problem."

I scoop another bite of my eggs. Chew. Swallow. In the light, the sparseness of Dean's apartment is more obvious. The bare walls and empty shelves are lonely. "How long have you been getting tired of your routine?"

"Awhile. But I didn't realize it until I saw you again."

"I mean that much to you?"

"I didn't think so, but yeah. You're the only woman I've ever trusted."

"You trust me?"

"Yeah."

"Even with everything with your mom?"

"I'm not gonna pretend that isn't in the back of my mind somewhere, but, yeah, I do."

"Oh." My cheeks flush. Somehow, this is more intimate than anything he's told me. It shouldn't be news—last night, he promised he'd stick around no matter what—but it is. I reach for the proper response. Find nothing. "These eggs are really good."

"Thanks."

"I didn't realize you cooked."

"I don't. I know a few things."

"So, I can cook?"

"Can?" He aches a brow. "Please. Take it off my hands. Unless you want to eat grilled cheese every night you're over here."

I stifle a laugh. "Is that really it?"

"Mac and cheese, too."

My lips spread into a smile.

"Spaghetti with broccoli and frozen meatballs. I can do that. Get veggie meatballs for you or leave them off."

"It sounds like your specialty."

He laughs. "It's... edible."

"High praise."

"I mostly do takeout."

"But you..." My eyes go to his bare torso. "You're super cut."

"And?"

"You don't get that cut eating mac and cheese."

He laughs. "I can cook chicken breast and broccoli too."

"Do you think... can I cook tonight if we come back here?"

"Sunshine, if we come back here I'm not gonna give you time to breathe much less cook."

~

THE SECOND I SLIDE INTO MY CAR, THE WALL BETWEEN now and later falls.

The test is the only thing on my mind.

I turn the key, press the brake pedal, bring the car into reverse. Try to focus all my attention on pulling out of this space.

Parallel parking is the worst.

No. I can't sell that to myself. Life changing tests are a hell of a lot worse than parallel parking. Especially when they're supposed to be normal and routine.

We need to do a scan every year for five years. Just in case your cancer is back. No biggie.

I guess it's no biggie for an oncologist. They eat, breathe, sleep cancer. As awful as that is.

"What did you do about your appointments?" I pull onto tenth. Head toward the freeway.

"Rescheduled them."

"You didn't have to."

"Yeah, I did."

"What did you tell your clients?"

"That I was fucking my apprentice and we needed to work some shit out or we'd be too distracted."

My cheeks flush. He's kidding, but, God, the thought of our eleven o'clock staring at us dumbstruck, whispering *so is she as kinky as she looks or what?*

He is kidding.

Right?

He looks to me with a laugh. "You're so fucking cute when you blush."

"I am not."

"Yeah, you are." He takes my free hand. Intertwines my fingers with his. "I'm gonna have to keep saying stupid shit."

"Do you ever stop?"

"I think it happened once."

My laugh breaks up the tension in my shoulders, but it's short lived. By the time I turn onto the freeway, it's back.

Dean is good at distracting me, but there's nothing distracting enough to block this from my mind.

It's a routine test.

It's going to be okay.

It's not a big deal.

I repeat the words over and over, but they do nothing to make it to my brain.

Still. I need to focus enough to drive to the damn hospital. It would be the worst kind of irony if I died in a car crash on the way to a test that's going to tell me I'm perfectly healthy.

I don't believe in much, not anymore, but I do believe in the universe's love of irony.

"You are kidding, right?" I ask.

"What do you think?"

"I'm never sure with you."

"Yeah. I told them I have a cold. That I don't want to spread it."

"Oh."

"I can call back and confess the truth."

"No. I don't want anyone to know—"

"That we're fucking?"

"That I was ever sick. People look at me differently. With pity in their eyes."

"I can see that."

"I hate it." Traffic is light. Blue sky and two-story houses whiz by the windows. Picture perfect Southern California. "I hate when people tell me I must be so strong or brave to make it through that. Like it's a character fault to have a terminal illness. My mom was strong. I wasn't. I was lucky."

"Not sure I agree with that, sunshine."

"Huh?" My eyes go to him. There's pride in his expression. It's weird, but not bad. Not even a little bad.

"It takes strength to get through that."

"Maybe."

"And it was fucking brave, telling me."

My eyes go back to the road. "I told you because I was scared. Not in spite of it."

"You have a higher opinion of me than I do."

"Maybe." The tall buildings of Century City whiz by the windows. Glass and steel against the blue sky. "You haven't looked at me with pity once."

"I don't pity you."

"I know." My fingers curl into the steering wheel. "That may not mean a lot to you, but it means a hell of a lot to me."

Chapter Twenty-Six

DEAN

Chloe is usually good at hiding her feelings.

Not right now.

Her fingers dig into the steering wheel. Her left foot taps the mat. Her shoulders climb to her ears.

I do my best to distract her with stupid shit—changing the radio to the Top 40 station to get her complaining about the inanity of pop music, teasing her about how much more comfortable she'd feel in sandals than combat boots, asking how she can have any color tattoos where the rest of her wardrobe is black.

For a while, it works.

The closer we get to Burbank, the farther away her thoughts are. By the time she pulls off the freeway, she's in some other place. Her eyes stay on the road, but her head stays far away.

A few turns and she pulls into the hospital's parking garage. The concrete structure drowns out the sun and the blue skies. Turns the world to a cold, grey place.

Or maybe that's my head going off someplace.

I'm not a daydreamer. Never have been. I got into art

because I wanted to do ink, not the other way around. But right now...

Fuck, my thoughts are a million places.

I thought I was scared for Ryan and Leighton and their inability to figure their shit out.

That was nothing.

How the hell am I going to handle it if something does happen to her?

I looked up the statistics this morning. There's almost no chance of a relapse after a double mastectomy. But if there is a relapse...

Odds aren't good.

Chloe parks on the third level. She leans back into her seat and plays with her keys. "I guess we should go do this."

"We have a minute."

"Barely." She turns to me, her eyes heavy with concern. "I'm sure they'll make us wait forever. They always do. I just... I want to be done with this."

"I know." I undo my seatbelt and move over the center console. Until I can wrap my arms around her.

She softens under my touch. "Sorry. I... I'm freaking out."

"Don't apologize."

"You're... it's weird, you being serious."

"Isn't it?"

"Can you... not?" Her laugh is soft. "This is serious. I know. But can we pretend like it's not?"

"Sure thing, sunshine." I pull back to release her. "But I gotta know something."

"Yeah?"

"That line last night about how you weren't still trying to get in my pants. That was bullshit, right?"

Guilt spreads over her expression.

"Fuck, should have known."

"That wasn't my primary intention. I swear." She opens the door and slides out of the car.

I follow her lead. Move around the trunk to wrap my arm around her waist. "So, what was it? Coming?"

"If I only wanted to come, I would have fucked myself."

"Go on."

"Oh my God." She hides behind her hands.

"I'm lacking details." I press my palm into her lower back to lead her through the parking lot.

Slowly, she brings her hands to her sides. "What is it you want to know?"

"About you fucking yourself? Everything."

"It's not that interesting."

"No, it's fascinating." We step into the elevator lobby. I press the down button. Watch it light up. "Did you fuck yourself in my bed?"

The elevator doors slide open. Chloe steps inside. She turns back to me with a coy smile. "Not answering that." She motions *come in*. Her expression stays easy. Distracted.

"That's a yes."

She presses the *Lobby* button. "I'm disregarding your question because it's ridiculous."

"In other words, yes." I wrap my arms around her waist.

She wraps hers around my neck. Looks up at me with need in her dark eyes. "Dean..."

"I'm happy to fuck you in this elevator. If that's your next question."

Her cheeks flush. "No. That wasn't."

"I know." I back her into the wall anyway.

Press my lips to hers anyway.

Her fingers dig into my hair.

Her lips close around my bottom lip. She sucks hard. Scrapes her teeth against my flesh.

Then she's parting her lips to make way for my tongue.

The reality of the day fades away. There isn't a single ugly thing in the world. Just her and me and all the need pouring between us.

The elevator's ding interrupts us.

The doors slide open.

"Fuck." Chloe pulls back with a heavy sigh. She turns to the door, eyes blinking, cheeks flushing with the sudden realization we have an audience. "Sorry."

The older couple standing in front of us laughs.

"You know how it is," I say.

They share a look. A best friends/siblings/been together forever and finish each other's sentences look.

I slide my arm around Chloe's waist and whisk her onto the sidewalk.

For a few moments, her posture softens. She relaxes as we cross the street, move into the teal lobby, find the elevator inside the building.

But the second we hit the button for the fifth floor, her shoulders are back up at her ears.

The easiness is gone.

And, this time, I'm pretty sure it's not coming back.

THE SECOND SOMEONE CALLS HER NAME, CHLOE JUMPS TO her feet. She presses her hands together and sucks a breath through her teeth.

I reach up. Take her hand. Squeeze tightly. "You ready?"

She pulls back, breaking our touch. "It shouldn't be long." She moves forward. To the technician in grey scrubs.

She follows him past the *patients only* double doors. Disappears into the testing area.

I'm not allowed back there. Not that she wants the support.

If there's something I've figured out sitting next to Chloe for the last twenty minutes, it's that she's determined to do this on her own.

It must have been exhausting going through treatment like that.

Feeling like sharing her dread was a burden.

Hell, I'm exhausted just thinking about it.

No. That's not quite right.

The thought of Chloe taking on the world alone doesn't make me tired.

It makes my stomach drop.

It makes my heart ache.

With every minute I wait, it gets more and more clear.

There isn't a chance in hell I can let her go.

Chapter Twenty-Seven

CHLOE

"**F**inished." The technician smiles as he walks me back to the changing area. "The office will call with your results."

If they're good.

If they're bad, they'll ask me to come in. As if that isn't as good as screaming *you're totally fucked*.

"Thanks." I move into the dressing stall. Shed my gown and step into my jeans. Socks. Bra. Tank top. I got to keep my underwear on. Not that it really made me more comfortable.

It's hard to feel comfortable in a plastic tube.

Especially when it's screening for cancer.

I toss my gown in the hamper and sling my backpack over my shoulders.

It's all waiting now. It will be a few days. It always is.

A few days of wondering if I'm dying.

Awesome.

I try to shake it off as I move through the sterile hallway, but it won't go.

This is a routine test.

A precaution.

The odds are almost nothing.

But if they aren't...

If this is it...

I move through the double doors. A dozen steps and I'm standing next to Dean in the bright lobby. The sun bounces off the white walls and the teal chairs, filling the room with warmth, energy, and a whole lot of irony.

He looks up at me with those bright blue eyes. "You okay, sunshine?"

No. But I want to get there. If I'm okay, I want to stop thinking about illness. If I'm sick, I want to stop wasting time.

He can get me out of my head.

He did last night.

And now... Well...

My fingertips graze his neck. "It's after my test."

His lips curl into a smile. "So it is."

"My place is ten minutes away."

His smile spreads over his cheeks. "I know."

"Then what are you doing sitting there?"

THIS IS THE SLOWEST DRIVE IN THE HISTORY OF THE world.

Every verse flowing from the speakers stretches on to eternity. I know the songs are four minutes each. But, God, do they really have to take forever to get the point?

Finally, I pull onto our street. Park in front of the empty house. Turn the car off.

The music ceases.

Our breath fills the tiny space.

His hand brushes my thigh as he reaches for his seatbelt.

It's only the lightest hint of pressure, but I feel it everywhere.

He was wrong to insist we wait until after the test. I'm no more relaxed than I was two hours ago.

But he can get me there.

I know he can.

I fumble over my seatbelt. My keys. The door handle. All of a sudden, I'm not an artist with expert control of my hands. I'm all thumbs.

There. My boots pound the pavement. Move closer to the door. My hand finds Dean's. The car beeps. Locked.

He intertwines my fingers with his.

It's sweet. But, right now, I don't want sweet. Right now, I want a dirty, messy, hungry fuck.

I slide my key into the door and turn the lock.

He brings his hands to my hips to pull me closer. My ass against his crotch. My back against his chest. My cheek against his neck. "You're nervous."

"It's been two years."

"Is that it?"

"I just... I don't want to think anymore." I turn the handle and press the door open.

He follows me inside. Studies the cozy living room the way he studies my mock-ups.

"What?" I lock the door. Toss my keys on the dining table. Our place is nice for what it is, but it's nothing compared to the Beverly Hills neighborhood where Dean grew up.

"I like it."

"Really?"

"Yeah. It fits."

"What about it?"

He motions to the huge TV, the black couch, the framed prints from the Met. "Everything." His fingers skim my sides as he moves closer. "If you're worried about your test, I get that. But I don't give a fuck about how big or fancy your house is. I've dreamed about being in your room since the tenth grade."

"For that long?"

"Yeah." He takes my hand and pulls me toward the stairs.

"Shouldn't I lead the way?"

"Probably, yeah, but one of us has to get to your bed."

"It's a twin."

He flashes me a devilish grin. "I can work with that."

My room is the first door to the right of the stairs. It looks out on the cozy street.

Usually, I enjoy the view of the neighborhood.

But right now?

Not so much.

I pull the sheer curtains to block out the world.

They cast diffuse light over the room.

Dean presses his ass against the door to close it. He looks around the space with a mix of reverence and curiosity.

His eyes pass over every piece of art—mine, others, magazine cut-outs, movie posters.

Over the full-length mirror across from the bed. "Fuck, sunshine. I knew you had it in you."

"Huh?" My brow screws with confusion.

He wraps his arms around my waist and whisks me to the spot in front of the bed.

The one across from the mirror.

He stares at our reflection as he drags my tank top up my stomach.

Oh. "I've never."

"You should."

"Now?"

"Unless it's too much all at once."

"No." Too much is just right.

I raise my arms so he can pull my top over my head.

He drops it on the ground in front of me.

His lips brush my neck as he unhooks my bra and slides it off my shoulders.

Usually, I don't like staring at my reflection.

Especially my unclothed reflection.

But there's something about his body behind mine.

His lips on my shoulder.

His hands on my skin.

Fuck, it's hot.

His fingertips brush my stomach.

My chest.

He cups my breasts with his hands.

Through the mirror, I watch him toy with my nipples. He runs his thumbs along my tender flesh. Softly at first.

Then harder.

Harder.

There.

A groan falls off my lips. My eyelids get heavy. Press together.

"Open your eyes." He nips at my neck. "I want you watching this."

I try to keep my eyes open, but it's a struggle.

This is too intense.

Too intimate.

His thumbs brush my nipples...

Fuck.

My sex clenches.

I reach for something to steady myself. Find him. My first two fingers slip through his belt loop.

I pull him closer.

Until his hard-on brushes my ass.

Mmm. "Fuck me. Please."

He drags his lips up my neck with the lightest hint of pressure. "This first."

His teeth scrape my ear lobe. It's soft. Enough I feel it, but not enough to hurt.

And, God, how I feel it.

Anticipation courses through my veins. Heat pools in my sex. My body whines *more now*.

I force myself to savor every ounce of need.

It feels so fucking good, Dean toying with me.

I watch him work. He sucks on my earlobe as he rolls my nipples between his fingers. Softer. Then harder. Then softer again.

Every brush of his digits sends a pang right to my sex.

My nipples tighten.

My sex clenches.

My fingers curl into his jeans.

I tug at the fabric. Pull him closer. Arch my back to rub my ass against him.

Our jeans are in the way, but I can still feel his hardness.

It steals my breath.

Sends another wave of desire racing through me.

God, I've never been so full and empty at once.

"Dean." I tilt my head to the other side, offering my neck to him. Offering everything to him.

He drags his lips up my neck with that same featherlight touch. "Watch."

I do.

He keeps one hand on my chest. Drags the other down my stomach.

He toys with my nipple as he unbuttons my jeans.

I release my hold on him. Bring my hands to my hips. Slide my jeans to my knees.

That's as far as I can get them without taking off my boots, but it's enough.

He presses his palm against me, over my panties.

The soft cotton fabric makes for perfect friction.

I'm already on fire.

I stare at our reflection as Dean teases me. He rubs me over my panties. He toys with my nipple. He rocks his hips, grinding his hard-on against my ass.

Anticipation and need overtake every last thought. I forget that it's been two years. That I have new tits. That the test results are waiting for me.

I forget everything but how badly I need him.

I rock my hips to grind against him. "Fuck me. Please."

"Here?" He motions to the mirror. His pupils dilate as he stares at our reflection. His breath hitches. His fingers curl into my skin.

He looks as needy as I feel.

And I want that more than I want to come. More than I want to forget. More than anything.

I want to drive him out of his mind.

Only...

How the hell do I do that?

I'm not a blushing virgin anymore, but I'm not some kind of sex goddess either.

I'm out of my element.

I make eye contact through the mirror. "Tell me what you want."

"I want you groaning my name like it's your favorite thing in the world."

My sex clenches. He's good at this.

He runs his fingertips over the waistband of my panties. "I want you coming on my cock."

Yes. My nod is heavy. Needy. Achy. Or maybe that's my everything.

"Turn around."

I try, but my jeans are at my calves. It's hard to move.

Dean wraps his arms around me. In one swift motion, he lifts me and carries me to the bed.

He lays me down flat on my back then drops between my knees.

Slowly, he undoes the laces of my boot and peels it off my foot.

Then the sock.

The other foot.

He rolls my jeans off my ankles and drops them on the ground in front of him.

Then he does the same with my underwear.

I stare down at him as he plants a kiss on my ankle.

He drags his lips up my calf with that same featherlight touch.

They brush the inside of my knee.

My thigh.

They go higher and higher and higher.

Until his fingers are curling into my thighs.

And he's so, so close to where he needs to be.

He digs the heels of his hands into my thighs, pinning me to the bed.

I look up for long enough to watch Dean plant his face between my legs.

He breathes warm air against my clit.

Then cold.

He does it again and again.

Until I'm dizzy.

He keeps a steady hold on my legs. Just enough pressure to keep me pinned. That I feel how in control he is.

I fall back on the bed as he brings his mouth to me.

His lips close around my labia. He sucks softly. Then harder. Then it's the soft scrape of his teeth.

He moves to the other side and does it again.

Again.

One hand finds his hair. The other goes to my sheets. Curls into the soft cotton fabric.

But that isn't enough to contain the anticipation coursing through my veins.

Nothing is enough to contain the anticipation coursing through my veins.

He licks me up and down. Slowly. Then faster.

Softly. Then harder.

His tongue plunges inside me.

I tug at his hair, pulling him closer. "Make me come." My hips shift of their own accord. "Please."

He pins me harder.

But he's merciful. He makes his way to my clit and licks me with steady stokes.

My eyelids press together.

My toes curl.

My nails dig into the sheets.

Every flick of his tongue winds me up.

He pushes me right to the edge. Until the pressure inside me is so tight I can barely take it. Until all I can feel is this deep, desperate, impossible need to come.

With the next flick of his tongue, I unravel.

"Fuck. Dean." I tug at his hair, holding him against me.

My sex pulses with my orgasm. Tension unwinds in a big, beautiful wave of pleasure. It crests and rolls through my torso, my limbs, my fingers and toes.

"Fuck." He nips at my inner thigh. "I love watching you come." He plants a soft kiss on my pelvis as he pushes himself to his feet.

He's quick about pulling his t-shirt over his head. It's not like when we were at the beach. It's not a show for my attention.

He needs to be naked now.

I need him naked now.

God, how I need him naked.

I push myself up. Reach for his jeans. The button is a struggle, but I manage to undo it. To unzip him.

He pushes the denim off his hips and shimmies out of it.

Then it's the black boxers.

Fuck.

He's bigger than I remembered.

And that piercing.

It's...

I'm...

Fuck.

I stare up at him as I wrap my hand around his cock.

He shudders as I grip him tighter.

I pump him with a steady stroke.

Then another.

Another.

He's warm and hard under my hand. And it feels so fucking good, watching bliss spill over his expression.

I wind him up with steady strokes, then I bring my hand to his tip and brush his piercing. The silver barbell is curved. It goes from the center to the bottom of his tip.

I tease one end with my thumb.

Tease the other with my index finger.

Dean's hand knots in my hair.

He blinks his eyes open. Stares down at me like I'm the best thing he's ever seen.

My anxieties vanish.

The way he's looking at me...

I don't have a doubt in the world.

I tease him until his eyelids flutter closed.

A groan falls off his lips. "Fuck, Chloe."

God, the way he says my name. I need more of it. I need all of it.

I scoot up the bed.

Then off it.

I lower myself onto my knees in front of him.

He presses his palm against the back of my head, urging me forward, begging for more.

Fuck, I want to give him more.

I want to give him everything.

I brush my lips against his tip as softly as I can.

His fingers dig into the back of my head.

His toes curl into the hardwood.

I tease him the way he teased me.

I flick my tongue against his tip. The warm, sweet flesh. The smooth, silver metal.

He shudders as I play with his piercing.

I do it again and again.

I do it until he's groaning.

Slowly, I take him into my mouth.

His hand knots in my hair.

The other goes to my shoulder. Then my chest. He toys with my nipple as I take him deeper.

Deeper.

Fuck, he tastes good.

It's been a long, long time since I've done this.

But he makes me feel right at home.

His hips shift ever so slightly. His groans bounce around the room. His fingers brush my nipple again and again.

He rolls it between his thumb and forefinger as I flick my tongue against the bottom of his tip.

I tap it against his piercing again and again.

Until his groan is agony as much as it's pleasure.

I wrap one hand around his cock. Pump him as I take him deeper.

Deeper.

As deep as I can manage.

Then I pull back and do it again.

His eyes blink open.

He looks down at me with heavy lids.

Desire fills his baby blues. It pours over his expression.

His brow knits. His lips part. His head falls forward.

I do it again.

"Fuck, Chloe." His fingers dig into the back of my head.

My sex clenches. My nipples tighten. My body begs for more, but this is exactly where I need to be.

His need is intoxicating.

It's everything.

I move faster.

Suck harder.

Get lost in the feeling of his firm flesh in my mouth.

His breath hitches in his throat.

His nails dig into my skin.

There.

I flick my tongue against his piercing.

Push him over the edge.

He pulls back as he comes.

He groans my name as he spills onto my chest.

Like it's his favorite word in the entire world.

Like it's everything.

When he's finished, he pulls me to my feet.

He wraps his arms around my waist.

And he kisses me like he's never going to let go.

Chapter Twenty-Eight

Dean joins me in the shower.

His hard, wet body presses against mine as we move past each other.

He runs his fingers through my hair as he helps me shampoo and condition. I rise to my tiptoes to do the same to him.

He catches me when I slip.

He presses his soft, wet lips to mine.

Rubs soap over my shoulders, arms, back, chest, stomach.

I take my time exploring every inch of his torso. Hard muscles. Soft skin. All those lines of ink.

He feels good against my fingertips.

Right.

I'm ready to spend eternity in the shower with Dean.

Until I hear the whir of the garage door.

Shit.

What the hell is Dad doing home?

I PRESS MY BACK AGAINST MY BEDROOM DOOR. SUCK A shallow breath through my teeth.

Today is out to get me. Or at least to give me an anxiety attack.

Dean chuckles as he pulls his boxers on. "Relax." He steps into his jeans. "I know what I'm doing."

Maybe he does, but I don't. "My dad has never caught me with a guy."

"He knows we're fucking."

"How do you figure?"

"The way he looked at me when I picked you up." He pulls his t-shirt on. "He was deciding if I was worth his daughter's time."

"And?"

"Pretty sure he liked me."

He did like Dean.

And he did send me that sassy text.

I'm sure Dad realizes I have a sex life. Even if I didn't have a sex life until last night.

Dean moves to my dresser. Opens my underwear drawer. Tosses me a pair of panties. "Though I'd prefer if you skipped them."

"How did you—"

"That pic you sent." He runs his fingers through his wet hair. "Fuck. I can't think about that or I'm gonna get hard."

"You remember it that well?"

His nod is pure need.

It's everything.

It's completely inappropriate with my dad's footsteps downstairs.

But it's still incredibly hot.

"You home, Chloe," he calls.

Fuck me. Seriously. How do people deal with having sex in high school? This is mortifying.

"Yeah. I'll be down in a minute," I say.

I fight my blush as I get into my clothes. I'm still wet. My jeans don't want to cooperate. I have to coax them into it.

There.

I find a bra in my drawer. A black tank top.

Dean wraps his arms around my waist.

His touch calms me instantly.

"You'll be okay, sunshine." He plants a kiss on my neck. "I promise."

I nod. He's right. This is no big deal. Just my dad getting home minutes after my boyfriend came on my chest.

Is Dean my boyfriend?

I can't even say *hey, Dad, you know my boyfriend*. More like *hey, dad, you know my boss, who I am clearly having sex with*.

Ugh.

Dean's chuckle bounces around the room. "How about you let me lead?"

I shake my head.

"You trust me?"

"Terrifyingly enough, yes."

"Then let me handle this."

Uh...

He holds his hands up. "Your call."

Dad did like him immediately.

Everyone likes Dean immediately.

Maybe he does know what he's doing.

"Okay. But if I give you the signal, that's it. I'm taking over," I say.

"What's the signal?" He chuckles.

I tap my nose three times.

"Sure." He motions after you. "I lead until the signal."

"Don't mock the signal."

"I wouldn't dare." He follows me into the hallway.

My fingers skim the railing as I move downstairs. My feet are still wet. My footsteps are slippery.

"Hey, Dad." I step into the living room. "What are you doing home?" I cross my arms reflexively. Is there really a better time to be defensive?

"Meeting finished early." His gaze shifts to Dean. "I guess I don't have to ask what you're doing here."

My cheeks flush. "We were in the neighborhood. For the test."

"Oh." Dad looks to Dean. "It's that serious?"

"Yeah." Dean steps into the living room. Runs his fingers through my wet hair. "Can I be honest?"

Dad laughs. "I should hope you're always honest."

Dean nods *true*. "I adore your daughter."

Dad's gaze flits from me to Dean then back to me. "And you, Chloe?"

"And I...?" Why is he being so cool about this? He just caught us in the act. After the act. Close enough.

"He's asking if you like me or if you're only in this for my body." Dean slides his arm around my waist. "No one would blame you for the latter."

"No. I like you a lot too." My cheeks flush. "Is this the time for this conversation?"

"I figured you'd have that worked out by now." Dad moves into the kitchen and grabs the coffee from a high shelf. "But Chloe has always been particular."

"I am not particular." My voice breaks into a teenage whine. "I just have high standards."

"Pretty sure that's another way of saying particular," Dean says.

"Maybe we should get out of your hair," I offer. "Traffic shouldn't be too bad yet."

"No. Stay for dinner." Dad smiles at Dean. "Unless you have plans."

"Can't think of anything I'd rather do," Dean says.

Dad beams. "I'll call Gia."

God help me.

GIA TWIRLS HER FORK, SCOOPING STRANDS OF PASTA. "So, Dean... what have you been doing since high school?"

Dean looks to me and raises a brow. *What's she getting at?*

I'm not really sure. Dad skipped the thorough grilling in favor of coffee (tea for us) and conversations about action movies. He gave us space to make dinner while he and Gia collaborated on the best way to torture us.

My older sister loves torturing me.

But then she's protective too.

I don't know if she's teasing me or calling Dean out.

I shrug. He might as well answer honestly. Dean is Dean. They're going to like him or not.

"I did my apprenticeship at this place downtown with the same guy who taught my older brother. It was a lot of grunt work and I made twenty bucks a day, but I got to learn to do ink. When my brother jumped ship to go to Inked Hearts, he got me a job. We bought the place from the previous owner last year." Dean sucks a noodle from his fork. Chews. Swallows. Smiles that wicked smile of his. *Take that, judgmental sister.*

"You're an owner? Hmm." Gia stabs a piece of broccoli with her fork. Stares at it like it did her wrong. "That's not what I would have guessed."

"I know. It's not fair. All this beauty and brains too." Dean shrugs with mock humility. "Don't worry. It was ego that got me to buy the shop. Not intellect."

This time, Gia shoots me that *what is he getting at* look.

This time, I know.

"You're smarter than you let on-" I stumble on my old pet name/insult for Dean. *Dick face* doesn't work anymore. But what does? "Sweetie." No. Too cute.

It does light up his eyes.

God, he has such nice eyes. That bright, clear, gorgeous blue.

"He's here with you. As far as I'm concerned, he's a genius," Dad says.

Gia laughs. "You're so cheesy."

"You'll be the same way when you have kids," Dad says.

My sister's gaze stays on Dean. "So, you really came with Chloe for her test?"

"Had to beg her, but yeah," he says. "Should have seen me. It was pathetic. I was on my knees."

"I bet." Gia smiles knowingly. "So are you two like... boyfriend girlfriend."

I clear my throat.

Dad shakes his head. "I asked the same thing hours ago. They still haven't worked out an answer."

Dean laughs. "I tried. But Chloe wouldn't hear it."

"We were cooking!" I take a deep breath and exhale slowly. Everyone here is on my side. It's too much attention, yes, but I can handle it.

"What do you think, sunshine, you want to be my girl-friend?" he asks.

My chest warms. "Yeah. Definitely."

"There you go." Dean shrugs like it's no big deal, but his expression betrays him. His eyes are even brighter. He's beaming like the sun.

"You call her *sunshine* when you're—" Gia motions to my bedroom upstairs.

God. I hide behind my hands.

Dean chuckles. "Pretty sure Chlo' will kill me if I offer that information."

"Could you not bring up my sex life in front of our father?" I try to ignore them in favor of my spaghetti marinara, but the rich, tomato flavor does nothing to distract me.

"You're too uptight, baby girl," Dad says. "This is the time in your life where you should be having fun."

My cheeks flame red.

This conversation needs to go away. Now. "Can you berate Gia for sticking with Mark then?"

"I tried for a long time," Dad says. "But she loves the guy."

Gia's eyes get soft. Dreamy. It's sweet. All this time and she's still the high school girl who giggled over their first kiss. She's still innocent. Cheery. Optimistic about the world.

Right now...

No, I'm not thinking about the test results.

I'm borrowing my sister's optimism.

And Dean's... well, I'm not sure how to describe Dean's outlook on life.

But I'm borrowing it.

"What was it that happened between the two of you? I think it was Chloe's junior year. One day, she went from going on and on about how much she hated you, to moping around the house in all black, hugging her sketchbook like it was her best friend." Gia's nose scrunches and she chews and swallows another broccoli floret. "I mean, it was barely different than normal. But it was noticeable."

I flip my sister off.

She returns the gesture with a hearty laugh. "See? She's always been kinda pissed. Not that I blame her. I was pissed at the universe after Mom."

Dean's eyes find mine. He raises a brow. *You want to take this, or should I?*

I nod *go ahead.*

He turns to Gia. "I was a stupid kid. Didn't realize what I had."

"So, you were always into Chloe?" she asks.

He looks to me. "I don't know what it is about you, sunshine, but you've always been under my skin."

"You know I'll kill you if you hurt her," Gia says.

Dean nods. "Wouldn't expect anything less."

Chapter Twenty-Nine

CHLOE

Dad and Gia revel in the chance to embarrass me. They spill every mortifying story—the first time I gushed about Dean, the first time I ranted about him, the sex dream I shared with Gia in confidence (she pinkie swore!), the time I wore my lap suit to a pool party, the day my kindergarten teacher called my parents because she was worried my drawings were too downer.

When we leave, Gia says goodbye with a tight hug and a quiet whisper. "Call me as soon as you know the results."

I nod like I'll tell her.

I will. Eventually.

After I process this without everyone else's feelings hanging over me.

I let Dean drive. Let my thoughts wander as the city whizzes by the windows. Los Angeles may not have much of a skyline compared to New York or Seattle, but the tall buildings are beautiful in the dark.

There's something about Southern California. The fluorescent yellow of street and city lights turns the sky a soft blue. Casts a cream glow over the grey tree trunks, the green leaves, the off-white pavement, the charcoal roads.

The sounds of grunge fill the car. Dean doesn't ask what I'm thinking and I don't offer. I just rest my head on the window, press my eyelids together, and let the stress of the day roll around my head.

I stir as he pulls off the freeway.

It's three turns to his place.

He finds a spot on the street. Of course. Lucky bastard.

The music ceases as he turns the car off. He spins the keys around his forefinger. "It's a long drive."

"It goes fast."

"You have to come back tomorrow morning. We have a ten o'clock."

I nod.

His lips curl into a half-smile. "Sunshine, I'm asking if you want to spend the night."

"Oh."

"Indirect isn't my strong suit."

"It was confusing, yeah."

"Let's try this again." He undoes his seatbelt and offers his hand. "You want to come in and fuck me?"

"Yes, please."

THE SECOND THE LOCK CLICKS, I POUNCE.

My hand goes to Dean's bright blue t-shirt. I grab the soft fabric and tug him closer.

He presses his palm to my lower back.

Brings the other to the back of my head.

Plants a long, soft kiss on my lips.

My stomach flutters. My heart thuds. My veins buzz with desire.

God, he's a good kisser.

But that isn't enough.

I slip my hand under his t-shirt. Press my palm against his soft skin. "Bedroom. Now."

He nods as he brings both hands to my ass.

In one swift motion, he lifts me into his arms.

I squeal as I wrap my legs around him.

"I can bench three hundred pounds, sunshine. You're nothing."

"I'm deceptively heavy." My fingers curl into his skin. "All muscle."

"Yeah. But still tiny." He kicks the bedroom door open. Takes three steps. Lays me down on the bed.

I stare up at him as he pulls off his t-shirt.

The moon streams through the windows, casting highlights over the lines of his body. God, those lines run deep. The man is built.

"Clothes off." He moves to the bedside table and pulls a condom from the drawer.

"You first." I push myself up. Crawl across the bed to his spot. Move onto my knees.

I run my fingers over his torso as I press my lips to his chest.

Fuck, he's so incredibly yummy. It defies logic.

This is what I need.

His body and mine and nothing else.

I was wrong before. I didn't need to rediscover my body before my test. The test itself is nothing. It's the results.

I need to find bliss now.

If I'm sick again, that's it. No more trying to forgive my body. No more waiting around while everyone watches me disappear. No more waiting, period.

This is my time.

I have to seize it.

Carpe fucking diem.

I'm a cliché, but I don't care.

Not right now. Not when I'm here.

I drag my fingertips down Dean's sculpted torso. Below his belly button. To that soft tuft of hairs.

My fingers curl into the waistband of his jeans.

I undo the button. The zipper. Go to push them off his hips.

His fingers curl around my wrist. "On your back." He climbs onto the bed next to me. Brings his hand to my cheek. "I need to be inside of you."

"I need to kiss you." I climb into his lap. One hand goes to his light hair. The other goes to his back.

My fingers dig into his skin as I bring my lips to his.

I suck on his bottom lip softly. Then harder.

He scrapes his teeth against my top lip.

His hands slip beneath my tank top. They go right to my breasts.

He traces the outline of my bra again and again.

His tongue slides into my mouth.

His thumbs slip into my bra.

He toys with my nipples as he kisses me.

I shift my hips, swing a leg over his so I'm straddling him.

He's hard under me. Even with our jeans in the way, I can feel him.

I grind against him, so my clit is rubbing against his length.

Fuck.

That's intense.

Pleasure pools between my legs. Every brush of his thumbs sends a pang of lust straight to my core.

My nails dig into his skin. My tongue dances with his.

I move faster. Kiss him harder. Kiss him with everything I have.

He pulls back with a heavy sigh. Drags his fingertips down my stomach. Does away with my tank top.

My hands go to the back of my bra. I start to unhook it, but my fingers freeze.

This is our third time being here, but it still feels new.

It's still terrifying.

Slowly, I slide my bra off one shoulder, then the other.

His eyes go wide as he takes me in.

His soft, low groan erases every doubt in my head.

In his eyes, I'm not weird or broken or pieced together.

I'm whole.

HE BRINGS HIS HANDS TO MY LOWER BACK. PULLS BOTH OF us up the bed. Straightens us.

He lies down, his head on his pillow, his back against the sheets.

His hands find my chest. He cups my breasts softly.

Not like they're strange and foreign.

Like he's reveling in the feel of them.

One hand plants between my shoulder-blades.

He pulls my body into his. Until my chest is against his mouth.

When his lips close around my nipple, I feel it.

The line between my body and soul dissolves.

I *am* my body.

I'm the tight feeling in my nipples, the ache between my legs, the pounding of my heart.

The last hint of tension in my shoulders melts.

The day fades away.

The future fades away.

Everything else fades away.

It's just me and Dean and all this bliss.

He strips me out of my jeans then presses his palm against me, over my panties.

I rock my hips, grinding against his fingers, reveling in the friction of the soft fabric.

It feels good, but it's not enough.

I need him inside me.

I shift sideways. Fall onto the bed on my back. Turn my neck so we're face-to-face.

God, I love his face. The blue eyes. The strong nose. The soft lips. The sculpted jawline.

"Fuck me." I push my panties to my ankles. Kick them off. "Now."

His nod is heavy. Needy.

He undoes his jeans. Arches his back to push them, and his boxers, off his hips.

They fall onto the floor in front of the bed.

Finally, we're exactly where we need to be.

Nothing between us.

He kneels next to me and tears the condom wrapper open with his teeth.

He drags his fingertips over my skin with a feather soft touch. Down my stomach. Up my thigh. Closer and closer and—

There.

His fingers brush my clit.

Softly.

Then harder.

He drags his hand lower. Teases me with one finger. Two.

Again.

Again.

There.

He slides two fingers inside me.

Fuck. The pressure of his digits is intense. But it's not enough.

"Dean." I arch my hips, pushing his fingers deeper.

My breath hitches as he drives into me.

I forget what I'm asking for. Only that I need it.

He rolls the condom over his cock.

Looks at me with this intoxicating mix of desire and need.

"Now," I plead. This feels so fucking good, but I'm greedy. I want more. I want everything.

"Spread your legs."

I do.

Slowly, he pulls his hand away. He brings his first two fingers to his lips. Sucks the taste of me from his digits.

My sex clenches.

He places himself between my legs.

His fingers curl into my hips as he lifts me into the air. Brings my body to his.

His tip strains against me.

Then it's one inch at a time.

He stares into my eyes as he slides inside me.

My fingers curl into the sheets. It's been a long, long time. This is a lot.

My lips press together.

I squeeze my eyes shut.

"Breathe, baby." He holds my body against his. Strokes the flesh of my ass with his fingertips.

I just barely nod.

"We can take this as slow as you need."

But that's the thing. I don't need slow. I need fast. I need him splitting me in half.

Deep breath.

Steady exhale.

We're making up, my body and me. If it needs slow, I can respect that.

Dean and I have a lot of time to fuck.

Well... we might not.

But we have all of tonight.

"Look at me." His voice is soft. Sweet.

I blink my eyes open.

God, there's something so intoxicating about the way he's looking at me. He needs me, yes, but it's more than a carnal thing.

He needs all of me.

I hold Dean's gaze as he pulls back then shifts into me again.

I'm ready. I'm wet. I'm antsy. I'm aching.

But the pressure is still intense. As much as I can take.

He lays me down. Lowers his body onto mine. One hand plants outside my shoulder. The other knots in my hair.

He strokes my temple with his thumb.

He brings his lips to mine.

He kisses me as he drives into me.

Slowly.

Softly.

Then faster.

Harder.

His tongue slips into my mouth.

His cock pushes deeper.

Bit by bit, my body relaxes. My legs wrap around his hips. My arms wrap around his chest.

I break out of the kiss. Stare up into his eyes. Nod. *Yes, more, please, faster.*

He holds me close as he rocks into me with long, steady strokes.

His groans vibrate down my throat.

He drives into me again and again.

Pleasure floods my pelvis. It spreads out through my torso, my limbs, my fingers and toes.

With every thrust, he winds me tighter.

I rock my hips, moving with him, pushing him deeper.

Deeper.

Fuck.

I pull back to groan his name.

My eyelids flutter open. The room is a blur of moonlight and white walls and soft sheets and skin and sweat.

And Dean.

I nestle my head in the crook of his neck.

I wrap my arms around him.

We stay locked together like that, holding each other, moving together.

He keeps that same slow, steady pace.

He fills me with deep steady thrusts.

I hold on to the bliss as long as I can. Until the tension inside me winds as tight as I can take it.

Then tighter.

Tighter.

Fuck.

With his next thrust, I go over the edge.

My nails dig into his back. My lips find his neck. I suck on his soft skin as I come.

My sex pulses with my orgasm. Pleasure spills through every molecule of my body. Everything goes white. Nothing but the pure, blinding light of bliss.

I suck a breath through my nose as I come down.

He looks down at me like I'm his salvation.

Maybe I am. If he really has been spending the last few years with that empty spot in his gut. The one that can only be filled with loving someone and letting them love you.

I want that so badly. To have that well of trust inside me. That willingness to drag someone through hell with me.

My eyes close.

My lips find his.

He kisses me as he drives into me. His strokes speed then steady.

I get lost in the motions of our bodies.

Until he's there, groaning my name into my neck, pulsing inside me.

Kissing me like I'm everything he needs.

Chapter Thirty

DEAN

At work, Ryan is sitting at the front desk, scribbling a mock-up into his sketchbook, cup of coffee by his side.

His eyes dart from his paper to me. "Can't remember the last time I saw that look."

I drop my backpack in my suite. Cross the room to the counter. "This is my everyday look."

"No." He stares into my eyes, picking me apart in that Ryan kind of way. "You're happy."

"I'm always happy."

He shakes his head. "You're always amusing yourself. But this is different. Like... no... that's not possible."

"No?" I hoist myself onto the counter. Tap my feet together. "Go on."

"Nah. I must be imagining shit."

"Yours is vivid."

His smile gets dreamy. He looks out the windows, taking in the blue sky and the ocean view.

He sighs that *I'm thinking about Leighton* sigh.

At first it was sweet. It was nice not seeing him a miserable shell of himself.

Then I got sick of the swooning.

But now...

Fuck, it's like I want to hug him or something. Don't get me wrong. I always want to hug Ryan. My older brother is squeamish about affection from anyone but Leighton. Hugging him is fucking with him.

And fucking with people is my favorite pastime.

Damn. I'm losing track of my point. It's Chloe. My brain keeps going back to her. The way her lips part with her groan. The way her back arches. The way she pulses around me.

But my brain doesn't stop at sex.

Her smile, her laugh, the trust in her eyes, the soft murmur as she falls asleep, the way her fingers curl into my skin when she's nervous—it's all bouncing around my brain.

"Fuck. That is it." Ryan drops his pen. "You're into someone."

"Get real."

"Wish I could." Incredulity streaks his expression. "How the fuck did this happen?"

I offer him my best coy shrug.

"Dean. Don't fucking tell me—"

"Wasn't gonna tell you."

"Don't tell me it's Chloe."

"Wasn't gonna tell you," I repeat.

His brow furrows. "Fuck. Seriously?"

Am I really this easy to read? "Don't know what you're talking about."

Right on cue, the bell rings. Chloe's footsteps move toward the counter.

Ryan's gaze flits from her to me. Then back to her. "Are you fucking Dean?"

Her cheeks flush. She stops dead in her tracks. Deer in headlights.

Busted.

Ryan shakes his head. "Ask you to do one thing."

"It's not like that." The earnest tone of my voice burns my ears. This is fucking weird. "It's serious."

"You're serious?" Surprise creeps into his voice. He looks to Chloe for some help, but she's still deer in headlights.

Slowly, she nods. "It is."

"Shit, really?" Ryan runs a hand through his wavy hair. "You two ever planning on telling the rest of us?"

"Not really, no," I say.

"With all due respect, Ryan—and I have a lot of respect for you—I'm not sure how it's any of your business," Chloe says.

Ryan chuckles. "You've been working here how long?"

"Three weeks," she says.

"You really think anything stays secret here?" he asks.

She laughs. "No. But... Um... you're not going to try to fire me or something?"

"No." His brow screws. "But... Not sure it's cool for you to stay Dean's apprentice."

"We'll work it out. Draw strict lines. Compartmentalize. Promise." Vulnerability fills her eyes. She can't lose this job. She'll die if she loses this job.

Ryan shoots me a concerned look. "Can you do that?"

"Yeah. No problem." Huge problem.

But I will figure it out.

Somehow.

RYAN STAYS AT THE COUNTER, COFFEE IN HIS HAND, EYES

on us, until his client arrives. He shoots me a *don't fuck this up* look as he moves to his suite.

I should borrow some of his caution—there are way too many ways this could go up in flames—but I can't seem to find any. My heart is too full. My body is too warm. My soul...

Fuck, this cheesy shit isn't me.

Even if I can't bring myself to care at the moment.

I take Chloe's hand and lead her to the office. Nerves fill her eyes as she looks back to Ryan, but he's not paying attention to us. He's already enraptured in his work.

"You think he's serious about the whole we shouldn't work together thing?" She presses her back against the door, shutting it.

"It's Ryan."

"Right. He's always serious." She digs her index finger into the pad of her thumb.

"He's not gonna fire you. I promise." I bring my hands to her hips and pull her body into mine. "He can't."

"'Cause you're all co-owners?"

I nod.

Her brow softens. "We're not making the best case for keeping work and play separate."

"He isn't here."

"Still." She leans closer anyway. Rests her head on my chest. Digs her fingers into my sides, pressing the cotton fabric of my shirt into my skin.

Yeah. We're doing a shit job compartmentalizing.

I'm here for a reason.

She's just so fucking distracting.

Her fingers skim the edge of my t-shirt.

Then they're on my skin.

Fuck, her touch does shit to me.

I force myself to take a step backward. "You finish Han for me?"

"Oh." Disappointment flares in her eyes for a second. She blinks, and it fades to that fiery determination. "Yeah. In my backpack. Give me a second."

I do.

She's conspicuous about opening the door wide on her way out then leaving it open on her way in. It's smart leaving the door open, proving we have nothing to hide, but doing it this much is like screaming *hey, we have nothing to hide.* Calls attention to us being alone.

He was right. It's not a good idea for me to teach her if I can't draw that line.

I've got to draw that line.

Somehow.

She sets her backpack on the desk, pulls her sketchbook from it, and flips to the right page. Anticipation spreads over her expression as she shows off the design.

"Is it perfect?" Her voice perks.

"Yeah."

"Really?" She taps her toes together. "Are you sure?"

Positive. If I was the type to get a joke tattoo, this thing would be going on my arm today. I roll my shirt up my sleeve. "Do me one last time, sunshine."

Her lips curl into a half smile. "Only one? I'm not sure I can promise that." Her ass brushes my crotch as she moves past me, to the scanner. She's quick about scanning, printing, and cutting out the mock-up. She's a pro now. "Within a week, you'll be begging for more."

"Will I?"

"Yeah. I already worked up a Lando and a Chewbacca for you. So you have options."

"You did not."

"Did too." She wets a cotton swab with rubbing alcohol and drags it over my shoulder. Her fingers skim my skin as she holds up my shirt. "C3-PO too."

"R2-D2?"

"And Luke. That one is probably the best. In my opinion."

"'Cause he's holding his lightsaber like it's a massive dick?"

"Maybe." She presses the paper to my skin then dabs with a wet cotton swab.

"Maybe?" I raise a brow. "That's it."

"You're being greedy. One free design at a time."

My gaze shifts to her sketchbook. It's still sitting face down on the scanner. I can't marvel at the design. But I know it well enough. "I am. This is good shit."

"You really think so?"

"I do."

She drops the cotton swab and peels the paper off. Her eyes go wide with enthusiasm. Her jaw drops. Her fingers curl. Her toes tap together. "Does this ever get old?"

Yeah. But not with her sitting next to me. Not with her reminding me what I want. "Only if you let it."

"Have you?"

"Yeah. But I'm getting it back."

She looks up at me with a wide smile.

Fuck, her smile does shit to me.

I feel it everywhere.

Her fingers curl into my skin. She takes a step backward. "You need to see this in the mirror."

She's right. I do. But her voice isn't *I'm excited about what you're teaching me*. It's *I never want to stop touching you*.

Still, I follow her into the main room. All the way to my suite. To the mirror.

Soft light streams through the sheer shades. The room hums with the sound of Ryan's gun and the quiet grunts of his client. Neither one of them is talking. Of course.

My gaze shifts to the mirror. "That really is fucking perfect."

Chloe's eyes light up. "You sure?"

"Positive. You aced this." I turn toward her. Let my fingers brush her shoulder. "Bring me Lando tomorrow."

She nods.

"And work up something else."

"What else?"

I rack my brain for something that's just challenging enough. "An abstract design. For my forearm. Something geometric."

"Where?" She traces my bare forearm with her index finger, from my wrist to the crook of my elbow. "All that. Or less?"

"All that."

"I think I need a ruler."

I arch a brow.

"You're obsessed." She traces the length of my arm again. Carefully. Like she's committing it to memory. "You have a problem."

The door rings. Bouncy footsteps move into the room.

Walker.

"Hey." He greets Ryan then moves into my suite. "We're doing karaoke tonight." He stops dead in his tracks when he sees us. "Oh." It's written all over his face. *You're already fucking her.*

I nod *yeah*. "You're late to the party."

He nods to Ryan. *Does he know?*

"Chloe broke on the cross." I run my fingers through her hair.

She folds her arms. "That's not why he figured it out." Her cheeks flush. "Hey, Walker. You're early, aren't you?"

"My noon asked to come in early." He looks at us like he's assessing our potential. "You really like Dean?"

"Tragic, isn't it?" she teases.

"Yeah." He nods. "But the heart wants what it wants."

Chapter Thirty-One

DEAN

L eighton jumps from her spot on the couch. She bounces to Chloe and throws her arms around her. "It's nice to see you again."

Chloe's eyes fill with surprise for a second. She blinks and it's replaced by friendly affection. "You too." She pulls back with a smile. "How is indie design treating you?"

"Good. Tiring." Leighton brushes a purple strand behind her ear. "Let's not talk about work." She looks back to Ryan, who's sitting on the bench next to Walker and Iris. "Let's not talk at all. Yeah?"

"Right here?" Ryan raises a brow.

"Yeah." She hikes her tight black dress, daring him. Fuck, she hikes it far.

His eyes fill with hunger

His tongue slides over his lips.

His—

Those are details I don't need.

Iris nods hello. "I'm not sure we've met." She stands and offers her hand. "I'm Iris."

Chloe nods. "I've heard a lot about you." She shoots Walker a knowing glance. "Your boyfriend is smitten."

"I'm pretty smitten." Curiosity fills her blue eyes as she looks to me. "It's weird, seeing Dean with someone."

"Oh." Chloe's cheeks flush. "Is that common knowledge now?"

Ryan nods. "News travels fast."

"And it's..." She pulls her arm over her chest. Curls her fingers around her tank top strap. "Is that cool?"

"Dean's in charge of teaching you. It's up to him how he wants to handle it." Ryan lifts his glass—filled with coke, not booze, since this place is alcohol free—to me. "To your ability to take responsibility."

Leighton climbs into Ryan's lap. Runs her fingers through his wavy hair. "Should we really toast to something that doesn't exist? That's bad luck."

"How could you say that, Leigh. I'm as responsible as they come." I press my palm into Chloe's back to lead her to the other bench. It's perpendicular to theirs, but it's opposite the TV. It's a nice spot.

Chloe's posture stiffens as she sits next to me. She looks at the four of them with nervous eyes.

Can't blame her.

They're staring like she's an exhibit at the zoo.

I'm not that much of a commitment phobic manwhore.

No... I am.

But they could be cool about it.

"You guys know you're not gonna see more unless you ask." I nod to my crotch. "I'm always ready for a show."

Leighton rolls her eyes.

Iris laughs. "You're not as bad as I thought at first, Dean."

Walker chuckles. "Sweetness, that was not a good compliment."

"He knows what I mean." She wraps her arms around her

boyfriend's shoulder. Rests her head on his chest. "You're actually kind of sweet. Protective." She looks to Chloe. "He's a good guy."

"But how'd you get past his personality?" Walker teases. "Must have been difficult."

"It was. But then I thought about it, and I realized that Dean is incredibly hot," Chloe teases back.

Leighton laughs. "Was that it?"

"Well..." Chloe taps her combat boots together. "I don't want to overshare, but I have to admit—"

"Oh God. I do not want to hear about his dick." Leighton makes a show of squeezing her eyelids together and holding her hands over her ears. "Tell me when it's over."

"It's Dean. It's never over." Ryan nips at her ear.

"Can't believe you thought I was into him." Her eyelids flutter open. She scrunches her nose *gross*.

"Yeah, wasn't like you two used to flirt nonstop." Ryan shakes his head *you're ridiculous*. He plants another kiss on his girlfriend's neck, then he turns to Chloe. "He treating you well?"

"Yeah. Surprisingly so," she says.

"Hey," I feign offense.

"Please. You're obnoxious on purpose." Her posture softens. Her voice eases. "You think it's adorable."

I bring my lips to her ear so I can stage whisper. "If you're gonna tell me you don't like it, I'm gonna check."

Her cheeks flush.

Iris laughs. "I have to admit. The Prince Albert thing—"

The door swings open. Brendon steps inside. His gaze goes right to Iris.

Then to me.

He raises a brow *really*. He's completely unmoved by my bullshit.

Kaylee, his now (finally) nineteen-year-old girlfriend, follows him into the room. Then to our bench.

She brushes her long blond hair behind her shoulder as she settles into her boyfriend's lap. "Dean, there's this idea in writing: less is more."

"Not following," I say.

"Maybe mention your dick less often. So it has more impact each time," she says.

"I get you. I'm making your boyfriend jealous," I tease.

She laughs. "Exactly. How did you figure it out?" She leans in to whisper in said boyfriend's ear.

He whispers something back.

Her cheeks flush.

She's not a blushing virgin anymore.

It was fun for a while, teasing Brendon about how much he wanted her. I pushed him so hard he bet me a hundred bucks she'd never been with anyone.

Asshole really thought I cared if his crush was fucking around.

I guess I did. Just not for the reasons he assumed. I wanted the two of them together.

Whether my friends believe it or not, I want them happy.

I do whatever it takes to make it happen.

Kay and Brendon made it, even if there was a lot of fallout on the path. His little sister, Kay's best friend, freaked about them getting together.

Right on cue, Emma steps through the door. She looks like she's headed to the clubs—dark hair in waves, makeup bringing out her dark eyes and red lips, tight dress, fuck me heels.

Brendon shoots her a *really, you're wearing that* look, but he keeps his lips zipped. They stay out of each other's business pretty well considering.

Emma surveys the room. Slowly, her gaze focuses on

Chloe. "I knew you liked him." She turns to her brother. "Did you know?"

"Everyone knew," he says.

"Everyone?" Chloe bites her lip. "Was it really that obvious?"

"Yeah. You guys bicker like Han and Leia," Walker says.

Iris whispers something in his ear.

He laughs and whispers back. "One more word and I will."

"Right here?" she asks.

"Fuck yeah." His fingers curl into her thigh, over her jeans. "Everyone can leave or watch."

"Can you give them that same less is more speech, Kay?" I ask.

"They heard it." She looks to Emma. Raises a brow.

Emma nods *yeah*.

They share a knowing look. A *we're best friends, we can nearly communicate telepathically* look.

"Excuse me. Restroom." Kaylee slides off her boyfriend's lap. She grabs Emma's hand on the way out the door.

"I think she likes Em better than she likes you," I say.

"I hate to agree with Dean, but that was cold." Leighton laughs.

"That's not it," Chloe says. "She's—" Her gaze shifts to Brendon. "Never mind. Girl talk."

"You know a secret!" Leighton claps her hands together. "Damn. Why are we at this all ages place? I can't get you drunk to get it out of you."

"I hold my liquor better than you'd think," Chloe says.

I motion *no way*.

Everyone laughs.

Chloe swats me.

Walker leans forward to pick up the mic. "Are we gonna

sit here or are we gonna embarrass the hell out of ourselves?"
He looks to me then to Ryan. "Do your thing."

Ryan and I usually duet a grunge number at karaoke. But
that's not what I want to do today.

I lean in to whisper in Chloe's ear. "Come up with me."

"And sing in front of people?" She shakes her head.

"Since when are you shy?" I ask.

"Since the day you met me in the ninth grade. That's a
terrible question."

"All right." I stand and offer her my hand. "What if I
promise to make it worth your while."

Her eyes perk. "Worth my while how?"

"I'll fuck you in the bathroom."

Her cheeks flush. "You would have done that anyway."

"Yeah. Definitely." I motion *come here*. "Shit. I wasn't
supposed to say that, was I?"

"You weren't," she says.

"Giving up my bargaining power." I shake my head with
mock shame. "Fuck. I need to work on my negotiation
skills."

She nods.

"Get up here with me because you want to."

She bites her lip.

"'Cause if you don't, I'm gonna have to do *Smells Like Teen
Spirit* instead of *Jeremy* and nobody wants that."

She nods with mock disgust. "That would be horrible."

∼

BY THE SECOND VERSE, CHLOE IS *IN* IT, BELTING OUT THE
song with everything she's got. When we finish, she hands
the mic to Walker, who regales us with his best Metallica
impression.

Bit by bit, she relaxes into the room. Sings along with

everyone, cheers, laughs, mocks me as senselessly as I deserve.

Everyone makes an effort to include Chloe. Hell, everyone likes her more than they like me.

Which is fine by me.

I don't live my life looking to be liked.

After a dozen songs, I lean in close and whisper in her ear. "Meet me in the bathroom in two songs."

She looks up at me and raises a brow *really*.

I nod *hell yes*. If she's not game for that, fine. But I'm taking her somewhere and fucking her.

She nods back, a much more timid *okay*, then she scoots to the other bench to get lost in Leighton and Iris's conversation.

I hang back. Watch Ryan serenade Leighton with her favorite song—this miserable, breathy number where the singer sounds simultaneously mid-fuck and about to break.

Personally, I don't see the appeal. But she laps it up like warm milk.

When Emma grabs the mic, I move to the door. Leave as inconspicuously as possible.

But the hallway isn't empty. Brendon is leaning against the wall, staring at me with a knowing look on his face.

I stare back. "Reliving a favorite memory?" Once upon a time, he popped Kaylee's cherry at this very karaoke. At least, that's the impression I got.

He shrugs *maybe*. "You really like her, huh?"

"Yeah, I do." My shoulders tense then relax. It's weird not firing back a joke. But it feels good, admitting it aloud. I want to scream it. I want to tell the entire world.

"You sure you know what you're doing?"

"Fuck no."

Brendon chuckles. "Sounds about right."

"Did you?"

He peers through the window on the door. Watches Kaylee clap over Em's performance. "Not for a second."

"Even after all that time pining?"

"Only made it worse."

"You ever figure it out?"

"Depends on the day."

"It's a hell of a thing, loving somebody."

His gaze shifts to me. His voice gets serious. Well, more serious. Brendon is always serious. "Is it?"

He's asking if I'm in love with her.

Fuck, I don't know.

I've never loved somebody. Never even thought about it. Certainly never considered it within the realm of possibility.

But Chloe...

"Fuck, you know that kind of insight is beyond my capabilities." I deflect with a joke.

But it doesn't fool him. He shakes his head *nice try*. "You want my advice?"

"No. But I'm sure I can't stop you."

"Yeah." His chuckle is soft. Knowing. "If you do love her, hold onto her. Don't let anybody, even yourself, convince you there's anything more important."

I shrug like his advice means nothing.

But that doesn't fool either of us.

Chapter Thirty-Two

DEAN

"**T**his is so much better than a karaoke bathroom." Chloe pulls my t-shirt over my head and tosses it aside.

"That's 'cause you have no idea how hot that bathroom is."

"I know enough." She reaches for my belt. Unfastens it. Pulls it from my jeans.

My hands go to her hips. I pull her body into mine. Lean down to press my lips to hers.

She rises to her tiptoes to meet me.

One hand knots in my hair. The other curls into the back of my neck.

She shifts her hips, grinding her crotch against mine. "Dean." Her breath catches in her throat. She forgets about teasing me. About banter. About everything but how badly she needs me.

"Yeah?" My fingertips skim the bare skin of her stomach.

"I'm glad I'm here."

"I'm fucking ecstatic you're here."

"I just mean..." Her brow furrows as she tries to find the words. When she doesn't, she shakes her head and brings her hands back to my jeans. "Thank you."

"For?"

"Everything." Her fingers dig into my sides. "Now take off your clothes."

"Which ones?"

"Uh-uh. No sass. All of them. Get naked and get on the couch."

"Yes, ma'am."

"Don't even."

"I never *have* been with a woman who wanted to be in control."

"I don't want to be in control." She cups me over my jeans. Groans as her palm brushes against my hard-on. "I just want you naked."

Fuck, all that denim in the way.

I can still feel the heat of her hand.

The friction of her touch.

My eyelids flutter together.

I want her badly.

But I still need to tease her. To keep this light. To get that laugh in my ears.

"How can you know if you've never tried it?" I peel her tank top up her stomach.

She lifts her arms over her head to help me.

Once it's on the floor, I bring my hands to her hips.

"That's a stupid question and you know it." She brings her palm back to my cock. Rubs me over my jeans. "Naked now."

"Sunshine, I'm not gonna do anything to stop exactly what you're doing."

"Oh." Her cheeks flush. "You're that—"

"Fuck." My nails dig into her skin. She's too fucking good

at this. She doesn't realize it either. She doesn't realize there's a sex goddess in those combat boots.

And, fuck, I can't take teasing tonight.

I need to be inside her.

To be one with her.

To be every cheesy cliché in the world.

I lean down to bring my lips to hers.

She meets me halfway. She kisses me softly.

Her lips part. Her groan vibrates down my neck.

Blood flows south.

No more talking.

It's not my body taking over.

It's my heart.

It's fucking weird. But right too.

I unzip her jeans and push them off her hips.

She shimmies out of them. Kicks them off her feet. Takes my hand and leads me to the couch.

I don't waste any time.

I pull a condom from my back pocket, do away with my jeans, and plant on the couch.

She looks down at me with hungry eyes. Like she wants to consume me. Like she wants every inch of me.

No. Like she needs every inch of me.

She slips onto the couch, her knees around my thighs, her body above mine.

Her eyes lock with mine as she wraps her fingers around my wrist and brings my hand to her chest.

I toy with her nipple with my thumb.

Her eyelids flutter closed. A groan falls off her lips. She's falling into that perfect trance. Where she's in a world of bliss and pleasure and nothing else.

She's already wet, but I warm her up anyway. My thumb goes to her clit. My index finger goes to her cunt.

She gasps as I slip a finger inside her. I watch pleasure spill over her expression as I push it deeper.

She brings her other hand to my cock. Wraps her fingers around me and pumps me with a steady stroke.

Fuck.

My thoughts scatter. The world fades away. Until she's the only thing I can see, touch, taste, feel.

She pumps me with steady strokes.

I drive my fingers into her.

The way she groans my name is ecstasy. But it's not enough. I need to be inside her.

I tear the condom wrapper open.

She stares down at me, watching as I slide the condom on.

Then her eyes are on mine.

They're wide with bliss, need, affection.

They're promising the world.

I want to take it from her. And to give it to her.

I want everything for her.

My hands go to her hips.

She stares into my eyes as I bring her body onto mine.

My tip strains against her.

Then it's one sweet inch at a time.

Fuck. She's soft. Wet.

Mine.

It floods my brain, my heart, my everything.

I need her to be mine.

All of her.

And I need to give her all of me.

But how the fuck do I do that?

I keep one hand on her hips to guide her.

I bring the other to the back of her head.

My fingers curl into her scalp as I pull her into a soft, slow kiss.

She wraps her arms around my shoulders.

I pull her closer.

Kiss her harder.

She rocks against me, rubbing her clit against my pubic bone.

Fuck, the friction of her soft, sweet cunt.

I groan against her lips.

She pulls back with a sigh of pleasure.

Her head tilts to the right. Her hair falls in front of her eyes. Her lips part with a moan.

"Fuck." Her nails dig into the tender skin on my shoulders.

I look up at her. Watch pleasure spill over her expression as she drives me deeper.

It hits me all at once.

I love her.

I'm balls deep in the woman who's owned my masturbatory fantasies since I was a teenager, and it's the only thing in my head.

The timing is fucked.

And it's perfect.

My fingers curl into her hips. I guide her body over mine, so she can drive me deeper again and again.

Fuck.

My balls tighten.

My eyes close.

I reach up for her. Bring my hand to her cheek. Rub her temple with my thumb.

She lets out a soft murmur.

Then she's wrapping her arms around me.

Bringing her lips to mine.

We stay locked together, rocking together, breathing together, hearts beating together until she's there.

She pulls back to groan my name.

Her pulsing pushes me over the edge.

Pleasure floods my body as I come. I hold her close. Groan her name into her neck as I spill every drop.

She looks up at me with hazy eyes.

Her lips curl into the perfect shy smile.

And it hits me again.

I'm crazy fucking in love with her.

Chapter Thirty-Three

CHLOE

When we aren't working, we're in Dean's bed. Kissing, touching, fucking, talking about everything and nothing.

My last bit of defenses crumble.

I forget about the test results. About the difficulty of drawing a line between girlfriend/boyfriend and teacher/apprentice.

I forget about everything but the comfort of his body against mine.

I shouldn't lose myself in his arms. I shouldn't let down my walls. I shouldn't let myself fall for someone. Not without knowing if I'm going to be around.

But I do.

I can't help it.

TIME IS FUNNY. WHEN I'M WITH DEAN, DAYS BLUR together.

When I'm not, seconds stretch into hours.

The week goes quickly. And slowly. Except for the *holy fuck am I going to die* question nagging at me, it's normal.

We work. We play. We fuck like rabbits.

Brendon makes a big deal of wishing me goodbye before he leaves for his mini vacation. He's taking his girlfriend back to New Jersey, to be with her parents for the one year anniversary of her grandma's death.

It's sweet.

And it's everything I'm avoiding.

It makes the voice in my head a hundred decibels louder.

Thankfully, the next day brings a distraction in the form of tattooed sex god Hunter Keating. (Okay, I don't know that he's a sex god, but that seems to be the case for most guys around here).

He arrives at the shop bright and early, fingers wrapped around a thermos of coffee, deep blue eyes filled with calm concentration, chip firmly on shoulder.

If anything, he looks more broody and intense than he did last week.

I guess it fits. He is filling in for Brendon. If this is Hunter's usual vibe, he more than belongs here.

Dean nods a hello. He motions to our suite, where I'm working on a mock up.

I shoot him a *what's that supposed to mean* look.

He chuckles. "I looked at you. That enough for a reaction, sunshine?"

More than enough. With everything going through my head... I need to be at his apartment. In his arms. In his bed.

I need the rest of the world to go away.

I stand, set my sketchbook on the chair, greet Hunter. "Hey Hunter." I offer my hand.

He shakes. "Good to see you, Chloe."

I nod.

"It's Chloe Grace Lee," Dean jumps in. "And she knows karate—"

"Aikido," I correct.

His voice stays bouncy. Proud. "Don't fuck with her or she'll fuck you up."

Hunter's eyes flit from me to Dean then back to me. He's trying to figure out why Dean is teasing me.

Okay, he's trying to figure out if we're fucking.

Dean's wearing his usual *I love starting shit* smile.

Does he care if Hunter knows?

There is something about this being *our* world. About having *our* secret.

Especially when...

Who knows what the hell happens after I get the call?

"Shit, you can cut the sexual tension with a knife, huh?" Dean winks at me. Then at Hunter.

I stare at my... whatever I should call him, trying to figure out his intentions.

There's something about his devilish smile, about the softness in his eyes.

He's trying to keep me here. To keep me present.

He's doing it in the most Dean way possible.

But, well, that's the man I... I can't use that word. Not yet. But, fuck, I really, really like him.

I take a deep breath. Shrug my shoulders. There's a lot to do today. I can't get sucked into thoughts about the future.

I motion for Hunter to follow me. "You're borrowing Brendon's suite for now." I lead him to the center suite. "Not that it's officially his. Now that you're working here—"

"I'm just filling in," he says.

I look back to Dean. He knows Hunter a lot better than I do, but there's no sign he knows why Hunter is all quiet and afraid of commitment.

God, he really is intense.

Hurt.

He's trying to hide it, but it's there. It's all over his expressive eyes.

Thank god for eyeliner and mascara, or I'd be cursed with the same problem.

"Been awhile, huh?" he asks.

"Yeah." I study Hunter. Fail to find a clue as to why he's walking around with the weight of the world on his shoulders. "How have you been?"

"Alright," he lies. "How about you?"

"I'm here." I turn to Dean. Motion *play along*. I need to step into a role. I need to be someone other than the girl waiting for her test results. "It's horrible torture, being here, but at least I'm learning."

"Oh yeah? You want to quit?" Dean teases.

I flip him off. "What if I do, Dick Face?"

He blows me a kiss. "You know I take that as a compliment."

My cheeks flush. "He's under some delusion that by calling him Dick Face, I'm saying his dick is beautiful."

"And?" Hunter asks.

"I've seen better." There's a wink in my voice.

Even though he's behind me, I can feel Dean's smile.

We're flirting through Hunter.

It's wrong. And weird. And hot as hell.

I take Hunter through everything in the suite. Explain the shop layout. Show him his schedule—when Emma isn't working, I'm the one in charge of it.

He nods along with everything I say, quiet and intense, then he falls back into work.

I take his lead. Try my best to focus on our first appointment. Fail.

My head keeps going back to the test results.

To the little matter of whether I'm going to live or die.

WHEN WE FINALLY BREAK, I'M DEAD TIRED. LEIGHTON wasn't kidding about tattoos being bad for your back. Hunching over clients all day is brutal.

I let Emma charm her way through check out, but she isn't her usual confident self. She trips over her words. Blushes endlessly. Shifts her weight between her feet nervously.

Her attention isn't on the client.

It's on Hunter.

She's as bad as I am.

As smitten as I am.

I wait until he leaves to approach the counter.

She folds her arms over her chest. Shakes off her blush. "What?"

"You know Hunter?"

"Oh. Well... Yeah." She bites her lip. "He and Brendon have been friends for a long time."

"Oh, he's the one—"

"Shut up." She motions to Ryan, sitting in his suite, working on a mock-up. "I don't need the lecture. Not from Ryan and not from you."

"I'm sleeping with my boss. You think I'm going to tell you not to go after someone working here?"

"Yeah." She brushes her dark hair behind her ear. "You can act all tough and no-nonsense, Chloe, but you don't fool me. Deep down, you're a softie."

"Am I?"

"Yeah. You probably have some sort of advice for me that belongs on a poster. *Follow your heart. Chase after your dreams. Today is a gift. That's why they call it the present.*"

I can't help but laugh. Emma is usually perceptive, but she's dead wrong about this. "Are you going to fuck him?"

"No." Her cheeks flush. "He thinks I should join a convent."

I shoot her a look.

She makes that *ugh, my brother is so annoying* sound. "Brendon asked Hunter to keep an eye on me. So... he's basically an annoying babysitter."

"You never had a crush on an older baby sitter?"

"Never."

"Then why do you keep staring at him?"

"I don't."

I nod *you do*. "He's staring back."

"You think?" She clears her throat. "I mean... it doesn't matter. We're friends. If that."

"You're not into him?"

"Yeah. Totally." She swallows hard. "Not at all."

"Uh-huh."

"Say I was?"

"Say you were."

"It wouldn't matter. Brendon will kill him if anything happens. And... Uh... Ahem." Her gaze shifts to something behind me. "Dean. Hey. Great work. Amazing. You're talented."

"What are you trying to hide?" Dean looks from Emma to me. His fingertips graze my hip for a second, then they're back at his side.

The stolen touches are divine. Wrong in the way that's so, so right.

"Nothing." Emma's dark eyes fill with nerves. She shoots me a *girl code, please* look.

I nod. Of course.

It's quite the thrill, being able to participate in the girl code again. For a long, long time, I've been on the sidelines. I've been avoiding connections.

Reaching out feels good.

Dean's fingers brush my wrist. "We've got two hours for lunch. I need the first one."

Emma raises a brow. "Keep it down."

His smile gets wicked. "If only." He takes a step toward the office. Motions follow me. "We're being good."

"You can be good?" Emma asks.

"Depends," he says.

She laughs. "On?"

"How much Chloe glares at me." His laugh bounces around the room. "You know that glare does things to me, sunshine."

I shoot him said glare.

He presses his hand to his heart. "Just kidding. It's more here." He presses both hands to his crotch.

Emma shakes her head *you're ridiculous*.

He really is.

In the best possible way.

I follow Dean into the office.

He leaves the door open. "You have your gun?"

I motion to the autoclave.

He nods and peels the gun from the device.

His fingers brush mine as he hands it over. "Today is the day."

"Huh?"

"You're ready to do skin."

My heart thuds against my chest.

My stomach flutters.

My breath catches in my throat.

I'm ready to do skin.

That doesn't feel possible.

But there isn't a single sign of teasing on Dean's beautiful face. He's dead serious.

I muster up all the confidence I have. "Okay." This isn't like before, where he dared me to tattoo his ankle. This time, I'm ready.

"It's up to you if you want to do me or yourself."

I nod.

"But you should know, I'm gonna watch either way." He winks. Back to teasing Dean.

But that feels right too. Teasing and serious Dean want the same thing. Both of them want a reaction.

They want love, attention, affection, respect. They're just going about it in different ways.

"Can I really do you?" I ask.

He raises a brow what do you think? "We should probably do the ink first."

My lips curl into a smile. "Should we?"

"Yeah. I'm a greedy fucker. I'm going to take the whole afternoon if you let me."

My shoulders soften. The teasing helps. This is a big, serious moment, but it feels wrong treating it with dry respect.

This is exactly how it should be.

"Do I have to do another star?" I ask.

"Or a spade or a heart. Your call."

My fingers curl around the metal. My call. Do I want my first piece of ink on me or him?

There's something so, so right about tattooing my teacher. And about tattooing Dean in particular.

But this is still my journey.

It should be me. "I want to do myself."

He pulls his cell from his pocket. "I can record it for later, right?"

"One picture."

"You into that?"

"Pictures?" Heat builds below my belly. I've never really considered the idea of recording myself, alone or with someone else, but the thought of doing it with Dean...

Fuck, it's hot in here.

My nod is heavy. Needy. Not at all professional. "Stop distracting me. I'm doing this thing."

He motions to the materials on the desk. Everything is here. Rubbing alcohol. Gloves. Tracing paper. Cotton balls. "Make the stencil."

I slide the gloves on, pick up the sharpie, and draw the perfect heart. A tiny, smooth thing with an arrow through the center.

He places his body behind mine, his chest against my back, his arm around my waist, his breath warming my neck.

Fuck, the heat of his body feels good.

Distractingly good.

Which is another point in the we can't handle keeping work and play separate column. But I'm not willing to give up either. Not right now. Not when I finally have everything I want.

"You sure you want something that tricky?" He brings his hand to the drawing. Traces its shape. "It will be easier if you lose the arrow."

"But it wouldn't be right."

He nods *fair enough*. Hands me the stencil.

I transfer the design and cut where I need to.

There.

It's ready.

But where the hell do I want this? I stare at the thick plastic like it has the answers.

Of course, it doesn't.

"Did mine on my ankle. It's tricky to get into position,

but it's a good spot. Easy to hide if you fuck it up. Especially if you live in combat boots."

"What if I decide I love sandals?"

He shakes his head with mock disgust. "I'll have to look outside to check if pigs are flying."

"See if hell has frozen over."

"Exactly, yeah. But I'm pretty sure it did last night."

"Huh?"

"Nothing." His voice drops to that soft, sweet tone. "Come on, sunshine. Sit down and ditch the pants."

"I could just roll them up."

"Where's the fun in that?"

I can't help but laugh. He's just so... Dean.

He makes me feel so warm and fuzzy. Like a birthday card, a tea on a cold morning, a sweater, a puppy.

Like every cheesy simile in the world.

God, the things he makes me feel.

They go beyond like.

But then...

If everything isn't okay...

I can't...

I can't think about that right now. I have to do this.

My first tattoo.

On my skin.

No pressure.

I set the stencil on the desk while I set up in the office chair. My inner left ankle will be easiest—I'm right handed.

I unlace my boot, kick it off, peel off my socks, roll my jeans to mid-calf.

There. Cotton swab. Rubbing alcohol. Stencil. Tape.

That's it.

I'm ready.

Technically.

Dean hands me the gun and a fresh pad of ink. I set the

latter on the table. Flip it open. Stare at it like that will give me a bit of courage.

Doing ink is terrifying enough, but doing it on my skin? God.

My stomach flutters.

My heart thuds against my chest.

My breath... I'm not sure I even feel my breath.

I bend my leg, set as much of it as I can on the desk. It's not the most comfortable position, but it gives me the perfect canvas.

My fingers curl around the gun.

"Take your time, sunshine." Dean's voice is sweet. Caring. Then it's silly. Teasing. "The shop is open until eight."

"Fuck you."

"We already hashed this out. After."

We did. But he was kidding. But then... I hope some of him meant it, because I'm already buzzing with adrenaline. By the end...

Fucking him is the perfect way to close this.

I suck a breath through my teeth. Exhale slowly. I've done this a thousand times on fruit. Skin is similar. It's just it's my skin and I'm going to feel the pain of the needle while I figure it out.

But this pain is nothing compared to what I've been through.

The buzz of the gun fills the room.

Needle to ink.

Then to skin.

Fuck. That stings. My breathing stops. My heart thuds. My hands get sweaty. Clammy.

But I manage to trace the stencil. Up and around, straight, then curved, again and again. The pain stays but it stops hurting. It becomes a part of my reality. A thing to face, not fear.

It's hard to explain, but the hurt feels good. It feels like I'm alive.

It takes two minutes to finish the design. I barely manage to breathe through it.

But I survive.

Fuck. My entire body buzzes enough to make up for the ceasing of the gun's hum. I go to push myself up, but Dean stops me.

He holds me against the chair, pinning me at my shoulders. "Aftercare first."

"Right."

"Let me." He pulls two gloves from the box and slides them on. Then he's kneeling between my legs, peeling off the stencil, rubbing lotion into my skin and wrapping my fresh ink in plastic.

His touch is soft, gentle, the touch of a lover, not a teacher. But right now, I don't care about the line blurring. Only about every single way I want him.

God, the ways I want him.

His fingers curl into my foot as he looks up at me. "There. Done."

"Done." I look down at the ink like it's my first. In a way, it is. It feels as badass as it did back then. And, well, I'm far from Dean quality, but this is at least a little better than that lopsided star. "What do you think?"

"It's perfect for you." He plants a kiss on my ankle, just above the ink. "And, fuck, this position is perfect for me."

Yes, it is.

I spread my legs a little wider.

His fingers curl into my thighs.

I'm about to dig my hands into his hair and order him out of his clothes when my phone buzzes against my thigh.

Fuck, that vibration...

I reach for the thing to silence it.

But it isn't a SPAM call.

It's the doctor's office.

"Let me take care of this first." I push the chair backward as I answer the phone.

Dean's blue eyes fill with concern. He's reading me too well. He knows it's the call.

He can't know.

"It's just my dad," I lie.

He nods like he believes me.

I don't stick around to figure out if he does. I answer the call. Bring the phone to my ear as I step into the main room. "Hello."

"Chloe, is that you?" Dr. Nguyen asks. I'd recognize his voice anywhere.

"Yes."

The air conditioner hums to life.

Angsty, breathy vocals drown out the quiet conversations.

"I'm calling about your test results," he says.

My stomach drops.

He isn't starting with *your test was negative. You're still cancer free.*

Which means...

Fuck.

"Oh." I swallow hard. Press my eyelids together. Cross my fingers. *Please be okay. Please be okay. Please be okay.*

"Can you come in later today?"

Fuck.

Fuck. fuck. Fuck.

My breath is shaky. Shallow. "You can tell me now."

"There was a spot on the scan. It's probably nothing."

Of course. It's always probably nothing. It's nothing until it's something.

"It looks like a cyst. But we want to do a needle biopsy to be sure."

All the breath leaves my body at once.

His words don't make it into my ears.

Probably isn't enough.

Maybe isn't enough.

This is...

I can't...

"When can you come in?" he asks.

The room is spinning. My head is fuzzy. Light. I...

I grab onto the wall for support.

It's just barely enough.

"I can have reception call you back when you've had time to process it. I know this can be scary, Chloe, but the odds of relapse after your procedure are low."

"And the odds of beating a relapse are worse."

His voice drops. "If it is cancer, we'll have options. At the very least, we'll be able to make you comfortable."

That's oncologist for *you're fucked but we'll drug you until you don't care.*

I try to process his words. To believe that the odds are low, that it's probably a cyst, that it's probably okay.

But I can't.

It screams in my brain.

You're sick again.

You're dying.

You're a noose around everyone's neck.

"Chloe? Do you want Amelia to call in a few hours?"

"I can come in anytime. As soon as possible."

"Wednesday at noon," he offers.

That is soon. "And we'll know then?"

"The results usually take a few days, but I can have the lab fast track it. So it's only a few hours."

"Thank you."

He says something in response, but I don't hear a word of it.

I end the call and slide my cell into my pocket.

Footsteps move into the main room.

They come closer.

Then Dean's fingers are brushing my shoulder.

And his chest is against my back.

And his words are in my ears.

"Everything okay, sunshine?"

Chapter Thirty-Four

CHLOE

It's such a funny question.

Is everything okay?

I spent the better part of a year coming to terms with the possibility of dying. Hell, after two weeks of chemo, it didn't seem like such a bad option. Certainly better than another round of the treatment that killed me from the outside. At least, if cancer took my life, I wouldn't go out feeling like I was dying. At least, not until the very end.

But things turned around. The tumor shrunk. The double mastectomy was successful. The disease didn't spread past my chest wall (pretty much a death sentence).

I was glad to be done with injecting poison into my veins and struggling through surgical recovery and waiting around in dull hospital rooms.

But I didn't know how to be alive anymore. I didn't know how to face my future. I had no idea what to do with the world of possibilities that opened up in front of me.

For so long, my only choice was what to watch on TV, which frozen dinner to eat, spending my energy on drawing or meeting Gia for coffee.

All of a sudden, I could do anything.

It paralyzed me for a while. I was stiff and awkward amongst the healthy. But I figured it out, bit by bit. I went to aikido. I swam laps at the gym. I took figure drawing classes and got new tattoos and begged artists to consider training me.

And then Dean came back into my life and he opened up everything.

My world, my body, my heart.

I thought I was okay with this possibility.

With him sticking by my side no matter what.

I thought I needed that.

No, I do.

But I can't do it to him.

I can't be the weight around his neck.

I know what it feels like, watching someone you love die. Wanting, more than anything, to save them, but knowing there's nothing you can do.

He can't save me.

But I can save him.

I have to.

"Chlo'." He rubs my upper arms with a soft, sweet touch. "Your dad okay?" He sells the words, but it's clear he doesn't believe me.

"Yeah. He's fine." I bite my lips. How the hell do I get out of this? We have an appointment in an hour and a half. We have work all week. I'm supposed to sit by his side and watch him all... all year.

But then this apprenticeship was never going to work out.

Not with the two of us desperate to tear each other's clothes off every three seconds.

And not if...

If I'm out of time, it's not as if I'll be able to learn to be a tattoo artist anyway.

"But I... Uh..." I can't tell him the truth. He won't take it. I need to convince him I want him gone. That it's because I don't love him. Not because I do.

Gently, he turns me around.

His hand goes to my chin. He tilts my head toward him. Until I'm looking up at him.

And he's looking down at me.

My eyes dart around the room. I look everywhere else. Anywhere else. The string lights. The framed art. The open office door. The windows looking out on the dirty Venice street. The beach beyond that.

The blue sky mocking me with its endless brightness.

"What's wrong?" His voice is soft. Loving.

"I was just thinking."

"About?" He cups my cheek with his palm. Catches a tear with his thumb. "You're crying."

"No." I shake my head, but it does nothing to stem the tears catching on my lashes. Fuck this. I can't cry in front of him. That's giving it away.

And, well, this isn't going to be like it was with my mom. I'm going to find the strength to convince him I can handle this. To convince him I'm okay.

I suck my breath through my teeth, but that doesn't help.

When I blink, tears catch on my lashes. Then they're everywhere.

The room goes blurry.

"I'm sorry." I rest my forehead against his chest. Dig my fingers into the soft fabric of his shirt.

"Hey." He wraps his arms around me.

One presses into my lower back.

The other curls into my hair.

"You're gonna be okay, sunshine. I promise."

I shake my head.

"Yeah. Maybe not for as long as either one of us would like, but you will be okay."

Fuck. He knows.

Of course, he knows.

Why else would I be bawling in the middle of the shop?

I...

I can't let him follow me down this road.

If I only do one thing, it will be this.

"Come on. I'll drive you back to my place. You can take the rest of the week off. Get your head on straight."

"But—"

"You're right. I'll cancel the rest of today's appointments."

"No, Dean." I try to push myself away from him, but I can't. He feels too good. "Stop. Listen."

He runs his fingers through my hair.

I look up at him. Finally.

There's hurt in his expression but just barely. Mostly, he looks confident. Sure. Like he's ready to do anything to make this better for me.

Maybe he is.

God, I hope he is.

"It's not that. It's probably nothing," I say. "Probably a cyst."

"You don't have to convince me of shit."

That's where he's wrong. I do.

And I have to sell the hell out of it.

"I'm fine. The follow-up is just a precaution."

His eyes bore into mine. They pick me apart. Demand every thought in my head.

"That isn't what I want to talk about."

"You don't want to talk about how your can—"

"Don't say it here. Please." I wrap my fingers around his wrists. "The thing is..."

He stares back, patient and caring.

"I think... No, I know... No... Forget the qualifiers. I'm breaking up with you."

Chapter Thirty-Five

DEAN

I blink twice.

It does nothing to change the situation.

Chloe is still standing in front of me, tears streaking her dark eyes, lips curled into a frown.

She's still curling into herself.

She's still about to break.

"I should go." She takes a step backward. "I'll call later. We can work out what I'm doing with the apprenticeship. I should probably be somewhere else anyway."

"I want you here."

"No. I... I can't be here." Her gaze meets mine for a second. She stares into me, offering something, an apology or an explanation, I'm not sure.

Then she turns and her gaze settles on her combat boot.

Her left foot is still bare.

"Oh. I should... I should get that. Then go." She slides her hands into her front pockets. Slowly, she turns back to the office.

I stare into her eyes, but she refuses to meet my gaze.

To say anything.

To offer a fucking clue.

"Why are you running away from this?" It's far too insightful, but that's what she does to me. She wakes up this other part of me. Fuck, I love that part of me.

"It's doesn't matter. I'm breaking up with you."

I reach for a response, but nothing comes.

This doesn't make any sense.

It's fucking bizarre.

There's no way she's okay. Not with the way she was crying. But her voice is calm and even. Like she's talking about the weather or her schedule or her favorite tea.

Not like she's weighing life and death.

She moves around me on her way to the office. Her movements are soft. Quiet. Emma's emo album drowns it out. I'm not usually a fan of this whiny chordspam, but, fuck, right now, the angst feels just right.

Chloe steps out of the office with her backpack around her shoulders. "I'm sorry."

"Then stay."

She shakes her head like she wishes she could.

Then she walks out of the shop and out of my life.

Chapter Thirty-Six

CHLOE

❧❧❧

It's a dozen blocks to Dean's place. And there's my old Japanese sedan. Black, of course. With black leather seats, of course. And a black steering wheel cover, of course.

I slide inside, put on my favorite grunge album, hold it together for long enough to drive to my place.

Every step feels like a million miles. Climbing up the stairs takes everything I have.

But it's worth it for the quiet solitude of my room.

The soft embrace of my grey sheets.

This is the bed where Dean and I...

He's all over this room. In the old movie posters—the ones we watched together. In the tattoo mock-ups hanging on the walls. In the framed art from high school.

The smell of the sheets.

The mirror.

And the girl staring back at me in the reflection, asking me why the fuck I'm running from the person I need more than anything.

Chapter Thirty-Seven

DEAN

The afternoon is a blur of ink, skin, shitty music, quiet conversations. I fail to bring my usual banter. I distract my clients okay, but it's dull as doorknobs shit. Weather. Sports. Celebrity and shop gossip.

I cancel my gym session with Walker.

Jog around the beach instead.

Fail to find clarity.

It's not in my shower, on the couch where I fucked Chloe last night, on any cop show on TV, in a takeout Thai feast.

My bedroom is a mess of memories and feelings.

The feel of her fingertips against my skin.

That short black hair in my hands.

That strawberry shampoo.

She's the only thing in my head.

I find my cell. Shoot her a text.

Dean: You get home okay?

It takes an eternity for her to reply back. But she does.

Chloe: Yeah, thanks. I'll get in touch in a few days to talk about my apprenticeship. Until then, I want to be alone. I really appreciate the opportunity. You're a great teacher. I know you don't believe it, but you're a great guy. Good luck with everything.

It's as courteous as can be.

Like she's already over breaking my heart and walking away.

Chapter Thirty-Eight

DEAN

"Where's your better half?" Emma takes a long sip of her coffee. Her dark eyes fix on mine.

It's weird. She's nothing like Brendon, but the two of them have the same stare. The *I don't know what you're doing, but I know it's wrong. I wish I could fix it, but, honestly, you're hopeless.*

"Taking a few days off." The words feel funny on my tongue. I'm no stranger to lying. But doing it with a straight-forward response? It's weird.

It's been twenty-four hours since Chloe walked out that door and it still doesn't feel real.

This is a bad dream.

Or maybe our whole relationship was a dream.

I was some better version of myself. She was exactly what I needed.

That kind of thing doesn't happen in reality.

Badasses in combat boots don't fall for assholes who threw them away.

"Why?" Emma's red nails tap the counter. She leans back

on her stool. Places one hand on her lap. The other flat against the plastic. "What did you do?"

"All right, all right. I confess. I got carried away last night. Baby I want to split you in half was supposed to be a figure of speech, but one thing led to another."

"Uh-huh. Right."

She's seeing through my bullshit.

Time to deflect. "What's the deal with you and Hunter?"

Her cheeks flush immediately. "Who?"

"The guy you were fawning over yesterday."

She plays dumb.

"Who's been your brother's friend most of your life?"

"What about him?"

"He was looking at you the way a dog looks at a bone."

"Can you blame him?" She motions to her tight tank top.

I chuckle. "It was more than that."

"He's a man. I have boobs. I understand how it works."

Her tits are nice, but that isn't why he was staring. "He was staring like he's into you."

"No. He's just babysitting me while Brendon is away."

"That your kink?"

"Haha." She makes a show of rolling her eyes.

"Please. Your brother is dirty as fuck. You think I'll buy you as vanilla?"

"What did you do to Chloe?"

"What did you do to Hunter?"

"I told him to drop the babysitter bullshit."

"Even though you kinda like it?"

"I do not."

I nod.

She shakes her head. But it's there in her dark eyes. She's into it. She's into him.

"You like a big, strong man looking out for you."

"What? Cause I have daddy issues? Get some original material."

"He's hot."

"So are you."

"Thanks for noticing."

She shoots me a *get real* look.

She takes none of my shit.

It's one of the things I like about her.

Only...

Fuck does it make me think of Chloe.

Of her bad ass smile and the hurt in her dark eyes.

It's easier teasing my friend than thinking about how I'm losing the woman I love. "You gonna fuck him or what?"

"You gonna fix this shit with Chloe?"

"You want to fuck him."

"There's a difference between finding a man attractive—"

"No. You want to tear his clothes off and ride him all night."

She tries and fails to play aloof.

Her teeth sink into her lip.

Her blush spreads down her neck.

Her chest heaves with her inhale.

It should thrill me, backing Em into a corner, getting her to spill.

But it doesn't.

It's empty. Same as my ten o'clock and my noon. And, fuck, the odds are bad that my one thirty will be any better.

"Just keep it to yourself." She presses her palms together. "Okay?"

No. Agreeing means this conversation is over. Which means I have no place to deflect. No armor. Nothing to stop her questions from piercing my gut. "I dunno. Seems like Brendon would want to know."

"You wouldn't narc and we both know it."

I wouldn't, but I can still bluff. "Try me."

"Sure." She stares me down. "Why is Chloe taking a few days off?"

"She has some shit to deal with."

"Which is..."

"None of your business."

"Why are you flinching when I say her name?"

"No idea what you're talking about."

"You do realize I was here yesterday when she stomped out the door crying?"

I shrug like I can barely recall yesterday afternoon.

"What the hell did you to do her, Dean?"

"Nothing."

"Well, fix it. I like her."

"I like her too."

"SO FIX IT."

"It's not fixable." The room hums with the sound of the air-conditioning. It competes with the chill, acoustic music flowing from the speakers. I'm not sure who picked this. Only that it's all wrong. Calm, peaceful vibes are the opposite of what I need.

My head is a storm. I need angry. Angsty. Miserable.

Emma slides off her stool. She moves around the counter and places herself next to me. "What happened?"

I shrug like it doesn't matter.

"Drop the chill act, Dean. It's obviously bullshit. What happened?"

"She ended shit."

"Why?"

"She didn't say."

"No way."

I nod. "Way." My voice cracks. Thinking about this is agony. But it's not like it's going anywhere. If Chloe is gone, if that's what she wants...

Nobody changes Chloe's mind. Not about anything.

Emma places her palms on the counter. Uses them to hoist herself onto it. "She really didn't say?"

"Yeah."

She taps her toes together. "But you..." She nudges me with her shoulder. "You must know why. What you did."

Why? "Maybe."

"Your eyes lit up. You know."

"Maybe."

"Well..."

I say nothing.

The door rings and Ryan steps into the shop. He holds his hand over his eyes, blocking the glare of the fluorescent lights.

Which is overkill, because he's bathed in sunlight.

Like an angel in all black.

Fuck, the sight of black jeans is a knife in my heart. That's all it takes. Black jeans.

There's no way I'm going to survive the next week.

Or the next month.

Or year.

"What did you do to him?" Ryan shoots Emma a curious look.

"Chloe ended things," she said.

"Fucking snitch." I pull out my cell. Open my address book. Scroll to *Brendon*. "Two can play that game."

"You think I'm scared you'll tell my brother I have a crush on a guy? And I don't... I don't even like him." Emma folds her arms, holding strong.

But the fear in her dark eyes gives her away.

"Yeah." I nod. Go to press dial.

She lunges for my phone.

I hold it over my head, but Emma is tall and she's wearing wedges. It's within reach.

I step backward.

Ryan moves between us. "Somebody explain."

"Emma has a crush on—" Damn, I can't rat her out. It's too low. "A client. He's coming in next week."

She flips me off.

Ryan looks to me with a *get real* expression. "You think I'm concerned about Emma's sex life?"

"If I was considering sleeping with a client, you'd crucify me," I say.

He rolls his eyes. Turns to Emma. "What happened with Chloe?"

"Yesterday, she came out here to answer a call. Then when Dean came out, she started crying. Really crying. And she stomped out of here. Dean looked miserable. And not even miserable for Dean. Straight-up heartbroken. He's been a shell of himself all day." Her eyes fill with concern.

I'm actively trying to piss her off and she's still concerned.

It's that bad.

"You got in a fight?" he asks.

"No. She ended things." Emma stares at the cell in my hand. "Are you going to put that away?"

"Not planning on it," I say.

Ryan shoots me a serious look.

Fine. I slide my cell into my pocket. It's not like I'm actually going to snitch. I need the damn thing gone. It reeks of Chloe and her cordial, all business text.

Ryan surveys the shop. At the moment, it's just the three of us. Walker is at lunch. Brendon is on vacation.

He looks to Emma. "Do me a favor, Em."

She smooths her dress. "Sure."

He pulls a ten from his wallet. "Grab a cup of coffee. Come back in twenty."

Her eyes go to the clock. "You sure you want to deal with him?"

"Who else is gonna do it?" he says.

"Fuck you." This is bullshit. I have an appointment in twenty minutes. I'm trapped here. I have to listen to his lecture.

I move to the Keurig in the lobby. Plug in a pod. Fill a cup with water from the cooler.

It's not like I'm gonna drink the shit tea this thing makes.

But I need some sort of distraction.

Ryan and Emma whisper. She nods in agreement then moves toward the exit.

"I'm sorry, Dean. I hope you two work things out." She pushes the door open. "Let me know if you need to talk." She steps outside and disappears in the afternoon light.

Ryan crosses the room to me.

He nods to the teal bench against the window. "Let's talk."

I stay put. "Let's not."

"What would you do if you were me?"

"Give you shit until you explained."

"So, skip the middle step."

It's a reasonable suggestion. But reasonable isn't appealing at the moment. Reason isn't getting me anywhere.

Things were good with me and Chloe. I was *there*. And now, exactly when she needs me, she's gone.

Reason suggests she doesn't trust me.

That, like everyone else, she sees me as a good time and nothing more.

Reason is my fucking nemesis.

Reason can die in a fire.

Tea fills the paper cup with a steady *drip, drip, drip*. It's total crap. It even smells like coffee.

Ryan takes a seat on the bench. Leans back. Rests his head against the window. "Never seen you this miserable."

"'Cause you haven't looked."

"I know you've been this miserable. But I've never seen you wear it with pride."

Pride is the wrong word, but he's in the right ballpark. I shrug. "Am I getting on your turf?"

"No." He folds one leg over the other. "Being an asshole isn't gonna get me to back off."

"It might. If I dial it up to ten."

He shakes his head. "I'm gonna babysit you until you spill." His voice is steady.

His expression is confident.

I know my brother.

He isn't going to back down.

But that doesn't mean I have to make this easy for him.

The Keurig spits out the last drop of tea. I wrap my fingers around the paper cup. Bring it to my lips.

It's terrible, but the familiarity is comforting all the same.

I take a seat on the bench opposite his. Sip my tea like this is a normal Tuesday afternoon. "How's your girl?"

"Good. How's yours?"

"You heard Em. She isn't my girl anymore."

He raises a brow *really, you're stopping there*.

Yeah. That feels like a good place to stop. I opened my heart with Chloe. Now she's gone. What's the fucking point?

"Why'd she end things?"

"Why do you care?"

"You're my brother. My friend. I love you."

"Didn't realize you could admit that."

He shoots me that same *really* look.

I nod. Yeah. Really. Ryan isn't the cuddly type.

"Did she end things?"

"What do you think?" The sass does nothing to soothe me. It's empty. Useless.

"You're only convincing me you need help."

I guess I do.

"Let's try this again." He turns so we're face-to-face. "Why did Chloe end things?"

I reach for a sarcastic response. Find nothing. I don't need attitude. I need understanding. And nobody gets heartbreak better than Ryan does. "She didn't say."

"You do something?"

I rack my brain for something, anything. "I fell in love with her."

"Does she know?"

"Maybe. I didn't tell her."

"You should."

Something tells me that isn't going to fix shit.

"You've got a knowing look, Dean."

I shrug. Fight my desire to push him away with a sarcastic insult. This whole opening my heart thing isn't my strong suit.

He doesn't buy it. "Why'd she bail?"

"She's dealing with some shit. She doesn't trust me to help her." That's the only explanation that makes sense.

"She trusted you to teach her."

"Yeah."

"To fuck her and not abandon her again."

"Who told you that?"

"You." His lips curl into a smile. "Just now."

"Fuck." I shake my head. "Rookie move."

My brother nods *yeah*. "I'd expect better."

"Give me a break. I'm heartbroken."

"You are."

"Don't gloat."

"No. Just... Never thought I'd see the day."

"Me either."

He motions for me to hand my tea over.

I do.

His nose scrunches as he takes a sip. "Is it supposed to taste like that?"

"Like shitty, watered down coffee? What do you think?"

He tosses the cup in the trash. "How did that go down?"

"We were at the same party, back in high school. I thought... I guess I thought that would end it. Get me to stop thinking about her. But it didn't."

"And then you bailed?"

"It was just before graduation, yeah."

"She must have hated you for that."

I nod. "And for a hell of a lot more."

"But she got over it."

"I thought so."

"She did. She's bubbly around you."

Maybe. I don't fucking know anymore.

"Yeah. She is. She's as happy as I am around Leigh."

"You're an obnoxious motherfucker now."

"Thanks." He leans back. Takes a deep, steady breath. Exhales slowly. "Have you considered that this, her running away, isn't about you?"

The suggestion cuts through my armor. Am I being an egomaniac about this?

"She's freaking out about something." He raises his brow, inviting me to explain.

I don't.

"Is it possible she's locking you out because she's scared?"

"Anything is possible."

"Maybe it has nothing to do with trusting you. Maybe it's all about her."

Maybe. She was really fucking insistent about how awful it was watching her mother die.

Is she trying to protect me?

After everything?

After begging me to stay?

It's possible.

It's a brighter idea than sitting around here moping.

Ryan runs his fingers through his hair. "You figured something out."

"Maybe."

"No. It's in your eyes. You know what it is."

I might. "How much time do you have until your next appointment?"

He looks to the clock. "Twenty minutes."

"You want to help me with this?"

"What do you think I'm doing sitting here?"

"A yes would suffice."

He smiles. "Not with you, it wouldn't."

Chapter Thirty-Nine

CHLOE

Tuesday stretches on forever.

I watch TV with my sketchbook and all the Earl Grey ice cream I can eat.

My heart begs me to turn my cell back on. To call Dean. To tell him how wrong I was. How much I miss him. How terrified I am to do this without him.

But I hold strong.

It makes sense, in my head.

I can save him from this. I want that for him. I want to spare him the pain I felt.

But, God, for me...

I want to hold onto him and never let go.

A LITTLE AFTER SUNSET, DAD KNOCKS ON MY DOOR. "DEAN called."

I wipe my tired eyes. If it's possible to run out of tears, I'm there. "Is everything okay?"

"He told me about the test."

Oh.

Dad knocks again. "Come downstairs. I ordered pizza."

"I'm not hungry."

"It's veggie combo."

My stomach growls. "With peppers?"

"Extra."

"Okay." I push myself up from my desk chair. My sketchbook is still sitting on my desk, still open to the page of my current work in progress. *Memento Mori* covered in lush orchids. As if I need to scribble "remember your mortality" on my skin to realize I could die at any moment.

But *Carpe Diem* still feels too fucking easy.

I slip into my hoodie. Pull the zipper to my chest. Play with my sleeves as I follow Dad down the stairs.

The house is quiet. Warm. Light.

The smell of pizza wafts into my nostrils. Cheese. Tomato. Peppers. Mmm.

I take a seat at the table.

He grabs two plates from the kitchen, sets one in front of me, slides into the seat next to mine.

Mmm. That looks as good as it smells.

My hands are greedy. I reach for a slice. Let it coat my fingers with grease and flour. "Thanks, Dad."

"Of course." He's more careful about taking a slice and setting it on his plate. "You want to tell me what happened?"

No. Not at all. I take a bite to buy myself time. It doesn't help. "There was a spot in my MRI results." I suck a breath between my teeth. "Dr. Nguyen thinks it's a cyst, but we need to do a needle biopsy to be sure."

"You don't sound confident."

"Can we not do this?"

"Do what, baby girl?"

I take another bite. Once again, chewing and swallowing fails to offer insight.

I have to woman up and admit this.

Deep breath.

Slow exhale.

"I don't want to hear that my health is hard for you." I press my fingertips together. "I know it is, and I'm sorry, but it's hard enough for me. I can't take your feelings on top of mine."

"Oh, Chloe... no."

"No?" My brow furrows. What the hell does he mean no?

Dad's expression softens. "I'm sorry if I made you feel like you needed to take care of me. After your mom... it was a bruise. But all I wanted was to support you."

"You did, but—"

"You had to reassure me that it would be okay. Just like your mom did."

I nod. "I don't want you to apologize for being worried about me. I was worried too." I swallow hard. "But I can't take it again. I can't take those scared looks, like I'm a vase that's gonna break."

Dad shakes his head. "You've never been fragile."

My shoulders relax. He's trying. I'm not sure if he's going to get there. But he is trying.

Maybe it's not the worst thing in the world, talking about this.

Letting my family support me.

I do feel lighter. Broader. Bigger.

Like I can take up space instead of curling myself into this tiny box that reads *Cancer Survivor*.

"Maybe. I don't know." I take a bite of my crust. Savor the fluffy doughy flavor. "I... I know you want to help, Dad, but I don't want to hear that the chances are nothing. Or that I should call Dean and make up and ask him to come. If I want to break up with him, I can."

His expression screws with confusion. "You broke up with him?"

"He didn't mention that?"

"No." Epiphany fills his eyes. "That explains a lot."

"Does it?"

Dad nods. "He was upset. It seemed unlike him."

"You barely know him."

"I could tell." Dad's smile is soft. "You think I let just anyone take out my youngest child?"

"I'm twenty-four. You don't get to screen dates."

"We're never going to agree about that."

"You really like him?"

"He makes you happy. He treats you well. Unless he has a drug problem I don't know about, I love him."

"No. He's a good guy." I take a bite. Chew. Swallow. But it no longer tastes like cheese and tomato perfection. "Is he okay?"

"Why don't you call and ask?" His voice drifts to that Dad *I know what's best* tone.

"No... I don't want him to get attached."

"He called to make sure someone was there to take care of you. He's already attached."

"But I can stop it from going further." I tear my crust into tiny pieces. "I remember. With you and Mom. It killed you, watching her die. Then losing her. Being without her. It's better if I spare him from all that."

His eyes turn down. "Baby girl..."

"But you... you never started dating again."

"I did."

"When?"

He arches a brow. "Is it that implausible."

"No. I just... you've never said anything."

"You think I want you screening my dates?"

"It seems fair."

He laughs. "Maybe. But that's the perk of being the parent. You don't have to play fair." He settles into his seat. "You're right. It was the most painful thing I ever went through, losing your mother. But I wouldn't trade that for anything."

"But—"

"No. You and Gia are the best part of my life. But even if your mom and I had never had kids, if it had just been the two of us, I wouldn't give up a single day of the happiness we had to erase the pain of losing her."

I swallow hard.

"This is life, baby girl. The highs and the lows. The pain that knocks you off course and the bliss that rights your ship. Loving someone, having that time with them, it's worth anything."

"But what if I'm—"

"He knows, doesn't he?"

"Yeah."

"So why is that your decision to make?"

"I don't know." I pull a green pepper from my slice. Eat it in two bites. "I just... I want to protect him. We're new. He can get over me. Find someone else."

"You sure about that?"

"No..." If Dean really went twenty-five years locking everyone else out, it's unlikely he's going to let anyone else in.

"And what about you? Are you going to be okay without him?"

"I'll feel better knowing I'm not hurting him."

"Keeping him from loving you?"

I bite my lip.

"What if he does already?"

"No. It's been nothing."

"Do you love him?"

"I don't know. Maybe."

"You must care pretty deeply to want to protect him like this."

"Maybe."

"What if your roles were reversed? If he was sick? Would you walk away to keep from hurting?"

"Of course not."

"Why not?"

"Who would do that?"

"But you'd get hurt."

"So? Life is getting hurt. You'll never experience anything good if you're afraid of getting hurt."

Dad smiles. "You took the words out of my mouth, baby girl."

Chapter Forty

S leep eludes me. I toss and turn. I think about tests and promises and the look on Mom's face when she told us she was dying. The way my heart broke right there, then broke into a million smaller pieces as I watched her slip away.

Grief fills my memories as moonlight flows through the curtains.

But something changes when the sun breaks the horizon.

Orange streaks across the sky.

Dad's advice starts to make sense.

The ugly memories fall back to happy ones. The way Dad held Mom after they thought me and Gia were upstairs playing. The way they whispered each other promises. *I'll love you forever, baby. I'm right here no matter what. Whatever you need, even if it hurts.*

The night they celebrated their wedding anniversary in the hospital, him in a fancy suit, her in a standard issue hospital gown, white and cream cupcakes on plastic plates.

That perfect day he showed her toward the end. The tea

room at the botanical gardens, the lush red roses unfurling for the sun, the flowering cherry trees blowing in the wind.

That look of peace in her eyes.

I didn't understand it when I was a kid. I was angry at the universe. I still am. But she had accepted it. She wasn't hurting anymore. She was savoring every last drop of life she had.

It's not like she was lucky to get cancer. I don't give a fuck that her illness made her appreciate what time she had left. There's no universe where it was a good thing.

But there's no way I'd trade never knowing my mother for never losing her.

And there's no way Dad would change a thing, if he could do it over.

And maybe...

I don't know.

I toss and turn until my alarm clock's beep grows too annoying to ignore. I strip, shower, dress, fix my hair and makeup. Today is a combat boots and dark eyeliner kind of day. Even if every day is a combat boots and dark eyeliner kind of day.

There. Perfect. I feel like shit, but I look badass. It's something.

Downstairs, I fix tea. Hustle though a breakfast of raisin bran and milk. By the time I'm setting the dishes in the sink, it's eleven thirty. I need to get my ass in gear. To face my fate. Even if it's bad.

I pull the door open, ready to block out the world.

But the world is there.

Dean is leaning against his car, sunglasses hanging in his bright blue t-shirt, eyes on me.

The storm clouds surrounding me dissipate.

With the sun bouncing off his light hair, he's positively angelic.

Maybe that isn't wrong.

Maybe it's every kind of right.

"I've got good news and bad news." He pushes off the car and moves up the concrete pathway. "Which do you want first?"

"The bad news."

"I'm not going anywhere."

"What's the good news?"

He closes the distance between us. Until he's standing on the porch a foot away from me. "I'm not going anywhere."

My lips curl into a half-smile. "What if I want you to leave?"

"Too bad."

"You're not respecting my wishes."

"Not if this is some way to protect me." He moves closer. "If you're sick of me. If you're done with me. If you were using me for my body, sure. I'll leave. I'll follow you to the hospital and make a scene. But I'll scram eventually."

I shake my head. "I'm not done with you."

"Then you're shit out of luck, sunshine." His fingertips skim my hips. "I'm not going anywhere."

My heart thuds against my chest.

He moves closer. Until he's six inches away.

His palm rests on my hips. The other goes to my cheek.

He rubs my temple with his thumb.

He stares into my eyes like I'm everything he needs.

God, those deep blue eyes...

I can't let him stay but I can't tell him to leave either.

"Dean." My eyelids flutter together. My head falls to one side. Into his palm. God, his touch feels good. Like everything I want. "You should go now. You should get out before you fall in love with me."

"Too late."

My heart thuds against my chest. I reach for a response, but my mouth is too sticky.

"I'm crazy in love with you."

"But it's barely been a month."

"I know. But I am." He slides his arm around me. Presses his palm into my lower back to pull my body into his. "It's okay if you don't feel it yet. Or if you're not ready to say it. But you gotta know I'm not going anywhere. I'm here. Whether you're sick or well or something in between."

"But..."

"No buts, sunshine. This is where I want to be."

"But..." It's the only response I have. My urge to protect him overwhelms everything else. Even that greedy part of me that wants his comfort. His affection. His love.

He loves me.

When I stare up into his eyes, I believe it.

I know it everywhere.

"I..." I suck a breath through my teeth. His touch feels too good. It's drowning out my senses. "I don't know if I can do this to you."

"You're not doing it to me. I love you, whether you want me around or not. And, fuck, if you are sick, I'll never forgive myself for missing a second."

"But..."

His voice is strong. Sure. "I'll never forgive myself for letting you suffer alone. So, if you're doing this for me, trust me. This is what I want."

"Dean..."

"Let me finish this, sunshine." He pulls my body into his. "I've spent my entire life avoiding connections because I was afraid of getting hurt. I'm not doing it again. Not when I've found the person who completes me."

Every part of me goes warm at once. It's cheesy. It's wrong for him. It's perfect. "Did you really just say that?"

"Yeah. No. Let me correct that. Fuck yeah."

I can't help but smile. "It was super cheesy."

"I know. But it was true." He stares down at me with every ounce of love and affection in the world.

It's there, in his eyes.

There's no way I'll convince him to leave.

And there's no universe where I should.

If things were reversed, if he was the one who might be sick...

There's no way that would scare me off. There's no way I would let go of what I have.

Fuck. It is just like *A Walk to Remember*.

I am a cheesy Nicholas Sparks movie.

But, dear God, please let me strip the bittersweet from that ending.

I rise to my tiptoes and press my lips to his.

He kisses back, soft, slow, sure.

I pull back with a heavy sigh. "I have to go. For my needle biopsy."

He motions to his car. "I'm driving."

"'Cause it's harder for me to get away?"

"Sunshine, you overestimate my intellect."

Chapter Forty-One

CHLOE

After the test, Dean and I wait in the hospital cafeteria. The bright, cheery room is all aqua walls and wide windows.

For once, it doesn't feel like the sunlight mocking me.

It feels...

This might not be, okay. But I'm ready to face reality. Whatever it is.

Dean distracts me as well as he can. We trade gossip about clients, and high school friends, and celebrities then we move on to movies, and food, and tea, and friends, and sex...

And, well, we kind of stick with that topic.

I'm on my fifth cup of tea when my phone buzzes with the doctor's number.

We take the elevator to the fifth floor. Walk the narrow beige hallway. Turn the handle to suite 505.

I step inside with all the strength I can muster.

Dean stays behind me, his hand still glued to mine.

The receptionist nods. "Chloe, he's ready for you."

He's ready for me. With my fate. With...

Fuck, I just have to know.

Now.

I squeeze Dean's hand as I cross the room. He follows me into the patient area.

"Suite three," the receptionist calls.

It's the first door on the right. A standard doctor's room. Teal patient bench. Plain grey chairs. Stool. White counter. White cabinets. Sink.

"You'd think the guy wouldn't make me wait anymore." I sit in one of the chairs and fold one leg over the other.

Dean sits next to me. He rubs the space between my thumb and forefinger with his thumb.

The soft gesture is comforting. Calming. Not enough, but some.

I rest my head on his shoulder.

Let my eyelids fall together.

No matter what, this isn't the end. At best, I have four more years until I'm in the clear. At worst...

God.

Please don't let it be at worst.

I inhale the moment. The soft touch. The warmth of his skin. The clean, linen scent of his soap.

The creak of the door.

Fuck.

I bounce in my seat. Pressing my palms into my quads does nothing to help. I'm crawling out of my skin.

I need to know.

I need it to be okay. But even more than that, I need to know.

Dr. Nyguen's eyes meet mine. "You're going to be okay, Chloe." His voice lifts. "It's a lipoma, a fatty tumor. Benign."

Benign.

"You don't have cancer."

That's...

I...

Fuck.

I jump out of my seat and crawl into Dean's lap.

"You don't have cancer." He reaches up. Rests his palm against my cheek.

I blink back a happy tear. "I..." I force myself to turn back to the doctor. "Is everything else okay?"

He nods. "We'll still need to do a scan every year, but it's just a precaution."

For once, I feel the truth behind his words.

It is just a precaution.

It's not a death sentence.

I...

"I'll give you two a minute." Dr. Nguyen laughs. "We'll call to schedule next year's MRI."

"Okay." I turn back to my boyfriend. "I..."

He catches a tear on his thumb. "Me too."

"Fuck. This is..." I press my forehead to his. "This is so good."

He nods. "Yeah."

"I'm really going to be okay."

"You're gonna be better than okay, sunshine. At least if I have any say in the matter." He brings his hands to my hips. Straightens my body so I'm perched on his thighs. "Gotta show you something."

"Yeah?"

He nods as he unbuttons his jeans.

"Dean, I-"

"Trust me."

That's not it. I don't trust myself. I want to pounce. I want to wrap my legs around him and fuck him until I forget the world.

I...

He rolls his jeans over his hip.

There's a flash of black.

Then all of it.

A shooting star streaks across his skin.

The same as mine.

"Wanted you to know I was all-in." He stares up at me. "Chloe, I love you so fucking much."

"I love you too." The words roll off my tongue without passing through my brain. But I don't need my brain right now.

I need my heart.

And my heart is sure.

And this...

Fuck.

I press my lips to his. "Promise you aren't going anywhere?"

"Not in a million years."

Epilogue

A sweet, slow song pours from the speakers.

Chloe wraps her arms around my shoulders. Looks up at me with a hazy smile. "I didn't think this was going to happen."

The hotel ballroom blurs into warm light and bright flowers as we spin. The dance floor is crowded with people in formal wear—does Chloe's sister even know this many people?—but it still feels like our universe. "Me either."

"Please. You've been insistent that Mark was just waiting for the right moment."

I can't deny the allegations. Ever since we made this official, I've been a fixture at Lee family dinners. I spent a lot of nights telling Gia that Mark would get his shit together. She spent most of them rolling her eyes and warning me not to hurt Chloe.

To be honest, I'd almost given up on the guy when he finally did pop the question. Fuck. That was only three months ago. Gia fast tracked the wedding. Dragged Chloe into a world of dresses, bouquets, seating arrangements.

It's been weird, seeing her all girly.

She looks gorgeous in her fuchsia dress and heels, but she doesn't look like *my* Chloe.

Like the girl who will threaten to throw me over her shoulder if I fuck with her.

"What?" Her fingers curl into my hair. "You're giving me a look."

Yeah. I am. This is getting me all gooey and romantic. Watching Chloe walk down the aisle with Mark's brother... it was so real. So close to what it could be. "Thinking about Mark and Gia's honeymoon."

"What about it?"

"Which of them prefers to be on top."

Her nose scrunches in distaste. "You're baiting me. I'm not taking it."

I shrug *suit yourself.*

She nods *I will.* For a long moment, her poker face is strong. Then it crumbles. "Well..." She draws circles on the back of my neck. "Which of them?"

"I think that's pretty obvious."

"Ugh. Why do I talk to you?"

"Good body."

"True."

"Cock piercing."

She laughs. "Yeah. That is fun." She looks up at me. "You aren't really thinking about their wedding night, are you?"

Not the way she means. Fuck, if that was us, I'd already have my arms around her. I'd already be carrying her across the threshold, laying her on the bed, fucking her brains out.

I wouldn't be here, thanking family members and coworkers for attending.

"You have that look again?" She presses her hips against mine.

"What look?"

"I don't know. It's weird. Like you're daydreaming."

"Guess I am."

Her fingers dig into my skin. She looks up at me, her dark eyes hazy with love, affection, champagne. "What about?"

"What I'm gonna do to you."

"Oh?"

I press my palm into her lower back. Pull her closer. "You know... I kind of thought you were going to invite me to Vegas after my last test."

"I considered it."

"But?"

"Couldn't find a place with Earl Grey cake."

She laughs as she flips me off. "You shouldn't mock your girlfriend."

"What if she's my wife? Can I mock her then?"

"Are you proposing?"

Fuck, I want to. I've been ready for ages. But I'm not narcissistic enough to ask my girlfriend to marry me at her sister's wedding. "I think Gia might kill me."

"Yeah. She would. For sure."

"It would be worth it."

Her smile spreads over her lips. "Can you imagine the look on Ryan's face if we showed up wearing wedding rings?"

I can't help but laugh. Ryan is still Mr. Romance. He still worships the ground Leighton walks on.

And he's still not a fan of me teaching Chloe.

I can't blame him. It took us a long time to figure it out. For a while, we completely failed at keeping work and play separate. Brought fights and flirting to work. Brought work home. Made use of the back room when we were supposed to be doing mock-ups.

But we did figure it out eventually.

We don't talk work at home.

Don't tear our clothes off at the shop.

All right. If I'm being honest, my love of watching Chloe

bloom as an artist is as much boyfriend as it is teacher.

I don't let my affection hold me back. I criticize her when she needs it. Push her when she needs that.

We both push each other to be better.

At work. At home. At everything.

A few weeks ago, Chloe started taking on clients. She's still doing free designs. Simple stuff like hearts, spades, words. She has another year before she's ready to fly solo, but she's well on her way.

"Ryan's gonna have to get over it." I press my lips to hers. Fuck, it feels so good kissing her. It warms me everywhere. "You think I'm going to wait until you're finished with your apprenticeship for that?"

"You think I'm going to say yes before that?"

"Only four hours to Vegas."

"I'll miss you too much if Gia murders you."

"Plus, you might be collateral damage."

She laughs. "Yeah. But we can still go. Put it all on black."

I shake my head. "I want lucky number thirteen."

"Is that black or red?"

"You're the expert."

"Uh... Black. Totally."

My smile spreads wider. She wants this too. But we really can't. Not with how much Gia and Chloe have been fighting over wedding planning. This shit is a stress factory.

And with their mom gone...

I know it's on Chloe's mind.

She's not over her doubts.

But she's getting there.

She handled her two-year scan with grace. She was nervous, but it was nothing compared to last year.

I was more of a wreck than she was.

Fuck, I was terrified.

I get it now, why Ryan was such a miserable wreck of

himself.

I loved Chloe a year ago. But after twelve months of waking up next to her, eating breakfast with her, fighting over the remote, trading barbs, watching her grow as an artist...

Every day, I'm a little more in love with her.

~

"Mmmm." Chloe kicks her heels off, one at a time. They bounce off the walls. Land on the carpet with a thud.

"You trying to wreck up our place?"

"Our place?"

"You're here five nights a week."

"It's close to work."

"That's it."

"Well..." She bends her arm over her head, reaching for her zipper. "You're here."

"I'm here."

"Yeah. And, well... Dad isn't ready to accept that I've moved out."

"Just Dad?"

"Just Dad. I swear." She doesn't quite reach the zipper. "Could you?"

"Come here."

She does.

My fingers skim her hips. The curve of her waist. The sides of her chest. I trace the back of her dress.

She leans into the touch. Lets out a soft murmur as her head falls to the right.

I take my time undoing her zipper then tracing a line up her spine. Her back is gorgeous. And it feels so fucking good touching her. She feels right against my fingertips. Like she's made for me. "You look gorgeous."

"Weird."

"Yeah. But gorgeous."

She pushes her dress off her hips. "You don't look half bad yourself, Maddox." She turns and gives me a long, slow once-over.

"Does that mean I look half-good?"

"Amazing. But not good, exactly. Like the devil you are."

"Go on."

"What's that movie where Satan is a lawyer?"

"I look like Satan?"

"Yeah. Kind of."

"That's the sweetest thing you've said to me in ages."

"I try." Her fingers brush my suit jacket. My bright pink tie. My oxford shirt. "You look like Dean."

"Should I not?"

"No. But—" She kicks her dress off her feet. "I don't look like me in that dress"

"'Cause you weren't wearing your combat boots."

"Oh my God."

"You should have insisted."

Her laugh lights up her dark eyes.

"I'm serious."

"You are not."

"They're the essence of Chloe."

"Sounds like a perfume."

"Does it smell like your cunt?"

Her cheeks flush, but she holds strong. "What else?"

"I'll take a hundred bottles."

"It's ten thousand dollars a bottle."

"Fuck. That's steep." I wrap my arms around her waist. Pull her body into mine. "Guess I'll have to savor you the old-fashioned way."

She squeals as I lift her into my arms.

She wraps her arms around my shoulders.

Rests her head against my chest.

I carry her into our bedroom.

Lay her down on our bed.

She leans back on her elbows. Spreads her legs in invitation. "Should I put on my boots for this?"

"Depends."

"On?"

"You want it soft and slow or hard and fast?"

Her eyes fix on mine. "Which do I get if I wear the boots?"

"Sunshine, if you put on those boots, I won't be able to control myself." I sit next to her and pull her into my lap

She giggles as I dig my thumb into the sole of her foot. "Uh-huh."

"I'll split you in half."

Her eyelids flutter together as I rub her feet. "Oh my God." Her back arches. Her lips part with a sigh. "Don't stop."

"Never."

Pleasure spills over her expression as I massage her tired feet. "When did you get so good at this?"

I'm not. I just do what I can. "You never let me take care of you."

"I do sometimes."

"When?"

"The test last month."

She did. And, fuck, it meant everything.

"I'm working on it."

"I know." I get that Chloe is tough and independent. That she'll always be able to fend for herself. But sometimes I want to take that weight for her.

Her eyes blink open. Find mine. "You're still wearing a lot of clothes."

I rub her feet a little harder. "You want me to stop?"

"No. But I want you to go too." She swings her legs to her

side. Her hands go to my shoulders.

In one swift motion, she climbs on top of me.

Her knees plant outside my thighs.

Her eyes fix on mine.

"You look so good in this thing." Her fingertips skim my neck as she undoes the knot of my tie. "But I still need to destroy it."

"Destroy it?"

"Are you negotiating?"

"Say I am?"

"Take off your clothes if you don't want them destroyed."

"Oh?"

She nods as she undoes my top button. Her fingers linger on my neck. My chest. My collarbones. "I need you naked."

"Why's that?"

"Uh-huh. No sass. I'm too tired for that."

"If you're tired, we can just cuddle."

She's quick about unbuttoning my shirt. "No."

"No?"

She nods. "I'll get the combat boots if that's what it takes."

I laugh. "You're dedicated."

"Too much talking." She pushes my suit jacket off my shoulders. Then the shirt. "Not enough sex."

My lips curl into a smile.

Her cheeks flush. "What?"

"Just thinking about how much I love you."

"I love you too. And, really, I can't wait to discuss that subject more." She shifts her hips backward to give herself room to undo my belt. "After I fuck you senseless."

Fuck, I love everything about her.

My palm goes to her cheek.

She leans into the touch with a soft sigh. It's equal parts *I love you too* and *hurry up and fuck me.*

She does away with her strapless bra.

I ditch my slacks.

Then the boxers.

She kisses me hard as she wraps her fingers around my cock.

Fuck.

Her lips part to make way for my tongue.

She pumps me harder.

Kisses deeper.

I toy with her until she's groaning against my lips.

Then I bring my hands to her ass, hold her body against mine as I scoot backward.

She stares into my eyes as she pushes her thong off her ass.

I help her slide it to her feet.

Trace a line up the inside of her leg.

Higher and higher and higher.

There.

My fingertips skim her clit.

Her nails sink into the sheets.

I love watching anticipation spill over Chloe's expression, but I don't have the patience for it today.

I need her coming.

My hands go to her hips. "Sit on my face."

She crawls up the bed, turns, plants her knees outside my cheeks backward.

Fuck.

My girlfriend is brilliant.

I dig my fingers into the flesh of her ass. Bring her cunt to my lips.

Tease her with a soft flick of my tongue.

Her nails scrape my chest. My stomach. My hips.

She claws harder with every tease.

Gets closer.

Until—

Fuck.

Her thumb brushes my piercing.

She wraps her hand around me. Pumps me hard as I lick her.

Pleasure floods my senses.

Then she lowers her body onto mine.

Brings that gorgeous mouth to my cock.

Toys with my piercing with her tongue.

And my conscious thoughts flee at an alarming rate.

She's too good at working that thing.

I'm gonna come way too fast.

She does it a little harder.

Harder.

My balls tighten.

The fluorescent light and low hum of the air-conditioning fades into one blur of Chloe.

She groans against my cock.

Presses her thighs into my cheeks.

Writhes against my lips.

I hold her in place as I work her.

With every breath, I lose track of another thought. But I don't need thoughts. My body knows what it's doing.

It needs her pleasure.

Period.

I find that spot where she needs me and lick her harder.

She takes me deeper.

There's something fucking beautiful about this, the two of us pushing each other to the edge.

But with the next flick of her tongue, I lose interest in poetry.

I lose interest in everything but making her come.

And coming inside her.

I pull back enough to groan. "Get on your stomach."

She pushes herself up, but I don't give her time to get into position. I wrap my arms around her waist. Pin her to the bed.

Her breath catches in her throat. "Fuck." She looks back at me, daring me to split her in half.

I hold her in place as I tease her.

My cock strains against her.

With one quick motion, I fill her.

"Mmmm." Her legs spread wider. Her groan gets louder.

I sink into our position, her back against my chest, her ass against my pelvis, her thighs against my hips.

She arches her back to meet me.

Fuck, that feels good.

Like it's where I belong.

But it's not enough.

I need her coming too.

My fingers dig into her hips. "Touch yourself. I want to feel you come."

"Dean..." She shifts to her right to make room for her hand.

I wrap my arm around her chest.

Pull her closer.

There's no space between us. All of her is against all of me.

She's all mine.

And I'm all hers.

She turns back. Brings her lips to mine.

I kiss her as I pump into her.

She rocks her hips with mine.

Strokes herself.

Pushes herself right to the edge.

She pulls back to groan. "Fuck. Dean." Her fingers curl into the white cotton sheets. "Dean."

My name rolls off her lips again and again.

Her cunt pulses around me as she comes.

Fuck, that feels good.

I lose track of everything but her flesh against mine.

A few more thrusts and I'm there.

I groan her name as I come inside her.

Pleasure floods my pelvis. It spreads through my stomach and thighs. It turns my world to pure ecstasy.

Once I've spilled every drop, I untangle our bodies and collapse next to her.

She nestles into my chest.

We lie like that until we catch our breath.

And then for a little longer.

She looks up at me with those almond eyes.

I rest my palm on her cheek. Rub her temple with my thumb. "Shower with me."

"Mmm. Yes." Her lips curl into a smile. "Get it warm for me."

"You know I love when you're bossy."

She pushes herself up. "You're ruining the moment."

No. The moment is perfect like this.

"Just shut up, okay?"

"Yes ma'am."

She laughs. "You're the worst."

"Thanks." I slide off the bed.

She shoots me that trademarked *you're ridiculous and I love it* look of hers.

Fuck, I love the way she looks at me.

I love those almond eyes. That wide smile. The shooting star across her hip.

I love every fucking thing about her.

I even love the four different kinds of black eyeliner on the sink.

And the dozen shampoos in the shower.

I turn the knob until the water is just right.

Something catches my eye. A flash of movement in the bedroom.

Both doors are open a crack. I can just barely make out the dresser.

Chloe pulls open her drawer. Grabs the white tank top she sleeps in.

Moves to the bottom drawer.

My drawer.

Shit.

She paws through my drawer, moving past pair after pair of jean.

She freezes.

That must be it.

Slowly, she pulls out the ring box.

Her eyes go wide as she flips it open.

I couldn't ask for her mom's ring—Mark beat me to that —but the ring I got is perfect for her. A round stone on a platinum band.

She slips the ring onto her left ring finger. Holds it up to catch every ounce of light.

Squeals the way she does when she perfects a tattoo mock-up.

Turns toward the hall.

I push the door closed just in time.

The water is hot as hell. Or maybe that's all the warmth flowing though my veins.

Her footsteps pad the hallway.

She slips into the bathroom with a goofy smile.

Fuck, it hits me everywhere.

I'm over the moon.

It's nearly impossible to keep a poker face, but I manage. "What got into you?"

"You did. Or did you forget?"

My smile spreads over my cheeks. "Sunshine, that was

terrible."

"You do better."

"I can't. You worked me too hard."

"Mhmm." She wraps her arms around my waist. Traces circles on my skin with her ring finger. "Just thinking... I love you so much."

"I love you too."

"Now get in the shower."

"Yes ma'am."

"I don't mean it like *that*." She drops her voice to that *I'm obviously talking about sex* tone.

"You sure?"

She pulls back with a laugh. "Can you even... ahem... this soon?"

"No. But I have hands."

"Oh."

I raise a brow.

"Okay... maybe I'll get a little bossy."

"Maybe?"

"If you're into it."

I step into the shower and offer her my hand. "Sunshine, you know the drill. Your wish is my command."

~

Want More?

Sign up for my mailing list to get an exclusive extended epilogue (if you're already subscribed you'll get this soon).

You can also join my Facebook group, like my page on Facebook, or friend me on Facebook.

Hunter and Emma's book, *Breaking the Rules*, is coming this fall.

Author's Note

Can I admit something? I'm writing this the morning I have to upload *Hating You, Loving You* to Amazon. I'm not usually a procrastinator. Deadlines stress me out and stress makes me shut down.

I try to stay a book ahead. I don't announce release dates until the manuscript is with the proofer and the cover is done.

But there are certain things I always put off. Epilogues are one. Author's Notes are another. The former is my private goodbye to the book, the point where it's really over. The latter is my public goodbye. There's no denying it now.

I'm done with the book. The end. Forever.

I'm attached to all my books. I love them in different ways. With some, it's a trial. Sacrifice and suffering and tearing my hair out wondering why it isn't working.

This book was the opposite. It was easy. It flowed.

I always felt like I knew Dean. It's funny. My husband listens to all my books—he's my audio proofer—and expresses his opinion with great enthusiasm. He hates Dean with a fiery passion (audio is currently in production, so we'll have to wait for his final opinion).

The other day, we were talking about *Hating You, Loving You* and I pointed out that I'm the most like Dean. I'm constantly saying dirty things, teasing people, enjoying my role as the funny one. He didn't want to admit it was true (insisted I'm like Dean without all the bad qualities), but, eventually, he agreed.

Dean has been one of my favorite characters. He lights up every page he's on. When I need a hit of humor, I bring him into the scene, and he always delivers. I have to admit that my husband is right too. There are a lot of places where Dean and I differ. I'm not a flaming extrovert. I'm not the life of the party. I'm not constantly showing off my abs (maybe, if I had abs...).

But I get that urge to make people laugh. To shrug off shit that bothers you. To pretend you're invulnerable. If no one knows you hurt, no one knows how to hurt you.

This was my first time writing an enemies to lovers book. Chloe and Dean are never enemies, exactly, more like rivals, but, it was still so much fun exploring that dynamic. I knew Dean needed a bad ass heroine, and Chloe really delivered. She's tough as nails. Sharp and guarded, but willing to let her guard down. That's where her strength really is, what real strength is—the willingness to be vulnerable.

It's something I've gotten better at as I've gotten older, but it's always a struggle.

It's the sharp parts that are the most fun (in life and in books). Writing Dean and Chloe's banter, watching her bite back, was pure joy. I love sharp, guarded characters. (If that isn't obvious already). I love her determination and her fearlessness.

Cancer is a weird topic. It's there in the popular culture, but it often feels like a concept more than an illness. Like it's a way of exploring the idea of life and loss. I hope this didn't feel like one of those "cancer books." I watched both of my parents survive cancer (one very treatable, one incredibly aggressive). Most of my information comes from their experiences, and from mine. It's not easy trying to soothe someone when you're just as terrified as they are. I wanted to explore that element of illness—the way we all try, and sometimes fail, to hold each other up.

Though, I suppose, all my books are about the way we try and sometimes fail to help and understand each other.

I dedicated this book to my husband to tease him. (He really hates Dean). But also because he's always holding me up. He's exactly the person I want by my side when times are tough. If I ever have to go through illness, I want him to be the person there, holding my hand.

This book is for him. But it's also for all the survivors out there. And for everyone who fought like hell and didn't make it.

As always, thanks for reading. I hope I'll see you soon for Emma and Hunter's book, *Breaking the Rules*.

Love,

Crystal

Acknowledgements

My first thanks goes to my husband, for his support when I'm lost in bookland and for generally being the sun in my sky. Sweetheart, you're better than all the broken bad boys in the world.

The second goes to my father, for insisting I go to the best film school in the country, everything else be damned. I wouldn't love movies, writing, or storytelling half as much if not for all our afternoon trips to the bookstore and weekends at the movies. You've always been supportive of my goals, and that means the world to me.

A big shout out to all my beta readers. You helped give me the confidence to put out a book a little more heartbreaking than usual. And also to my ARC readers for helping spread the word to everyone else in the world.

A special thanks to my fellow pop-punk addict, Molle, for fangirling over music with me, for talking me through my business decisions, and for reminding me that loving my work matters as much as all the marketing money in the world.

Athena Wright, you are the best author friend a girl could ask for. Thank you for your feedback, for being my chat buddy, and for always being there to give me the perspective I need. And thank you for mocking me when I deserve it and telling me no when I need to hear it.

Thanks so much to my editor Marla, my designers Okay Creations and Tempting Illustrations, and to all my beta readers.

As always, my biggest thanks goes to my readers. Thank you for picking up *Hating You, Loving You*. I hope you'll be back for *Breaking the Rules* (Emma and Hunter's book), coming this fall.

Stay in Touch

Sign up for my mailing list to get an exclusive extended epilogue (if you're already subscribed you'll get this soon).

You can also join my Facebook group, like my page on Facebook, or friend me on Facebook.

More books about the men of Inked Hearts are coming soon.

Emma and Hunter's book is coming soon. Turn the page for a teaser!

Breaking the Rules - Special Preview

EMMA

<u>Sign up for my mailing list</u> to be notified as soon as *Breaking the Rules* is live.

There's something wrong with my brother. Seriously. There isn't a single spec of dust in the living room/ kitchen/ dining room combo. Every dish is in its place. The stainless steel fridge is shiny and bright. The black leather couch is spotless.

If it weren't for the sound of the shower upstairs, I'd swear this place was uninhabited.

"Brendon." I kick off my work flats. Move across the living room. Up the stairs. My fingers trail the railing. Then it's the tips of my red nails. "Can we talk?" I swallow the *I need to beg you for a favor, though we both know it's not really a favor to ask if I can stay in my bedroom.*

The shower turns off as I step into my old bedroom. It's no longer a beautiful disaster. No clothes on the floor. No electric purple comforter askew. No lyrics scribbled on the desk.

It's an Ikea showroom.

Not Emma Kane's bedroom.

The bathroom door opens.

Footsteps move into the hallway.

"Seriously, Brendon. What the hell is this?" I turn to the noise. Pull my bedroom door open.

But that's not my brother.

It's...

Fuck.

I try to force myself to make eye contact, but I can't.

He's dripping wet.

Naked.

Huge.

"Emma?" His voice is the same as it always was.

It brings me back to a million afternoons here.

His devilish smile.

The spark in his bright blue eyes.

The way he'd wink when I caught him and Brendon drinking out on the patio.

But what the hell is Hunter doing here?

Naked.

And dripping wet.

And incredibly huge.

I try to pull my gaze from his crotch.

Fail.

I'm going to die of embarrassment.

I'm going to die right here in the hallway, no college degree in hand, no boutique kicking ass, no reports of excellence.

I'm going to die of embarrassment and my tombstone is going to say *Emma Kane, full of untapped potential, disappointment to her late parents, and especially to her brother.*

At least she had great hair.

"Fuck. Sorry." He turns and marches into the bathroom.

I try to peel my eyes up his body, but I can't.

He's so naked.

And I'm so...

Into it.

After *that*...

It's been weird with guys. Different. Uncomfortable.

But seeing Hunter naked...

I don't know.

It's been a long time. Years.

But he was Brendon's best friend for a long time. And he was always good to me.

He consoled me after my first rejection.

He taught me every swear word I know.

Gave me my first sip of booze.

I had a huge crush on him.

Dreamed about kissing him.

And then about more.

About so much more.

"You okay?" He steps into the hallway.

Finally, my eyes obey my command. They trace a line up his long, lean torso. The dreamcatcher tattoo on his chest. The strong chin. The piercing blue eyes. They're familiar and they're so fucking intense.

They're staring into me.

Through me.

"Emma?" He asks again. With extra concern. "Are you okay?" His voice drops to something closer to a whisper.

It's not even remotely close to a *baby, I want you whisper*, but that's still where my head goes.

He's only wearing a towel.

And he's still so wet.

I...

He...

God, he's beautiful.

"What are you doing here?" I press my palm against the

door frame. Dig my toes into the carpet. Whatever my control freak brother wants to believe, this is my house too.

"Brendon didn't explain?"

"No."

"I'm staying here for a few weeks."

I just barely nod.

"And I'm filling in at Inked Hearts. While he's in New Jersey."

"Oh." It's the only thing I can say. Of course the one guy who makes me blush is the one filling in at Inked Hearts. Of course he's house sitting the one time I want to stay here. "That's great."

"You sure?" he asks.

"Yeah." I trip over my tongue. It's not like me. I don't get flustered in front of guys. Even ones wearing only my raspberry towel. But after *that*... Fuck, I don't know anymore. "You'll fit right in."

"You work the front desk?"

"Yeah. Sometimes." I take a step backwards. Suck a breath through my teeth. Hunter is still wearing a towel. My brain is still struggling to function. It's still screaming *Hunter. Towel. Wet.* It's a cavewoman who can barely put words together.

Though there's a certain flow to *Hunter. Towel. Wet.*

There is something poetic about it.

God, after that...

It's been awhile since I've felt like this about anyone.

"I should get dressed." He nods to the office.

"Right." I press my lips together. He's so... This is so... I'm so not doing this. "And I should..." Break the news to my brother than I'm crashing his bachelor pad. "Do you know when Brendon will be back?"

Hunter shakes his head.

"I'll text him. You can, um... I'll see you later."

He nods *sure*, turns, and disappears into the office.

I press my bedroom door closed.

Then I slide to the ground and I die of embarrassment.

Sign up for my mailing list to be notified as soon as *Breaking the Rules* is live.

Also by Crystal Kaswell

Sinful Serenade

Sing Your Heart Out - Miles

Strum Your Heart Out - Drew

Rock Your Heart Out - Tom

Play Your Heart Out - Pete

Sinful Ever After – series sequel

Dangerous Noise

Dangerous Kiss - Ethan

Dangerous Crush – Kit

Dangerous Rock – Joel

Dangerous Fling – Mal

Dangerous Encore - series sequel

Inked Hearts

Tempting - Brendon

Playing - Walker

Pretend You're Mine - Ryan

Hating You, Loving You - Dean

Breaking the Rules - Emma + Hunter - coming fall 2018

Sign up for the Crystal Kaswell mailing list

Made in the USA
San Bernardino, CA
17 August 2018